"De la Rosa presents politics and history not as lists of bills and battles, but as things that upend lives and bruise hearts. . . . Intensely dramatic." —*The New York Times Book Review*

"De la Rosa spins a richly original historical romance."
—*Boston Globe*

"Sisterhood, espionage, and an unstoppable romance between two passionate leads—*Isabel and The Rogue* is utterly delightful and charming and not to be missed!"
—*USA Today* bestselling author Evie Dunmore

"A clever and resourceful Isabel Luna heats up the pages with a dangerously charming captain while working together to aid her beloved Mexico against the French. An exciting and equally steamy romp!" —*USA Today* bestselling author Amalie Howard

"It doesn't get any better than Liana De la Rosa, and with her wallflower-and-the-spy outing, *Isabel and The Rogue*, she cements her reputation as a shining star of historical romance."
—*USA Today* bestselling author Eva Leigh

"De la Rosa cracks open the stuffiest of Victorian ballrooms, showing that the world is much bigger than England and that history is made by acts of hero- and heroine-ism, both small and large." —*Oprah Daily*

"Filled with history, wit, intrigue, and, above all, chemistry, *Isabel and The Rogue* is everything a romance should be and more." —Felicia Grossman, author of *Marry Me by Midnight*

"The well-written story has a rich combination of suspense and complex character development, not to mention a red-hot scene when the two are trapped underneath a desk together, but what will stick with readers is the dramatic and moving ending. An excellent author's note adds welcome context to a book that brings to life an underreported story of the Victorian era so well." —*Kirkus Reviews* (starred review)

"In this exquisitely written second installment of the Luna Sisters series, after *Ana María and The Fox*, De la Rosa again skillfully blends elements of historical fiction and romance, transporting readers to Victorian London with a complex and compelling Latina protagonist." —*Library Journal* (starred review)

"De la Rosa gives every character a chance to shine in a world filled with parties and intrigue that comes alive with sparkling dialogue and scintillating chemistry. Readers will eagerly await the story of Isabel's younger sister, Gabriela." —Shelf Awareness

"De la Rosa brilliantly continues on an upward literary trajectory in her second Luna Sisters title, following *Ana María and The Fox*, delivering another flawlessly crafted romance. . . . An entrancing love story expertly seasoned with sensual spice." —*Booklist*

PRAISE FOR
ANA MARÍA AND THE FOX

"Pleasingly subversive."   —*The New York Times Book Review*

"The Luna sisters are a force to be reckoned with."
                                        —*Entertainment Weekly*

"Truly a delight! A breath of fresh air in the landscape of historical romance."
            —*New York Times* bestselling author Sophie Jordan

"*Ana María and The Fox* is a pitch-perfect romance with a remarkable amount of both charm and chemistry."   —BuzzFeed

"Downright enchanting."   —PopSugar

"A lush, immersive, and evocative romance full of fascinating historical detail. An enchanting love story with a fierce, complex heroine and a swoonworthy hero. The Luna sisters have arrived . . . and the London season will never be the same."
            —*USA Today* bestselling author Adriana Herrera

"The perfect blend of romance and intrigue written in the most gloriously lush prose."
            —*USA Today* bestselling author Alicia Thompson

"Ana María is a feisty, fresh, and fabulous heroine, and I fell *hard* for her swoony hero, Gideon. This book is pure magic!"
            —Minerva Spencer, award-winning author of
                                        The Dueling Duchess

"De la Rosa deftly weaves together a delicious slow-burn romance with danger, intrigue, and sisterly bonding. Full of riveting details, *Ana María and The Fox* is a breath of fresh air in historical romance!"

—Alexis Daria, international bestselling author of
A Lot Like Adiós

"De la Rosa's writing sparkles, and her characters are both admirable and memorable. With plenty of humor, history, and, of course, spicy love scenes, *Ana María and The Fox* is an absolute must read for fans of historical romance."

—Elizabeth Everett, author of *The Lady Sparks a Flame*

"Liana De la Rosa fulfilled every historical romance craving I had and then some with *Ana María and The Fox*. The Luna sisters are the headstrong, politically savvy, and intelligent Mexican heroines I have always dreamed of reading about!"

—Isabel Cañas, author of *Vampires of El Norte*

"When a historical romance can combine a swoonworthy love story with a rich historical setting, it goes on my keeper shelf. *Ana María and The Fox* does this and so much more. It was absolutely delightful to watch Ana María's bond with her sisters grow all while the reserved hero is falling head over heels in love with her."

—Harper St. George, author of *The Stranger I Wed*

"Thrillingly different. . . . A new direction for historical romance."

—*Kirkus Reviews* (starred review)

"This delectable Victorian Latinx romance from De la Rosa will delight fans of sexy historical romances with strong social justice plots such as Alyssa Cole's The Loyal League titles and Evie Dunmore's A League of Extraordinary Women series."

—*Library Journal* (starred review)

"De la Rosa turns the world of Victorian London's high society upside down with this impressive series launch."

—*Publishers Weekly*

"The perfect blend of historical fiction and romance."

—HipLatina

Gabriela
and
His Grace

A LUNA SISTERS NOVEL

Liana De la Rosa

BERKLEY ROMANCE
NEW YORK

BERKLEY ROMANCE
Published by Berkley
An imprint of Penguin Random House LLC
1745 Broadway, New York, NY 10019
penguinrandomhouse.com

Book design by Tiffany Estreicher

Library of Congress Cataloging-in-Publication Data

Names: De la Rosa, Liana, author.
Title: Gabriela and His Grace / Liana De la Rosa.
Description: First edition. | New York: Berkley Romance, 2025. |
Series: Luna sisters novel
Identifiers: LCCN 2024045670 (print) | LCCN 2024045671 (ebook) |
ISBN 9780593440926 (trade paperback) | ISBN 9780593440933 (ebook)
Subjects: LCGFT: Romance fiction. | Novels.
Classification: LCC PS3604.E12266 G33 2025 (print) |
LCC PS3604.E12266 (ebook) | DDC 813/.6—dc23/eng/20241001
LC record available at https://lccn.loc.gov/2024045670
LC ebook record available at https://lccn.loc.gov/2024045671

First Edition: August 2025

Printed in the United States of America
1st Printing

The authorized representative in the EU for product safety and compliance is
Penguin Random House Ireland, Morrison Chambers, 32 Nassau Street,
Dublin D02 YH68, Ireland, https://eu-contact.penguin.ie.

For the lionesses. The fiery ones,
who burn bright to warm those they love.
May you always find a safe place to rest.

GABRIELA
AND
HIS GRACE

1

London docks, March 1867

Gabriela Luna rarely made a decision she regretted. Sure, there had been a handful of occasions where she'd acted rashly and without thought. Like the time when she was fifteen and had slapped Don Ángel, patriarch of the powerful De la Cruz tobacco empire, across the cheek when he'd uttered a disgusting comment about her mother marrying a Purépecha, the crack echoing through the stunned assembly room. Or when she had pointedly corrected Vizconde Alborada for misnaming the Juárez law during dinner at a party hosted by her parents. Or even when she'd abandoned a waltz with a marquess's heir in the middle of a dance floor when he'd insinuated "mixed-blood" women were more hotheaded.

But now, as she stood on the grimy docks, staring at the steamer ship rocking gently to and fro on the murky waters of the London harbor, Gabby recognized the uncomfortable lump in her throat as an error in judgment.

"Isabel said in her letter that there will be a conveyance to collect you at Altamira when the ship docks." Her eldest sister,

Ana María, worried her lip. "I know I shouldn't fret because Isa would never leave you waiting, but I'm going to anyway because I won't be there to help you should you need it."

It was just like Ana María to fret over her safety. And Gabby would miss her terribly for it.

"I'll be fine. Once I'm back in Mexico, I'll have my feet under me and will have no problem finding assistance." She smiled and tapped the back of her sister's hand. "I'm not afraid of doing things on my own."

"I know, querida." Worry lines still bracketed Ana María's eyes. "I take some solace in the fact that you won't be completely alone. Señorita Moreno will make excellent company on the long voyage."

Gabby inclined her head as she slid her gaze to where Miss Lucia Moreno stood. The young woman appeared to be a few years older than her own four and twenty, a modest but well-trimmed cloak wrapped around her trembling frame. From what their tío Arturo had said, Miss Moreno had been raised in England by two Mexican-born parents but was now traveling to Guanajuato to care for her ailing grandmother. Tío had thought the young woman could serve as Gabby's traveling companion, and Ana María and Gideon, her husband, had quickly agreed. Miss Moreno appeared friendly enough, and it would certainly be nice to have company on the trip across the Atlantic.

A trip she was still uncertain she should be making.

"You remembered to pack the parcel I put together for Isa and Mother, right?"

"Of course I did." Gabby grabbed her hand. "I have the parcel, your letter, and photos of Estella. I won't let anything happen to them."

Ana María swallowed as her eyes danced over Gabby's face.

"I'm sorry. I know it's silly to worry about such a thing. It's just . . ." She looked to where Gideon stood, their young daughter smacking his cheek with her chubby hand. "I want them to know how happy I am here. That I may not have married who they wanted, but I married who *I* wanted. Does that make sense?"

"Of course it does." Gabby watched as her sister admired her little family. Her baby niece, Estella, had quickly become Gabby's favorite person in the world, and she was loath to say goodbye to her. But in the four years since she and her sisters had fled their home in Mexico City as the French army marched on the capital and sailed to London for refuge, Gabby had itched to return. Her life among the British aristocracy was not as bad as she liked to complain it was, especially since it allowed her infinitely more freedom than she experienced under the watchful eye of her father, but Gabby felt ill at ease. With Liberal forces reclaiming power in many parts of Mexico, her father would eventually turn his attention to his youngest daughter and invite her home. But Gabby was tired of waiting on tenterhooks, and was no longer inclined to await an invitation.

"Always a matador, ready to face down a bull," Isabel had said once, and Gabby had been hard-pressed to disagree. And after the incident at the Wright ball, a return seemed warranted.

"But, Ana"—she cleared her throat—"you don't have to prove anything to Mother and Father. Your life here in London, with Gideon and Estella, is testament enough to your happiness."

"You're right. I don't." Ana María's throat bobbed, and her dark eyes turned glassy as they held hers. "And neither do you. You know that, right?"

Damn her sister for being so perceptive. Gabby managed to

hold Ana María's stalwart gaze out of sheer tenacity. "I'm not trying to win—"

"Yes, you are, querida. I think you want to show Father that you can be an asset in the war. And you would make a wonderful diplomat because you know how to put others at ease even while you push to get what you want." Ana María stepped forward to press her cheek to Gabby's, and her voice dropped as she continued, "You are more than enough, and you always have been. Return to Mexico because you miss Mother and Isa. Or to escape the machinations of these idiot fortune hunters—"

Gabby huffed a strained breath in her ear. "I think a break is needed, don't you?"

Ana María's brows dipped low. "I worry for you."

"Well, you'll have nothing to worry about if I'm in Mexico."

"I'll just have a new set of things to worry about," her older sister quipped.

Gabby pressed her lips together for a moment. "I tire of feeling like a prize, and by men who don't truly know me or even care to. They're more concerned with my dowry, or my connections to you and Gideon, or even Isa and Sirius, for all that they live in Mexico. I just want to be wanted . . . for me."

"As you deserve to be." Ana María leaned back to consider her. "But returning to Mexico means you will have new battles to wage. Are you prepared to do that?"

Her older sister did not need to explain what she meant. A sob lodged in Gabby's throat, and she struggled to breathe around it. She'd fled Mexico City with her sisters and had lived a happy life in London ever since. But just the thought of seeing her father again, of experiencing the push and pull of coveting his approval yet needing to rebel against it, turned her stomach. But if anyone knew what it was like to be a stranger to your own father, it was Ana María. Gabby wrapped her arms around her sister's shoulders and hugged her close.

"Maybe this time I can make him see." Blinking rapidly, she pulled back to meet her sister's gaze. "Maybe this time he'll want to."

Ana María nodded, a hint of a smile on her lips. "Maybe he will. I will pray he does. But do not ever forget, querida, that there are those of us who know the real Gabby and love her immensely. You'll always be welcomed with open arms."

"And she loves you, too." Gabby took a step back and straightened her spine. She would not cry.

Before she could say anything else, Gideon came to stand at Ana María's side, and baby Estella immediately reached her eager arms toward Gabby. Without a moment's hesitation, she scooped her niece into her arms and cuddled her close, inhaling deeply of her sweet baby scent.

"I'm going to miss you so much, mi amor," she said, pressing a kiss to Estella's soft cheek. "Are you sure I can't take her with me? We'd have so much fun together and she'd have the entire crew wrapped around her chubby finger even before we left British waters."

"But then her papa would unravel, because she has him tied up in knots, too," Ana María said with a laugh, linking her arm through Gideon's and smiling up at him.

Gabby had once thought her brother-in-law a dour man, an adjective so foreign now as she watched him gaze fondly upon his wife and young daughter. "Estella will one day visit her mother's homeland, but preferably not when she's so young."

"Or without her parents," Ana María added, arching a brow.

"You're no fun," Gabby murmured as she kissed the baby's cheek again.

Estella remained unconcerned, more interested in gnawing on the dimpled fist in her mouth.

Before Gabby could say anything else, a figure appeared at her right elbow, her familiar rosewater scent wafting above the stench of the sea.

"Well, darling," Viscountess Yardley began, tapping Gabby on the arm, "While I disagree that you should let that foul earl chase you from London, I am happy you will have an opportunity to hug your mother again."

Gabby exchanged a glance with her sister, who merely pressed her lips together as she looked between Gabby and the viscountess. For his part, Gideon pivoted away, but not before Gabby spied a muscle twitching in his jaw.

Lifting her chin, Gabby said, "I'm not being chased away, I'm simply reevaluating my options."

Ana María snorted but said nothing. Gabby had always made it clear that she wanted to return to Mexico at some point, and with Maximilian and his imperialist supporters quickly losing ground now that the majority of French troops had withdrawn and the United States continued to send aid to Juárez and the Republicans, now seemed an appropriate time.

And if it also saved her from the unscrupulous actions of a cash-strapped earl, well, then Gabby would take advantage of the opportunity, even if her family did not approve.

"It's also true that I've missed our mother a great deal." Gabby studied her niece's perfect face instead of meeting her sister's or the viscountess's gazes. "Let us hope she will be happy to see me. I haven't exactly asked for permission to return."

"Aah, but you did. You asked me."

Gabby laughed as Tío Arturo joined them. He was correct, of course. She may not have received her parents' permission to return to Mexico, but her uncle, as the Mexican ambassador, was well versed in the conditions surrounding the war, and had been comforted by word from her sister, Isabel, that travel would not be compromised. And after the debacle at the Wright ball, Tío was even more inclined to allow her a graceful escape.

She had been relieved by his support, especially as Ana María, Gideon, and Lady Yardley had objected quite soundly. But she suspected Tío Arturo understood the deep burning desire that flared in her chest to step on Mexican shores once again. She missed home and everything associated with it . . . well, *almost* everything.

This time would be different, though. Her teeth clamped together. She was a different Gabby than she had been: more mature, savvy, and sophisticated. She would show her father that she could be an asset to the Luna family, just as her sisters were. No longer would he view her as—

Determined to lighten her mood, Gabby shook away such thoughts and turned her attention to Gideon, who surveyed the crowd on the docks as if he was searching for someone. "I can't believe you changed your mind about me leaving, Gideon. I thought I was going to have to resort to bribery . . ." Gabby narrowed her eyes. "Or maybe even battery, to convince you to let me return home."

Gideon didn't smile—he saved all of his smiles for Ana María and Estella—but there was a spark in his dark eyes that Gabby had long recognized as amusement. "Let's just say that once I learned you wouldn't be traveling alone, my concerns over your safety lifted a tad."

"I've always appreciated your concern," she allowed, "but I'm certain Señorita Moreno and I will be perfectly fine."

Her brother-in-law's lips twisted in a manner Gabby had never seen before, and she frowned. "What?"

With quick movements, Gideon scooped Estella from her arms and propped her against his chest. Gabby didn't miss Ana María's quiet laugh. "As much as I'm sure you and Miss Moreno are capable of caring for yourselves, there will be another on the ship to provide you assistance should you need it," Gideon said.

Jerking her chin back, Gabby looked from Gideon to her sister, whose attention was focused on her daughter. Ana María refused to meet Gabby's eyes. When she turned his way, Tío Arturo was studying the ship's masts. Lady Yardley, however, stared back at her with a broad smile. Dread dropped in Gabby's stomach like a rock.

"Who?" she demanded, spinning about in a whirl of skirts, her eyes darting about the busy docks. A name flashed in her mind and she drew up short, her breath catching. Surely not. Of all the people who would be traveling to Altamira, it couldn't be *him*.

Gritting her teeth so tightly her jaw ached, she pivoted, following the direction Gideon searched. It was then that the crowd shifted and her gaze collided with a familiar pair of blue eyes and her skin flushed so hot, Gabby was certain she would combust. Without a thought, she stomped her foot and shrieked, "Ay, no!"

Sebastian Brooks, the eleventh duke of Whitfield, knew better than to expect an effusive . . . or even a cordial greeting from the likes of Miss Gabriela Luna. But he certainly hadn't expected her to exclaim so loudly she'd frightened several of the sailors working on the gangplank.

Sighing, Sebastian plucked his spectacles from his face and massaged the bridge of his nose. The voyage to Altamira was scheduled for twelve to fourteen days, and then the carriage ride to Dawson's home would take five to six days. Surely he could survive three weeks in Miss Luna's company.

Even across the sixty or so feet between them, Sebastian could see the disbelief and frustration sparking in her greenish-brown eyes.

"And here I thought you were a rake about town, Your Grace." Brodie, his valet, stopped next to him, his head cocked to the side. "But that lass appears angry enough to bite through steel."

Sebastian snorted as he slid on his spectacles. Brodie had worked for him for nigh on a decade, and he was used to his easy manners and glib tongue. He continued to employ the man despite his propensity for bringing Sebastian down a peg because, frankly, no one dressed Sebastian quite like the burly Scotsman. He should have foreseen Brodie's delight at Miss Luna's fiery disdain for him.

Three weeks, he reminded himself. Just three weeks, and he would be in Mexico with his old friend Sirius Dawson, touring the silver mine that had single-handedly brought the Whitfield dukedom out of arrears.

Brodie whistled through his teeth. "She truly dislikes you, doesn't she?"

"I assure you the feeling is mutual," Sebastian said, tugging on his cuff links.

"Sure it is."

"What is that supposed to mean?" he growled, glowering down at his valet.

Unmoved by Sebastian's annoyance, Brodie lifted a shoulder. "It means that I don't believe you, Your Grace."

Sebastian leaned on his onyx-and-gold-tipped cane as he lifted a brow. "My opinion of Miss Luna does not require your approval, Brodie."

"Of course not," the valet replied, unimpressed. "But I do so look forward to watching that lovely lass tie you up in knots these next few weeks, especially as you'll have nowhere to go to escape her."

Clenching his eyes closed, Sebastian exhaled a long breath. Between the sharp-tongued Miss Luna and his shrewd valet, he was bound for purgatory.

Pushing his spectacles up the bridge of his nose, Sebastian pulled his gaze from Miss Luna's scowling face to where Fox stood with his infant daughter in his arms. Looking amused. The damn man was almost smiling. Something about the scene made him think of James and David.

"Do you think they'll be okay while I'm gone?"

His valet didn't need Sebastian to explain whom he was speaking of, for the older man nodded. "They know you're coming back. That you wouldn't have left in the first place if the trip hadn't already been planned. Old Mrs. Evers and the staff will take good care of them."

Sebastian knew that, of course, but unease still turned his stomach. "I'm going to tell Mrs. Evers you call her old."

"Now you're stalling, Your Grace. You're gonna have to speak with Miss Luna eventually," Brodie offered, most unhelpfully.

"Yes, I am aware. But after this moment, it will be almost impossible to be away from her, so I am reveling in my freedom while I can."

With a long exhale, Sebastian set off toward the group waiting at the edge of the gangplank, their expressions ranging from polite regard to open hostility. Doing his best to avoid Miss Luna, Sebastian exchanged greetings with Lady Yardley, then Mrs. Fox, and then Mr. Valdés. When he finally stretched out a hand to his friend, Sebastian couldn't keep himself from squeezing Fox's hand tightly.

"It would seem she did not take the news well," he murmured quietly, careful not to be overheard.

Fox shook his head, amusement still evident in his expression. "I'd say her reaction was very much in character."

Sebastian couldn't argue with that. He'd known Miss Luna would be upset when she learned he would also be on the voyage to Mexico, and he also knew she was not a young woman who hid her emotions behind a veneer of placidity. Sebastian had never doubted where he stood with Gabriela Luna, and try as he might, he couldn't help but respect her for it. The majority of people he met acquiesced to him and his desires simply because he was a duke, and Sebastian had come to value those friends who were not swayed by his title. Gideon Fox was one such friend; Sirius Dawson another. And while Sebastian would never call Miss Luna a friend, her fierce resistance to treating him as anything other than a bug beneath her fashionable shoe was a trait he found both vexing and charming.

Fox took a step closer to him then, his voice dropping an octave. "I'm sure the voyage will have its trying moments, but I am much relieved that you will be there should Gabby require your assistance."

"But who will protect me from her?" Sebastian volleyed, affecting an affronted look.

Fox didn't have a chance to respond because Sebastian felt a tap on his arm. Clenching his jaw, he looked down, not at all surprised to see Miss Luna's hazel eyes glaring up at him.

"What, exactly, are you doing here, Your Grace?"

Her tone was clipped. Commanding. Sebastian stifled an inner sigh. "I was invited to attend the board of directors meeting for the Camino Rojo mine."

Miss Luna's nose crinkled. "Isn't that the same mine Captain Dawson has invested in?"

Sebastian nodded. "He is the one who courted my involvement in the venture. I've been hoping to visit the operations since I first threw my support behind it."

"Oh." She blinked for several seconds. "Does that mean you will also be a guest of my sister and Captain Dawson?"

Now it was Sebastian's turn to blink. "I had assumed you would be staying with your parents. Surely you're anxious to be reunited with them."

Her face darkened. "Of course I am eager to see them, but I would much rather stay with Isa."

"I don't understand—"

"All aboard!"

Sebastian took a step back, unease curdling in his stomach. In a daze he watched as Miss Luna turned from him in a huff, before she launched herself into her sister's arms.

The gravity of their situation crashed onto his shoulders like an anvil. Not only would he be sequestered on a ship with Miss Luna for weeks on end, but they would also be guests in the same house. Christ almighty, what had he agreed to?

"It won't be so bad, Whitfield." Fox clapped him on the back, while the infant Miss Fox reached her plump arms to him. Without hesitation, Sebastian brought her into his embrace. "Despite how your interactions have gone to this point, Gabby is a clever and kindhearted young woman. I'm certain the two of you could be friendly . . . if you tried."

"I believe you mean that Miss Luna is *wickedly* clever and *selectively* kind." Sebastian arched a brow. "I have no qualms being friendly to her, but I rather doubt she'll reciprocate."

Fox met his gaze directly. "Then don't antagonize her."

Scoffing, Sebastian rubbed the backs of his knuckles along the baby's downy cheek. "Miss Fox, I implore you to remind your dear father that your great friend the Duke of Whitfield would not know the first thing about antagonizing others. He is a virtuous saint of a man."

Little Miss Fox gurgled what was surely her agreement, and Fox chuckled. Since his marriage to Ana María, Gideon smiled and laughed more often, a feat that no longer shocked Sebastian. Perhaps one day he would be lucky enough to find such happiness—

"Write when you can. I'll be very interested in all your observations about Mexico, the workings of the mine, and how Dawson and Isabel get on." Fox hesitated, plucking his daughter from Sebastian's hands and propping her on his hip. His expression returned to the serious facade he was known for. "Please keep an eye on Gabby. She is brimful of self-assurance, but from what Ana has said, there are those in Mexico who will delight in stripping her confidence away. She'll need an ally, whether she knows it or not."

An uncharacteristic ache thrummed in Sebastian's chest, and he slid his gaze to where Miss Luna shared tearful good-byes with her family. She had gone out of her way to avoid him over the last few years, and he'd done much the same. Heaven knew Sebastian didn't need to subject himself to her cutting remarks. But the idea of someone trying to humble the indomitable Gabriela Luna seemed unforgivable.

Clearing his throat, Sebastian finally said, "And you trust me to be her ally?"

Fox shook his head. "I trust you with her life."

2

Gabby stood on the deck of the ship, her gaze fixed on the rapidly disappearing shoreline. If she squinted her eyes, she could just barely make out Ana María holding Estella, her arm raised in farewell. Gabby's eyes burned with unshed tears, and she curled her hands into fists to keep them at bay. She'd cried enough for one day.

So much about life felt like a long series of goodbyes. First she'd said goodbye to her mother when they fled Mexico, then when Isabel returned home without her. Now to Ana María. Whether Gabby returned to London or stayed in Mexico, she was destined to say goodbye to someone, and that harsh truth was a sharp knot in her throat.

Which made her angry. Gabby despised being vulnerable. Hated crying, for she'd long ago learned that her tears were useless. But she especially hated crying now that she knew the Duke of Whitfield would witness her pain. Oh, he had quietly boarded the ship after exchanging goodbyes with her family, and had not lingered on the deck to observe her as she clung to her niece and plied Estella with kisses and whispered words of love. The duke had not seen how Gabby held tightly to Ana

María as her sister said a prayer for her safety and happiness. Had not heard Lady Yardley confess, in a broken voice, that she would miss her.

No, the Duke of Whitfield had given Gabby her space to mourn this parting, but just knowing he was close unnerved her. He had unnerved her from the moment she'd met him . . . which had always confused her, because the duke had never frightened her. Yet being in his presence had always left Gabby feeling decidedly on guard. And with so much about her reception in Mexico unknown, Gabby already had more than enough to worry about.

"The water is so much bluer than I was expecting."

Gabby swiveled her head, the tension dissipating when her gaze met Miss Moreno's. The young woman's cheeks were flushed from the wind, but there was a sparkle in her amber eyes. While Gabby's emotions were in tumult, Miss Moreno— Lucia—appeared happy. Excited, even.

Forcing her thoughts back to the other woman's remark, Gabby finally said, "London has so grievously polluted its waters, it's easy to believe the ocean is supposed to be a dank grayish brown. But I assure you that the sea is composed of the loveliest blues and greens in the world. You'll see the variations best when we reach the Caribbean."

"I look forward to it." A smile stretched across Lucia's lips. "I confess, this is my first time traveling outside of England, and I am both elated and scared to see more of the world."

"Such a conflicting mixture of emotions I can understand." Gabby quirked her head. "Your parents emigrated to London from Mexico some years back?"

The other woman nodded. "Almost thirty years ago. I was born in London, although my parents spoke of Guanajuato so much, I feel as if I know it, too."

"Is that where you will be traveling to when we land?"

"Sí. Mi abuela todavia vive en la Guanajuato." Lucia looked out on the choppy waters of the bay. "We've never met in person, so I hope she is as agreeable as she comes across in her letters."

"For your sake, I hope so, too." When Lucia laughed, Gabby smiled. "What made you decide to visit now?"

"My father remarried." Lucia's pleasant expression faltered. "My mother died five years ago, and it had been just the two of us ever since. Until three months ago, that is. When he met Mrs. Grayson."

Although Lucia's tone was guarded, Gabby could detect a whole cache of hurt in her words. She could only imagine what sort of circumstances had forced Lucia to flee the only home she'd ever known for a land she'd never visited.

"I'm certain welcoming a new person into your home after so long had been very difficult."

"It was time for me to venture out." Lucia clasped her hands together, her chin tilting up. "I'm well past the age my mother was when she met and married my father, and she would have wanted to see me settled. And as I've yet to find a man I could envision as my husband in England . . ."

"It is a bachelor wasteland," Gabby declared, chuckling when Lucia laughed outright.

"Perhaps I will have better luck in Mexico." Lucia sighed, her eyes wistful on the horizon. "Or perhaps I will find purpose in caring for my grandmother. I like feeling useful, and recently I've felt like a burden."

Useful. It was a word Gabby had never heard used to describe herself, and she longed for there to be a reason to. Ana María had found a purpose collaborating with Gideon on his work as a member of Parliament. And Isabel had saved President Juárez's life and now worked for the First Lady of Mexico to aid rebel soldiers and their families in the fight against the French. Meanwhile, Gabby had languished in one boring ballroom after the other, the pretty Luna sister but nothing more. She prayed, with all of her heart, that returning home to Mexico would give her a sense of purpose, just like Lucia.

Gabby laid a hand on the other woman's arm. "I think it is quite brave of you to travel to Mexico on your own when you're unsure of what to expect when you arrive."

Lucia pivoted, a dark brow raised. "I've heard I can say the same of you."

"Perhaps." Her mouth went dry. "At least my older sister, Isabel, knows I'm coming."

"Do you think your parents will be upset?" Lucia asked, her eyes wide.

Gabby shrugged, while her gut roiled. "Knowing my father, most definitely."

Movement from the corner of her eye caught her attention, and Gabby turned with a scowl to see the Duke of Whitfield on the other end of the deck, conversing with the ship's captain. Of course he would seek out the most powerful man on the ship, Gabby thought disdainfully.

"My word, Señorita Luna, that's quite the scowl." Lucia clicked her tongue. "Your sister said you were not fond of the duke, but I suppose I didn't realize how much until just now."

"Sí, bien." She paused, biting her cheek. "He is . . . not my favorite person."

"It would seem not." The young woman studied the duke askance. "I wonder why you hold him in such low regard."

Shuffling on her feet, Gabby risked a glance in the duke's

direction, her frown deepening to see him now laughing along with a group of sailors. "I will tell you if only to caution you to avoid him as much as you can."

When Lucia nodded, Gabby held up her hand, ticking off her fingers. "Whitfield's presumptuous, vain, and arrogant. He believes himself to be the smartest person in any room he steps into and must always have the last word. He's a rake of the highest order, and his list of paramours could probably circle London twice."

"Now that last part does not surprise me," Lucia said, angling her chin to observe the duke and the group of men he stood within. "He's quite handsome."

"I suppose so," Gabby agreed reluctantly. It would be a lie to deny that the Duke of Whitfield was attractive. Even if one ignored his rich dark hair and striking arctic eyes, his broad shoulders always seemed to be in danger of splitting the seams of his dress coats. She'd often noted how he prowled through a crowded ballroom, a bud of resentment blooming across her skin as she took in his easy feline grace. Gabby hated that she noticed the handsome figure the duke cut, but she was never one to lose her head over a pretty face. She'd maneuvered through elevated social circles long enough to know that a comely appearance hid all manner of sins.

"So the Duke of Whitfield is a libertine who would take advantage of a young woman on her own," Lucia said, clasping her hands together.

"No." Gabby was surprised by her own sharp tone. Ignoring the other woman's cocked head, she continued. "Whitfield would never prey upon a defenseless young woman."

Lucia frowned. "I don't understand. If he's all the awful things you said, surely my reputation, if not more, would be endangered by him."

Gabby pressed her tongue to the back of her teeth, wavering on whether to concede the point. But no, it wasn't fair. "While he's not someone I would engage with, it doesn't mean that Whitfield is dangerous. I'm certain Gideon would not have entrusted us to Whitfield's care if he wasn't convinced of the duke's honor."

She knew that to the depths of her soul. Whitfield was a scoundrel, but he was an honorable one . . . of sorts. Yet despite knowing the duke would never harm her, Gabby would never trust the man. There was just something about him and his piercing blue eyes that sparked every one of her defenses.

Rather than explain this, Gabby spread her palms. "You must decide for yourself how you intend to interact with the Duke of Whitfield. If at all. I merely wanted to share what I knew of his reputation, but I don't think those things make him a threat to your safety and well-being."

Lucia flashed a bemused smile. "I don't know, Señorita Luna, a handsome face paired with an arrogant confidence has always been a danger to young women."

Gabby glanced in Whitfield's direction, somehow unsurprised to meet his gaze. He held hers for only a heartbeat, then dipped his head politely and looked away.

"Not all young women," she murmured, a smirk settling on her lips. "Oh, not all of us."

In an instant, Gabby was back in the darkened hall of Montrose House as she made her way to the retiring room. When soft moans had met her ears, Gabby couldn't stop herself from peering around the cracked doorway on her left, a gasp catching in her throat. She had met the Duke of Whitfield earlier in the night when he had ignored proper protocol and introduced himself to her directly. Gabby had been charmed by his confidence, and then struck by his droll wit, especially when he had made her laugh with his insightful commentary about those in attendance. The intense manner in which he watched her while she spoke, as if he were keen to hear every thought in her mind, had been incredibly flattering, and she had accepted his request to share a waltz despite her reservations that a handsome titled man could be anything but a rake.

So Gabby had paused when she spied him seated in an armchair, his head tilted back and showcasing the long line of his throat, his eyes clenched closed. One of his hands was tangled in the blond curls of a woman who kneeled in between his spread legs. Heat had coiled low in her belly to see the pleasure etched on his striking face, but before Gabby had an opportunity to ponder what exactly the woman was doing to elicit such a response from him, footsteps had echoed from down the hall. The duke's gaze had suddenly collided with hers, and Gabby had slapped a hand to her mouth to stifle her surprise. Horrified and embarrassed, she'd grasped her skirts and dashed away. When Whitfield had approached later in the evening to claim her hand for their waltz, she'd arched a brow at him and turned away.

Her cut direct of the Duke of Whitfield had been a minor scandal and had colored her reputation for months afterward, but Gabby had not cared. The duke had revealed his true nature, and no amount of glib compliments, shrewd words, or clever blue eyes would ever convince Gabby that he was worth her time or attention.

Even if the memory of Whitfield's pleasure in that dark room had been impossible to forget.

"Surely there's more to him than just that," Lucia offered now, yanking Gabby back to the present.

But a murmured "perhaps" was all Gabby was willing to concede.

. . .

"Your Grace, I hope your accommodations meet with your approval," Captain Navarro said, stepping from an interior door and offering Sebastian a crisp bow. "You are in our largest guest chamber, and it was recently updated not a month past with the finest in furnishings."

"I believe I will be quite comfortable for the voyage to Altamira," he replied.

Sebastian tapped his cane as he glanced about the activity on the deck. Fellow passengers spoke in various groupings, with many lining the railing that overlooked the lower deck where the sailors congregated and the deep blue waters beyond. Like Sebastian, several sets strolled the deck in a circuit, greeting other first-class passengers along the way. Now that the captain had halted his promenade, Sebastian's gaze immediately landed on Miss Luna—Gabriela—in her jade-green travel ensemble, the sea breeze tossing strands of her mahogany hair against her wind-chapped cheeks. She stood at the railing near the bow of the ship, chatting with a petite dark-haired woman he was not acquainted with. Fox had mentioned that a young woman would be traveling with Gabriela as a companion, so he assumed that was she. Sebastian was certain he would make her acquaintance at some point or another on the trip, and was certainly in no rush to engage with Gabriela so soon after departing.

He blinked when he realized the captain was speaking to him. Something about taking a tour of the bridge? "I thank you for the offer, sir, and it's one I will gladly accept once I've become accustomed to the movements of the ship."

Captain Navarro raised his brows. "Haven't quite gained your sea legs, Your Grace?"

"Unfortunately, no." Sebastian's chuckle was dry. "I'm sure they will come to me in the next day or so. Or at least I hope."

"Indeed." The older man cocked his head. "I assume you have much experience traveling abroad."

"Unfortunately, no." Sebastian fought to keep the embarrassment from his cheeks. "As my father's heir, the late duke forbade me to travel any farther than Paris, lest I come to harm. And since becoming Whitfield, I have been tending to the needs of the dukedom. This trip to Mexico is a first for me, and I find myself quite curious to explore the country. The wife of a close friend is from Mexico, and she speaks lovingly of her homeland."

"Sí, Señorita Luna's sister." When Sebastian nodded, Captain Navarro smiled. "Señor Fox was quite adamant that I keep his young sister-in-law from harm."

"He was quite adamant with me, as well." Sebastian scoffed. "But I assure you that Miss Luna is quite capable of taking care of herself."

He darted a look in her direction, startled to discover her gazing at him. Sebastian met her stare for only a moment before glancing away with a nod. Politeness was not hard, after all.

"I have found that you never know what kind of Mexican woman you'll encounter. In Spain, where I am from, the women are demure and feminine. They're pious and dutiful, and loving wives and mothers." The older man's tone turned contemplative as he studied Miss Luna and her companion. "But in Mexico, the women are . . . harder. Quick-tempered. I'm sure it's from their mestizo blood."

Sebastian didn't bother to hide his frown. "Mestizo blood?"

Captain Navarro braced a hand on the railing, a relaxed posture that set Sebastian's teeth on edge. Not that he expected proper decorum on the deck of a ship, but the older man's ease hinted at a familiarity that had not been earned. "When you mix Spanish blood with . . . lesser varieties, well, you're bound to produce inferiority."

"Are you saying that Miss Luna is inferior?" Sebastian was surprised he was able to say the words around his gritted teeth.

The older man must have noted the anger in his tone, for he dropped his arm immediately, his eyes wide. "I would never dream of saying such a thing to her."

"I should hope not, for her displeasure is a thing to fear." The captain opened and closed his mouth, but before he could respond, Sebastian stepped close to his side. "Miss Luna is the epitome of not just beauty and grace, but intelligence and bravery. If I learn that she is treated with anything less than the utmost respect by you or any member of your crew, I will be incredibly vexed. Do you understand?"

Captain Navarro swallowed. "Of course, Your Grace." Taking a step back, the man bowed stiffly. "Enjoy the rest of your day, sir," he said, disappearing into an interior passageway.

Sebastian stared at the empty doorway for a long moment, replaying Navarro's words in his mind. He was not naive to the fact that the Mexican people were maligned by many Europeans, most especially their former colonizers. But for anyone to assume Gabriela was somehow inferior was unfathomable to him. Sebastian knew she didn't need him to defend her, and he wasn't certain he even liked her, but good God, no one would ever insult Gabriela Luna within his hearing.

Tapping his cane on the wood beneath him to relieve the abundance of annoyance he now felt, Sebastian glanced up and down the deck. The promenade was dotted with passengers dressed in their most luxurious furs and wraps, as if they were preparing for an evening at Covent Garden. Sebastian swallowed a snort when an older couple dressed in tails and diamonds dipped their heads to him, like they were passing one another in the receiving line at a grand ball. The ship may be in fine, excellent shape, and Sebastian was all for greeting fellow passengers, but he was keen to leave behind the pomp and circumstance of the London social scene. The promise of weeks away from the critical stare of the ton that had been an oppressive presence in his life since the moment he came down from university made Sebastian want to laugh. Loudly and obnoxiously. David would be delighted by his uninhibitedness.

But Sebastian didn't need to draw more attention to himself than his title already did.

So instead, Sebastian tugged on his waistcoat and meandered away. While he greeted fellow passengers with polite murmurings, Sebastian pondered how this would be his reality for the next eight or so weeks. If he were careful to avoid the mundane, this trip could be an adventure, and Sebastian welcomed it. After a lifetime spent in limbo, always waiting, first for his father to return and then for him to die, Sebastian was eager for something new.

With a sigh, Sebastian turned from the circuit he walked and directed his steps toward his cabin. Brodie would still be sorting through his trunks and arranging his wardrobe, but Sebastian had a task to see to. He'd promised his brothers that he would write to them every day he was away, so Sebastian may as well get started on his first letter. Sliding his gaze to the bow of the ship where Gabriela laughed with her companion, Sebastian snorted. If only he had pleasant company to keep.

3

Threads of gold, pink, and violet were just weaving across the horizon when Gabby stepped out of the interior passage and onto the promenade deck. Wrapping a shawl tightly around her shoulders, she shivered in the early morning air, white halos of steam puffing from her lips.

It wasn't like her to awaken before dawn, but she'd not yet adjusted to the pitch and roll of the ship, which had jerked her awake more times than she could count. Gabby had stared at the ceiling of her cabin for long minutes, listening to Lucia's even breaths, feeling as if the room were shrinking in around her. She'd always despised confined spaces, and with her head pounding, she escaped for the welcoming expanse of the ship deck. Tipping her head back, Gabby sucked salty sea air into her lungs and then expelled it, and her discomfort, in a long whoosh.

And then she heard it. Coughing, followed by a gagging noise that made Gabby's nose crinkle. Apparently someone was struggling with motion sickness, and she pivoted to see if she could offer assistance . . . only to draw up short. For, leaning against the railing, a sickly tinge to his pallor, was Whitfield.

He dragged a handkerchief from his coat pocket and wiped it across his brow, his shoulders heaving with his labored breaths. Had Gabby ever seen him so discomposed? She couldn't recall, and sympathy swelled in her chest . . . which she resented. The duke didn't deserve her sympathy.

Still, Gabby wasn't heartless, and with a sigh she quietly made her way to him. "You don't strike me as a man to be felled by seasickness."

Not exactly kind, but she reasoned it was the best she could do.

Whitfield's frame instantly stiffened, before his shoulders drooped. Turning his chin, he glanced back at her and offered a brief smile. "Well, you are in good company, for I didn't expect it, either."

Gabby hummed in the back of her throat as she took a step closer. "I must say—"

"Must you?"

"—that I almost believed you incapable of human afflictions," she continued, as if he hadn't spoken. Gabby didn't let any man speak over her. "You being a duke and all."

He opened his mouth to respond, but the ship dipped sharply then, and Whitfield turned to grip the railing with both hands. His head dropped forward, and it took him a moment to say, "I don't know what I did to offend Poseidon."

A laugh bubbled up her throat, but she quickly swallowed it. Gabby wrapped her shawl tighter about herself even as she inched closer. "Isa had horrible seasickness on our voyage to England. I had never seen her so listless."

"Listless. That's an appropriate word to describe how I'm feeling." Whitfield's chest rose and fell with a sigh. "First your warm welcome, and now this stingy greeting from the sea. This trip across the Atlantic seems determined to humble me."

Heat rushed up her cheeks. "Yes, well, that was not well done of me. I was surprised . . ." She dropped her head. "And I acted rudely. I apologize."

She glanced up to find Whitfield looking at her, his brows now high on his forehead.

"Don't look so shocked," she snapped . . . and then bit her tongue. After a pause, Gabby licked her lips and tried again. "I know when I'm in the wrong."

"So you know when you're in the wrong, yet choose to not always confess it." His eyes narrowed. "Is that it?"

Gabby considered this for a moment, and eventually nodded. "I have a healthy dose of self-awareness . . . although I'm often lacking in empathy. And patience."

"Hmm," the duke said, turning to stare back out on the ocean. "I wouldn't say you're uncaring."

"You wouldn't?" Gabby's brow furrowed.

"I'm well aware you have no care for me, Miss Luna," he said on a snort, "but I'm not ignorant of how you give it to others."

"What do you mean?"

The corner of Whitfield's mouth kicked up. "I know of the charitable ventures you engage in."

"Oh," she murmured, dropping her gaze to study the planks beneath her feet. Gabby should have known the duke was aware of the work she had done with her women's group. Although they had fundraised to provide aid to widows and young mothers within Whitechapel and beyond, they had begun to organize an official effort to petition Parliament to take up the right of women to vote. Gabby had worked alongside several friends to gather signatures for the petition, and she felt terrible that she had left before all the signatures had been acquired.

Another thought that plagued her was how she would fill

her time once she arrived in Mexico. Ideally, Gabby would like to aid the resistance in some way. Perhaps she could assist Isabel in her work for Señora Maza de Juárez or even act as a diplomat, earning the regard of imperialists, who would be keen to form alliances now that the French empire was crumbling. But such plans would matter only if her father didn't immediately send her back to England for not asking to return—

"What charitable or political causes will you commit yourself to once you return to your life in Mexico?"

Gabby blinked. Of course Whitfield would ask her such a thing. But Gabby was done considering her future in Mexico when so much about it seemed uncertain. So Gabby rushed to divert the attention from herself.

"I didn't know you were invested in the Camino Rojo mine," she blurted out, containing a cringe over how forceful her voice sounded.

If Whitfield thought it strange, he didn't show it. Instead, he raised a shoulder as he carefully folded his handkerchief and put it in the pocket of his coat. "My letter to you announcing the news must have been lost in the post."

Gabby's mouth wobbled as she bit back a laugh. "How terribly rude," she finally managed.

The duke's eyes darted to her for a moment, and he promptly looked away again.

Silence enveloped them but it was not uncomfortable. Gabby was usually on edge when she was around Whitfield, always ready to return his pointed jests with barbs of her own.

But there was no bite in Whitfield's jests now, and Gabby didn't have the energy to reignite their war of words. Not when the ocean breeze sifted through her hair and cooled the fire of her temper.

"Are you excited to be returning home?"

Gabby blinked as she glanced at him. "*Excited* is a strong word."

The duke pivoted to perch on the railing, his arms crossing over his chest. Once again it appeared his coat seams were fighting a tense battle. "Relieved, maybe?"

She considered this for a moment. "Relieved, yes. Eager, definitely."

"Eager to see your parents?" Whitfield asked.

"My mother," Gabby said succinctly.

"Aah," he said, and nothing more. But it contained a depth of understanding she had not expected.

Gabby rested her hip against the rail. "I assume Gideon has told you of my father."

Whitfield nodded. "He has. So has Dawson."

Now it was her turn to say *Aah*. Gabby had no desire to speak about her father or even to bring thoughts of him into this peaceful moment. He waited for her on the other side of the ocean, whether he knew it or not, and the thought of his reception made her stomach turn. Gabby was thankful that Whitfield did not push the topic. He could have used whatever he knew of Elías Luna and his relationship, or lack thereof, with his youngest daughter to humiliate her, but he didn't. Perhaps it was an olive branch. Perhaps they could call a ceasefire to their contentious interactions while away from London. Perhaps Gabby could return his circumspection with discretion of her own.

Perhaps.

Neither of them said anything more, and the only sounds were the cresting waves and the gulls squawking overhead. Gabby found herself staring at the horizon as the sun prepared to peek over the ocean, a sense of purpose, of hope, swelling in her chest.

Movement in the waters below caught her eye, and she gasped.

"Look, Whitfield, do you see there?" Gabby exclaimed, gesturing to the figures streaking in the water next to the ship.

The duke took a step closer to her, his gaze following the direction she pointed. "Wh-what are they?"

"They're dolphins!" Gabby laughed as she clapped her hands, looking up at him with a smile. "I was told they like to swim in ship wakes. They're considered good luck, you know."

A hint of a smile softened his face, even as he continued to stare down at her and not at the beasts that zipped along in the blue waters below. "I didn't know."

"Well, you do now." Turning back to watch, Gabby laughed again when a dolphin leapt out of the water, its grayish body graceful and carefree. "Aren't they wonderful?" she cried into the wind.

"Indeed," he murmured before pivoting to face the ocean again. "I could use a little luck right now."

So could she. Gabby closed her eyes, soaking in the moment and all the positive energy it presented. She never would have imagined the Duke of Whitfield would be by her side in such a moment of hopefulness. Gabby decided she could afford to share this moment with him . . . for a spell, at least.

Sebastian didn't quite know how he had found himself the recipient of one of Gabriela Luna's smiles, but he would not complain. It overtook her whole face and blazed in her greenish-brown eyes.

Not that she was miserly with her smiles, but the offerings she flashed at social events were different. They were polite, friendly, and usually without depth. Gabriela knew how to navigate a social situation with a kind word and an attentive gaze. She deployed her laughs and smiles with a military precision, a talent Sebastian recognized because didn't he do the same?

But in this moment, with the salty breeze in her hair, and her gaze sparkling with unfettered delight, Sebastian was afraid to move or say anything to pop this idyllic bubble he had found himself in with her.

He'd barely slept an hour the night before, his stomach roiling with the waves, and Sebastian had been embarrassed by the number of times he'd emptied his stomach in the small bucket in his room. As soon as he heard the call of seagulls outside, he'd stumbled from his confining, foul-smelling cabin to the haven that was the ship deck. Aside from the sailor in the crow's nest above, he'd been blissfully alone. Without worrying that he was behaving crudely, Sebastian clung to the rail that overlooked the waters and prayed for relief from the malaise that clawed and twisted his insides.

Instead of relief, Gabriela had appeared, her sleep-softened face an unjustly cruel punishment because he knew she would delight to find him in his current state. Yet Gabriela had surprised him. She'd been sympathetic to his plight, and even apologized for her curt greeting the day before. For a second, Sebastian wondered if he had hit his head at some point during the night, because he could not understand why she had stowed away her caustic remarks, especially when he was so vulnerable.

But then Sebastian wasn't giving her the credit she deserved. While their interactions had always been marked by acrimony, Gabriela was well liked by his fellow peers. She was known for her friendliness and kindness just as much as she was known not to suffer fools. Sebastian had always regretted that their association had started so poorly, a fault he took responsibility for.

He'd initially been captivated by her beauty, by the teasing lilt in her voice, the taunting light that shone in her eyes. Yet instead of approaching her with respect and a sincere earnestness to meet her, Sebastian had been a rogue. In turn, she'd met his sarcasm with jaded jeers of her own, and Sebastian was thankful for the space her well-deserved dislike of him necessitated. Gabriela Luna was dangerous, and he'd endeavored never to get close enough to her to learn how much.

Yet she stood by his side now, laughing gaily at the dolphins that raced alongside the ship, and Sebastian swallowed. He could almost believe their conversation was one shared between friends, and that terrified him. Sebastian may have promised Fox he would ensure Gabriela remained safe, but he did not owe her friendship. Acrimony was safe territory, and while Sebastian was loath to upset the precarious affinity stretching like a web between them, Gabriela would be safer if he ushered their interactions back to familiar battlegrounds.

"If you'll excuse me, Miss Luna." Sebastian pulled his watch out of his pocket and consulted the time, more so for an excuse not to look at her. "As you can imagine, I slept poorly last night and I find myself exhausted."

"Por supuesto." She shuffled on her feet, and Sebastian risked a glance at her face. Her forehead was crinkled as she looked up at him. "I hope you adjust to the movements of the ship soon, Your Grace."

"Thank you. I do, as well." Running a hand through his hair, he laughed dryly. "With my luck, I won't get used to it until the day before we reach port."

"Nonsense," Gabriela declared, luring his gaze back to her eyes. "I strongly believe our dolphin friends are a sign of good things to come."

"For you, no doubt."

Gabriela shook her head. "And for you, as well. You were here for their antics, after all."

Sebastian pressed his lips together as he stared at her. She was including him in her good fortune? Christ, that would not do.

"I don't know that I believe in luck, Miss Luna. Good or bad," he heard himself say.

Her brows stitched together. "Why not?"

"Because to believe in luck is to relinquish a measure of control." A deplorable request, as far as Sebastian was concerned. "If luck is responsible for the good and bad things that happen in our lives, does that mean we have no say in its direction?"

"A rather sobering thought, and one I had never considered before." Gabriela angled her head, a silky curl falling against her cheek. "Can luck not just be a little of happy happenstance? The universe righting itself in some way?"

"But does it need to be righted? Maybe things happen the way they're supposed to. Maybe good things happen to good people, and bad things come to those who deserve them." Sebastian leaned close, doing his best to ignore her floral scent. "If bad luck comes to me, we both know I deserve it."

Gabriela tilted her chin up in that pert, challenging manner he'd come to know her for. "I agree. Whatever comes your way was certainly earned." She sank into a curtsy, her expression arch. "Rest well, Your Grace."

Sebastian watched her walk away, stopping to greet a group of older women who had just stepped out onto the deck. She easily assimilated herself into the group, even though he was certain Gabriela had just met the women the day prior. Still, the smile she wore was devoid of its vivacity. Its brightness had been dulled. His words had done that to her, and he was sad for it.

Releasing a deep sigh, Sebastian returned to his room, intent on claiming that nap he had spoken of. When he opened the door, however, he found Brodie sorting through his cravats and ties, arranging them by type and color across his bed.

"Already started your day, I see," the older man drawled, barely glancing up from his task.

"I had a terrible night," Sebastian declared, pulling his coat from his shoulders and tossing it on a rack by the door. "The floor pitched and rolled, and I could barely withstand the nausea."

"I could tell by that bucket in the corner."

Sebastian winced when he realized said bucket had been cleaned and emptied while he was gone. "Thank you, Brodie."

The valet nodded. "I asked the kitchen staff to prepare you a pot of mint tea. They assured me they would provide a few lemon wedges, as well. Hopefully that will help settle your stomach."

"Good man," Sebastian said, easing into the small armchair tucked under the one window in the room. He could barely fold his body into the seat, but Sebastian had practice maneuvering around furniture not fit for his large frame. His father had often lobbed cruel remarks about his height and the broadness of his shoulders and chest, bemoaning how unfashionable his only son was. But Sebastian had never desired to be a dandy like his father, who had run in Beau Brummel's circles. He could do nothing about the natural way his body was built, and so he exercised regularly to make it strong and purchased larger furniture to accommodate it whenever he had the funds available to do so. Thanks to the success of the Camino Rojo mine, such items had become easier to acquire.

"I saw you on the deck earlier," Brodie said, his voice deceptively innocent.

Sebastian was not fooled. "Hmm."

"I'm sure it wasn't your first choice to be discovered by a beautiful woman while you were shooting the cat." Brodie glanced up, a devilish grin stretching his lips. "What a sight you must have made."

Unwilling to encourage the valet's teasing, Sebastian reached for a book on the cramped side table and flipped it open to the spot he left it at the night prior.

"Did she scold you?" Brodie pushed.

Sebastian scoffed. "Of course not."

"I don't know why you would say *of course*. It's not like I know the lady."

"Well, I do. And Miss Luna is not the type of person to scoff at another's suffering." Sebastian tried to focus his gaze on the words before him, but they swam out of order, leaving him feeling more vexed than he had been when he walked in the door.

Brodie propped a hand on his hip. "What did she do then?"

"You are the most annoyingly tenacious man I have ever met." Sebastian threw his hands in the air. "Do you know that?"

"Of course." Brodie scowled as if Sebastian had declared the sky was blue. "That's why you keep me around. You like it when people stand up to you. They so rarely do."

Whatever response had been perched on his tongue was quickly swallowed in the face of Brodie's words. Sebastian strategically surrounded himself with people who stood up to him. Who didn't hold his title in such a high regard that they believed telling lies to his face was kinder than sharing the truth.

"That's why you like her."

Sebastian jerked his chin back. "I beg your pardon."

"Miss Luna." Brodie spread his palms, an exasperated note to his voice. "You've always had a soft spot for her because she doesn't put up with your shit."

Cotton seemed to fill his ears, and Sebastian stared back at his valet—his brazen, ludicrous valet. "I don't have a soft spot for Miss Luna. Or *any* woman."

"Well, now that's bullshit." Brodie snorted, picking up a stack of handkerchiefs and walking to the wardrobe. After wrestling them into their designated space, the valet pivoted to look at Sebastian. "How long have I worked for you?"

"Ten very long years," Sebastian drawled, rubbing his brow. The beginnings of a megrim were already creeping along his scalp.

"And in those ten years, there is only one lass you've mentioned with regularity." Brodie arched a brow in that annoying manner of his.

"Because she is a terror. Anytime I encounter her in public, we're guaranteed to engage in a sparring match, and frankly it's exhausting." Sebastian sighed. "She's exhausting."

Except she hadn't been that morning. She had been effervescent. While he had been feeling like the sludge stuck at the bottom of a Thames ferryboat, Gabriela had been pleasant and kind . . . and dangerous. Sebastian was used to her hostility. Her carefully veiled insults. The way her lip curled whenever she was forced to speak with him. Anything less than the full weight of her disgust felt foreign. Fake.

"Well, if I may speak plainly, Your Grace, you can be exhausting, too."

Sliding his gaze to Brodie, Sebastian slowly arched a brow. "I doubt you've ever not spoken plainly to me."

The older man nodded. "Well, there are very few people who can put up with you, Your Grace."

Tipping his head back, Sebastian groaned. "You make me sound like an unfortunate, incurable malady."

"No need for the dramatics," Brodie said, laughing. "But you respect people who stand up to you. And so you respect Miss Luna."

"Uhh," Sebastian paused, his jaw working as he tried to decipher what the valet was on about. "I do respect Miss Luna, but I don't understand why that matters."

Brodie threw his hands up into the air. "Because I've never known you to respect a woman before."

"That's nonsense." Sebastian narrowed his eyes. "I respect Mrs. Fox."

"She's married to your friend," Brodie pointed out.

"Yes, well." Sebastian ran his palms over his thighs as his mind churned. "I respect Mrs. Evers."

"I should hope you'd respect old Mrs. Evers. She damn near raised you, or so she likes to claim." Brodie crossed his arms over his chest. "The old biddy would whack the back of your head if you were to ever talk back to her."

Mrs. Evers was the longtime housekeeper at Whitfield Manor, and had been a fixture in his life from the time he was a small boy. Sebastian had offered her a pension to retire more than a half dozen times, but Mrs. Evers always said she'd leave her post when a new Duchess of Whitfield arrived at the manor. He thought it an amusing declaration at one time, but now it filled him with guilt.

Until recently, Sebastian had been unable to afford to take a wife, thanks to his vile father. And even if he could, he could not think of a single woman he'd be willing to shackle himself to for the rest of his life. A night spent together in shared pleasure was one thing; a life lived together for eternity was quite another.

Brodie's voice interrupted his memories. "Have you thought of anyone else who'd be willing to put up with you?"

Sebastian arched a severe brow. "I'm a duke. I'm sure there are multiple ladies who would be willing to put up with me, as you say, for a duchess coronet."

"Ain't that the truth." Brodie sorted through various soaps, salves, and colognes. "But how many of them are *you* willing to put up with?"

Zero. Sebastian leaned forward to prop his elbows on his knees. "Why are we even talking about this, Brodie?"

"I have no notion, sir." The valet shrugged. "I just assumed you wanted to talk about how every lass in the United Kingdom, and probably soon Mexico, will want to marry you because you're a duke. And an impeccably dressed one at that."

"You're cracked," Sebastian declared.

"I may be, but I also make sure you look the part of a dapper duke, so . . ." Brodie spread his palms, his teeth flashing with an impish grin.

Sebastian rolled his eyes and pointed at the door. "Get out."

"I'm working here," Brodie complained, gesturing to the jars and bottles arranged before him.

"The only work you're doing is testing my patience." Sebastian toed off his loafers and sank onto the bed, ignoring the valet's disgruntled sounds when the glass containers clinked together. "Go have breakfast and come back later."

"Oh, very well," Brodie grumbled, gathering up the bottles. "I'll make sure that pot of tea is delivered."

"Good man," Sebastian called as the door shut, finally stretching out on the bed.

And Brodie was a good man, even if he damn near drove Sebastian to Bedlam.

4

"There now. You look much better after your nap, Your Grace," Brodie said as they passed each other in the corridor later that morning.

"Thank you," Sebastian said, tugging on the brim of his hat as he stepped into the bright afternoon sun.

He felt remarkably better after he had slept for several hours, the nauseated sensation that had ached like the devil in his gut over the last day finally subsiding. Sebastian was relieved, having almost convinced himself that he would never grow accustomed to the rocking of the ship. But he had managed to keep down the contents of his stomach since that morning, when he'd shared a conversation with Gabriela, and now he sucked a greedy draw of sea air into his lungs. He was beginning to feel like his old self.

Sebastian was stopped not long after he began his jaunt around the deck by a couple he had met the night prior. Over roast beef tenderloin and pudding, Sebastian had learned that the gentleman, Mr. Conner, was a railway representative traveling to Mexico by invitation of the Maximilian government to assist the Imperial Mexican Railway Company with finishing work on the line between Mexico City and Veracruz. Mr. Conner indicated construction had resumed three years prior on the almost decade-long project, but it had been hampered by the occupation. He was surprised the imperial government was willing to continue work when the majority of French troops had withdrawn. Still, his employer, the Great Western Railway, saw the invitation as an opportunity to stake an early claim in the development of railway lines throughout Mexico.

Their discussion naturally turned to the political turmoil that had gripped Mexico for the last handful of years, and how the Mexican empire appeared to be on its last legs. Sebastian fancied he kept his finger on the pulse of what was transpiring in Mexico, if only to ensure his investment in the Camino Rojo mine continued to flourish, but no one could speak to the prevailing attitudes of the Mexican people quite like Gabriela Luna.

Throughout dinner, Sebastian had done his best to ignore the corner of the dining room where Gabriela had sat with her companion and an older couple. If anyone on the ship understood the complexities of the political and social situation in Mexico, it was her. Like her older sisters, Gabriela was well versed on the machinations of the Juárez government, and she was quite vocal of her pride for her homeland and countrymen. It was she who should be speaking with Mr. Conner about how the railways could open Mexico to commerce and trade in ways that kept it isolated in the current system of transportation. It was Gabriela who could discuss why French imperial representatives had reached out to British railways, and whether they had also been in discussion with American companies, as well.

He'd been tempted to invite her to join his conversation with Mr. and Mrs. Conner, eager to pick her mind about the various situations and scenarios they discussed, but Sebastian had hesitated. Gabriela could barely tolerate him on a good day, so he wagered she would have no patience for him on a day when she had said a tearful goodbye to her family.

However, after their conversation that morning, perhaps he had been mistaken.

"Your Grace, it's good to see you again," Mrs. Conner said now, smiling as she sank into a curtsy.

Sebastian grasped her hand. "It is good to see you as well, Mrs. Conner. Mr. Conner." He nodded at the other man. "I hope the day has been kind to you."

"Indeed," Mr. Conner replied, and his wife nodded in agreement. "We actually just met a lovely young woman returning home to Mexico. I believe you know her."

The man's words ended with a lilt, his brows rising in question. Sebastian dipped his head. "Miss Gabriela Luna, I assume."

"Yes. She's delightful," Mrs. Conner said, looking over her shoulder with a smile.

Following the direction of her gaze, Sebastian spied Gabriela standing with a group of women under the awning. She had changed from the nondescript gown she'd worn in the early morning hours, now fully in her role as the charming and wealthy Mexican heiress she was known to be. Sebastian had rarely been subjected to her charm . . . but then hadn't she directed some at him that morning?

Sebastian leaned on his cane and pinned Mr. Conner with a look. "You know, sir, if you want to discuss the current political landscape of Mexico, you should speak with Miss Luna."

The older man frowned, his gaze darting to his wife. "I should?"

"Yes. Her uncle is the Mexican ambassador to England, you know."

The man's expression morphed from dubious to interested in a heartbeat, and Sebastian swallowed back a smile. "I did not know that. How interesting."

"Indeed." Sebastian glanced at Gabriela again, watching as she laughed. "Miss Luna's family is very well connected within Mexican politics, and I'm certain she possesses an astute insight into the climate and the various players you will encounter if the Great Western Railway truly wishes to broker deals within Mexico."

Mr. Conner turned fully to look at Gabriela. "She doesn't appear to be much older than our daughter, Claire."

His wife chuckled. "She doesn't, but then think of how clever and observant Claire is."

"An excellent point." Mr. Conner patted his wife's hand. "Would you be so kind, my dear, as to ensure we dine with Miss Luna this evening?"

"Of course." Mrs. Conner turned to Sebastian with a smile. "Will you dine with us as well, Your Grace?"

"I'd like that," Sebastian said. Oddly enough, he meant it.

The older couple said their goodbyes and moved off to continue their walk, leaving Sebastian alone. He wandered to the railing, his thoughts mulling over the conversation with the Conners. With a sudden jolt, Sebastian realized that he'd perhaps shared more about Gabriela than she may have wanted. He'd disclosed her familial connections merely to bolster her authority on such topics, but it was possible that she did not desire to make her ties to Mr. Valdés known. The majority of the ton were still unaware that the Luna sisters were the ambassador's nieces, their relation not disclosed out of a desire to protect the young women. Sebastian had only learned the truth when Mrs. Fox was abducted by French sympathizers several years past. Gabriela may have made her home in England for the better part of four years, but most in the ton were ignorant of the political power her family wielded.

And Sebastian had just divulged it like he was passing along the race times at the Epsom Derby.

Glancing at Gabriela askance, Sebastian resolved to apologize and let her know of his misstep. Preferably before dinner. Not now, of course, as she appeared diverted by her present company. Soon, though, Sebastian would swallow his pride and confess what he'd shared. He certainly deserved whatever tongue-lashing she subjected him to.

A familiar figure on the main deck below him snagged his attention, and Sebastian squinted his eyes to make out what Brodie was about. The valet appeared to be taking part in a . . . dice game? Brodie crouched in a circle with a handful of sailors, some sort of activity happening in the center that Sebastian couldn't quite make out. Whatever they were doing, the men were laughing loudly, calling insults to one another that Sebastian could just barely hear above the roar of the sea and the noise on the promenade deck.

Without another thought, Sebastian made his way to the servants' stairs that connected the upper deck to the steerage deck below. Passengers were only permitted on the promenade deck with proof of a first-class ticket, and first-class passengers rarely traversed to where the steerage passengers and sailors mingled. Once he stepped onto the lower deck, Sebastian swiped his hands on his thighs and looked around. Several men glanced in his direction, but none spoke to him or asked why he was there. So Sebastian did what he always did: prowled forward like he knew what he was about.

As he approached the group of men, Sebastian was able to make out that they were indeed playing a game of dice. But instead of playing for money, they appeared to be wagering with a clutch of small pins worth an amount known only to the men playing. Whatever the case, the sailors appeared to be having a riotous time, the cacophony both grating and tempting.

Sebastian wanted in on the fun.

Nudging Brodie with his shoe, he waited for the older man to look back at him, stifling a chuckle when the valet's eyes went wide. Brodie jumped up with a quickness that belied his age, rubbing his hands together. The group of men behind him fell silent and still, their gazes heavy on Sebastian.

"Your Grace, whatever are you doing here?" his valet asked, the normally jaunty tone to his voice missing.

"I'm here to play dice," he said, tapping his cane on the ground.

"You are?" Brodie took a step back. "I didn't know you played dice."

Sebastian raised a shoulder. "There's a first time for everything. And since you all seem to be enjoying the action, I thought it would be diverting to learn."

He could practically see Brodie's brain turning over his words, considering them from all sides. The older man seemed to come to a decision when his lips mashed together. "Play is quick, so it's best to pay attention to learn the rules."

Ah, so Sebastian wouldn't be receiving a breakdown of the rules. All the better to swindle a new player. What was Brodie up to? Sebastian trusted him implicitly, but that certainly didn't mean the valet wasn't a troublemaker.

"Very well," he said, nodding. "I'll watch a few games until I grasp the rules and flow of play."

Several of the men chattered to each other in Spanish, not bothering to hide that their words were about him as they stared at him openly. Sebastian didn't think it was the appropriate time to reveal he understood them, having employed a Spanish tutor the same day he sent Dawson his first investment check.

Brodie knew of his Spanish lessons, but he smartly held his tongue.

Play resumed, and after a half hour of watching rounds of play, Sebastian felt he understood the rules of the game and he fancied he could hold his own for a few throws of the dice.

His first throw was four ones. The men erupted, and Sebastian laughed as hands clasped his shoulders in praise. Triumph filled his chest, and Sebastian outright grinned as his opponents slid their pins to him. Although he'd eventually learn what the pins were worth, victory was its own reward.

Play continued, with Sebastian winning more rolls than he lost. He learned the names of several of the sailors, and soon found himself taunting and teasing them in ways he was certain they had not expected from an English duke. So intent was he on the game, on the rowdy bubble that encompassed them, Sebastian didn't notice how late it had become until he glanced up and spied the sun dipping low over the horizon.

Dusting his palms on his thighs, he offered the men a smile. "I must ready for dinner, but thank you for allowing me to join your fun."

Sebastian exchanged friendly handshakes and goodbyes with the sailors, and then made his way toward the stairs, Brodie following close behind.

"I'm right surprised by how well you caught on to the game," his valet commented as they stepped onto the promenade deck, and flashed a grin at the footman who stood nearby, before directing it at Sebastian.

"Why should you be surprised?" Sebastian scowled. "You know I enjoy games of chance."

A feminine snort met his ears. "You enjoy games of chance but don't believe in luck?"

Fighting back a jolt of surprise, Sebastian slowly pivoted until he met Gabriela's cheerful expression. And why did her sparkling hazel eyes suddenly put him on edge, in more ways than one?

Gabby had watched Whitfield play dice with the sailors from the railing for the better part of an hour. It had taken that entire length of time for Lucia to convince Gabby not to march down there and ask to join the fun. But Gabby could not remember ever seeing the duke so carefree, and her gaze had been glued to him as he laughed and exchanged barbs with the sailors, an odd heat creeping along her skin.

Surely she'd been out in the sun too long.

Still, her feet remained rooted in place long after Lucia had returned to their room, and even as she watched Whitfield walk up the stairs toward her. When she'd overheard a snippet of his conversation with the older man accompanying him, Gabby couldn't help but interject.

The duke stared down at her, his mouth lifting into a hint of a smirk. "Games of chance are about probabilities. But even if they were about luck, someone told me, just this morning, that I would have a lucky day. It seems they were right."

"Of course they were. I offer you my congratulations," she said, swallowing around her suddenly dry throat. Forcing her gaze away from his, she turned to survey the man standing just behind the duke. The older gentleman's attention swung between her and Whitfield, as if unsure whether they would bicker or not.

"Did you watch the game, miss?" the man said, stepping from behind the duke to offer her a bow.

His Scottish brogue drew a smile to her lips. "I did. I would have joined the action if I could."

"You've played before?" Whitfield asked, his brows stitching together.

"This is not my first sea voyage, Your Grace." Gabby shrugged. "I played dice many times during my trip to England."

"I imagine your older sisters had an opinion or two about that," the duke quipped.

Gabby clutched her hand to her chest. "A Luna with an opinion? Surely you jest."

Whitfield snorted, but the Scots gentleman took a step closer to her. "What's this you said, miss, about His Grace not believing in luck?"

"Just that the duke declared he doesn't believe in luck. *Things happen the way they're supposed to*," Gabby said, mimicking Whitfield's imperious tone as best she could.

"Said as if good luck didn't smack him on his bare bottom when he was born the son of a duke." The Scotsman snickered, and Gabby found herself laughing along with him. She looked up to better gauge Whitfield's expression.

To her surprise, the duke merely shook his head at the Scotsman, amusement etched into the lines of his face. Gabby had never heard anyone tease Whitfield in such a personal manner, although Gideon had mentioned that he and Sirius Dawson worked hard to keep the duke's ego in check. Still, the older man did not appear to be some illustrious figure . . . so who was he?

"Your Grace, would you be so kind as to introduce us?" Gabby asked in her sweetest voice.

Whitfield sighed. Gesturing with his hand to the man at his

side, he murmured, "This is Mr. Charlie Brodie, my valet. Brodie, this is Miss Gabriela Luna. She is Mrs. Fox's youngest sister and the bane of my existence."

"Your Grace," Gabby cried, beaming up at him, "I had no notion you held me in such high regard. To be *the* bane of your existence is a compliment I had not dreamed possible."

"One person's dream is another person's nightmare," Whitfield volleyed, although there was no bite in his tone.

"Tell me truthfully, sir," she said, dropping her voice as she leaned toward him. "Did you think you were in a nightmare when you saw me on the docks yesterday?"

The duke angled his large body closer, and Gabby tried not to inhale too deeply of his crisp, woodsy scent. "I almost threw myself into the harbor." A pleased sort of smile flitted across his face as she chuckled. "I was aware you would be there. Fox knew better than to surprise me."

Gabby huffed. "But Gideon was perfectly happy to surprise me."

"Probably because he knew you would never board the ship if you were aware I would be on it, too."

"That's not true." Gabby tapped her fan against his arm. "*I* would have thrown *you* into the harbor."

That damn smirk flashed again. "You are ruthless, Miss Luna."

"Dios mío, Whitfield, you really must cease with the compliments lest my head grow too big for this hat." Exaggerating modesty, Gabby patted her simple straw hat with a gloved hand.

"Oh, I like you, miss."

Laughing, Gabby turned to Mr. Brodie. "You just like me because I'm not afraid to tease His Grace."

Mr. Brodie stroked his chin, his assessing gaze on the duke. "No doubt that's part of the reason."

"You two are incorrigible," Whitfield grumbled, rolling his eyes. Looking to the Scotsman, he cocked a brow. "Don't you have to prepare for dinner?"

"Oh, very well." Mr. Brodie executed a quick bow. "It was a pleasure to meet you, Miss Luna. Have a lovely evening."

"Igualmente," she murmured. Inhaling a deep, satisfying breath, Gabby turned toward her chamber, when the duke's voice drew her up short.

"Miss Luna, a moment of your time, please."

Only Whitfield was capable of rendering his tone both commanding and entreating all at once. Gabby suspected it had something to do with his deep timbre, which filled the dips and bumps of her spine whenever she heard it.

Gabby gave herself a shake. How silly.

Spinning about, she linked her hands together as Whitfield snatched his hat from his head and ran his fingers through his dark hair. He had taken his gloves off for play, and Gabby observed how his long fingers sifted through the strands, the movement hinting at his agitation.

"Miss Luna, I fear I may have overstepped."

Her brow furrowed. "What do you mean?"

Glancing about them for a moment, Whitfield seemed satisfied that no one was close. Clearing his throat, he continued, "I believe you've met Mr. and Mrs. Conner."

She nodded. "Earlier today. They were quite cordial."

The duke nodded in turn. "We spoke earlier, as well. And during our discussion, the conversation turned toward the political and social climate in Mexico."

"Oh," Gabby said dumbly. Her mind raced with possibilities

of what could have been discussed. The tense way Whitfield held himself now set her teeth on edge. "Was something said that I should know about?"

"Unfortunately yes." The duke moved a step closer, and Gabby's heart lurched at the somber expression on his face. "I, quite inadvertently, mentioned that you possess close ties to Mr. Valdés."

An alarm sounded in her head, and Gabby stumbled back a step. Whitfield grasped her by the elbow, though, his blue eyes wide on her face. His closeness grounded her, and Gabby sucked in a breath, expelling it slowly. While there were those within the Home Office who knew she was the niece of the Mexican ambassador, her tío Arturo had done his best to hide the connection out of an abundance of caution. After Ana María was abducted by a French sympathizer, they all agreed his reticence to make the connection known was wise. And now Whitfield had disclosed it to a couple she had just met.

"What did you say?" she asked around her parched throat.

The duke's jaw worked for a moment, his gaze fixed on his feet. "I mentioned that if anyone knew about the political climate in Mexico, it would be you, as your uncle was the Mexican ambassador to England. You're quite clever and knowledgeable, so you instantly came to mind."

"Oh," she whispered, confusion muddling her thoughts.

"But I should have been more mindful of your safety, and I am sorry for not taking better care of it," Whitfield said, his eyes flashing to hers.

Relief . . . and something she dared not identify, coiled warmly in her belly. That wasn't so bad. It wasn't as if he shared that her father was the infamous Elías Luna, close adviser to Benito Juárez. "Is that all?"

"I said that you had insight into the major political players

Mr. Conner would encounter if the Great Western Railway decided to broker a deal with the government." Whitfield's grip on her arm tightened. "I didn't realize until afterward how it could put you in danger."

The Duke of Whitfield had recommended her to speak on the political matters concerning Mexico? A foreign surge of satisfaction pulsed hot in her blood. Had anyone ever thought her knowledgeable enough to comment on such things? People often asked Ana María about the resistance against the French, and she had the benefit of receiving regular updates through Gideon's connections within Parliament and the Home Office. But Gabby knew things as well. Isabel wrote to her frequently of her exciting work with Señora Maza de Juárez, and Gabby routinely dined with her tío Arturo so she could meet his Mexican guests and learn what she could about her countrymen's struggle against imperial rule. But no one had ever thought to ask for her opinion on the matter.

No one except Whitfield. Gabby's throat worked on a swallow as she considered what that meant.

Not that it had to mean anything.

He stood before her now, his hand still on her elbow and an apologetic look on his face. Gabby was certain he had not meant to put her in danger, and truly, had he? Tío Arturo was the ambassador far away in London. Revealing that she was his niece was not so dangerous, for her connection to Elías Luna, who was resented and respected in equal measure by both Liberals and imperialists alike, was still unknown.

With that in mind, Gabby laid her hand over Whitfield's and squeezed it for a moment. "Thank you for letting me know, Your Grace. I'll make sure to proceed with care should Mr. or Mrs. Conner attempt to discuss Mexican politics with me."

Whitfield glanced down at her hand, only then seeming to

realize he still held her. His fingers slowly peeled away, and he swallowed as he took a step backward. "I'm positive they'll bring it up. They were quite desirous to learn everything they could about the prospects available to Mr. Conner's employer."

"Surely Mr. Conner is looking for Great Western to form an alliance with Mexican railway officials, especially seeing as how Juárez supporters would probably favor offers from American railways over British ones," she said.

His brows rose. "Do you think so?"

"I do and I suspect you agree." Sweeping her gaze about to confirm their privacy, she whispered, "Britain has not intervened with the French, while the United States continued to send weapons and other supplies to the resistance, even while they waged their own war with the Confederacy." Gabby smirked up at him. "Juárez will want to reward that sort of loyalty."

Whitfield's crisp gaze traced over her face. "That's why I recommended the Conners speak with you."

"Because I can anticipate how Mexican sentiment will run?" she asked, cocking her head.

"That and because you're quite astute."

The duke spoke so casually that it took Gabby a heartbeat to grasp his meaning. Blinking, she ventured, "Are you paying me another compliment, Your Grace?"

"It would appear so." Whitfield plopped his hat on his head and withdrew his gloves from his pocket. He winced as he slid one over his hand. "It has to be the sun. I must be suffering from sunstroke."

Perhaps she was, as well, for Gabby could not stop staring at how his long, graceful hands flexed as the buttery-soft kid leather stretched over his fingers. Jerking her gaze away with a start, she reached for her poise when she found the duke watching her with an amused light in his eyes.

"Thank you again for the warning, Your Grace," Gabby hastened to say, grasping her skirts as she turned to depart.

"See you at dinner, Miss Luna," Whitfield called after her, and Gabby's shoulders tensed.

Glancing back at him, she nodded. "I suppose you will."

And why did that promise not feel as vexing as it would have just days ago?

5

Sebastian was ten minutes late for dinner, which meant he had at least ten minutes of annoyance built up in his veins. Setting his jaw as best he could, he nodded politely to the footman who opened the dining room door, and paused just inside the entry. The room was relatively small, as first-class dining was a newer concept aboard passenger ships, so it was not hard to spot his dinner companions. Sebastian stifled a sigh when he saw Mr. Conner raise his hand in greeting, and he regretted accepting the man's dinner invitation. After an afternoon spent around rambunctious men, Sebastian would have preferred to sit in the corner and eat his meal in silence.

Or perhaps share a private dinner with a quick-witted and pretty partner whose recent scolds had been more gracious than he'd expected—

"Your Grace, I'm happy you can join us for dinner again tonight," the man said as he extended a hand in greeting. "I took the liberty of requesting a glass of that port you favored last night."

Sebastian inclined his head. "Thank you, Conner." Glancing to the man's right, he nodded. "Good evening, Mrs. Conner."

"Good evening, Your Grace," the older woman said, a welcoming smile warming her face. "I believe you know Miss Luna," she said, indicating the person sitting on her right.

Releasing a quiet breath, Sebastian finally allowed himself to glance at the woman whose presence shined bright in his peripheral vision, but whom he steadfastly refused to seek out. "Miss Luna," he murmured simply, sinking onto a chair beside her.

"Your Grace," she said, all formal politeness. As if they hadn't chatted with each other just an hour or two beforehand. "I hope you've recovered from your diverting afternoon."

Sebastian slid his gaze to her, keeping his eyes locked with hers. It was a challenging task, for she was wearing a rich aubergine color that brought out the pink hue in her cheeks, and abruptly he was swamped with a desire to drag his tongue along her skin and discover where else it would flush pink.

Clearing his throat, he finally said, "I did, thank you. A nap was warranted."

"Whatever entertainment did you find this afternoon, Your Grace?" Mrs. Conner asked, her gaze darting between him and Gabriela.

"Well, ma'am," Sebastian began, mulling over what he wanted to share. A game of dice with the ship's crew was not exactly a genteel pastime. "I spent some time on the lower deck with the sailors. They are an energetic bunch and taught me a thing or two about the mechanics of the ship."

There. A vague answer that in itself was not a lie. Sebastian risked a glance at Gabriela, but she was smiling benignly at Mrs. Conner as if his reply were the truth.

For her part, the older woman stared at Sebastian for a heartbeat before looking at Gabriela. Whatever Mrs. Conner saw on her face seemed to placate her, for she eventually nodded.

"That must have been quite interesting to learn about the ship's engineering."

Sebastian nodded, thankful for a reprieve when a footman brought him that glass of wine. He took a sip as Mrs. Conner turned the conversation to mundane observations about the trip, and Sebastian listened in a detached manner, following the ebb and flow of the conversation but only contributing to it with short nods and grunts. Gabriela, however, was adept at asking questions or adding supportive commentary in a manner that was natural and effortless. When Mrs. Conner asked a question about Gabriela's connection to Mr. Valdés, she artfully sidestepped it with a vague response immediately followed by a question about Mrs. Conner's children. The skill with which she deflected the attention away from herself made him snort in amusement.

The waiter arrived just then with the next course, and Sebastian assumed his response had been overlooked. He should have known Gabriela had noticed.

"What did you find amusing?" she whispered, leaning close so that her floral scent wove about him.

Holding his breath for a moment, Sebastian finally said, "You dance with expert precision."

Her forehead puckered for a second, and then her lips curved up. "Years of practice, Your Grace."

Sebastian dropped his head in her direction to murmur, "I had not realized. You've never attempted diplomacy with me. You've always been more than willing to confront me directly."

Gabriela clicked her tongue, quickly pressing a napkin to her mouth. "You would have seen through any attempt I made to deflect. Just as you did now."

That was true. Sebastian would not have let her get away with anything less than a candid answer. The fact that she knew such a thing about him, and thus never attempted to give him anything but the most brutal candor, made his ribs tighten in a manner he didn't understand.

"I appreciate your honesty," Sebastian said.

"Of course. I'd have to care to lie, Whitfield," she said, batting her eyes up at him.

"Ouch." He clutched at his chest.

Although she tried to stifle it, a giggle slipped out. "As if I could ever possess the power to truly hurt you."

Before he could toss back a response, a throat cleared across the table. Sebastian looked up to find Mr. and Mrs. Conner regarding them.

"I forgot that you two are closely acquainted," Mrs. Conner said, slowly stirring her soup.

"I wouldn't say we're *closely* acquainted—" Sebastian began.

"His Grace is good friends with my brother-in-law," Gabriela hastened to explain.

The older couple followed Sebastian's and Gabriela's rushed explanations with avid eyes.

"You're referring to Gideon Fox, are you not?" When Gabriela nodded, Mr. Conner's gaze turned shrewd. "He's made quite a name for himself in Parliament. I'm sure he's been able to use his connections to help you keep tabs on what's happened in Mexico since you've been gone."

"His contacts within the Foreign Office have been quite informative." The corner of Gabriela's mouth curled. "I'm sure His Grace has contacts within the Foreign Office, as well as both houses of Parliament, and beyond. If only he would use his great privilege to support worthy causes—"

"Like, say, urging the Crown to support Juárez's resistance," Mr. Conner interjected, flashing a knowing look at Sebastian.

"Precisely," Gabriela said primly.

Sebastian fought the urge to run his finger under his collar. "I confess that in the five years since I've officially taken up the mantle of Whitfield, I've yet to vote my seat. The machinations of Parliament have always seemed so incredibly tiresome."

"It is a tiresome task I know many women would happily take upon themselves, and excel at, were they permitted to," Gabriela pointed out, her brows high.

"As you said, it is a privilege." Sebastian held up his hands to stave off additional retorts. "I have no defense. Perhaps upon my return to England I can finally see to my duty, if only to save myself your ire."

A deceptively sweet smile touched her lips. "You should use your privilege to help those pushed to the margins, be they man, woman, or child. To protect those in danger. You can make the halls of Parliament listen."

Angling his chin, he snagged her gaze with his own. "And what issues would you champion? The occupation, of course, but what else, Miss Luna? If I recall correctly, your women's group sought universal education."

"That is but one of the many worthy issues I would advocate for, in addition to a married women's property law." Gabriela's shoulders sank. "One of the hardest parts of leaving England was saying goodbye to the friends I made within my women's group. We had made strides to join with other like-minded reform groups to organize a petition to submit to Parliament demanding the right to vote."

"You would have been a fierce proponent for it," Sebastian said sincerely.

Color touched her cheeks, but she did not smile. "I envy your position of power, sir. Your easy access to intelligence. What a relief it would be to have some sort of regular insight into my family's safety. To be able to fight for their freedom in a tangible way."

Sebastian didn't know what to say, especially as shame twisted in his gut. He'd always been aware of the power of his birthright, even when the dukedom's coffers were near empty, but he'd never considered all the ways it protected him. Sebastian had very little family to care about until recently, and he certainly never cared about his father's well-being. The late duke had been an absent parent. But his mother had always ensured Sebastian knew he was loved and cherished. After her passing, there was no one to care about his safety and yet he'd never felt vulnerable . . . until recently. He could only imagine the fear he'd experience if James and David were in danger.

Gabriela didn't have to imagine. She had attended social events with a smile, behaving as if she hadn't a care in the world, when in reality her family lived each day under foreign occupation. Their safety and livelihoods balanced on a precarious invisible line. Such resilience and bravery briefly robbed him of breath.

Sebastian did not miss how her lip trembled slightly when she said, "There have been several moments when I have outright feared for my parents' lives. It's not an experience I ever hope to relive."

"I should think not."

Sebastian only realized he'd spoken when Gabriela laughed dryly. Her expression turned serious, though, and she fidgeted with the napkin in her lap. "I've found there's a special sort of helplessness to being separated from those you love the most. How can you ensure their safety, their happiness, ensure you're not forgotten, when you're so very far away?"

"How long has it been since you left Mexico, Miss Luna?"

Mr. Conner asked, peering at her curiously even while the waiter took away his empty soup bowl.

"Four years." Her hazel eyes fixed unseeing on a point across the room. "My older sisters and I were sent away the night after Puebla fell to Napoleon's troops."

"How frightening," Mrs. Conner murmured.

"Indeed, it was. But I don't remember feeling fear at the time."

"What did you feel?" Sebastian heard himself ask.

Gabriela looked up at him, humor lighting her face. "Anger. I was so angry to be sent away. It felt like a cowardly move to leave and not stay and fight."

Mr. Conner scoffed. "But you and your sisters were not soldiers."

Sebastian slid his gaze back to Gabriela to see her reaction. Mr. Conner's argument was sound as far as Sebastian was concerned, but if he had learned anything during their long acquaintance, it was that Gabriela Luna could find a thread of an argument and pull on it until it became a rope.

"One does not have to wield a weapon to fight a war." Gabriela tapped her fist on the table. "We could have transcribed messages or written correspondence between resistance members throughout the country. We could have served as nurses or cooks or seamstresses. I would have gladly mucked out horse stalls and fed livestock if it meant I could have stayed in Mexico and supported the struggle against the French."

"I can't imagine you mucking out horse stalls," Sebastian said.

"And I wouldn't have imagined you seasick, but it seems we both possess limited imaginations," she shot back.

Sebastian leaned back in his seat, his glass of wine dangling from his fingers. His brow crinkled when he noticed Gabriela slide her gaze to his hand, her eyelids dropping and hiding her thoughts.

"I beg your pardon," he said, "but I have a very healthy imagination. It's how I am able to survive the endless monotony of social events during the season."

He'd expected her to respond with disgust, but instead Gabriela grinned. "Is that why you have that faraway look in your eye whenever I spy you at a ball or dinner party?"

"Probably." Sebastian considered her over his glass. "I know you believe you would have aided the war effort in practical ways, but I'm convinced you would've been on the back of a giant steed, leading Porfirio Díaz's troops in a battle charge."

Her brows rose high on her forehead. "You think I'm capable of being a Mexican Boudicca?"

Sebastian shrugged, mindful that he was once again skirting along the edge of another compliment. "You have always been quite fearsome, Miss Luna. I have no doubt you'd have the French swimming back to Paris if they ever encountered you on a battlefield."

Gabriela met his gaze, her hazel eyes burning, but Sebastian could not grasp any notion of her thoughts. Whatever she planned to say was lost, though, when Mrs. Conner cleared her throat.

"I wouldn't dream of calling you fearsome, Miss Luna"— she flashed Sebastian a censorious look—"but you do strike me as a woman not to be taken for granted."

"Thank you, Mrs. Conner." A flush colored Gabriela's cheeks. "I learned at a young age that if I wanted people to pay attention to me, I had to make myself known. As a girl, I did that by behaving deplorably. But as I've grown older, I like to think I've channeled that irritability into productive avenues." She suddenly jerked her head in Sebastian's direction. "Like keeping His Grace's ego in check."

Mr. and Mrs. Conner burst out laughing, and Sebastian was

content to allow himself to be the brunt of the joke. "She once gave me the cut direct in front of an entire ballroom of people," he conceded.

"And he deserved it." Gabriela tipped her chin up, her eyes sharp chips of hazel glass.

Sebastian dared not argue. His regret of how he ruined their promising start festered still. Eventually, Mr. Conner was successful in returning the conversation to talk of the Franco-Mexican War, and Sebastian ate his meal while Gabriela hypothesized why Maximilian and the French had lost support throughout the country.

"I suspect that once the Civil War ended in the United States"—Gabriela ran a finger over the rim of her teacup—"Napoleon realized Juárez's greatest ally was now at liberty to provide him support."

Mr. Conner leaned forward in his seat. "Am I mistaken in my understanding that Emperor Maximilian has angered many of his imperialist supporters?"

"From what I've learned, yes." Gabriela leaned forward in her seat. "I believe the monarchists expected Maximilian to undo the reforms Presidente Juárez championed, like the curtailing of power and privileges the Catholic Church has wielded within Mexican society, but he didn't. Maximilian has been much more moderate than anyone expected, almost as if he wants the support of not just monarchists, but Liberals, as well. He even offered Juárez the post of prime minister."

"Did he really?" Mr. Conner exclaimed.

Gabriela nodded. "Of course the presidente refused, and the United States has only ever recognized him as the rightful leader of Mexico. But the thing I find so humorous about the situation is that in another world at another time, I can imagine that Presidente Juárez and Maximilian could have been friends."

"Do you think so?" Mrs. Conner asked with a chuckle.

"I really do. From what I've learned from family"—she briefly met Sebastian's gaze—"Juárez has quite enjoyed how Maximilian has eschewed imperialist expectations."

Isabel Dawson had no doubt shared that nugget of information with Gabriela.

"Do you believe it's these signs of strain that caused Maximilian's government to contact the Great Western Railway?" Mr. Conner asked, his food and drink long forgotten. "Perhaps as a means of generating goodwill among the people?"

"I have no doubt." Gabriela sighed, her shoulders falling. "But I think—I *believe*—the French will be long departed by the time construction is complete."

"Is that why you're returning now?" Mrs. Conner asked. "Because you have hope the French government will topple?"

Her jaw worked for a moment, but eventually Gabriela said, "It's not a hope. It's a certainty. The end of the occupation is in sight."

Despite the forcefulness of her words, Gabriela's hand shook as she reached for her teacup. Sebastian had never asked Fox why she was so intent to leave England. What Gabriela chose to do was not his business. But her obvious discomfiture gave him pause. If her reason for returning to Mexico was that the war was ending, why would she be agitated now? Should she not be elated? Was there another reason why she fled London?

Taking up his own glass of wine, Sebastian took a large sip and forced the questions from his mind.

6

"How was dinner with the Conners last night?" Lucia asked as she and Gabby began their second circuit around the narrow promenade deck.

They had wandered outside after a late breakfast of poached eggs and sausage, and Gabby had eagerly soaked up the warmth. She'd had a fitful sleep the night before, once again stressing over the reception she would receive once she arrived in Altamira. Gabby had thought she'd successfully convinced herself that regardless of what her parents, or more specifically her father, thought of her return, she was not beholden to them once she arrived. Isabel had offered Gabby a home with her and Sirius, and Gabby was more thankful than she could say.

Yet Mrs. Conner's questions during dinner had started the wheels of anxiety churning in her mind once again. Had she made the right decision to depart for Mexico without telling her parents? Ana María had cautioned her to at least send a letter to their mother, but Gabby had refused. María Elena Luna could be more stubborn than her husband, and would have insisted upon her obedience. Besides, Gabby was four and twenty years old, and did not need permission to make decisions in her own life.

It was a mantra she repeated to herself on a loop, although the message had not quite sunk in.

A shoulder bumped into her own, and Gabby jerked her head around to find Lucia staring at her with a bemused expression. "Did you hear me?"

"Lo siento," she murmured, bumping Lucia's shoulder in turn. "Your question actually sent my thoughts spiraling into a replay of dinner."

Lucia frowned. "Oh. I hope it's not an unpleasant reflection."

"Not at all." Gabby adjusted the set of her hat as they stepped out from under an awning and directly into the sunlight. "Mrs. Conner was gracious and asked interesting questions. And Mr. Conner was intent on learning everything he could about the political landscape in Mexico, especially since the troop withdrawal announcement."

"That announcement is the only reason my father allowed me to even consider traveling to live with my abuela," Lucia said, a crinkle in her nose.

"It's the only reason my sister Ana María let me leave, as well." Gabby toyed with the strings of her hat. "Although my parents will argue that despite the French departing, the troops are still a threat."

Lucia turned to look at her, her eyes wide. "Are you worried for your safety?"

Gabby immediately shook her head, although unease swirled under her ribs. "No, not really. When my sisters and I first arrived in London, my tío Arturo was late in collecting us from the docks. We were set upon by footpads."

"You were not," Lucia exclaimed, smacking Gabby's arm.

She laughed. "We were. Isa stabbed one of them in the arm, and I was prepared to stab another in the eye, but my uncle's men arrived just in time."

Clutching at her chest, Lucia shook his head. "Well, I am relieved you and your sisters were rescued, but now I wonder if I should have asked for more people to collect me from the docks than just my cousin José."

Gabby wrapped her arm around Lucia's and leaned into her side. "Don't worry. We'll find a way to get you safely to your abuela's house."

"Gracias," the other woman murmured, squeezing her arm.

Turning the corner in the circuit, both women pulled up short, because there across the deck was the Duke of Whitfield surrounded by a group of noisy, laughing children.

Her gaze focused on Whitfield, who was perched on the balls of his feet. He seemed to be sketching out something in chalk along the deck, with five or six children in a semicircle around him, inspecting his work and calling out instructions in turn. The children spoke over one another, the pitch of their voices competing with the shrill calls of the seagulls swooping overhead, and Gabby could make no rhyme or reason of what they said.

"He's drawing them a hopscotch court."

Swallowing back a gasp, Gabby and Lucia spun about to see Mr. Brodie leaning upon the rail, a delighted smile on his face.

"He is?" Gabby asked dumbly.

Brodie gestured to Whitfield with his chin. "His Grace challenged the moppets to a game of hopscotch."

"He did?" Gabby and Lucia said in shocked unison.

Mr. Brodie brandished a hand. "Just because he's a duke doesn't mean he doesn't know how to play hopscotch."

"I thought that was exactly what it meant," Gabby confessed, smiling when the older man coughed a laugh.

"Nah, His Grace has always been good with children. Hosts a fishing day at Whitfield Manor, and makes sure the local schoolhouse is fully stocked with books and supplies." Brodie considered Whitfield as he dutifully drew a square to the exact specifications of a girl with red pigtails. "I believe he respects their bluntness."

Gabby snorted. "I can't say I blame him."

Lucia had wandered closer to the duke and his gaggle of friends, and Gabby hastened to catch up.

"Tell me, Gabby—" her friend began

"Oh, I don't think I'm going to like this," she interjected with a sigh.

Lucia smirked, before she gestured with her chin to Whitfield. "Will you add this to your list of the duke's faults?"

Annoyance rang in Gabby's ears, and she fought the urge to walk away. She knew Lucia was not being rude, and yet Gabby so disliked her opinions and viewpoints being challenged. Whitfield was very much an unrepentant rake who had provoked her more times than she could count. Unfortunately, it would seem that he was also quite good with children. Gabby didn't know how to feel about such a revelation, and she scowled openly as she observed the duke stand and dust the chalk from his hands. His large, graceful hands—

Blast it, what was the matter with her?

"Miss Luna, what have I done to upset you today?"

Gabby stiffened, her gaze flying to Whitfield, who stared back at her with his brows raised.

"I—uhh, I—" She bit her tongue when the duke snorted.

"You were scowling as if I stole the last biscuit on the tea tray."

Doing her best to project blithe indifference, Gabby lifted a shoulder. "Come now, Your Grace, I never scowl. I am cheerful at all times."

"Except to me," he pushed, his voice becoming more animated the more she argued. "Are you upset because you were not invited to play?"

The children all turned to look at her as one, and Gabby rocked back on her feet. Even Lucia glanced at her with a grin.

Gabby immediately shook her head. "Oh, I don't think—"

"Come now, miss," Brodie interjected, sauntering from his spot on the rail to stand beside her. "Surely you're amenable to play a simple game of hopscotch with the children."

The glare Gabby shot him should have reduced him to ashes. As it was, it merely made Brodie cackle.

"You must have played when you were a girl," Whitfield said, watching her closely.

Not willing to admit anything, Gabby looked down at her feet. "I'm not exactly dressed for it. No doubt my skirts will get in the way."

Gabby was not prepared for the way her stomach swooped when Whitfield dragged his gaze down her body . . . before sliding it slowly back up to meet her eyes. "Yes, they would probably be a hindrance. Perhaps your friend would like to play instead. Her skirts aren't nearly as voluminous as yours."

Reluctantly, Gabby pivoted to Lucia. It was true that the profile of her friend's gown was much less pronounced, and if Lucia's wide grin was any indication, she would be more than happy to accept the invitation.

After taking a pause to calm her annoyance, Gabby placed a hand on Lucia's arm. "Whitfield, this is Miss Lucia Moreno. Lucia, this is His Grace, the Duke of Whitfield."

Gabby clamped her teeth together as Lucia and the duke

exchanged greetings and then when Lucia stepped forward to join the children in the game. She tried to look unbothered as the group all but forgot her when the marker was thrown and play began, twirling her hat ribbon around her finger and politely following the action. But she was an outsider to the fun, watching as Lucia lifted her skirts and successfully hopped over the marker Whitfield's team threw. Her teammates roared with delight, even while the duke and his followers booed and hissed good-naturedly.

She did not like being left out, and a sour taste filled her mouth. It reminded her of being a young girl, and watching as Ana María, and sometimes Isabel, were dressed in their finest gowns and brought out to meet their father's guests. They were his perfect, lovely daughters whom he wanted to parade about like dolls, and Gabby had hated not to be invited. Her mother claimed it was because she was too unruly; too brass, too incorrigible, too much. It wasn't until she grew older that Gabby learned if she wanted to capture her father's attention, she needed to play by his rules.

It certainly helped that her beauty matured as she aged, and her company was sought after by suitors and her father's allies alike.

Yet the sting of being excluded, of being ignored, was a phantom pain that sometimes struck her without warning . . . as it did now.

"I must say, Miss Luna, I'm surprised you didn't play," Brodie said from her side, his eyes trained on the hopscotch court.

Gabby shrugged. "I probably would have, if not for my skirts."

"Were you worried you would lose to His Grace?"

Swiveling her head, she pinned the older man with a glare. "Por supuesto que no."

Brodie hummed in the back of his throat, and Gabby knew he did not believe her. His doubt sparked her anger.

"You know what," she growled, pushing her parasol into his hands. "I *will* play."

Hefting up the bulk of her skirts, Gabby marched to the court, her eyes narrowed on the duke.

Gabriela Luna was a thunderstorm. Sebastian had always thought it, but he was reminded of the comparison as he watched her stalk toward him with lightning flashing in her hazel eyes and thunder in every step she took across the deck. He slowly planted his hands on his hips as he waited, steeling himself for the onslaught.

"She doesn't look happy, does she?" Little Samuel Ellis murmured, his lip stuck between his teeth.

Miss Catalina Ortega cocked her head, her pigtails falling across her shoulders as she studied Gabriela's approach. "Did you do something to upset her, Your Grace?"

"If I did, I have no notion of what." Sebastian narrowed his eyes when Gabriela did the same. "She's probably annoyed I'm breathing."

Catalina nodded her head in understanding, while Samuel frowned.

Gabriela came to a stop before him, her musky violet scent filling his senses. "I'd like to play."

His lips twitched around a smile. "Did Brodie bully you into it?"

"Perhaps," was all she allowed.

"He does it to me all the time." Sebastian barked a laugh when Gabriela spun about on her heel to shoot Brodie a glare, no doubt realizing how the Scotsman had manipulated her. "It's sort of comforting to know I'm not the only one he manages."

She rubbed her temple. "He knew just how to spark my temper."

"Or your competitive nature," Lucia Moreno said, coming to join them.

"Or that." Gabriela's throat worked on a swallow. Not that he noticed. "I should have known better than to let him provoke me."

A strange sensation burned in Sebastian's gut to discover he understood the frustration Gabriela was feeling. He liked to think he was a logical, dispassionate man, ruled not by his heart but by his head. It had been an uncomfortable realization that his mood—his pride—could be ignited with the right sort of provocation. Brodie had perfected the talent, and while Sebastian knew the valet did so only to encourage him to get out of his own way, it still chafed.

Just as Gabriela's talent to provoke him did. The thought irritated him to no end.

"Whether Mr. Brodie convinced you or not, you should play." Miss Moreno squeezed her arm. "It's the most fun I've had so far."

"Perdóneme," Gabriela cried, her face twisted in faux outrage, "but I thought we've had an entertaining time together."

"Well, aside from the time I spent with you, of course," Miss Moreno hastened to add, and the women shared a laugh.

Sebastian was almost certain the women had met only a few days ago on the docks, yet they now appeared to be confidantes. Once again, he marveled at Gabriela's ability to make friends wherever she went.

He tapped his cane on the deck to draw their attention. "Are we ready to resume play, ladies?"

The women exchanged a smile, but then Gabriela surprised him when she crouched before Catalina and Samuel, who'd been lingering nearby. "I would love to play, but I am afraid I may need some help. It's been so long since I've played hopscotch, and I could use a refresher. Would the two of you be willing to review the rules with me? I noticed that you're both talented players."

Biting back a sigh, Sebastian watched as the children succumbed to Gabriela's charm, eagerly explaining the fundamentals of hopscotch.

The next ten minutes passed by quickly, with the children alternating between shouting encouragement or instructions at Gabriela. She caught on quickly because really, it's not like they were playing chess. It was bloody hopscotch.

It was the reason Sebastian suggested it to the children to play in the first place. He'd been walking along the deck after an early breakfast when he'd seen young Samuel, Catalina, and a group of their friends moping about, bored and directionless. From Sebastian's own experience, bored and directionless were a dangerous combination. It reminded him of his brothers, whose small, frail bodies were brimful of rambunctious energy. Somehow or another, Sebastian found himself outlining a hopscotch court on the brick patio at Whitfield Manor for the boys, and the trio spent hours hopping about. Members of the staff eventually joined them, for their laughter had been infectious.

An ache throbbed deep in Sebastian's chest whenever he thought of the boys, but playing with the children now had dulled it slightly. The activity, and the children's near-constant chatter, had also quieted the anxieties about the Camino Rojo mine that had been plaguing him since he left London. The children were occupied for a spell, and so was Sebastian. It was a mutually beneficial situation.

Until Gabriela arrived. She'd directed only a handful of

comments at him, yet she had become the center of his attention. Sebastian fidgeted with the chain of his pocket watch while Gabriela patiently listened to her pint-size teachers explain the mechanics of hopscotch, and he did his best to avert his eyes when she lifted her skirts to hop down the court. Not that Sebastian had ever been tempted by the mere flash of a woman's ankle. Now, the gentle slope of her calf or the sensual silky skin between her thighs was a different matter—

Sebastian clamped his jaws together as he tore his gaze away and focused on the white-tipped waves dotting the horizon.

"Are you ready to join us, Your Grace?"

Jerking his eyes from Gabriela, who had just tilted her head back to laugh at something Brodie said, Sebastian turned to meet Miss Moreno's amused gaze.

"Is Miss Luna done practicing?" He leaned his cane against the railing and moved toward the court. "Is the novice ready to test her newfound skills?"

"I believe I am." Gabriela spread her arms to encompass the children. "Thanks to my new friends, I may be unstoppable."

Sebastian held up his hands. "I don't think the world could handle an unstoppable Gabriela Luna."

Her eyes twinkled as she moved a step toward him. "I would only use my powers against Napoleon and the French."

"I'm not sure I believe you." He edged closer. "Viscount Mathers once said you were ferocious, and I quite agree."

"Mathers." Gabriela said the name with a roll of her eyes. "The viscount continued to speak over me and interrupt, even when I kindly pointed out his rudeness. He deserved the setdown he received."

"Oh, I quite agree." Sebastian pressed his lips together to

keep from smiling when her eyebrows flew up. "Mathers is a rude bore, but that doesn't negate the fact that your willingness to scold a member of the peerage for his bad behavior makes you ferocious."

"Or an idiot." Her expression slipped for a second, but it was enough for Sebastian to glimpse a smidge of regret in her hazel gaze. But Gabriela quickly recovered, and the curve of her mouth turned impish. Sebastian was immediately on guard. "Regardless, I hope to be a ferocious hopscotch competitor, right, children?"

The throng of urchins cheered loudly, and Sebastian shook his head in faux outrage.

Rubbing his hands together, he reached out to take the token from Samuel, and walked toward the court he'd drawn on the deck with chalk. Sebastian pointed the token at Gabriela, infusing a taunting note to his words when he said, "I can be a ruthless competitor, too. You'd underestimate me at your peril."

Gabriela winged up a brow and then prowled toward him. "Let us have a true competition, then. Would you be willing to make a wager?"

Ignoring how Miss Moreno gasped, Sebastian curled his palm around the token and slipped his hands into his pockets as he considered this overconfident virago. Christ knew it was no hardship to look upon her. It had been her beauty, after all, that had drawn him to her in the first place. With her silken mahogany curls, delicate features, big striking eyes, and graceful figure, Sebastian had been captivated. But he should have known her angelic persona was just a ruse for her fiery disposition.

And he'd been burned one too many times.

"What did you have in mind?" Sebastian finally asked.

Gabriela shrugged, twirling a hat ribbon around her finger.

"If I win, you have to promise not to antagonize me when around my father."

He frowned. "I wouldn't dream of doing that."

She mashed her lips together. "Be that as it may, I would prefer not to have my temper sparked in front of him."

Various thoughts darted about his head, such as why Gabriela would be worried about such a thing. And did Sebastian provoke her temper so easily that she would be concerned he'd do so—

"And what of you?"

Gabriela's voice wrested his attention, and he flattened his mouth into a line. What did he want? If he were making a wager with any of the degenerates he encountered at the gaming hells he used to frequent, Sebastian wouldn't think twice about fleecing his opponent . . . but of course he couldn't do that to her.

"Dance with me at a time and place of my choosing."

Sebastian had no notion of where the idea came from, and based on how her eyes widened, Gabriela was as surprised as he was.

"Dance with you?" She wrinkled her nose. "Why would you want to dance with me?"

He shrugged, feigning an indifference his pounding heart did not echo. "We've never danced together, and that seems like something I should rectify."

"We've never danced together?" Gabriela pulled her chin back. "How is that possible?"

Snorting, Sebastian said, "Would you have consented to dance with me if I had asked at any point in the last four years?"

Pink crept over her cheeks, but Gabriela met his gaze head-on. "I suppose we'll never know because you never asked."

She could play coy, but they both knew that she would have

turned down any request Sebastian made with a firm no. Why would he subject himself to the ignominy?

Sebastian held his silence, however, because there was no point in arguing with Gabriela if he didn't have to.

Staring at him for a moment longer, Gabriela shook out her skirts and turned to the children. "I accept the duke's wager. Shall we begin?"

Gabriela's team began to play, with Catalina and Miss Moreno successfully navigating down the chalk-drawn court. When it was Gabriela's turn, she hefted her skirts up, flashing the trim curve of her calf, and completed her circuit with only a wobble here or there.

"You're lucky your hoopskirt didn't swing like a pendulum and knock you off balance," Sebastian told her as she deposited the marker in his outstretched hand.

She grinned. "Truth be told, I was worried about that exact thing happening."

Sebastian shrugged. "There's still time yet. Don't call bad luck upon yourself."

"For a man who doesn't believe in luck, you sure do talk about it frequently," she pointed out dryly.

Palming the marker, he chuckled. "Yes, well, I do enjoy being a contradiction."

Her answering laugh followed him to the court, where his team, made up of Samuel and Tommie Morrison, made quick work of their runs down the court.

"Come on, girls," Gabriela called, clapping her hands together as Catalina prepared to toss the marker. "We can do it."

Biting back a smile, Sebastian watched as Catalina and then Miss Moreno hopped across the court. When it was Gabriela's turn again, Sebastian looped his hands behind his back and wandered a few steps closer. After she had tossed the marker, he watched in amusement as her brow scrunched in concentration and she nibbled her lip, lifting her skirts and skipping through the first few squares.

Unable to resist the urge, Sebastian cupped his hand to his mouth and called, "Pendulum!"

Gabriela glanced back at him with a scowl, but the movement was enough to throw her off balance. As Sebastian bit his tongue, she wobbled on her booted foot, her arms flailing wildly as the bulk of her skirts swished around her ankles and she tried desperately to regain her balance. But with her center of gravity lost, Gabriela eventually stumbled to the side, just barely catching herself before she fell.

"That wasn't very nice," Brodie grumbled behind him.

It hadn't been, and Sebastian was sorry for it. He'd only meant to tease her, but he knew now that all he'd done was distract her.

Locking his jaw, Sebastian approached her, extending a hand to assist her. Gabriela glanced at his hand for a moment, her eyes striated chips of glass, before she grasped it and shook it.

"Good game," she said simply.

Sebastian frowned and then shook his head. "That was unki—"

Without a word, Gabriela spun away from him and walked to where Catalina, Samuel, and the other children were gathered, offering her apologies for losing the game. For their part, the youngsters seemed unconcerned with the loss, and instead called her a good sport and proceeded to pepper her with inane questions about what her favorite dessert was or whether she'd rather be a fish or a bird.

Sebastian collected the chalk and exchanged a few words with the parents who came to gather their children for luncheon.

He noticed Gabriela and Miss Moreno standing together at the railing. The flush was still high in Gabriela's cheeks, and he knew her loss was smarting. Snippets of their conversation met his ears, and he realized they were speaking in Spanish.

"I can't believe I let him distract me."

"Gabby, you act like losing to the duke is a personal insult," Miss Moreno remarked.

Gabriela fidgeted with the fit of her gloves. "Because it feels like an insult. I despise losing. And it's a million times worse to lose to him."

"But why? I don't understand."

Gabriela sighed, dropping her hands at her sides. "Because now I have to dance with him."

"The injustice of it all." Her friend laughed. "I just assumed you hated losing to him because who likes to lose in front of a handsome man."

Sebastian bit back a snort. As if Gabriela gave a whit for his looks—

"Whitfield's good looks are of no consequence." Although she glanced at him over her shoulder for a tense heartbeat.

"How could they not be?" Miss Moreno spun about, her back pressed to the railing. Her gaze swept over him in inspection, and Sebastian feigned an interest in the activities on the lower deck. "He's an Englishman with a title and power that could aid the Juárez cabinet in being rid of the French once and for all—"

"He's shown no interest in assisting the war effort before," Gabriela scoffed.

"Well, perhaps you can convince him. And if not you, his handsome looks will mean every prominent Liberal family will be dangling their daughters before him like livestock at market. Will you be content to sit by and watch it happen?"

Was that how it would be for him once the ship docked in Altamira? Had he traded one set of marriage-minded mamas for another, just in a different locale? Unease soured his mood . . . and that was without allowing himself to consider what Gabriela would think if her Mexican countrywomen were paraded before him.

For her part, Gabriela shook her head, glimpses of her crinkled brow visible from Sebastian's vantage point. "Whitfield's future has nothing to do with me. He barely tolerates me—"

"That's not true," Miss Moreno interrupted, her voice forceful.

Sebastian's stomach dipped. Whatever carefully achieved apathy he may have felt toward Gabriela Luna had changed. Oh, she could still be overbearing and antagonistic, but he had come to understand that she was more than just that. He had softened toward her . . . just a bit.

Sebastian moved a step closer, intent on saying something to put her mind at ease over the game, when she spoke.

"We shouldn't discuss this any further because the duke approaches."

Miss Moreno glanced over at him and met his gaze. "He doesn't speak Spanish, so it's not like he knows what we're saying."

"I suppose that's true," Gabriela said, turning to face him. Her hazel eyes studied him for a moment, and Sebastian raised his brows in response. "He really is unfairly handsome. The women in Mexico will be beside themselves once they catch a glimpse of his blue eyes."

Sebastian's steps halted at her claim, because this was the first time Gabriela had ever hinted she found him attractive. Certainly they had made inconvenient eye contact across any number of ballrooms, and Sebastian's anatomy had been only too willing to showcase its interest in the lovely brunette, but he'd always squashed such thoughts. Gabriela was Fox's youngest sister by marriage, and a hellion with a serpent tongue to boot.

The bolt of heat streaking down his spine now to settle low in his gut was an aberration he would quickly suppress.

Stopping before the women, Sebastian whipped his hat from his head and pressed it to his chest. "Ladies, am I to assume you're discussing me?"

Miss Moreno ducked her head, crimson coloring her pretty cheeks, but Gabriela tilted her chin up and met his gaze with her own. "Come now, sir, of all the topics we could discuss, why would we discuss you?"

Hellion, indeed. Sebastian just barely managed to contain his smile. "More appropriately, as two unmarried ladies, why wouldn't you?"

Much to Sebastian's surprise—and delight—she laughed. A sunburst of laughter that made the day suddenly seem brighter. "Despite your faults, Your Grace, your sense of self is unmatched."

Sebastian rocked back on his feet. "Oh, my dear Miss Luna, if I were to claim to have an equal, it would be you."

Sebastian managed to capture the surprise that fired like a cannon blast deep in her hazel eyes. He allowed himself a brief moment to enjoy her satisfaction.

"May I escort you ladies to lunch?" he finally said, breaking the silence. "If you're anything like me, you're famished."

Gabriela's brows stitched together. "Do you want to dine with us so you can taunt me with your victory?"

At any other time, he would have fired back a sarcastic remark about sore losers, but he resisted. Sebastian didn't like losing, either. "It was a silly game of hopscotch. I had the benefit of playing without heavy skirts, which worked in my favor."

"No one distracted you, either," she remarked, then her shoulders sank with a sigh. "And now I'm in your debt. When do you plan to claim your dance?"

Sebastian flicked a hand, allowing just a tinge of arrogance to curl his lips. "When you least expect it." When she made to argue, he shook his head. "Rest assured that my request will not come at the expense of your good name."

She stared at him for a long moment, her bottomless gaze darting over his face as if looking for any signs of duplicity. But Sebastian was not lying; he would rather jump into the North Atlantic than knowingly embarrass Gabriela Luna in any way.

"Very well," she said, nodding.

With that settled, Sebastian reiterated his earlier question. "May I escort you to lunch?"

Miss Moreno readily agreed, while Gabriela nodded.

"I'd like that," she said, flashing a quick grin that hit him right in the solar plexus.

7

It was a very odd thing for Gabby to encounter Whitfield and not immediately feel her hackles rise.

But so it was, even now, as she watched him chat with several gentlemen across the first-class deck. Ever since their hopscotch match and their luncheon afterward, she and the duke had seemed to come to an unspoken agreement that they would avoid each other. Because it was obvious Whitfield was avoiding her. He went out of his way to walk on the opposite side of the deck and sat for meals either before she did or well after he knew she would. Gabby appreciated his circumspection because she wasn't exactly keen to interact with him, either. Not because he'd been rude to her or even because he was a bore; neither was true. If Gabby were honest, Whitfield was a diverting conversationalist, and she'd enjoyed his company of late. And that was the thing; Gabby did not want to like the duke. He was a depraved rake, and she refused to think of him in any other manner, even if she was beginning to realize there was more to the man beneath his arrogant facade.

So she forbade herself to think of him . . . which meant she needed to avoid him. If Whitfield learned she was softening to him, he would be insufferable. More so than he already was.

Gabby clung to this thought as she covertly tracked Whitfield's movements while she walked next to Lucia, doing her best to attend to her friend's chatter.

"—and Mrs. Sanderson mentioned that she'd be happy to ask their driver to deliver me to my abuela's house because they would be heading in that direction anyway. I told her it was incredibly kind of her to offer, but the Duke of Whitfield had already offered to procure a private carriage and outriders for me and José when we docked."

Stumbling to a halt, Gabby whipped her head about to look at Lucia. "Whitfield is renting you a private carriage?"

Her friend slowly nodded, a divot between her brows. "He is. We shared an early morning walk yesterday, and he offered when he learned I was nervous about traveling to Guanajuato with only my cousin."

"You walked with the duke?" Gabby asked, frowning outright.

"Did I not tell you?" Lucia cocked her head to the side. "We chatted for at least a half hour. I can't tell you how relieved I am that he offered to assist me, and before I could even ask."

Gabby dropped Lucia's gaze to stare at the horizon. An odd mix of emotions churned in her chest, and she swallowed the knot that abruptly lodged in her throat. "That was kind of him."

And it was. Not just for Whitfield to come to Lucia's aid, but to engage her in friendly conversation. Yet why did the knowledge that Lucia and the duke spent time together, without her, leave her clenching her teeth until her jaw hurt?

"Have I said something to upset you?"

Shaking her head, Gabby flashed her friend a smile. "No. I'm just surprised you spent time alone with the duke."

Lucia scoffed. "Well, we weren't really alone, were we? There were several other passengers on the deck when Whitfield and I chatted, and truthfully, I would not at all be surprised if the duke sought my company because Mrs. Attmore had been chattering his ear off about her daughter."

"There's nothing mothers of unmarried daughters desire more than a bachelor duke," Gabby grumbled.

"Especially when he's charming. And has stunning blue eyes," Lucia said, with a laugh.

"Stunning?" Gabby rolled her own eyes. "I wouldn't call them stunning."

Lucia tapped Gabby's skirts with her parasol. "That's because you don't like him."

"That's not true," she responded, more sharply than she had intended. Pressing her lips together, Gabby paused before she said, "My dislike for him may have lessened over the course of this trip."

Her friend stared at her, laughter in her gaze. "Even though he beat you at hopscotch?"

"I assure you I'm quite over it."

And she was . . . for the most part.

"Well, it seems that if the duke returned any aversion toward you, it may have lessened, as well," Lucia said, walking away at a leisurely pace.

Gabby hastened after her. "What do you mean?"

"What I mean is that Whitfield mentioned that he learned a good deal about the current political climate in Mexico from you." Lucia lifted a shoulder. "He seemed impressed with your nuanced perspective."

"Oh," Gabby whispered, turning her chin away. She'd

impressed Whitfield? Gabby had certainly never sought the duke's good opinion, but she couldn't deny that her chest felt tight at the thought she may have earned his respect. Because whatever Gabby thought of the Duke of Whitfield, she knew earning his esteem was not easily done. They were alike in that way.

"Have you put away your quills?"

Blinking, Gabby met Lucia's amused gaze. "Qué?"

Lucia smiled as she moved away a step. "You bristled like a porcupine. I've noticed that your initial response to new information tends to be a defensive one. As if you aren't sure if it's a threat or not."

Gabby scowled . . . but it melted from her face when Lucia winged up her brows, as if to say, *See?* With a sigh, she pinched the bridge of her nose and counted to five. Lucia wasn't wrong. Almost by default, her natural response was to be wary of new people and observations, using her smiles as a shield. It took her time to lower her guard, which was why most of her interactions, and even friendships, were surface level. Gabby had no desire to share her true self with every miss, rake, and gentleman she met.

"Yes, well. I've been trying to be better about that." She paused, a new thought striking her. "How do you know about porcupines? I didn't think there were any in Britain."

"There are not," Lucia conceded with a chuckle. "But my father used to call my mother his beloved puercoespín, because like you, she was of a fiery temperament."

"That's sweet." Gabby smiled. "Did your mother appreciate the sentiment, though?"

"She did." Lucia's gaze turned wistful. "They truly loved each other."

Gabby thought of her own parents, who so often argued.

She'd always believed her father was the dictator in the relationship because of his more vocal and arrogant manner, but with maturity, Gabby now realized the ways her mother manipulated her father to get what she wanted. What would her childhood have been like if they were loving, attentive parents, like Lucia's? How would her life be different now?

It took her a moment to clear her throat. "I'm glad you have those happy memories of them together."

"Me, too. Remembering the love and respect they shared for each other has convinced me that finding such happiness in marriage is possible." Lucia grinned, the deep dimple in her right cheek flashing. "If not necessarily probable."

"Do you wish to marry?" Gabby asked, resuming their walk.

She saw Lucia nod from the corner of her eye. "Of course. Aren't all Mexican women, and even British women for that matter, taught that finding a husband and becoming a mother is their one goal in life?"

"Oh definitely." Gabby swayed her shoulder into Lucia's. "Marriage has always seemed like an inevitability, but it's never been something I desired."

"Truly?" Lucia turned to look at her as they walked. When Gabby nodded, she laughed in turn. "I suppose I'm not surprised. Now that I know you better. You don't strike me as the kind of woman to allow a man to tell her what to do."

"Indeed, I'm not." And yet hadn't she done just that with her father? Gabby shoved aside that thought. "I like the idea of a partnership between spouses. Ones like my sisters share with their husbands. Did you know that Gideon actively includes Ana in his work in Parliament?"

Lucia shook her head. "Everything I've read about them in the papers or seen with my own eyes says there is a good deal of love and respect between them."

There was. Seeing her eldest sister so happy, and her brother-in-law so infatuated with her, brought Gabby a joy she didn't think possible. And if Isabel's letters were any indication, her marriage to Sirius was just as happy. And yet . . .

"I'm thrilled that Ana and Gideon share such love, but what if they didn't? What if he was authoritative or, God forbid, abusive? What recourse would Ana have? As her husband, Gideon owns her. He owns her body, he owns any wealth she brought to the marriage, he owns any child she delivers. Under the law, she has no control over her future, and I find that terrifying."

And Gabby was not being dramatic. Society, and thus the laws enacted within it, were not created to give women a voice. To give them power. Quite the opposite, in fact, and that knowledge infuriated her. Gabby hated that at some point in the future, whether she wanted to or not, she would have to choose between masters: her father or the nameless, faceless man who would one day be her husband.

"The older I become, the more I realize what a perilous existence it is to be a woman." Lucia sighed, and wrapped her arm around Gabby's. Pressing close to her side, she whispered, "That's why it's important to have friends to help make the way forward less unpleasant."

"I agree." Gabby squeezed her arm. She had her sisters and now Lucia. She was rich in friends, and so very grateful.

"It looks like you swallowed your tobacco instead of spitting it out."

Smothering a sigh, Sebastian turned away from the porcelain bowl he was washing his hands in and accepted the towel Brodie extended to him. "You know I don't chew tobacco. Foul habit."

The valet waved away his response. "It looks like you swallowed a mouthful of gin when you were expecting brandy. Better?" he asked, cocking his brow.

"Quite." Sebastian wandered from the dressing room to the bedroom, his eyes drifting along the trunks Brodie was packing. "I can't believe we dock in Altamira tomorrow."

"Is that why you were scowling? Because the voyage is coming to an end?"

"Christ, man, I wasn't scowling," Sebastian growled.

Brodie planted his hands on his hips. "Well, now you are."

Sebastian raked a hand down his face. "It's obvious you want to discuss my . . . expressions? Have at it, then."

"I just want to know what you were thinking that had your face scrunched up like that," Brodie said, gesturing to Sebastian with his chin.

Dropping into an armchair, he leaned back, propping an ankle on the opposite knee. Folding his hands over his stomach, Sebastian speared Brodie with a look. "I was thinking how very relaxing and enjoyable this trip would have been had I not employed the nosiest valet in all the United Kingdom."

That was a lie, of course. Sebastian had been thinking of Gabriela. Of how she'd flashed him the smallest hint of a smile when he'd seen her earlier on the first-class deck. Sebastian hadn't been able to attend to the conversation he was engaged in because he was so surprised.

He'd made sure to keep his distance from her since the lunch they shared after the hopscotch match. Sebastian had found himself charmed by her company, especially when the topic turned to Mexico and Gabriela had entertained him and Miss Moreno with what they should expect when they arrived. It had been apparent in the lilt of her voice and the sparkle in her eyes that she adored her homeland, and Sebastian had been entranced.

And that was a problem. Sebastian could not afford to be bewitched by the youngest Luna sister. Even if for some unfathomable reason Gabriela's opinion of him had somehow changed, her future was in Mexico while his was home in England. Unlike his friend Sirius, who moved to Mexico to be with his wife, Isabel, Sebastian had vast responsibilities to the dukedom. And there were David and James to consider. He wouldn't dream of abandoning the boys after finally finding them. A trip to Mexico to ensure the financial future of the dukedom was a necessity; deserting them at Whitfield Manor was a cruelty.

No, Whitfield's future depended upon the Camino Rojo mine, but Sebastian could not make his home in Mexico because of it. Thus, whatever new, uncomfortable feelings bloomed whenever he was around Gabriela Luna would just have to be ignored.

Sebastian wished he were as adept at ignoring his valet.

"You say the trip would be relaxing and enjoyable without me, but you would be bored to tears," Brodie sniffed, before looking pointedly at the half-filled trunks. "Plus, your attire would be dreadful."

"Now, I won't argue that point." Tilting his head back, Sebastian stared at the paneled ceiling. "Are we still set to dock at noon?"

"Last I heard." Brodie moved to the sideboard and removed a stopper from a bottle of brandy. Pouring two fingers into a tumbler, he brought it to Sebastian. "The lads in the bridge said we've made excellent timing."

They had. And the weather had been clear, aside from a

passing thunderstorm they weathered somewhere off the coast of Cuba. The resulting choppy waters had sent Sebastian to bed early, where he battled the return of his motion sickness. He was thankful cerulean skies and crystalline waters greeted him the next morning.

"And we're certain Dawson's men will be there to meet us when we arrive?"

Sebastian studied the amber liquid in his glass for a moment. Of course Sirius's men would be there. His friend had indicated as much, and the retired military captain's word was ironclad. Plus, Sirius wasn't just collecting Sebastian and Brodie, but Gabriela, as well. And Sebastian had enough self-awareness to know that Gabriela was the more valued guest.

"Captain Dawson's secretary sent along the name of a gentleman who would meet the ship at the docks." The valet patted the front pocket of his coat. "And I have his information right here."

"Good." Sebastian sipped a mouthful of brandy and winced at the bite. "Don't mind me. I just find myself anxious now that we will be disembarking soon."

"Perfectly understandable, if you ask me." Brodie took several of Sebastian's dinner jackets from the dressing room and carefully arranged them in a trunk. "The secretary's note also indicated the trip to Captain Dawson's home from the port will take almost a sennight."

"I recall reading that." Sebastian sighed, sinking farther into his chair.

"How far is your silver mine from where we'll be staying?" Brodie asked, glancing at him over his shoulder.

"Sirius purposely withheld that information. He said that while monarchists had abandoned his area of Mexico, he didn't want it known an English duke was arriving to tour the mine operations." Sebastian ran his fingers through his hair. "But from what I can gather from the references he's made, it's within a day's ride."

"That's some good news. I'd hate to have to lug your trunks all over Mexico," Brodie said with a chuckle.

"Yes, it would be a real pity for you to have to do your job." Sebastian rolled his eyes. "Perezoso."

"Does Miss Luna know you speak Spanish?"

Sebastian frowned at Brodie's back. "Why do you ask?"

The valet raised a shoulder. "I overheard her speaking with Miss Moreno, and it occurred to me that they could openly be discussing you or any of the other passengers and no one would know. Seems it would be a great way to learn exactly how that pretty lass feels about you."

"I don't need to eavesdrop on Miss Luna to know how she feels about me." He took a bracing gulp of brandy. "She's always made her opinion of me abundantly clear."

"And her expressions certainly let you know your place with her." Brodie barked a laugh . . . and abruptly grew sober. "But I think she's softened toward you a little."

Sebastian's heart lurched out of rhythm, and he scowled at his nonsensical response. "Why do you say that?"

"Well, as I said, her expressions are quite telling, and Miss Luna has never seemed concerned with schooling them for your benefit. But lately, I've noticed she doesn't scowl in your direction like she did when I first met her. She still watches you, except now it seems she does it out of curiosity rather than self-preservation."

Sitting up, Sebastian set his empty tumbler aside. "Miss Luna watches me?"

Brodie scoffed. "Of course she does. Most of the women on the ship do. You're a bloody duke, Yer Grace."

"A fact I'm aware of." Still, he had no notion Gabriela was keeping tabs on him, and was surprised by how delighted the thought made him.

She probably just wants to make sure to avoid you. That thought deflated his mood, and he shared the idea with Brodie.

"Miss Luna has been avoiding you, hasn't she?" Brodie replied, with a sad nod of his head.

"I beg your pardon, but *I've* been avoiding *her*."

Why Sebastian felt inclined to make this clarification, he didn't know, but he immediately wished he could recall it when his valet turned around and planted his hands on his hips. An ecstatic grin spread his weathered cheeks taut.

"Now why would you be wanting to avoid the lass, Yer Grace?"

Clearing his throat, he said, "We've managed to set aside some of our acrimony for each other, and I would hate to resurrect it by being too much in her pocket. We'll be spending even more time together once we reach Mexico. Better to create some distance to keep the peace."

There. That sounded perfectly reasonable. Sebastian almost smiled at his well-crafted argument.

"I think it's because you've found she's just as bewitching as you feared." With a decisive nod, Brodie turned back to packing the trunks.

Sebastian really should think about sacking his valet.

8

Gabby was home.

The thought sent a rush of elation zinging through her blood, and she clutched her reticule to her chest as she spun about and took in the busy docks around her. Wagons piled high with crates and trunks bumped over the craggy cobblestone roads, dodging pedestrians while food vendors with pushcarts shouted their offerings to the freshly disembarked passengers and sailors. A malodorous scent crept along the boardwalk but was undercut by the salty breeze sweeping inland from the sea.

What delighted Gabby the most about the commotion was that almost every conversation, every shout, was in Spanish. Or Nahuatl. Or Purépecha or another native language. Closing her eyes, she tilted her head back and allowed the Mexican sun to welcome her back with a warm caress to her face.

"I wish we didn't have to say goodbye."

Lucia stood a few feet away, nervously clutching her bag. Her dark eyes were wide as she scanned the activities around them, and when she looked back at Gabby, there was more than a dose of fear in her gaze. Without a moment's hesitation, Gabby stepped forward and wrapped her arms around the other woman.

"I wish we didn't have to say goodbye, either. I wish you were going with us." Gabby squeezed Lucia tight. "But if your family proves to be overbearing and tries to marry you off to a man you don't esteem, I will do everything I can to help."

"You've been very good to me." Lucia stepped back and smiled, her eyes watery. "If I were to ever have had a sister, I would have wanted her to be like you."

"That is—" Gabby abruptly pressed her lips together. When she was certain her voice would not break, she said, "That's one of the nicest things anyone has ever said to me."

Lucia reached for her hand. "It's true."

Gabby shook her head. "I know what a good sister is like because I have two of the best sisters in the world. I hope that one day I'm able to introduce you to them."

"I would like that very much." Lucia's eyes traveled to a spot over Gabby's shoulder. "It appears my carriage is ready."

Following Lucia's gaze, Gabby spied Whitfield speaking with an older gentleman in a broad-brimmed straw hat and a younger man in overalls. The men stood next to the attractive rented carriage Whitfield had procured, and it looked exceedingly more comfortable than the various wagons and hackneys that rumbled down the street.

"It will be a much pleasanter ride in that than it would have been in the conveyance my abuela had instructed my cousin to rent," Lucia said, relief in her words.

"Your cousin appears relieved at your change of fortune." Gabby smiled as she took in the man. "The ride to Guanajuato will take several days, so it's best to be comfortable."

"We need Mr. Conner and his railway to start laying tracks as soon as possible." Lucia laughed. "Then we can visit each other more easily."

Gabby heartily agreed.

The women continued their chatter as they made their way to where Whitfield stood at the carriage with Lucia's cousin. Gabby's skin prickled when she met the duke's eyes. They had yet to speak that day, although she knew they would be spending a good deal of time with each other as they traveled to Isabel and Sirius's home. The specter of a smile that turned up the corners of his lips gave her hope they could continue their genial accord.

And if Whitfield could greet her graciously—for him, at least—well, she could do the same. As they came to a stop before him, Gabby bobbed a quick curtsy. "Good day, Your Grace."

One of his black brows winged up, but his glacial eyes sparkled behind his spectacles. "I'm sure it is a good day, Miss Luna, for you're closer than ever to being reunited with your sister."

Gabby's answering grin was crooked, and a bubble of excitement swelled in her chest. "I am more delighted that I can express to see Isabel again. And to see her married. I expect Captain Dawson to be a very good husband to her."

"Sirius quite lost his head over your sister, so I have no doubt that he dotes on her to an embarrassing degree." Whitfield watched her over the top of his spectacles when she scoffed. Eventually he turned his gaze to Lucia. "I'm sorry that we must say goodbye, but I hope your trip to Guanajuato is comfortable."

"And thanks to you, it will be," Lucia proclaimed. Turning to Gabby, her smile faltered. "I will miss you."

"And I you." Gabby bussed both of her cheeks before hugging her again.

Gabby stood next to the duke as they watched Lucia's rented carriage rattle over the cobblestone streets heading west. She was sad to see her friend go, and hoped Lucia was treated kindly by her abuela and family.

"Thank you for organizing a carriage to deliver her," she whispered, unsure if Whitfield would hear her but suddenly needing to say the words. "That was a very generous thing for you to do, especially since you have no responsibility to Lucia."

"Of course I have a responsibility to her." Whitfield made a sharp noise in the back of his throat. "She is a young woman in need of help. What sort of gentleman would I be if I didn't aid her to the best of my ability?"

What sort of gentleman would he be? Gabby looked up at him, taking in his handsome profile. The sharp set to his jaw. The long sweep of his lashes. She was slowly discovering that Whitfield was much more the gentleman than she had ever given him credit for. The realization made her stomach clench tight.

Stepping back, Gabby fanned her face as she scanned the crowd. In her last letter, Isabel had written that Sirius's men would meet them on the docks, but she'd yet to see them. Gabby hoped nothing had happened in the last twelve days to change the plans—

The duke let out a bark of laughter as he strode forward through the crowd. Gabby frowned as she watched him, curious what he'd found so amusing when a familiar blond head appeared above the array of people. When Whitfield exchanged a hearty hug with the man, Gabby rushed toward them.

"Captain Dawson!" she cried, most inelegantly. But Gabby

was so relieved to see the man she didn't care. Dashing to him, she pressed two quick kisses to his cheeks in greeting.

"Miss Luna," he said, whipping his hat from his head and flashing a friendly smile that brightened his angelic face. "Es lindo verte de nuevo."

Gabby gasped. "Señor, hable español muy bueno." She clapped her hands together. "Estoy impresionada."

The captain laughed. "Gracias, hermana. I've worked hard to learn the language, seeing as how Mexico is my home now. I still struggle with the pronunciations at times, but I try."

"And trying is what matters." Gabby's gaze wandered over his face before fixing on the gold band on his hand. Sirius seemed different somehow. While he'd always been charming and gregarious, something about him was now lighter. Happier. The knowledge that life in Mexico, a life with Isabel, made Captain Sirius Dawson happy filled Gabby's chest with a warm glow. "I trust my sister is well?"

"She is. Isabel wanted to come with me to collect you both, but she was pulled away when a letter arrived from Señora Maza de Juárez." Reaching into his coat pocket, Sirius withdrew a small wrapped package. "She insisted I give this to you immediately."

Puckering her brow, Gabby ripped open the packaging and found a brown leather-bound book. With a flick of her thumb, she ruffled the pages and stopped when she spotted Isabel's familiar script.

Querida,

You're here! I'm positive I will know the moment you step foot on Mexican soil because my heart will sing. While I wish I was there to greet you myself, please know I will be thinking of you and praying your trip here is a speedy one.

Also, I imagine that you're nervous about returning. About seeing Mother and Father again. If anyone understands the mixture of emotions you're probably feeling, it's me. So please allow me to remind you of a few things I know about Gabriela Elena Luna Valdés:

You are wickedly smart.

You are kind and empathetic.

You are more than your pretty face, and anyone who reduces you to the sum of your outer beauty without celebrating your stunning inner beauty is a fool, and you don't suffer fools.

Father may never recognize these things about you, hermana, but it doesn't mean they aren't true. You are worthy and deserving of love and every wonderful thing . . . but you might have to reach out and grab those things for yourself. And if you need my help, I will be at your service in a heartbeat. Whatever happens when you arrive, you won't be alone.

Use this book to record all your ideas, all your observations, and all the wild emotions society dictates we suppress. Fill these pages with every whisper, every outraged cry of your heart . . . and if you wish to share them with me, I will listen.

Always, Isa

Gabby stared down at the book for a long moment, rapidly blinking back the tears that clouded her vision. How very much like Isabel to send her such a message. To remind Gabby of her love, because Isabel, and Ana María, knew best how painful their father's criticism—or worse, his indifference—could be. But Isabel's words were a perfect reminder that the Gabriela Luna who fled Mexico ahead of the advancing French troops was not the Gabriela Luna who was now returning.

"Isabel has missed you very much," Sirius said quietly.

"And I her," Gabby managed around the tears in her throat. Which was why she was not upset that the work Isabel did for First Lady Maza de Juárez kept her away.

Pressing her lips together, Gabby looked up and wasn't surprised to see Whitfield watching her, a soft look on his face. Her throat bobbed as her mind raced with what she should say, or if she should say anything at all.

Thankfully she was saved from her internal battle when a group of men appeared behind Sirius.

"These gentlemen will store your luggage in the wagon, and we'll be on our way. Señora Medina, who will be traveling with us to visit her own sister, is already in the carriage." Sirius stepped back as the men made quick work of storing their steamer trunks in one of the waiting wagons. "We should arrive home in five days, four if we're lucky."

"Are we heading west?" Gabby asked, dropping her voice.

Sirius scanned the docks before answering with a curt nod.

Whitfield moved closer, dropping his head. "Do you expect us to encounter any . . . difficulties on the road?"

"No." Sirius glanced at the men storing their luggage before sliding his gaze to the duke and then to her. "The imperial government is on the verge of collapse, but Maximilian still has his supporters. So we are continuing to be careful. Until President Juárez marches into Mexico City with his cabinet behind him, we are taking all precautions."

"Very wise," Whitfield murmured, and Gabby nodded her agreement.

Taking another look at his timepiece, Sirius snapped it closed and tucked it into his coat pocket. "Let's be on our way. The longer we tarry here, the more attention we call upon ourselves."

An understatement, for sure. Gabby had noticed the stares directed their way. She blamed Whitfield. With his long, broad frame, he was easily a head taller than the majority of the crowd. Paired with his quality attire and the arrogant manner in which he carried himself, it was obvious he was someone important. Someone of worth.

Gabby rolled her eyes. She knew it wasn't the duke's fault he was so tall . . . and handsome . . . but really, he could do more to blend in.

Deciding to ignore him completely, Gabby looped her arm through Sirius's. "I would be much obliged if you took me to my sister."

The blond captain smiled down at her, his blue eyes twinkling. "I assure you that my wife wants nothing more."

The manner in which Sirius said *my wife* made her pause, and Gabby stared up at him, her gaze intense on his. "You love her, don't you?"

Sirius blinked, a crinkle in his brow. He must have read something in her eyes, for his expression turned earnest and he patted the back of her hand. "More than the moon and stars and every bright thing in this world."

"Bueno," Gabby said, nodding her head firmly. "She deserves nothing less."

The corners of Sirius's lips tipped up. "I quite agree." Gesturing with his head to the waiting carriage, he said, "Shall we?"

Casting a quick glance at Whitfield, who appeared just as impatient to be on the road as she was, Gabby smiled. "Yes, let's."

· · ·

The trip to San Luis Potosí was oftentimes uncomfortable, and Sebastian was thankful the windows on the conveyance they traveled in could be opened completely to welcome in a fresh breeze . . . at least until they began to ascend into the mountains and the air turned thick and humid. By the end of the second hour on the road, Sebastian's arse hurt almost as much as his head, and the beds he slept in each night of the journey had done nothing to assuage his pains. Despite the weariness of travel, Sebastian had never been bored, for Gabriela Luna was anything but boring.

She regaled them with Mexican folklore, tales of brave Nahuatl warriors who battled fierce jaguars and other fearsome creatures, sometimes with the added contributions of Señora Medina. Gabriela spoke of the history of Mexico, and how the Spanish ruled over the country with a harsh fist, their shadow still lingering on the land in a myriad of ways. She discussed the social hierarchy, and how the more Spanish blood one could claim, the higher your status. For a man of her father's antecedents—a Purépecha man from Michoacán—his success, both politically and personally, was almost an anomaly.

Yet Gabriela always spoke of her father, and even her Spanish-born mother, with a hint of resentment. Sebastian understood her hostility. Didn't he harbor a lifetime's worth of bitterness and anger toward his own father? After meeting James and David, Sebastian would raid his father's grave simply to spit on his corpse. If he knew anything about anything, it was that parental relationships were often fraught with trauma.

"We've been living just outside of San Luis Potosí for the last two months," Dawson—Sirius—explained now as the carriage took a right turn in the road. "The Juárez regime held it for a time, and the president even declared it the new capital of the country after the French took Mexico City. But Maximilian targeted it for that reason, and the president and the cabinet were forced to flee."

"But you're there now?" Sebastian asked, confused.

Sirius nodded. "Strides were made to retake it, and the city has been returned to Liberal control."

"Goodness," Sebastian drawled, "you sound as if you know what you're talking about."

"Only because my wife is so very intelligent," Sirius said with a laugh.

A pleased sort of warmth wrapped around Sebastian's ribs. Sirius was his oldest friend. They'd been young, rambunctious lads together at Eton, and they had seen each other through any number of firsts. When Sirius had returned from the war in the Crimea not just physically injured but mentally and emotionally broken, Sebastian had felt helpless to aid him. Eventually, with time, Sirius seemed to recover and earned a reputation as a rake about town, although Sebastian sensed his friend still carried a deep grief within himself.

So to see Sirius now, with his blond curls longer than he'd ever seen them, his skin tanned, and his smile broad, happiness was evident in every part of his being.

What would such happiness even feel like? Sebastian wondered.

"How close do you and Isabel live to our parents?" Gabriela asked suddenly.

Sebastian frowned at the abrupt question, because shouldn't she know such a thing? Sirius's expression was kind, however. "They live a fifteen or so minute walk from us, in the grand villas on the other side of the town square."

That answer seemed to please her, because Gabriela nodded before staring out the carriage window again.

Over the next several miles Sebastian watched Gabriela become uncharacteristically quiet. There were no more stories or witty observations as the terrain turned arid and the sun blazed overhead, San Luis Potosí moving ever closer; instead, Gabriela sat silently in the corner of the carriage next to Señora Medina, her arms wrapped about herself, and her expression shuttered. Whatever was wrong with Gabriela was certainly none of his business . . . or so Sebastian told himself as the carriage made its way over the rocky road.

The sun had dipped low on the horizon when the pitch of the dirt road gave way to cobblestone streets, and Sebastian peered out as they entered an attractive town, the narrow streets lined with colorful buildings. In some ways the community reminded him of the little village near Whitfield Manor in Gloucestershire, with each home nestled against its neighbor, but the houses here were painted in an array of colors, each more cheerful than the last. Climbing vines clung to the facades, their blooms a vivid splash of the rainbow, and every pedestrian they passed called out a hello, greetings their outriders returned with polite regard.

"I've never been to San Luis Potosí," Gabriela said into the silence, her gaze fixed on the passing scenery.

Sebastian winged up a brow. "You haven't?"

"It's not exactly a day trip from my old home in Mexico City. We are several days north of the capital, at least," she murmured. "It's very charming."

"Indeed it is. We've moved with the cabinet three times since we've been married." Sirius called out, "Hola," to a small group of women they passed. "And this is by far our favorite location."

"It must have a superb lending library or bookstore for Isabel to be comfortable here," Gabriela quipped, glancing over her shoulder at Sirius with a small smile.

He barked a laugh. "You know your sister well, for San Luis Potosí has both."

Gabriela dipped her head and returned to studying the passing sights. It took Sebastian a tad longer to follow suit. For truly, whatever was the matter with her? He had never seen her this . . . this . . . subdued. It was almost as if she was awaiting bad news. Or anticipating something terrible. He wished he knew what disturbed her, so that he could attempt to rectify it. Sebastian had little practice dealing with the varying emotions of womanhood, but staring at Gabriela's solemn profile, he decided he would do his best to put her at ease.

After delivering Señora Medina to her sister's home, the carriage rumbled along for another ten minutes before it jerked to a halt, and Sirius swung open the door without waiting for an outrider or footman. At the end of a red-tiled walk sat a pink stucco cottage tucked between two Mexican elm trees. Isabel stood in the doorway, dressed in a simple green gown and backlit by lamplight, her rich black hair coiled attractively on her head. Sirius tore his hat from his head, wrapped his arms around her, and kissed her full on the mouth. His old friend had never been so demonstrative with his feelings, and Sebastian didn't know whether he should blush and look away, or laugh.

Sliding his gaze to Gabriela, he found her staring at the couple, her lips stretching wide in a smile.

Sebastian stepped down from the carriage and promptly turned to offer her assistance. In the past, Gabriela would have spurned his gesture with an arch look, but this time, she said nothing, continuing to watch the couple as she slipped her hand inside his.

"He really does love her, doesn't he?" she whispered hoarsely as she stepped down.

"It certainly seems like it." Sebastian squeezed her hand briefly before releasing her.

Gabriela grasped her skirts and dashed down the tiled walk toward her sister. Sebastian ambled after her, suddenly feeling as if he was intruding.

As he watched Gabriela embrace her sister, their watery laughs filling the small courtyard, he wished, not for the first time, that he'd had siblings to share the long, lonely days of his childhood with. Thinking of siblings made his thoughts turn to James and David, and all the ways he would ensure their childhoods were happier than his had been . . .

An hour later, they sat on a veranda that Sirius called a *patio*. Ceramic pots stained in beautiful reds and blues dotted the space, showcasing a plethora of plants Sebastian had never seen before but whom Isabel had been happy to name. Aloe vera, agaves, crowns of thorns, and prickly pear cacti welcomed guests to the tiled patio with their foreign beauty. A large raised garden bed lay near the door leading into the kitchens, and Sebastian spied tomatoes, squash, various varieties of onions, brightly colored peppers, and even a stalk or two of corn. But what really drew Sebastian's interest were the potted fruit trees that lined the western edge of the patio, blocking the late afternoon sun. There was a large lemon tree, a smaller lime tree, and even an orange tree, and Isabel had plucked a perfectly symmetrical orange for him to enjoy. Sebastian tore into the peel while they enjoyed a glass of wine after dinner, and smiled as the juice ran over his fingers and hands.

"You act as if you've never eaten an orange before," Gabriela said. The words were sharp, but a quick glance at her amused expression told Sebastian that she was teasing, and not being critical.

"I've never eaten an orange directly off the tree." He studied a segment in the soft glow of the candelabra, before he popped it into his mouth. A zesty sweetness danced over his tongue and down his throat. "It's superb."

"It's late in the year for oranges, but the yield has been particularly sweet." Sirius took a sip of his claret. "I've eaten more oranges off that tree than I care to admit."

"He will never have to worry about scurvy," Isabel added, a smile in her eyes.

The conversation turned to the Dawsons' new life in San Luis Potosí, where they had been living for only a short time. Sebastian learned about the history of the region and how the imperialists held the city until Liberal forces had recently pushed them out as they gained the upper hand in many northern strongholds. He asked questions about Isabel's work for the First Lady of Mexico, and while he listened with genuine interest, Sebastian couldn't help but notice the look of pride on his old friend's face as he gazed at his wife.

Soon, the sisters wandered off so Isabel could show Gabriela her room, leaving Sebastian and Sirius on the patio with the crickets and soft hum of the village around them. They spoke for a spell about current events in London and the business of politics. They discussed the bills Gideon Fox was championing . . . and then the softening of his character since his young daughter was born. Sebastian asked questions about the Camino Rojo mine, and being able to do so in person rather than through letters assuaged any concerns he had about the project. He looked forward to visiting the operations within the next day or two.

Sirius's mien suddenly sobered, and he swished the remainder of wine around in his glass. "I'm sure you're wondering about Gabby's solemn mood in the carriage earlier today."

Sebastian nodded. While Gabriela's demeanor had turned cheerful once she was reunited with her sister, Sebastian had not forgotten her melancholy.

"Did Fox, or even Ana María, tell you about why she was returning to Mexico?"

"No." And Sebastian could not believe he hadn't questioned it. He obviously knew that after the French troop withdrawal, exiled Mexicans had been returning home. But Gabriela seemed to live a full, busy life in London. Why would she leave it behind? "The only thing Fox said was that there were *those in Mexico who will delight in stripping her confidence away.*"

"Aah." Sirius took a gulp of wine and set his glass on the table with a thud. "To put it succinctly, Gabby was anxious to leave London because her suitors were becoming aggressive. According to letters I received from Fox and Mr. Valdés, they were worried she would be forced into a compromising position. No doubt the rumors of her dowry have made her a target."

He'd heard the rumors. It had been whispered that the Luna sisters had fled Mexico with a fortune in gold, jewels, and property deeds. It had never been any of Sebastian's business, but both Fox and Dawson appeared to be living in comfortable luxury with their Luna brides.

Sebastian's lip curled. "I had no idea Miss Luna was battling such fortune hunters. I wish I had known when I was still in London so I could do something about it."

Just the idea of a chinless second son attempting to compromise Gabriela in the darkened corridors of a ball made Sebastian want to put his fist through a window.

"I'm sure Fox or Mr. Valdés would have prevailed upon you if they felt they needed to." Sirius's blue eyes skated over Sebastion's face before he turned his attention to the darkened garden. "But that is why Gabby is here now."

"You'd think she'd be happy to be here, then. She appeared so forlorn in the carriage."

Sirius cocked his head. "That is probably because Mr. and Mrs. Luna are unaware that Gabby intended to return. She didn't wish for them to know."

Sebastian pulled his chin back. "Whyever not?"

"Because she knew her father would not have consented. Although the end of the war is nigh, it's not over yet, and I imagine Mr. Luna would prefer not to worry about Gabby or her safety."

"Even knowing that she was the target of fortune hunters?" When Dawson nodded, Sebastian's confusion intensified. "I don't understand."

Sirius snorted. "Welcome to the world of Elías Luna. I've now known him for two years, and he is still very much an enigma."

Sebastian set down his glass and leaned forward, propping his elbows on his knees. "Did he think Miss Luna would be a distraction?"

"I think Mr. Luna simply wants Gabby to obey. He sent her to London, and he expects her to stay there until he summons her. Mr. Luna doesn't want to think about her unless he has to. Unless thinking about her benefits him at the moment." Sirius shrugged. "I suspect he would welcome Gabby's return when he was ready to marry her off, but until then, I doubt he's inclined to concern himself with his youngest daughter."

The idea of the stern Mr. Luna brokering a marriage deal for Gabriela left an unpleasant taste in Sebastian's mouth. So, too, did the idea of the spirited Gabriela Luna as a docile crea-ture. Of her being ignored. Sebastian had tried to ignore her for the better part of four years, and it had been a Sisyphean task.

"We're to dine at Mr. and Mrs. Luna's tomorrow after Mass." Sirius flourished a hand. "You'll be able to meet one of the most powerful men in Mexico for yourself."

"Charming," Sebastian sighed, before swallowing the re-mainder of his brandy.

9

Gabby sat side by side with her sister, their hands clasped, in the cozy bedchamber that would be her home for the foreseeable future. The lone window looked out upon a pink trumpet tree ablaze with bright magenta- and rose-colored blossoms, and Gabby spied bees buzzing about its blossoms. Neither of them spoke, and Gabby was thankful for the silence. It allowed her to breathe in Isabel's familiar vanilla scent and soak in the bright warmth of her presence. Like a hothouse plant that had suffered through the dreariness of winter, Gabby could practically feel herself bloom now that she'd been reunited with her sister.

"I'm so glad you're here," Isabel whispered, swiping her thumb over Gabby's knuckles. "I know it's going on two years since we've seen each other, but it's felt like ten."

"Twenty!" Gabby countered, resting her head on her sister's shoulder.

Isabel laughed. "But you're here now. Although I'm sorry it took the crass actions of a vile nobleman to force your hand."

A long sigh fluttered Gabby's lips. "I was such a fool. Lord Carlisle always seemed harmless enough, but I should have known better. I'd heard the rumors of his insolvency, so I should have been wary when he began paying me more attention."

"It's not your fault, querida." Isabel gripped her hand tighter. "I only wish I had been there to see the wrath Gideon brought down upon the man. Sirius said his anger was palpable even in writing."

"Gideon's anger was nothing compared to Ana's." Gabby snorted. "I'm certain she would have marched to the earl's townhome with a torch to demand blood . . . if she could have found a torch."

"I can't say I'm surprised. Ay Dios, how I miss her." Isabel moved back until Gabby met her gaze. "How is she? Tell me about the baby."

Gabby was only too happy to talk about their older sister Ana María and the happy life she lived with her husband and daughter. Gabby showed her sister the photographs Ana María had so carefully packed, and put an arm around Isabel as she cooed over the baby niece she'd yet to meet. Gabby squeezed her tight when Isabel shed several tears.

Eventually, the conversation turned toward Isabel's days in San Luis Potosí, and every word her sister used to describe the life she'd built with Sirius was infused with satisfaction. Isabel's dark eyes sparkled as she spoke of decorating their new home and combining her library with Sirius's. She also described her work with the First Lady of Mexico, and Gabby asked a plethora of questions about the current political atmosphere, curious if her ideas on how to aid the resistance would work. Gabby wanted to contribute . . . she just wasn't sure exactly how.

Abruptly, Isabel turned about to face her directly, her eyes wide. "So, you and the duke appear to have reached an understanding."

Gabby scowled. "Why do you say that?"

"Because you're both here and haven't bickered with each other once," Isabel replied, her lips quirked.

Gabby's scowl deepened, although she wasn't sure why. Hadn't Whitfield proven himself to be thoughtful? Attentive? Amusing company? Did she really want to share those new insights with Isabel?

Dropping her gaze to the counterpane, Gabby lifted a shoulder. "Perhaps away from London and the crush of society, Whitfield isn't as bad as I've always believed him to be."

To Gabby's relief, her older sister merely arched a brow before changing the subject, and Gabby was thankful.

The following day, Gabby found herself seated next to her sister as they left the parish church where Isabel and Sirius attended Mass. Her fingers were tangled in the skirts of her cotton day dress to keep them from shaking—

"I would tell you to stop fidgeting, but I understand why you're nervous."

Gabby's shoulders drooped, and she forced herself to untangle her fists from her skirts. Just thinking about seeing her parents again after four long years away made her heart pound and her palms clammy. She almost wished Isabel and Sirius attended services at the Catedral de San Luis Potosí, where her parents did, so their reunion could be done before God and all his saints, because Gabby knew her father would not dare to be anything but gracious to her if he knew there were onlookers.

It was bad enough that their reunion would be witnessed by Whitfield. Gabby knew she was being unfair to him. The duke had wished her a good morning at the breakfast table and then silently sat through Mass and the ride to her parents'. He'd done nothing to antagonize her, aside from being his handsome, aloof self. Yet those glacial eyes of his missed nothing, and Gabby knew he was aware of her growing discomfort. She wanted to be angry at his presence, but she couldn't drum up the emotion. Since they had left Altamira, Whitfield had given her as much privacy as their narrow confines allowed, yet he'd still been there, his shadow eclipsing everything in the vicinity. No doubt he was wondering who this timid miss was that had abruptly replaced the fearless Gabriela Luna she had worked hard to be.

Gabby glanced across the carriage at him now, not surprised to meet his gaze. Whitfield held her stare for only a heartbeat, and then he nodded and returned his eyes to the window.

Knowing he was paying attention, however, made Gabby straighten her spine. Her heart might be churning away like a locomotive down the track, but she was not about to lose a grip on her sensibilities. Not for her father, and certainly not for the Duke of Whitfield.

"Is there anything I should know before we arrive?" Gabby asked, relieved that her voice did not shake.

Isabel's lips pursed, and she looked to Sirius, who sat across from her. "Father has been in one meeting or another as el presidente and the generals strategize how to defeat Maximilian and the remaining monarchists. Mother has said that he leaves early in the morning and returns late at night. The only time I've seen him myself is when we visit on Sundays."

Gabby couldn't say she was surprised. She'd long thought her father's work for Presidente Juárez was his true love. Elías Luna had never willingly sacrificed time away from his career for his family, and Gabby would have been shocked if he'd suddenly learned to do so now.

"Who is usually in attendance for lunch on Sundays?"

Whitfield asked, and Gabby worked not to jump at the sound of his voice.

"It's only been family." Isabel ticked off her fingers. "Our father's brothers, Tíos Xavier, Diego, and Angel. Our mother's sister, Tía Susana, and her husband, Tío Ernesto. Fernando Ramírez attended last week with Señora Romero."

"Really?" A grin stretched Gabby's lips taut. "I'm surprised Mother was willing to welcome Señora Romero."

Fernando Ramírez had at one time been engaged to their eldest sister, Ana María, but the engagement was broken when she married Gideon instead. Gabby did not feel sorry for Señor Ramírez—their arrangement had been a political one negotiated by her father. And despite the engagement, Señor Ramírez continued to carry on his longtime affair with Señora Romero. It had been a slight on Ana María, as far as Gabby was concerned, and her opinion of the man had never recovered.

Isabel and Sirius laughed in unison. "She is not terribly fond of the woman," Isabel said, "but Mother is too well bred to object. Plus, you know she would never contradict Father."

Now it was Gabby's turn to laugh. "María Elena Valdés de Luna contradict her husband? No!"

"Some things never change, querida," Isabel said, a sad look fluttering across her face. "Even when we want them to."

Mashing her lips together, Gabby glanced away. Señora María Elena adored her children, but she loved her husband more, and Gabby knew better than to expect differently.

Silence settled on the carriage again, and Gabby leaned back on the squab, determined to steal the last moments of peace that she could before her world was tipped upside down. Sucking a great breath of air into her lungs, she inhaled and chanced another look at Whitfield, finding him considering her with a face devoid of expression.

Gabby bristled nevertheless, resentful that the duke was witness to their sorry family dynamics. "We've given you plenty to sneer about, haven't we, Your Grace, with our rather crude peek of the inner workings of the Luna family."

"Not at all. Family dynamics are often messy. And nonsensical." Whitfield plucked his spectacles from his face and then extracted a handkerchief from his coat pocket. He held her gaze while he cleaned the lenses. "In truth, I wish my mother was still here for me to complain about. Certainly she would have found plenty of things to criticize me for."

Oh. Whitfield's bald honesty took Gabby by surprise, and she struggled with how to respond.

"We are both lucky to escape the imagined censure of our mothers," Sirius said, his expression a mixture of understanding and amusement.

A smile flashed across the duke's face. "Indeed. But rest assured, I, too, had a father who seemed to take particular delight in pointing out and mocking my many flaws. Nothing I might encounter while dining with your family will shock me more than what I have experienced at the hands of my own."

Gabby opened her mouth to respond—with what, she didn't know—and abruptly closed it with an audible click. Whitfield hadn't said anything condescending, rude, or even mocking; rather, he had been empathetic. Gracious, even.

"Let us hope that everyone is on their best behavior, and Gabby's homecoming is met with all the excitement and relief it deserves." Isabel's voice was firm, and when she twined her fingers with Gabby's, she squeezed them tight. "And I am certain our parents will be delighted to meet you, Your Grace."

"Your father, especially." Sirius scoffed. "Any connection he can make to further his own ends is met with open arms."

Gabby snorted. "I bet he was pleased to learn you would be his son-in-law."

"He would have been more so if I held the title and were not merely the second son," Sirius said, grinning at his wife across the cab.

While her sister and brother-in-law shared a laugh, Gabby's stomach dropped when the carriage came to a stop. Suddenly the moment she had been dreading was here, and she wasn't sure how to act. Or what to say.

"You'll be fine, querida," Isabel whispered close to her ear. "You are a grown woman who has earned the respect and admiration of many. You championed causes that would make life better for women. You no longer need to ask for permission to live your life as you want to."

"Father would have something to say about that," she replied with a frown.

"Por supuesto. Still, you are my and Sirius's guest and don't have to subject yourself to Father's company any more than you desire."

Gabby considered her sister's words as she watched Isabel exit the carriage. When she was the last occupant left in the cab, she stared down at her trembling hands. She was tempted to close the door and ask the driver to take her back to Isabel's house.

Just then, Whitfield appeared in the carriage doorway, the sun streaming around him and obscuring his expression. His words were soft when he asked, "Have you changed your mind? I'd be happy to be a distraction if you wish to slip away."

Well. What a surprising offer. Forcing down a swallow, she finally said, "That is very kind of you. But I've never run away from a challenge before, and I'm not about to now."

There was a smile in his voice when he said, "Bravo, Miss Luna. There's that fiery spirit that's burned me more times than I can count."

"Burned you?" Gabby smirked. "Are you saying I've left you with scars, Your Grace?"

"Scars are a sign of a battle well fought." The duke looked over his shoulder for a moment, allowing Gabby a glimpse of his profile. "From what I can infer, you've earned your battle scars."

Gabby dropped her head. "Perhaps."

"In that case, they've provided you with armor. Let them protect you as you venture into the lion's den." Whitfield extended a hand to her. "Plus, you will not be without friends."

A blasted knot lodged in her throat, and Gabby paused as she fortified her emotions. Finally rising to her feet, she stepped from the carriage door, allowing Whitfield to assist her down. Taking a moment to shake out her skirts, Gabby sucked a bracing breath into her lungs and glanced up . . .

Only to see her father glowering at her.

Watching Gabriela's confidence wither away in the face of her father's displeasure made Sebastian's scalp prickle with anger. And no small amount of alarm.

"Tilt your chin up," he whispered through the side of his mouth. "You've done nothing wrong and have no reason to cower."

"That's easy for you to say," Gabriela hissed . . . although she somehow managed to keep her expression composed. "You're not the subject of his ire."

"True, but then I could be." Sebastian patted the back of her hand. "I have a talent for aggravating members of the Luna family, and am more than capable of doing so now."

"Estúpido," she murmured, although Sebastian was pleased to see some of the color had returned to her cheeks.

He didn't have an opportunity to say anything else, for Mr. and Mrs. Luna stood before them. Sebastian inclined his head, allowing himself a quick moment to study them. His first realization was that Gabriela inherited many of her mother's features, from her sleek mahogany hair, to her heart-shaped face, to her sparkling hazel eyes surrounded by lush, ebony lashes. But Mrs. Luna had hints of gray around her temples, and a fullness to her figure that spoke of her maturity. The older woman studied him unabashedly in return, those familiar yet foreign eyes sweeping over his form.

"Mother, allow me to introduce you to—" Gabriela began, but María Elena cut off her words as she swept her daughter into an embrace.

"Mi hijita," the older woman crooned, pressing kisses to Gabriela's brow and cheeks, before she stepped back to cup Gabriela's cheeks between her palms. "I did not know you would be here. Isa, why didn't you tell us your sister was coming?"

Isabel opened her mouth to respond, but Gabriela interjected. "I asked her not to because I wanted to surprise you."

"Surprise us?" Mrs. Luna crinkled her nose. "Why would you want to do that?"

"Yes, Gabriela," Mr. Luna said, speaking for the first time. "Why would you choose to surprise us? Surely it would have been wiser to ask if it was a safe time for you to return to Mexico?"

Sebastian narrowed his eyes. Shouldn't Mr. Luna greet his

youngest daughter before he scolded her? His wife certainly had, as she clutched Gabriela close even now. Yet Mr. Luna merely stared at her with his brows stitched together.

Gabriela's own gaze turned steely. "And yet here I am, happy and healthy."

"Señor y Señora Luna," Dawson interjected, stepping forward and flourishing a respectful bow, "le presento al Duque de Whitfield."

His clever friend. Sebastian met Dawson's gaze for just a moment, signaling his gratitude for the intervention. Without missing a beat, Sebastian first greeted Mrs. Luna by bowing over her hand, a teasing smirk on his lips. True to his experience with older women, Mrs. Luna simpered. Sebastian almost laughed himself when he heard Gabriela's soft snort.

"Señor," Mrs. Luna said, stepping away from her daughter and sinking into a graceful curtsy, "bienvenidos a Mexico."

"Gracias, Señora Luna," he said, dipping his head. "Contento de estar aquí."

"You speak Spanish?" Gabriela cried, slapping a hand over her mouth, her cheeks red.

Somehow, Sebastian managed not to smile. "Sí. I've been practicing since I first invested in the Camino Rojo mine."

"I see," she whispered, releasing his gaze to glance at her mother, and then her sister. "So this whole time . . ."

Sebastian knew it hadn't been sporting of him to not disclose that he could speak her native language, but he'd found the forthrightness in which she wielded her bilingualism charming. And Sebastian knew that if Gabriela was aware he could understand the thoughts she shared so freely in Spanish, she would cease to give him that peek behind the lovely and unflappable mask she presented to the world.

He didn't have a chance to respond, because Mr. Luna

stepped forward then, extending his hand. "Es un placer conocerlo."

Elías Luna was exactly the enigma Sebastian had been told to expect in that he wasn't what Sebastian had expected at all. With the top of his head barely reaching Sebastian's shoulder, Mr. Luna should have appeared small, and yet he carried himself with all the confidence of a man used to looking down on others. His skin was a warm brown, weathered by the years and the stresses of a career in politics, his hair a distinguished silver. And because of a life spent in the eye of political and cultural storms, there was a probing quality to Mr. Luna's dark gaze, as if it could pierce right through to the heart of a person and unearth their carefully hidden desires.

Mr. Luna reminded Sebastian of his own father, although the men looked nothing alike. Yet Sebastian sensed the same appetite for power, the same selfish determination, the same coldness he'd always seen in the late duke. It made Sebastian take a small, unconscious step toward Gabriela, as if he could somehow shield her from her father's ire. It was a very chivalrous urge that was completely foreign to him, and he was certain Gabriela would not be pleased by it.

"Es un placer, señor," Sebastian murmured, gripping the older man's hand in a firm shake.

Mr. Luna stepped back and turned to Sirius, who stood nearby with Isabel. "The duke is a friend of yours?"

"Yes. We've been friends since we were boys," Sirius said, flashing an easy smile. "When I first learned of the Camino Rojo mine, and how the owners were seeking more investors, I immediately thought of Whitfield."

Mr. Luna's lip curled up ever so slightly. "It is too bad the owners made the opportunity available to outside investors, instead of seeking capital *and* keeping it inside Mexico's own borders. Mexican silver should be controlled by Mexican hands."

Aside from a small tic in Sirius's jaw, he appeared completely unbothered by the older man's words. Sebastian guessed this was not the first time Sirius had heard such a claim. His friend might well agree with Mr. Luna, for he certainly had a point. The French, and the Spanish before them, had stripped Mexico of its riches, so Sebastian could understand Mr. Luna's desire to safeguard such valuable resources.

Which was all well and good, but Sebastian was willing to argue the point.

Sebastian tapped his cane on the ground, pleased to see the action drew Mr. Luna's attention back to him. "While it's true I'm just another privileged British man with a title, I do have a great respect and appreciation for the Mexican people. I've learned much from your daughters about the illegal occupation you and your countrymen have been fighting against. And seeing as how two of my close friends are now your sons by marriage, I feel a strong affinity for the people here. I'm quite pleased to have this chance to strengthen the diplomatic bonds between our two countries, because despite its might, Mexico cannot face the world alone."

Sirius pressed his mouth together and looked away. Gabriela wrinkled her brow as she stared at him. He didn't have time to consider whether her expression was one of frustration or approval, for Mr. Luna cleared his throat.

"I'm always interested in forging a mutually satisfying alliance." The older man turned toward his wife, and pressed his hand to the small of her back, ushering her toward the towering double doors that stood behind them. "Let us eat so we may discuss further how England and Mexico can assist one another."

"Well done," Sirius whispered before he and Isabel followed the older couple.

Watching them walk into the villa for a moment, Sebastian eventually pivoted to Gabriela. She was worrying her bottom lip, but she stopped immediately when she sensed his regard. "Were you going to tell me? That you can speak Spanish?"

He couldn't suppress his smirk. "Por supuesto. Eventualmente."

Huffing a breath, Gabriela swung her gaze to the empty doorway. "So diplomatic bonds, is it?"

Sebastian shrugged. "Your father is a statesman. I figured such things would interest him."

Her shoulders sank. "And deflect attention away from me."

"Is that not what you wanted?" Sebastian moved toward her. "I apologize if I overstepped."

Gabriela locked her hazel eyes with his. "Yet if my father's not annoyed with me, will he be bothered to consider me?"

"Do you truly feel it's one or the other?" Sebastian asked.

"You will have the extent of your trip to decide for yourself." Her lips tipped up in a sad mimic of a smile.

Unsure of what to say, Sebastian offered her his arm. "Shall we?"

Her resigned sigh made an ache strum under his ribs. "I suppose we shall."

10

"So Ana María married a member of Parliament and Isabel married an earl's son." Her father peered at Gabby over his tumbler. "And what of you, Gabriela? What have you done?"

What had she done? The strides she'd made with her friends to advance women's voting rights and married women's property reform, as well as the fundraising she'd done to aid women and children in need, didn't seem nearly as grand as her sisters' accomplishments, and she was offended on their behalf that their father had reduced their successes to their marriages. Both had aided Mexico in its fight against the French.

Yet before she could launch a defense of her sisters, the Duke of Whitfield cleared his throat.

"Miss Luna is a belle of the ton."

Gabby jerked her chin back, and she darted her gaze to Isabel, who shook her head in confusion. There was no way her father would be impressed with such a moniker, and Gabby wasn't sure she was flattered by the title. Once again, her worth had been reduced to her appearance—

"Of course she is," her mother said, reaching out to squeeze her hand. "You've only grown more beautiful, mi hijita."

Mr. Luna, however, scowled first at the duke and then at her. "Be that as it may, I fail to see how that is an accomplishment."

Keeping her chin high was a struggle.

Whitfield leaned back in his chair, his glass of tequila dangling from his fingers. "Allow me to elaborate, then. As a young, unmarried lady, there is only so much Miss Luna can do to call attention to the illegal occupation of Mexico. But what she can do is be a face for it. And she's done just that. Miss Luna has earned friends among influential members of the ton, the very members who hold the ear of the queen and her advisers, and the prime minister and Parliament. She speaks of her countrymen's continued struggle against Maximilian and his supporters, and brings a sense of familiarity to the cause because people have come to know her and respect her. I know my own appreciation for the resiliency of the Mexican people is a direct reflection of those same traits I see in your daughter."

Somehow Gabby kept her countenance impassive, even while she struggled to breathe. She knew that Tío Arturo had hoped she and her sisters could serve as goodwill ambassadors for the people of Mexico, but Gabby had often wondered if she had succeeded. Her temper flared with unfortunate public regularity, and she had responded sharply to various gentlemen more than once. How frequently she extended "goodwill" to her British neighbors was in question.

"All three of your daughters have been an asset to the Luna family name," Sirius interjected. "And certainly not because of the men they married."

"Hmm," Mr. Luna hummed, his shrewd gaze pinging between the occupants of the table before settling on the duke once again. "How do the British people view Mexico and its illegal occupation?"

Whitfield stared into his glass for several seconds. After taking a sip, he said, "I think the fact that most members of the ton even know about the conflict here in Mexico is a direct result of your daughters. They speak passionately about their home here and how they were forced to leave it due to France's aggression. Not only does Miss Luna charm society members at social events and gatherings, but Mrs. Fox works with her husband to propose laws and policies that will not only benefit those who live within the empire, but bolster the empathy and understanding between our two countries."

Gratification spread from Gabby's chest through her limbs to tingle in her fingertips. Had she really drawn British attention to the war effort in Mexico? Was it possible all those boring evenings she'd plastered a smile on her face and traded inane chatter had not been endured for naught? Dios mío, Gabby had always hoped she'd have an opportunity to be brave and help her countrymen in some grand manner, as her sisters had. But if Whitfield was to be believed, perhaps just smiling and laughing was an act of defiance unto itself.

The simple fact that the duke lauded her efforts to amplify the conflict in Mexico among her neighbors in the ton was praise her father would never have given her if the roles were reversed.

And Whitfield didn't have to do it. He could have been honest about the British public's apathy for the occupation, or how any event outside of England, and to a greater extent Europe, would never generate the sort of interest as a homegrown affair or threat.

However, Whitfield did not do that, and Gabby was grateful. She snagged his gaze and dared to smile at him. Just a little.

"I'm sure Ana has not been able to assist her Señor Fox as

much as she used to now that the baby is here," Mrs. Luna said, a fond look bringing life to her face.

"Estella definitely dominates her time, but Ana still manages to host dinners and lunches, organize parish events, and accompany Gideon to fundraising affairs. And Gideon is a doting father. He's quite a serious man, you know, but he seems to come alive whenever Ana and Estella are near." Gabby reached into her reticule. "Have you seen a picture of them?"

Her mother sat up straighter. "Ay no, but I would love to."

Extracting the envelope with photographs that she'd shown Isabel the day prior, Gabby rose to her feet and spread them on the table before her mother. One featured Ana María and Gideon, one was of Ana María with little Estella, and the last one was of the family of three together, the baby nestled in Gideon's arms and Ana María's hand on his shoulder.

"Que guapo," her mother whispered as she gingerly picked up the picture of the three members of the Fox family. Her hazel eyes grew glassy as she studied it. "Ana looks so, so . . . orgulloso."

"She does," Isabel agreed, coming to study the picture over their mother's shoulder. "But then she should be. She has a husband who loves and respects her, and a beautiful baby to call her own. Look at her cheeks!"

Gabby laughed, pointing at the photo of Ana María and Estella. "She's only six months old, and she already has the entire household wrapped around her little finger."

"And not just the household," Whitfield interjected. "Miss Fox bosses *me* around and she can't even speak yet."

"You love being ordered about by beautiful ladies," Gabby quipped.

The duke inclined his head, his blue eyes sparkling behind his spectacles. "It seems I do."

A bolt of heat shot through Gabby's blood, and her mouth went dry. She darted her attention to the photographs, but she struggled to focus. All she could see was the knowing look in the duke's gaze as he murmured those words. Surely he hadn't meant to imply—

"Señor Fox is very handsome," her mother murmured, oblivious to the tension percolating in her youngest daughter. "He cuts quite a figure."

Mr. Luna snatched the photograph his wife held out to him and considered the subjects in it. "I didn't know he was a Black man."

The table went quiet, and Gabby's irritation sparked. She may have a difficult time defending herself from her father's slings and arrows, but Gabby had no such compunction defending others.

Handing the picture of Ana María and Estella to Isabel, Gabby knotted her hands together at her waist. "Gideon's grandmother escaped from the American South many years ago. His father was a Scot. He graduated from Cambridge and worked hard to earn his seat in Parliament, and has earned a reputation as a shrewd, ambitious politician."

Mr. Luna's expression did not change as he considered the photograph, yet Gabby knew her father. He was not pleased with what he saw.

"Isabel mentioned that you, too, worked hard for your success, Mr. Luna," Sirius said, his tone friendly but his gaze sharp.

"Is that true, Señor Luna?" Whitfield inquired, setting his empty glass on the table and leaning toward her father. "I'd enjoy hearing how you came to have the ear of President Juárez."

It was just the right thing to say to Elías Luna, who never shied from discussing his rise from his humble beginnings in

Michoacán to his place as a close adviser to the president of Mexico. Signaling for a manservant to bring the men another round of tequila, her father regaled them with tales of traveling miles down craggy and steep dirt roads to reach the school where he first learned to read and write. Later he told of meeting Benito Juárez while the men were law students, before they both worked as law clerks for criollo solicitors in Mexico City. When President Juárez had been elected as governor of Oaxaca, her father was a member of his cabinet. The two Indigenous men had supported each other through the years, serving as allies in a political world aligned against anyone who could not boast Spanish antecedents. It was a chip her father carried on his shoulder even now.

"While I'm certain the path you took to arrive where you are today was fraught with challenges, you have much to show for your hard work. A lovely wife"—Whitfield looked to her mother with a nod—"three discerning daughters, and now a granddaughter—"

"Gah, I am surrounded by females," her father grouched, swiping his hand through the air dismissively. "There is no Luna man to carry on the tradition."

Gabby flinched.

"That seems rather unfair. From everything you have told me about your values and the dreams you hold for Mexico, it is your daughters who embody the future of those very things." Whitfield lifted a shoulder. "Señora Fox aids her husband to draft legislation to lead England into the future. Señora Dawson works for the First Lady of Mexico, helping to care for those who fight the imperialists. And Señorita Luna here uses her considerable charisma to lobby for reforms and win friends among the very people whose support President Juárez needs if he is to win the propaganda battle against the French."

Her father drummed his fingers on the tabletop, his dark eyes fixed on Whitfield's face. "Is that how you see them? My girls?"

Whitfield leaned back, his posture one of easy confidence. "I do, indeed. I see three young women I think you should be proud of, because I certainly am."

"Bah. I should have had sons," her father pushed, waving his hand.

"And yet it is your daughters who will care for you in your old age. Who will ensure that your last remaining years on this earth are ones of comfort. Of respect. Sons go off to join their wives' families, but daughters keep you as a part of theirs." Whitfield cocked a brow. "If you give them a reason to."

Suddenly Gabby didn't know what to do with herself. She reached for her cup of coffee, but the delicate china rattled in her trembling hands. Setting it back down, Gabby twined her fingers in the skirts of her day dress and willed her heart to stop thundering in her ears. No one ever confronted her father.

Yet Whitfield had. The duke had politely shined a light on Ana María's and Isabel's accomplishments . . . and even her own. Gabby had been acquainted with Whitfield long enough to know that he was not inclined to offer compliments. Flowery platitudes to soften the miens of judgmental dowagers, sure, but authentic, sincere compliments? Definitely not.

Yet Whitfield has complimented you numerous times on this trip . . .

Her father was staring at the duke with his brows knit together.

"Gabriela," her mother said suddenly, snapping Gabby's attention to her. María Elena's gaze slid from her husband to Whitfield. "Tell us about the work Ana María and her Señor Fox are engaged in right now. From what I understand from her letters, they've hosted several dinner parties and engagements to secure support for some sort of enfranchisement proposal."

The tension in the air dissipated, and Gabby's frame relaxed. After taking a sip of coffee, she smiled at her mother and explained the reform proposal.

"The man either hates you or respects the hell out of you."

"Yes, well, I'm quite used to inspiring such conflicting emotions in others," Sebastian murmured, propping his leg on his opposite knee.

After lunch had ended, Sebastian had returned with Sirius and Isabel to their home while Gabriela had stayed to spend time with her mother. Her shoulders had been tense and her jaw hard as she watched the group depart.

Yet when Sebastian had taken his leave of her, the smile Gabriela had directed up at him was unlike any she had ever bestowed upon him before. It brightened her whole face, as if the sun were contained within her chest.

Sebastian replayed her look now as he sat with Sirius on the patio at Casa Inglesa, the name the locals had given the home after Sirius and Isabel had moved in, glasses of lemonade in hand. Isabel had correspondence for Señora Maza de Juárez to see to, and had excused herself to the attractive study that was all her own in the front of the home. Sirius had mentioned how he'd commissioned the construction of six large bookcases to store Isabel's extensive collection of books, explaining that he wanted her to have a grand library and study to call her own. As a result, Isabel had an impressive office that rivaled any Sebastian had seen in a grand Mayfair townhome.

Sebastian's parents had never cared for each other the way Sirius so lovingly tended to his wife's happiness. He could admit, even in the dark recesses of his own mind, that while he was pleased for his old friend, he was also jealous. Horribly jealous, for Sebastian knew such affection would never exist between himself and whichever unlucky woman became his duchess.

The memory of Gabriela's bright smile flashed through his mind, and Sebastian tipped his head back and drained the last of his lemonade.

"Is he what you expected?" Sirius asked, nodding his head in thanks to the manservant who refilled Sebastian's glass.

Sebastian worked his jaw as he considered this. "I don't know what I expected. I had heard enough stories from you and Fox, and even Miss Luna herself, to know her father was a hard man. And he was, most definitely, that."

Sirius arched a brow. "I sense there is an unspoken *but* in your words."

"But," Sebastian emphasized the *T* sound, "he was not as intimidating as I anticipated."

"Really? Why not, do you think?"

"Because he reminds me of my father."

Only Sirius would understand the gravity of such a claim. As Sebastian's oldest friend, he had met the late duke a handful of times, most notably when Sebastian had almost been sent down from Eton after the secret gaming hell he'd organized, complete with dealers and courtesans from London, had been discovered. It had been after his mother's death when Sebastian was grieving, angry, and desperate for a distraction. His father had arrived at the school and met with the headmaster, and while Sebastian was unsure of exactly what the old duke had said, Sebastian had been allowed to stay. But it was his father's ear-blistering scold afterward that had been humiliating, especially because the duke had berated Sebastian in front of Sirius. His friend had never said anything directly about the cruel things the late duke had said that day, but whenever Sirius mentioned Sebastian's father, it was with a hint of disdain.

Which was why comparing the old duke of Whitfield to Mr. Luna felt so appropriate. Sirius appeared to agree, for he lifted his glass in toast to Sebastian.

"There have to be good fathers in the world, right?"

"Fox is a good father," Sebastian shared. "He dotes on his daughter . . . and his wife."

"And are you surprised by that?" Sirius chuckled. "Fox had a good father himself, from what he has said."

"And of course the man died young. All the good ones do, apparently," Sebastian said with a sigh.

"Let us not talk of fathers anymore. Perhaps one day you and I will be blessed to have our own children, and we will work to give them everything we were denied." Sirius glanced back at the house, no doubt envisioning where his wife was now working.

"That day may never come for me."

His friend frowned. "Why do you say that?"

Sebastian lifted a shoulder. "Who's to say I want to carry on my father's cursed name? Heaven knows he's wreaked havoc on numerous lives all over England." He thought of James and David, and a knot of anger lodged in his throat. "Perhaps his legacy should die with me."

A silence unfurled between them, and Sebastian cursed himself. Regardless of what Sirius knew of his childhood or his father's many sins, Sebastian didn't need to unload his bitterness onto his friend. He despised melodramatics, and he refused to behave in such a way when he could help it.

"But then your mother's legacy would die, too." Sirius uncurled a finger from around his glass to point at him. "And it seems to me that her good name deserves to be honored more than your father's."

That was not what he had expected. Sebastian looked out into the quickly darkening garden. Crickets chirped from between the spines of agave plants, and the breeze rustled the boughs of the piñon tree overhead. Tilting his head back, Sebastian spied a star or two shining in the twilight sky, and when he found the Ursa Major constellation, he felt the stress lift from his bones. The constellation was a bit higher in the sky in England than it was here, but the familiar sight was there nonetheless, and the connection to his home made his chest swell with wistfulness. Sebastian was thankful to have had the opportunity to travel to Mexico, to visit his friend and explore additional ventures that could aid the dukedom. He was also finally able to see the world in all the ways his father had denied him.

Yet Sebastian missed Whitfield Manor. Every brick, every window, every door, every rose blooming in the garden and blade of grass on the rolling lawn spoke of his mother. Of the late Duchess of Whitfield's great love for the estate and every person who worked there.

He missed James and David, who were just coming to consider the manor home. Sebastian was determined to make it as warm and welcoming as his mother had made it for him.

Yes, he thought, blinking rapidly. Let his life be a testament to her. His father could rot in hell.

Eventually, Sebastian cleared his throat and said, "So we visit the mine tomorrow. What should I know to be prepared?"

The men spoke of the operations at the Camino Rojo mine, the miners' compensation and accommodations, the connections to the surrounding community, and which other board members would be in attendance for the meeting and tour. Sirius's knowledge of the day-to-day operations was surprisingly vast, and he admitted that the geology and engineering involved in the venture had fascinated him. Plus, the mine had shown Mr. and Mrs. Luna that Sirius was not afraid of hard work.

"The fact that I invested in the mine from its infancy and benefited from its success has shown Mr. Luna I am a man who makes prudent and clever decisions." Sirius's mouth suddenly stretched wide. "Or at least that's what I overheard him tell several gentlemen at a dinner party."

"The highest of compliments from a man such as Mr. Luna." Sebastian raised his glass to his friend. "Bravo."

Sirius barked a laugh. "My involvement in the mine is not something I did to earn his approval, but if it makes our interactions less fraught for my wife, then I welcome it. Plus, it has allowed me to share its success with friends," he added, gesturing to Sebastian with a dip of his head.

"And I am thankful you thought to offer me the opportunity." Sebastian cringed. "I had long since resigned myself to the idea that I would have to barter off a duchess coronet to the highest bidder."

"Now you can be an independent duke, without need of a wealthy bride to save you." Sirius's chuckle echoed about them. "Now if you take a wife, it will be because you equally annoy each other, and not that *you* will endure the annoyance to save the dukedom."

Sebastian shook his head. "At least my staff won't have to worry about me bringing an American dollar princess to Whitfield Manor to be its duchess."

"Are they worried you'll bring home a Mexican heiress?" Sirius's expression morphed from one of amusement to acute interest.

A pair of hazel eyes flashed in his thoughts, and Sebastian ruthlessly pushed the visual away.

Instead, he made a show of requesting a glass of brandy from the manservant. "I'm certain that by this point, they'd be delighted if any heiress took pity on the fool that I am and deigned to make an honest man out of me."

Sirius lifted a palm. "You would only be so lucky."

Now it was Sebastian's turn to be serious. "Indeed, I would be."

11

"How did you learn about this place?" Gabby asked, pushing the carriage curtain aside to look out at the nondescript adobe building that resided near the edge of San Luis Potosí.

"Señora Maza de Juárez." Isabel slid kid gloves over her hands and grasped her reticule. "You know part of my work for her is creating a network of physicians, nurses, and clinics that are available to assist Liberal soldiers and their families. This is one such clinic."

While Isabel had mentioned in her letters that her duties required her to work with the families of soldiers, Gabby had not considered what that entailed. Her interest was piqued.

"Do you have business here today?" she asked, adjusting the fit of her hat.

"I don't," Isabel answered, whispering her thanks to the footman as he helped her from the conveyance. Glancing back at Gabby, she cocked a brow. "I thought you might be interested in visiting. You've written many times about your women's club and how you and its members were lobbying for not only the rights of women, but for greater access to the sort of care and support that would help women lead fuller, more in-dependent lives."

Unsure of what to say, Gabby nodded and scrambled out of the carriage after her. She grasped Isabel's arm as her sister came to a stop in front of the wooden door.

"If you decide to stay in Mexico—"

"Why wouldn't I stay in Mexico?" Gabby demanded, her hand tightening on Isabel's arm.

Her sister huffed a breath, her expression a combination of exasperation and affection. "I don't want to assume I know the plans you have for yourself, querida. Perhaps returning home will help you to realize you feel more yourself in London. Or, as I'm hoping, by introducing you to the staff at this clinic, you discover that the work which brought you a sense of purpose can also be done here in Mexico."

"Oh," Gabby whispered. Isabel knew her so well, and yet it still caught Gabby unawares to be understood so deeply. Her older sisters were the only people to ever truly know the Gabby who dwelled deep within her heart. The Gabby she still wrestled to understand herself.

Releasing a long breath, Gabby dropped her hand from Isabel's arm and squared her shoulders. "I look forward to learning more."

Isabel's lips tipped up ever so slightly, and she knocked on the door.

They were ushered inside a surprisingly large room that opened into an atrium. Large, narrow windows lined one end of the room, and beyond them was a lush garden filled with various flowering shrubs, succulents, and vines. Gabby spotted several benches and even a swing affixed to a piñon tree, where several children took turns pushing one another. Bordering all sides of the garden were archways, some containing glass windows and some not.

"What a calming space," she murmured, watching the children play.

"That was our goal," Doctora Jimenez said, coming to stand next to Gabby. Isabel had introduced her several moments prior as the head midwife and nurse at the clinic. Isabel explained that the older woman was called a doctor because had women been allowed to attend medical school in Mexico, Doctora Jimenez would have been one of the first graduates. "Señora Dawson was instrumental in the clinic's construction and design."

Gabby turned to gape to her sister. "Why didn't you tell me you were so intricately involved? You led me to believe you were simply creating a list of clinics that provided this kind of care."

Isabel waved a hand as she walked to a window, peering outside. "Sirius and I have our own charitable ventures, and this clinic began as one of them."

"Faith, Isa." Gabby stared at her sister with wide eyes. "I'm in awe of you."

"There's no reason to be. I'm not the one doing all the hard work." Isabel gestured to Doctora Jimenez with her chin. "Most of the patients are women and children. Many of whom are mestizos who do not have the sort of access to quality care that our criollo or peninsular neighbors do. It's a disparity we wished to address, even if only in this small way."

"Small way?" Gabby spun about in a circle. "It wouldn't be small if like-minded Mexicans invested in such clinics across the country. Can you imagine the impact an enterprise like that could have?"

Isabel and Doctora Jimenez exchanged a look. "Actually we can."

Gabby chuckled. "Of course you can." Turning to the older woman, she inclined her head toward the atrium. "Would you mind giving me a tour of the facility, doctora?"

Doctora Jimenez smiled. "It would be my pleasure, Señorita Luna."

An hour later, Gabby and Isabel sat side by side in the carriage, deep in discussion about the visit to the medical clinic.

"What sort of plans have you and Doctora Jimenez's team discussed?" Gabby inquired, excitement creeping along her skin. When was the last time she was this zealous for anything? Maybe when her women's group had organized in earnest a suffrage effort and had begun collecting signatures for a parliamentary petition for women's right to vote. Gabby had known that if such an act were passed she would be excluded, as she was not a British citizen, but the effort needed to start somewhere. And if it were successful in England, Gabby could take that success and what she learned from it, and bring it to Mexico . . .

"Our main focus is to expand the clinic itself. We would like to add more examination rooms, a dedicated room for surgeries and procedures. Contamination is a concern, you know?" Isabel said, tapping the back of Gabby's hand. "Plus, we need a constant flow of new supplies, for there are many things we cannot reuse despite what some *supposed* medical experts say."

The way Isabel's lip curled surprised a bark of laughter from Gabby. "Are these medical experts men?"

"Your question doesn't require an answer because you already know." Isabel glanced outside. "We're almost home. I'll explain more of our plans over lunch. How does that sound?"

Bumping a shoulder into Isabel's, Gabby grinned. "That sounds marvelous."

The sisters dined in the bright sunroom at Casa Inglesa and discussed the clinic and Isabel's work over a meal of tortillas and beans with salsa and sliced avocado. Gabby sighed happily. Reaching for her glass of horchata de arroz, she sipped a mouthful and savored the sweet flavor.

"I haven't had this since well before we fled to England," she said, studying the flecks of cinnamon that drifted about the creamy liquid. "It's just as refreshing as I remembered."

"When Sirius and I wed and set up our household, finding a cook was one of my first priorities." Isabel reached for a sweet-potato-and-chorizo empanada and placed it on the plate in front of her. "Mother helped me sort through the candidates, and I'm quite pleased with Señora Montez and her cooking. She was even willing to move with us to San Luis Potosí, and we are so grateful. Sirius has said he doesn't know how he survived so long without Mexican cooking."

"I don't know how I survived this long, either," Gabby quipped, taking another sip of horchata.

"Speaking of Mother," Isabel began, "how was your visit with her yesterday?"

The sweet taste on Gabby's tongue abruptly turned bitter. Her shoulders fell as she placed her glass on the tabletop. Of all people, Isabel understood the complicated relationship Gabby had with their mother. As the youngest, Gabby was a reminder to her father that she was not the son he long desired. Then her mother would send her away, as if by not seeing Gabby, she'd be able to erase her inability to birth her husband's heir. Worst still, their father often pitted Gabby and her sisters against one another in some sort of macabre competition for his approval, so she didn't have Isabel or Ana María to turn to for support until they'd arrived in England. Therefore, much of her childhood was spent alone in her room or wandering the grounds of the villa.

Expelling a breath, Gabby said, "It went well, I suppose."

Isabel raised her brows. "Just well?"

"You know how Mother is." Gabby picked at a crack in the table with her fingernail. "She wanted to know about life in London. The parties I attended and the people I've met. Tío Arturo. Did I fall ill on the voyage because I'm too flaca?"

"Ay," Isabel grumbled with a roll of her eyes. "She asked the same of me."

"She wanted to know more about Estella, and for me to describe Ana María and Gideon's home," Gabby continued.

"Mother was very interested in how many rooms they had. And how large their staff is."

It was Gabby's turn to roll her eyes. "Naturally."

"Did she ask you about your suitors? She asked me all about Lord Westhope until Sirius arrived," Isabel said, a fond curve to her lips.

"I'm to blame for her knowing about Lord Westhope. He was so kind, and I was thrilled he was enamored of you." Gabby feigned a wince. But truly the viscount had been infatuated with her sister, and had Isabel not been in love with Sirius, it was possible she would now be a viscountess. "But I should have kept that information to myself."

"Don't apologize, querida. Mother just wants us all to marry and have babies," Isabel said with a snort.

"Which is why she asked about Lord Carlisle's proposal."

All the humor bled from her sister's face. Isabel slowly dusted off her hands with a napkin and gently set it on the table next to her half-eaten empanada. "I didn't realize she knew about the earl."

Gabby shrugged, glancing away. "I'm guessing Ana told her."

"Did Ana also tell her that the earl's proposal constituted him accosting you in the drawing room at the Wright ball in hopes of forcing you into marriage?" Isabel bit out around her teeth.

The sound of a throat being cleared whipped Gabby's head up. Sirius and Whitfield stood awkwardly on the threshold.

"Good afternoon, darling," Sirius said finally, crossing the room to press a quick kiss to Isabel's temple.

The duke remained in the doorway, his gaze locked on Gabby. His expression was unreadable, but something about the way he held himself, as if he would be trembling if he weren't so disciplined, left her on edge. Was he angry?

"Mrs. Dawson," Whitfield voiced as a greeting, although he held Gabby's gaze as he pulled out a chair next to her and sat. "Miss Luna."

"Your Grace." Fighting the urge to fidget, Gabby wrapped her fingers around her napkin and squeezed it tight.

She had hoped the duke would not ever be privy to her shame. But what made her ears hot and her throat tight was the knowledge that the Earl of Carlisle was Whitfield's friend. She'd read any number of on-dits about their exploits together.

She could only imagine what the duke must think.

Whitfield didn't speak for several moments, and only the hum of Isabel and Sirius's conversation reached Gabby's ears. She wasn't sure what they were saying—their voices mere whispers at the end of a tunnel—but every fiber of Gabby's being was trained on the man next to her. Some innate part of her perceived Whitfield's distress. His agitation. His emotions didn't spark fear in her, but they made her restless and uneasy.

The housekeeper appeared in the sunroom at that moment

to exchange a word with Isabel and Sirius, and Gabby felt the duke lean toward her.

"Are you well?"

She could pretend his question was one of polite inquiry. Was Gabby well at that moment? Not particularly, but she knew that was not what Whitfield was asking. So she answered him truthfully.

"I am. Now."

Although Gabby did not emphasize *now*, he seemed to sense its importance nonetheless.

A manservant placed a glass of lemonade on the table before Whitfield, and she watched from the corner of her eye as he grasped it and took a large gulp. Setting it down with more care than it deserved, the duke scrubbed a napkin across his face.

"And before?"

Gabby fought the urge to nibble her lip. "I was not injured."

Not physically, although she did her best to leave her mark on the earl. The situation had angered her more than anything else, for the earl had forced her into a position where her reputation could have been harmed. The Luna name had been threatened, as had the small slivers of autonomy she'd grasped in England.

Just thinking about the fleeting minute of helplessness she'd felt in the drawing room at the Wright ball made her jaw ache from grinding her teeth together.

"I see." Whitfield dragged his thumb back and forth through the condensation on the side of the glass. "I saw him at the club before we departed, and he was sporting a green and yellow bruise near his eye. I assume that was from you."

"It was," she declared crisply.

"Good girl."

Inhaling sharply, Gabby shot her gaze up to his. Even behind his spectacles, Whitfield's eyes were warm. A little of that warmth nestled in her chest, and Gabby's hands unfurled from around her napkin.

"Tell me," the duke said after a pause, his voice barely above a whisper. "Would you feel safe returning to London, if that were your wish?"

Gabby snorted just as softly. "Of course."

Whitfield nodded. "So you did not return to Mexico because you were made to feel uncomfortable or unsafe?"

Now Gabby hesitated. This was not a yes-or-no question, and she bit the inside of her cheek as she contemplated her response. Everything about the duke's taut frame told her that he was anxious for her answer.

Angling her head toward him, Gabby said, "There's a difference between uncomfortable and unsafe. I was the first but not the latter."

"Yet you should never be either."

A breath stammered in her lungs, and Gabby turned to look at him, her mouth ajar. Whitfield's arctic irises stared down at her. "I would never presume to think you require protection from anything. Indeed, I'm certain every creature under the sun trembles at the sound of your name."

"Now's not the time for flattery," she murmured, her lips trembling over a smile.

"But if you are ever in need of . . ." His eyes searched hers. "*Anything*, I hope you know that I will help. Without question. Without delay."

"I know." Gabby said it without thinking. But it was true. And she wouldn't take back the words. Lifting her chin, she nodded once. "I know, Your Grace, and I am thankful."

. . .

"You didn't tell me it was Carlisle," Sebastian snarled the second Sirius shut the door of his study.

Gabriela and Isabel had retired after lunch to the latter's office to pen letters to their sister and friends in England, and Sirius had all but herded Sebastian into his study. No doubt because his friend knew he was holding on to his anger by the thinnest of threads. But now that the women were on the other side of the house, Sebastian was at liberty to set a spark to the tinderbox of emotions inside of him.

"Because I knew it would only upset you." Sirius grasped a bottle of liquor from the sideboard. Bypassing the snifters, he snatched up two shot glasses. "And I was right. Now take a seat."

Sebastian did as he was told, but only because he was too enraged to argue with Sirius's high-handed ways. Thankfully, his friend slid a shot glass filled with tequila to him, and Sebastian downed it in one bitter gulp. The liquid burned down his throat and settled in his gut, where it immediately extinguished some of the rage bubbling inside of him.

Feigning a calmness he didn't feel, Sebastian unbuttoned his coat and leaned back in his chair. "Tell me what happened."

Sirius propped his hip against the desk. "I don't know all of the details, and anyway those are for Gabby to share."

When Sebastian glared at him, his friend held up his hands in surrender.

"What I do know is that Carlisle accosted her as she was walking to the ladies' retiring room at the Wright ball, and refused to let her leave. She assumed he was waiting for them to be discovered together."

"Of course he wanted them to be caught." Sebastian worked his jaw. "How did she escape?"

"From what Isabel has said, Gabby punched him square in

the face when he tried to kiss her." Dawson huffed a chuckle. "Apparently he dropped to the ground immediately, and Gabby fled to the ballroom unscathed."

"Physically, at least. But I'd imagine such an encounter would leave its own sort of scar," Sebastian said with a sigh.

And Carlisle had left scars, because Gabriela had practically curled in on herself when she'd realized Sebastian overheard what happened. Like a flower closing its bloom.

At that moment, Sebastian would have happily throttled the earl.

"I can't believe Fox didn't tell me." Sebastian prowled to the sideboard and poured himself another shot of tequila. He welcomed the burn. "He could have let me know at any moment leading up to our departure. Hell, he could have told me when he wished me goodbye on the docks."

"Why would Fox tell you?" Sebastian pivoted to see Sirius staring at him incredulously. "You and Gabby have been at odds since you first met. It's possible he didn't trust you with the information."

That stung, and Sebastian clamped his teeth together and stared out the window. While it was true that he and Gabriela had traded more barbs than they had polite conversation, he would never want to see her harmed.

Sebastian carefully set his empty glass upon the sideboard before he shattered it against the wall. "I never would have thought Carlisle capable of such reprehensible behavior. I knew he played deep at the card tables and hadn't kept a mistress for the last few years, but he was the same arrogant rake he always was."

"He's in debt. From what my men have been able to uncover, he owes a sizable sum of money to various lenders all around London." Sirius scrubbed his hand down his face. "I can imagine he was growing desperate, and thought the pretty young Mexican heiress would do very nicely as his wife."

Despite having moved to Mexico, Sirius still kept in regular contact with the men he served with in the Crimean War . . . men who were adept at surveilling and gathering information should Sirius ever need it.

"The Whitfield dukedom was in a sizable amount of debt, as well you know, but I never schemed to ruin a young lady." Just imagining the earl touching Gabriela made his head pound.

"Indeed, you did not. But then you're a gentleman."

Reclaiming his seat, Sebastian ran a hand over his face. "I've tried to be, as of late."

"I noticed," Sirius said simply.

Sebastian took a moment to gather his thoughts as he adjusted the fall of his waistcoat. "After my mother died, I was angry. That she was taken from me so young while my piece-of-shit father continued to run the dukedom into the ground and wreak havoc across England." He thought of his brothers and ground his teeth together. "Yet despite my hatred for the man, in many ways, I fear I may have become just like him—"

"No. Do not even think the words," Sirius declared, his eyes chips of granite.

"So emphatic," Sebastian murmured around the knot in his throat.

His friend spread his palms. "You may be a prat, a snob, and a rogue, but you're not cruel, Sebastian. You've been a good friend to me."

"And you to me." Desperate to return their conversation to lighter topics, Sebastian pounded his fist on the desktop. "I really wish the earl was here now so I could mar his other eye."

"He would be here if you had shared the investor information with him." Sirius cocked his head. "Why didn't you?"

Sebastian crossed his arms over his chest and glanced out the window. "I'm not sure. He just didn't seem like a good fit for the venture."

"Your judgment was sound, it seems." Sirius quirked a brow. "So tell me what you thought of the mine."

Now this was a topic Sebastian was keen to discuss, and discuss it they did. For the next hour or two they pored over the notes they'd taken at the board of directors meeting, analyzing the projections for output over the next quarter, as well as expenditures. Seeing the Camino Rojo mine's operations in person was worth the trip to Mexico all on its own. Of course Sebastian trusted Sirius and the information he shared, but observing the extraction-and-cleaning process with his own two eyes had been revealing. It had also been a relief, because it was clear that the operators had organized the production in an efficient manner that took advantage of the landscape but didn't exploit it. And because the Camino Rojo mine was within an hour's ride of San Luis Potosí, the men who worked there had reliable housing available to them and their families, as well as a thriving community that was not dependent upon the mine but certainly benefited from it. Sebastian's experience with the dukedom had taught him that content, well-paid workers were a sign of a healthy enterprise.

"When we were departing, Señor Ortiz mentioned a dinner party he's hosting. Is that tonight?" Sebastian asked.

Sirius nodded. "His villa is not far from Mr. and Mrs. Luna's home. They will be in attendance, as well."

"I see." Sebastian searched his memory for a connection between Ortiz and the Lunas, but could not recall one. He asked Sirius about it.

"Ortiz has financially supported Juárez and members of the cabinet throughout the occupation," Sirius said. "Mr. Luna has a talent for winning the favor of men with money and power."

"I have no doubt about that." A new thought occurred to Sebastian, and he chuckled. "Miss Luna must have inherited that skill from him."

Sirius's mouth quirked. "I think you may be right, for Gabby certainly knows how to win admirers."

"She would make a fine diplomat." Sebastian tapped a finger against his lips. "As long as her admirers didn't try to take advantage of her beauty and charm."

"It's a good thing, then, that she has family and friends who are determined to protect her, should she need it," Sirius responded, giving Sebastian a pointed look.

At any other time, Sebastian would have pushed back on Sirius's unspoken assertion. However, he couldn't drum up the indignation, for Sebastian was pleased to be considered her friend.

Gabriela could certainly take care of herself, but it didn't mean she should always have to.

12

"Gabriela, really, where is the rest of your gown?"

Curling her tongue against the roof of her mouth, Gabby commanded herself not to respond in frustration. A lifetime as the youngest daughter of Elías Luna had taught her that her father was more than a match for her temper.

Pursing her lips, Gabby spun about in a circle, allowing the skirts of her scarlet silk gown to billow around her. It was a stunning dress, and her mother had gasped when she'd walked into the room, her eyes turning glassy as she gazed at Gabby. María Elena had invited both Gabby and Isabel to prepare for the Ortiz dinner at her home, and although neither of the sisters had been keen on the idea, in that moment with her mother looking at her with pride, Gabby was happy she had accepted.

Until her father's curt reception when they arrived in the drawing room.

What made Gabby particularly bitter was that he had not spoken a word to her—not through the hour they spent visiting with María Elena—until now. To criticize her appearance.

Her father was looking at her now, though, his dark, dark

eyes slits of displeasure and his lip curled in distaste. Gabby practically preened.

"This is a Worth gown, Father. The House of Worth dresses only the most elite women in Europe." She ran her gloved hand over the black-and-gold-embroidered moons and stars that cascaded like a meteor shower from the cinched waist. "A German prince, a cousin of the late Prince Albert, insisted I dance a waltz with him when he saw me in this gown."

"Of course he did, mi hijita. Eres muy bella," her mother crooned, adjusting the red rose that was tucked in Gabby's hair.

"And did this prince ask to marry you?"

"I don't wish to marry every man I meet, Father." How Gabby managed not to scowl, she didn't know. Instead, she flipped open her fan and considered him over it. "Anyway, he was a minor prince of a small principality, and I have no wish to spend my life in a drafty castle in Bavaria."

Ignoring the soft snort from Isabel, Gabby fanned her face, hoping she appeared as unbothered and confident as she strived to be.

"I fail to understand what the point of a pretty dress is," her father's gaze moved over her features, "or a pretty face for that matter, if they do nothing to win you an influential husband."

Acid singed the back of her throat, and Gabby swallowed reflexively. Never one to give up easily, Gabby cocked a brow. "What sort of influential husband do you wish for me, Father? A Mexican with peninsular connections, or a European who will further elevate the Luna name?"

The room fell silent. Isabel, her mother, and the servants all latched their eyes on her father, and Gabby couldn't help but smile. She relished any opportunity to lob probing questions his way.

To his credit, her father seemed to carefully consider his answer. While Gabby spun her skirts back and forth, doing her best to appear unruffled, Elías studied her.

Propping his arm on a chairback, he finally said, "Either would suffice, mi hija. Your sisters married clever British men with an eye for reform and progress. Values that have made me proud. They've made Benito proud."

Gabby cocked her head. "I've yet to meet a man who upholds such values, so I've focused my energies on more productive paths." She folded her hands at her waist as if she were preparing to give an oral presentation. "I attended the events that Tío Arturo deemed important, and I charmed the gentlemen he identifies as influential and powerful within Parliament and beyond."

"Arturo has had nothing but glowing things to say about Gabriela in his letters." Her mother reached out to squeeze her hand. "He said the name *Luna* is synonymous with intelligence, beauty, and Mexican pride."

She had no notion her tío had shared such sentiments, and Gabby flushed.

"*Intelligence, beauty, and Mexican pride,*" her father repeated, considering her with an intense stare. After a pause, he gestured to a manservant for a beverage. "It seems to me that beauty is your only attribute, for surely if you possessed the other two, you would have already secured the hand of a powerful husband and been filling your nursery with Mexican babies."

Flames of humiliation licked up her throat, and Gabby fought the urge to pick up her skirts and dash from the room. She longed to be somewhere, anywhere, that allowed her to escape the derision on her father's face.

"That's unfair, Father."

Gabby and her father turned in unison to Isabel, who stood nearby in a striking green gown. Her sister was usually reserved around their father and rarely spoke unless spoken to, but Isabel was staring directly at Elías now, her shoulders thrown back and her head high.

"Gabby may be beautiful, but she's also clever and discerning. She can step into a room, quickly identify the most important people in it, and win their regard. She's used that talent time and again while we were in London, and earned the respect of many." Isabel's gaze turned soft as it landed on Gabby. "It's a rare and valuable skill to be able to put others at ease. To convince them you have more in common than not. It is a skill that will be needed when Presidente Juárez attempts to unify a fractured Mexico. Those who have stood with the French will soon have to decide if they will cling to the remnants of imperial power or embrace a new progressive future for Mexico, and Gabby can eloquently argue for such a future. Tell them about those ideas you shared with me."

Ay, she hadn't expected to be thrust into center stage, and her hands shook as she gripped her fan. She risked a glance at her father, finding Elías staring at her, confusion carved into his brow. This was her chance to create a place for herself among this new Mexico taking shape, and she was determined to be poised and articulate as she did so.

Licking her lips, Gabby began, "I know Maximilian and the French have not yet surrendered, but I'm sure Presidente Juárez has already begun to look to the future and how to unite the republic—"

"Of course Benito has," her father snapped.

Gabby inclined her head, refusing to let his cutting tone bother her. "I think that in order to do so, a concerted effort needs to be made to bring the influential peninsular and criollo families who supported Maximilian back into the fold. They need to have an invested stake in Mexico's future. I think we can do this in several ways—"

"*We?*" Elías quirked a brow. "There is no *we* here, Gabriela. The only way you would be involved in such a venture is if you were pledged to marry into one of those families."

To her great frustration, Gabby felt the flames of her temper fan to life. Yet she did her best to sound undaunted when she said, "Brokering marriage agreements for political power is woefully old-fashioned, Father. There are more effective ways to unite the people of Mexico—"

"Perhaps. But I'd rather you use the skills Isabel claims you have to find a husband," he declared, raising his glass for a drink.

Before Gabby could growl a retort, the butler entered the room and announced that the carriage awaited them. And just like that, the conversation was over.

"I'm sorry, querida," Isabel whispered as they accepted wraps from a maid. "We knew he wouldn't be an easy audience."

"I suppose I'll have to try again." Gabby sighed. "And it's I who owe you an apology for asking you to accompany me this evening. You could be with Sirius now instead of listening to Father complain about my unmarried state."

"I'm glad I'm here with you." Isabel weaved her arm through Gabby's, and together they followed their parents to the waiting carriage. "You should not have to defend yourself from Father on your own. And it's easier for me to weather his tirades now that I have Sirius to support me."

"He loves you very much," Gabby said, smiling.

"I know he does." Isabel patted her hand, a fond look on her face. "And you deserve a man who will love you just as much. Don't let anyone force you to give your hand away."

"I won't," she murmured. Although Gabby wondered if her life would be easier if she capitulated to her father's demands instead of always fighting against them.

The ride to the Ortiz villa was not long, and soon Gabby found herself within a crowded drawing room standing next to a Spanish gentleman who claimed to want to know about her time in England yet interrupted her constantly.

"I was in Europe last summer to visit my family in Valencia. We originally had plans to spend a fortnight in London to partake of the culture before traveling to Sussex for the derby, but we decided to visit Rennes and then Paris instead." Señor Valenzuela studied her over his glass of port. "Have you been to France?"

Gabby gaped at the man for what felt like a full minute. How he could ask such a question simply shocked her. "Considering the French have illegally occupied Mexico for years, no, I have not possessed any interest in visiting France."

Rather than showing embarrassment, Señor Valenzuela chuckled as if she had told a joke. "Well, then you missed an opportunity, for the French are very cosmopolitan. They have brought a refined influence to society in Mexico City."

"I believe we have different definitions of *refined*, señor," she murmured, glancing about for an escape.

And that's when she saw him. Whitfield stood in a circle of men and women, her father by his side. While the duke always cut an impressive figure, something about his presence now—his broad shoulders, the twinkle in his eyes behind his spectacles, the way his long fingers wrapped around his glass of wine with ease—left Gabby flushed. She'd thought him handsome from the first, but now with the tan he'd earned on their voyage serving as a complement to his dark hair and piercing blue eyes, he was devastating.

She didn't appear to be the only person Whitfield had this effect on, for women all about the room had their gazes trained on him. Over fans and glasses, eyes studied his every movement, and a foreign and uncomfortable blaze burst to life in her gut. Gabby wasn't surprised the duke was garnering such attention—she had even predicted it on the ship. Yet the prickles of jealousy that slithered along her skin at seeing Whitfield not just admired by the women in the room but *coveted* frustrated her to no end.

Her mood soured further when she noted how her father appeared resolved to keep the duke by his side. Standing between Whitfield and Sirius, Elías was a king surrounded by his court. It made Gabby want to scream.

Instead, she swiped a glass of mezcal from a passing servant and swallowed it in one cutting bite.

"Ay Dios, señorita, you know how to make an impression."

Gabby spun about, her brows arching when her gaze landed on a gentleman she did not recognize. He was young, perhaps Ana María's age, yet he carried himself with a confidence that belied his years. With his dark hair a little too long, and his chin and cheeks covered by dark stubble, he should have looked unkempt. Instead he was rakish, in a dangerously appealing way.

Gabby was instantly intrigued.

Flicking her fan open, Gabby met the stranger's dark gaze. "I'm almost afraid to ask what sort of impression I've made."

The stranger cocked his brow. *"Almost?"*

A slow smile tightened her cheeks. "I've never been afraid of a man's opinion of me."

His laugh echoed around the room, and it was a very nice laugh. Gabby couldn't help but smile up at him.

"I'm Pedro Carrasco," he said, grasping her hand and bringing it to his lips. "And you are Señorita Gabriela Luna, yes?"

"I am." Gabby tilted her head. "How is it you know who I am but I don't know who you are?"

Señor Carrasco dipped his head shyly, but Gabby was not convinced he was at all shy. "I may have asked who the stunning woman in the red gown was."

"Aah," was the only attention she paid his compliment, because she was much more interested in who he was. "And how did you come to be here tonight?"

"I was invited by Señor Ortiz." The man took a step closer to her. "He is a new investor in my . . . enterprise."

Gabby arched a bow. "Enterprise?"

"My brother, Diego, and I are mining consultants." Señor Carrasco grabbed two glasses of mezcal from a passing servant and handed her one. "We grew up in Chile in a family of gold and silver miners, and have developed an eye for mining design."

"Design? How do you mean?" Gabby asked.

"When you mine, you don't just stick a shovel in the ground and dig, hoping you'll find something. It takes planning, so you are not wasting resources. Once a deposit is located, how will extraction begin? How should the infrastructure for the mine itself be constructed? What sort of equipment is needed? How many miners can safely work within the mine at any given time?" Señor Carrasco ticked these items off his fingers. "These are just a few of the many considerations that need to be taken into account, and Diego and I are hired to oversee these details."

"Oh," Gabby murmured, blinking. "I've never really considered everything involved with such an operation."

"But why would you? I learned the importance of such

things because my father, my tíos, my primos risked their lives every time they went into the earth." The Chilean man's expression abruptly brightened. "But such things have also brought me here to Mexico, where I can meet interesting and lovely women."

Gabby just barely managed not to roll her eyes. "Will you be visiting the Camino Rojo mine while you are in San Luis Potosí? My brother-in-law is on the board of directors."

"Captain Dawson, yes?" At Gabby's nod, Señor Carrasco nodded. "I met him and his friend, the duke, today at the board of directors meeting."

Without thought, Gabby glanced to the other side of the room, where Whitfield still stood with her father. She swallowed when her gaze met his, especially because his expression was a marble mask.

Gabby pointedly turned back to Señor Carrasco. "I assume you're adept at dealing with spoiled Europeans who think they know everything about everything?"

"I'm excellent at managing them." The Chilean man's mouth stretched in a grin. "I bet you are, too. A beautiful woman only wears red if she has a man she hopes to charm."

Gabby fluttered her lashes. "I beg your pardon, señor, but nothing I do is ever for a man's benefit."

And with that salvo, Gabby threw back the entirety of her second shot of mezcal.

Señor Carrasco's laugh echoed around the room. "You took that shot like you know what you're about."

"Come now, my mother may be a peninsular, but I am a Mexican through and through." Gabby grinned. "If you learn anything during your time here, let it be to never underestimate a Mexican woman."

"I wouldn't dream of it," the Chilean said, admiration in his voice.

Fighting the urge to look in her father's direction—*Whitfield's* direction—she lifted her chin. Her father may think to ignore her, but Gabby would make herself memorable tonight because she refused to be underestimated.

Good God, she was wearing red.

Sebastian had never seen Gabriela Luna in red, yet he was now certain she should wear nothing else.

He and Sirius had arrived at the Ortiz manor house a half hour earlier, and Sebastian felt like he was only now able to catch his breath. His friend had said the evening would consist of an intimate dinner party, followed by cards, dancing, and discussion. However, the atmosphere they arrived to was anything but intimate.

The Ortiz villa was ensconced by a wrought iron gate, with a long cobblestone entrance that the carriages trudged down to deliver their occupants to the residence. Just outside the gate, however, was a gravel street leading to a teeming city square. Vendor booths and wagons were arranged throughout the space, with peddlers selling various textiles and wares, while others offered delicious-smelling foods like empanadas, roasted corncobs, tamales, and tacos. Musicians with violins, guitars, and trumpets serenaded the crowd, and several couples twirled and stomped to the melodies. Men, women, and children of all ages appeared to take part in the festivities, and Sebastian itched to abandon the Ortiz gathering and join in the community fun. He'd have to find trinkets for the boys, because once he told them of the fiesta, they'd never forgive him if he didn't.

"It is not uncommon for impromptu fiestas to form whenever

the upper class host a gathering," Sirius said, following Sebastian's gaze to the activities in the square. "Sometimes Isabel and I will steal away from whatever event we are at to enjoy the action."

Sebastian snorted. "I don't blame you. Are you sure we can't join the fun now?"

"Let us put in an appearance before we flee for more diverting entertainment." Sirius smoothed his hands down his lapels as the carriage slowed. His hand twisted the door lever as soon as it came to a stop. "Plus, I'd like to see my wife," he called over his shoulder as he bounded down the carriage steps.

"Of course," Sebastian murmured, shaking his head as he followed his friend. He couldn't imagine what it would be like to truly miss a woman and desire her presence.

So it was a disconcerting realization to feel as if his lungs could finally fill with air when he laid eyes on Gabriela standing across the candelabra-lit room. It was as if he had been anticipating just this moment when he would see her again. Sebastian shoved the uncomfortable epiphany away and swiped a beverage from the tray of a passing footman.

Oh, but he watched her. In her red gown, which sat off her shoulders and showcased the delicate cut of her jawline and her strikingly symmetrical profile, Gabriela was exquisite. The burnt sienna curls that cascaded about her shoulders gave her a freshly ravished look, but the red roses tucked within them lent an ethereal halo. Even now as Sebastian stood next to Señor Luna among a group of guests, the conversation ebbed and flowed around him but he struggled to attend to it. He had no notion of how he was expected to act like nothing was amiss when the sight of Gabriela in red had quite literally knocked him senseless.

And blast it all, she stood chatting with Señor Carrasco, the charismatic Chilean whom Sebastian had met at the Camino Rojo board meeting. If her dimpled smiles were any indication, the man had managed to charm his way into her good graces . . . but Sebastian drew a grim sort of satisfaction from the muted light in Gabriela's gaze. He'd glimpsed her across any number of ballrooms, drawing rooms, and dining tables, and Sebastian fancied he was a bit of an expert on the varied expressions of Gabriela Luna. And the current expression on her face hinted at amusement and nothing more.

Or so he hoped.

"How have you been enjoying your time in Mexico, Your Grace?"

It took Sebastian a second to understand the question was directed at him. In truth, it was the pressure on his arm that finally drew his attention. Glancing down, Sebastian found a feminine hand wrapped around his forearm. It belonged to a woman who had been introduced to him not long after he'd arrived. She appeared to be around his age, and was quite elegant and attractive.

If the hungry look in her eyes was any indication, she would also happily welcome him into her bed. Sebastian had lost track of how many months it had been since he'd last enjoyed a turn in the sheets, so the advances of a pretty and willing partner should have stoked the fire in his blood.

Yet he was decidedly cold.

"Señora Delgado, correct?" When she smiled, Sebastian continued in Spanish. "My time in San Luis Potosí has been edifying. It's a beautiful city filled with interesting people doing important things."

The woman's crimson lips tilted up. "Your Spanish is quite impressive, Your Grace."

"Thank you." Sebastian dipped his head. "When I first signed on as an investor of the Camino Rojo mine, I promptly found myself a Spanish tutor."

"Are there many Spanish speakers in London?" Señora Delgado sidled closer to his side.

"As with any large, cosmopolitan city, there are. Plus, I had an advantage in that I'm on friendly terms with the Mexican ambassador to England." Unconsciously, Sebastian glanced in Gabriela's direction. The color was high in her cheeks as she stared up at Carrasco. Unease prickled along his scalp. "Señor Valdés has been a staunch advocate for Mexico."

"That is how you are acquainted with the Luna family, yes?" she asked.

Sebastian inclined his head. "That is one way. But I am also associated because two of my closest friends have married Señor Luna's daughters."

Recognition flared in her dark eyes. "Of course. The British captain, Señor Dawson. He married the morena daughter."

A frown immediately tugged down Sebastian's lips. He was obviously aware of Isabel Dawson's darker skin, but for it to be the first adjective used to describe her seemed like a sin. Swallowing his irritation, he finally said, "Yes. The captain and I have known each other since we were boys. His marriage to Isabel Luna has made him very happy."

Señora Delgado glanced to the left, and Sebastian followed her gaze to where Sirius stood with Isabel near the perimeter of the room. They appeared completely engrossed in each other, as if they were the only two people about. Sebastian quickly looked away when his friend brushed a curl from Isabel's cheek, his knuckles lingering to caress her skin.

"They are an interesting pair," the woman by his side murmured.

"They complement each other," Señor Luna said, pivoting to join their conversation. The man's dark eyes studied Sirius and Isabel, his mien contemplative. "My wife and I did not think Isabel would marry at all. For truly, who would want a dark-skinned mestiza with more brains than beauty?"

Sebastian locked his teeth together so forcefully they clicked.

"Yet Dawson arrived from England already infatuated with her." Señor Luna shrugged. "He is charming, and stands to make a fortune with that silver mine. And Isabel's clever and reserved nature is an asset for her work with the First Lady. Yes, they seem quite content with each other. Isabel has far exceeded any expectation I had for her."

Catching a passing servant's eye, Sebastian gestured to his empty glass. He needed fortification.

In comparison, Señora Delgado's lips curled up in delight. "And your eldest daughter is married to a politician in England?"

"Sí. Ana María's husband is a member of Parliament and has already made a name for himself." The older man glanced at Sebastian. "Is that not true, señor?"

"It is." Sebastian accepted a new glass of tequila from the servant eagerly. "Fox may one day be prime minister."

Señor Luna smiled, and it did nothing to soften his features. "An alliance worthy of a Luna."

Sebastian took a long sip of tequila.

Señora Delgado had managed to press herself into his side, and Sebastian held himself stiffly. "You have another daughter, do you not, Señor Luna? Has she married a British man, as well?"

At just that moment, a peal of laughter sounded above the din. Sebastian didn't have to look to know it was Gabriela, but his eyes immediately went to her. She was holding an empty shot glass, her dimple flashing as she laughed along with Carrasco.

"Ay no." Elías Luna rubbed at his brow, his own gaze fixed on the other side of the room. "My youngest daughter remains unwed still."

"Maybe she's waiting for just the right sort of gentleman to make a proposal." Señora Delgado tapped Señor Luna on the arm with her fan. "A titled gentleman? Or maybe a handsome Chilean."

His stomach dropped, watching as Carrasco gazed down at Gabriela.

"Or a duke," Señor Luna quipped, turning to face Sebastian and raising his glass.

Unsure of what to say, Sebastian merely tipped his head in acknowledgment.

"Aah, is that the next match in the making?" Señora Delgado's eyes narrowed on him. "Are you hoping to take the last Luna sister off the marriage market, Your Grace?"

Before Sebastian could formulate an answer, Señor Luna snorted loudly. "Gabriela is meant for a Spaniard. With her güera beauty, my hope is for her to marry into one of the powerful Spanish families who have thrown their support behind the French. El presidente needs their allegiance if we are to successfully rebuild after Maximilian is deposed."

"How shrewd of you, señor," Señora Delgado said.

"Plus, let us be honest," the older man continued, his lip curled, "Gabriela may be beautiful, but she's hardly bright enough to hold the attention of the duke here."

Sebastian scowled outright. "That's patently untrue."

"Is it?" Señor Luna cocked a brow, seemingly surprised.

Doing his best to suppress the anger that locked his jaw tight, Sebastian nodded curtly. "There is no doubt Miss Luna is beautiful, but if all you see is her beauty, you're missing the fire, the depths that make her incomparable."

"With all that fire, she should have been born a boy." The older man shook his head. "Instead, that girl has always been difficult and always will be difficult, and I'll have my hands full finding a peninsular husband willing to put up with her."

Any words Sebastian had intended to utter were stolen from him on a silent gasp when a pair of hazel eyes collided with his. Hazel eyes that had grown shiny with unshed tears. He had been so incensed by Señor Luna's sentiments that he hadn't noticed that Gabriela had come to join their group until that moment when she spun about on her heel and bolted, her red skirts streaming in her wake.

No one else seemed aware she had overheard them, for Señor Luna and Señora Delgado continued to chatter. But Sebastian could not erase the picture of her stricken expression from his mind. Tossing back the remainder of his beverage, Sebastian set down his glass on a nearby table.

"If you will excuse me," he murmured, and walked away without giving either Señor Luna or Señora Delgado a chance to respond.

They deserved no such niceties.

13

If she hadn't had that second glass of mezcal, Gabby never would have cried.

As it was, her father had an uncanny talent for knowing exactly how to reduce her to tears.

Angrily swiping at her cheeks, Gabby pushed her way through the guests that filled the Ortizes' home to the front entrance. Without a backward glance, Gabby grasped her skirts and darted down the cobblestone drive toward the music and laughter that emanated from the town square. Footsteps sounded behind her, and she looked over her shoulder and saw that one of Sirius and Isabel's grooms was following her, and a flash of affection for them spread through her limbs, for she knew they had sent him to guarantee she was safe.

Even though her walk was not a long one, Gabby's evening slippers were more appropriate for genteel gatherings than mad dashes over graveled streets, and she limped slightly as she reached the center of activity. Gabby paused as she took in the crowds around her, a smile slowly sliding onto her lips. Hefting the bulk of her skirts in her hands, Gabby crisscrossed her way through the various stalls and wagons, stopping to allow a milliner to place a stylish hat on her head to model. She did so happily, before she wandered to where a temporary stage had been constructed under a large piñon tree. Lanterns hung cheerfully from the boughs, and a large group of children sat in a cluster before the stage, their excited chatter filling the air with anticipation. Gabby watched with a grin at the puppet show that commenced, laughing at the performance along with the children.

After the show had ended, Gabby discovered a wagon that had been transformed into a traveling bookstore. Narrow bookshelves lined three sides of the wagon and were filled with novels, poetry collections, history tomes, and more. Many were in Spanish and French, but a surprising selection were in English, and Gabby energetically searched through the assortment, grabbing first one book and then another, trying to decide which one Isabel would like more. When the elderly bookseller noted Gabby's interest, he assisted her with selecting several different books for not only her sister, but herself, as well. Gabby owned very few books of her own, always content to borrow from her older sister. But now that Isabel was married, Gabby would have to acquire and curate her own library. The idea made her more enthused than she'd anticipated.

After she paid for her selections, the bookseller had wrapped them and agreed to hold them until she collected them later, leaving Gabby to meander to where a six-member band played an eclectic arrangement of musical styles. At one point they played a waltz, but they weaved in a distinctly Mexican flair with the sound of the guitar. Gabby swayed side to side as she watched couples twirl around the makeshift dance floor.

"I believe you owe me a dance."

Gabby jerked back, her eyes flying wide as she pivoted to find Whitfield standing several paces away. The bright chandeliers in the Ortizes' home had highlighted every detail of the duke's beauty, but the same was not true here in the town square. The sparse lighting from torches and lamps elongated the shadows, hiding his expression. Yet the dim illumination also made Whitfield appear taller, broader, and more . . . *dangerous* than ever before.

Suddenly Gabby could imagine Whitfield cloaked in darkness, awaiting his lover for an assignation. How would a woman possibly say no to such a man? She shivered.

"Are you cold?" he inquired, moving closer.

"No," she said hastily, ignoring the gooseflesh that crept along her skin. Clearing her throat, she glanced back to where the band played. "I'm surprised you're here."

"I seem to surprise you a good deal," he drawled, coming to stand beside her. His woodsy scent flooded her nose, and Gabby closed her eyes for a moment and simply inhaled. Why did he have to smell so damn good?

"You do," she managed to murmur, fluttering her eyes open and glancing up at his face. "This trip has been illuminating in more ways than one."

Whitfield inclined his head. "For me as well."

Gabby nibbled on the inside of her cheek for a moment. The duke knew why she had fled the party, so it seemed prudent to confront what her father had said and put the shame behind her. "Thank you for what you said."

"What I said?"

"To my father." She swallowed. "I'm sure it's been quite enlightening to see how the lauded Elías Luna really feels about his youngest daughter."

"I meant every word." The duke rocked back on his feet. "And it has been enlightening, actually."

Gabby wanted to ask how, but her mouth was abruptly desert dry.

To her horror, Whitfield turned on his heel and faced her directly, his blue eyes snaring hers even in the poor lighting. "It has given me insight into the person you are. Why it often feels as if you are constantly on the offensive. As if you're expecting verbal attacks instead of compliments. It's because you've been trained to expect such things."

The music and the sounds of the crowd faded away, and all Gabby could hear was the duke's voice. His calm, soothing tenor curled about her.

"It's also why you're a defender. Why you rush to protect others. Your sisters, definitely, but also your friends. Acquaintances. I compared you to a Gorgon once. Do you remember?"

She nodded, her tongue stuck to the roof of her mouth. Two years prior Gabby had attended a horse race with Isabel, where they'd encountered Whitfield. When he called her a Gorgon, she hadn't been sure if it was a compliment or not, and Gabby suspected that was the point. Everything about the duke left her off balance.

"I'm sure you thought I said it in jest, but I meant it earnestly." Whitfield took a step closer, his gaze unwavering on hers. "You are a fearsome champion of others, but you take up no weapons to defend yourself."

"I do." The words were broken, watery, but Gabby forced herself to say them. "It's just so hard with . . ."

"With *him*." The duke's tone was gentle. "Why is that?"

Shaking her head, she dropped her chin to her chest. Gabby could not believe she was on the verge of tears before the Duke of Whitfield yet again. She was horribly embarrassed . . . but she also longed to wrap her arms around his waist and nestle into his broad chest. Nothing sounded more comforting, and Gabby held herself stiff as a board so she would not give in to the desire.

"Dance with me?"

Gabby frowned. "You really want to dance?"

"I do." Whitfield smirked, and that familiar expression made her smile. "Plus, as I said, you owe me one."

The music changed then, and so did the dancing. Quirking her lips, she said, "Do you know how to dance el jarabe tapatío?"

Furrows creased his brow as Whitfield stared at the couples positioning themselves as the first trumpet notes filled the air. "I do not. I swear I just heard a waltz."

A giggle burst from her mouth, and Gabby pressed a hand to her lips. But Whitfield's disgruntled expression made her laugh harder.

"They did play a waltz earlier, but not anymore," she managed.

The duke's frown deepened, although there was an amused light in his eyes as he watched her laugh at his expense. When Gabby finally calmed herself, Whitfield studied the dancers, who tapped and twirled around each other.

"Have you danced . . . ?"

"El jarabe tapatío. No, I haven't," she said, turning to watch the dancers with him.

"Why not?"

Gabby lifted a shoulder. "The dance was only becoming popular when we fled to London. I was too young to dance it before that."

Whitfield nodded and, after a heartbeat, glanced down at her. "I'm willing to try it, if you are."

"You are?" Gabby blinked at him, suddenly lightheaded. "Truly?"

"Truly. Although"—he removed his hat and rubbed the back of his neck—"I will probably look like a fool."

"We can look foolish together, then," she proclaimed, extending him a hand.

The duke stared down at her hand for a moment and then slid his pale blue eyes up to meet hers. Her palm already prickled with awareness, and he'd yet to touch her.

Whitfield slid his fingers around hers. "Let's be fools together."

Sebastian had no idea what he was doing, but he was very happy to be doing it.

How could he not be when Gabriela looked at him like that? With that radiant expression she had never directed his way because he'd ruined any goodwill she may have felt toward him by acting with his cock and not his head.

He didn't have a chance to contemplate the thawing of their animosity because the dance's steps required all his concentration. They were unlike anything Sebastian had ever danced before, and involved a dramatic stomping, tapping, and spinning. Everything about dancing the waltz was stately and refined, but el jarabe tapatío was infused with life. With vitality. It was a dance that was made for Gabriela, who was the most vibrant person Sebastian had ever met.

Even now, as she twirled her bulky skirts as best she could and kicked her slippered feet in a close approximation of the steps the other couples were engaged in, she glowed. Gone was the brokenhearted young woman he'd watched flee the Ortizes' opulent home, and in her place was this vivacious beauty who was beaming her brightest smile at him. At Sebastian, who had only ever earned her scowls. He wanted to hold his breath, afraid that, like a bubble, her esteem would not last.

Yanking his gaze away from her spirited face, Sebastian studied the other dancers, determined to mimic their movements. The man and woman next to them moved toward each other on the beat, their heads angled as if to kiss. They danced one, two beats, and then twirled apart.

Sebastian rotated until he faced Gabriela again, and she seemed to read the intention on his face because she arched a brow. When the tempo swelled, he moved close to her, his eyes fixed on hers while he tilted his chin. His heart skipped a beat when she did the same, her face so close he could count the smattering of freckles on the bridge of her nose. Without conscious thought, Sebastian glanced down at her mouth. He'd noticed it before—of course he had, he was no monk—but never had her lips looked so perfectly kissable. It would be just a move of inches to claim her mouth, as his mind and body had been begging him to do since . . . forever.

Christ. Sebastian somehow managed to use the movements of the dance to save him from making a fool of himself in front of every resident of San Luis Potosí in attendance, for he knew Gabriela would not take kindly to being kissed against her will. Wasn't that why she was in Mexico now? Because another *supposed* gentleman had thought to take advantage of her? He refused to be so boorish.

Thankfully, Sebastian was not required to touch her. If they had danced a waltz together, he would be free to rest his hand on her waist. To touch her palm to his. To feel her body step and sway in harmony with the music. But the damn el jarabe tapatío required him to have his hands knotted behind his back. To have her so temptingly close but so far away made it the most frustrating dance Sebastian had ever engaged in.

They moved together again, and this time Gabriela positioned her chin so that her mouth was at the right height and angle to be kissed. He clamped his eyes shut to block out the temptation, but Sebastian could not stop her violet and amber perfume from filling his lungs. Her luscious scent seemed to settle on his tongue and twirl about his mouth.

Sebastian almost groaned aloud at the taste.

His eyes shot open in time to catch the playful light that flashed in her hazel gaze before she pivoted away. What had he gotten himself into? Sebastian had managed to spend three weeks with Gabriela Luna, and a single dance, one that prohibited him from touching her, threatened to be his undoing. As it was, his wild attraction to her was making itself inconveniently known, and Sebastian prayed the dance would end soon before he embarrassed himself.

For once Providence heard his plea, and the last strums of the string instruments reverberated through the air. With a dramatic flourish, Gabriela grasped her skirts and sank into a graceful curtsy.

"That was . . ." She peered about them before meeting his gaze. "Fun."

Widening his stance, and hoping to relieve his straining cock, Sebastian said, "Once again, you sound surprised."

"Because you're making a habit of surprising me, Your Grace." She shook out the fall of her dress and adjusted the fit of her gloves. "I thought perhaps we'd be so concerned with the correct footwork and movements that we wouldn't enjoy the dance itself. But after a while, I didn't even care if I was doing it right."

"Neither did I," Sebastian chuckled. "As I'm sure you could tell."

"I thought you were very elegant."

He went still, even as he battled a grin. "What was that? I didn't quite hear you."

Gabriela cut him a sharp look. "We both know you heard me."

"I beg to differ," Sebastian pushed, daring to move closer. "Would you be so kind as to repeat it?"

Raising her hand, Gabriela poked him in the center of his chest. "I said you're an arse."

In a flash, Sebastian grabbed her wrist and reeled her against his chest. He expected her to be surprised, maybe pull back and attempt to step away from him. But instead, Gabriela's eyes dropped to his mouth for an electric instant, and then slowly rose to meet his.

God damn this woman.

Wetting his lips, he whispered, "You always have the prettiest compliments to share with others but never with me, and I find myself hungry for them."

As double entendres went, his was heavy-handed. But this seemed to delight Gabby, because she giggled.

"I *am* very generous with my praise." Her voice dropped further when she said, "But compliments taste much sweeter when they've been earned."

Sebastian dared to run his thumb over the back of her knuckles. "And have I not earned them?"

Gabriela's brows rose, and she stared up at him for a fraught second. Then her pink tongue darted out and ran across her bottom lip, and—

"Gabby, there you are. I've been looking everywhere for you."

They stumbled apart as if they'd been burned. Sebastian reached out to steady her, but Gabriela pulled away, and his arms dropped to his sides. He watched in a daze as she turned to converse with her sister, the color high in her cheeks. It took him an embarrassingly long moment to understand that Sirius now stood at his side.

"You look like someone just punched you in the face," his friend said, staring at Sebastian intently.

"I'm sure there are many who would relish the opportunity to do so." Sebastian scrubbed a hand over his chin. "I'm just a little knackered after that dance."

"Juan, the groom, said you and Gabby danced el jarabe tapatío." Sirius clicked his tongue. "I'm sorry I missed it."

Sebastian snorted. "I'm sure you are. Have you ever danced it?"

"Lord, no." Sirius clapped him on the shoulder. "I have no qualms with leading Isabel out for a waltz or a minuet. Even a Scots reel. But Mexican dances are for people with more rhythm than me."

"Well, my mother worked to ensure that I didn't trip over my own feet when I stepped onto a dance floor, so I hope I didn't look too ridiculous." At that moment, Gabriela threw back her head to laugh at something Isabel said. Sebastian's gaze lingered on her. "Thankfully, I had a graceful partner."

"Yes, it seemed you two were quite . . . absorbed with one another."

Sebastian looked at his friend askance. "What is that supposed to mean?"

"What do you think it means?" Sirius crossed his arms over his chest and stared back at him with a smirk.

Spinning on his heel, Sebastian stalked toward the Ortiz villa. "I have no interest in playing guessing games with you."

"Don't leave." His friend yanked on his arm. "Christ, Sebastian, you have no problem teasing others, but heaven forfend others tease you in turn."

Tugging his arm away, Sebastian smoothed his palms over his sleeves and then his lapels. Sirius was not wrong, and yet he couldn't possibly exchange lighthearted banter when his whole body felt as if it were vibrating like a tuning fork. That damn dance had changed how he looked at Gabriela Luna—no, that wasn't true. This whole blasted trip to Mexico had done that. It had thrust her from the "lovely but shrewish and completely unavailable" category he'd long ago placed her in, to a woman he surprisingly understood and sympathized with. Whom he desired, not just for her stunning beauty, but because she made him feel needed. For while she was defending everyone else, whom did she turn to when her sword grew dull?

"Is everything all right?" Sirius asked, his brows pulled low. "Isabel and I saw Gabby dashing out of the gathering, and she appeared upset. And now we've found the two of you together, and you're as prickly as a cactus."

Was everything all right? *No*, it bloody hell wasn't. And yet Sebastian had no desire to tell his friend how Gabriela Luna had knocked him off his feet again and again. Instead he cleared his throat, and said, "Miss Luna overheard unkind remarks from her father, and was understandably upset. I like to think that making a fool of myself dancing the tapatío has improved her mood."

If the smile brightening Gabriela's face now as she chatted with Isabel was any indication, it had helped a little. And that damn smile made Sebastian's chest a tad lighter.

"That man," Sirius growled, swiping a hand over his brow as he stared at the sisters. "Well, whatever you did or said appears to have worked, although let's hope no one has anything to say about the two of you being alone here."

Sebastian scowled. "We're hardly alone." He emphasized his point by waving a hand at the surrounding crowd and even Juan, who stood nearby.

"Propriety is just as valued here as it is in London." Before

Sebastian could argue, Sirius jerked his thumb at his wife. "Isabel wanted to visit the book peddler. He only comes through San Luis Potosí every few months."

Sebastian blinked, embarrassed he had been woolgathering about Gabriela when his friend was speaking to him. Clearing his throat, he murmured, "A welcome visitor, I'm sure."

"Indeed. So I'm going to escort her and Gabby there." Sirius inclined his head. "Did you want to meet us at the villa?"

He hesitated. Sebastian knew he should return to the safety of the Ortiz gathering, yet he didn't move. Locking his teeth together, Sebastian slid his gaze to Gabriela at just the moment she glanced at him. Their eyes held, and while Sebastian could read nothing of her thoughts in her stare, he found himself shaking his head.

"I'll accompany you," he said shortly.

14

When Gabby fluttered her eyes open, it took her a moment to remember where she was. For a fortnight she'd awoken in her parents' villa, yet Gabby continued to experience the same confusion, because it did not feel like home.

Stretching her arms overhead, she sat up and rubbed the heels of her palms into her eyes. Dropping her hands, she slowly focused on the painting on the wall. It depicted La Virgen de Guadalupe when she appeared to Juan Diego and asked him, in Nahuatl, to have a church erected on the spot where they stood. Gabby knew for a fact that this was not the only painting of La Virgen in the house, but this particular one had always been her favorite because depictions of the four apparitions were included. As a child, she used to imagine the cherubs, who frolicked along the border, their reverent eyes turned upon Mary, were her friends. Her youthful thoughts made her laugh now, almost as much as they made her want to cry.

A maid had left a tray with chocolate and a pan dulce on a side table, and Gabby smiled as she padded to it. Taking the cup of chocolate in hand, she wandered to the window and pushed the curtain aside. From this angle, she could just make out the table on the terrace where her father sat every morning to read reports and the latest news. However, he was not there now, and Gabby remembered that he would be meeting with Presidente Juárez to discuss the latest news from the siege of Querétaro. She was relieved she would not have to tiptoe around him, as she had been since the start of her stay. A stay she had felt forced into, if only to escape her own roiling emotions.

After she and her sister had collected their books and left the town square to rejoin the Ortiz dinner, Gabby had thrown herself into socializing. She'd talked and laughed with any number of people, although she could not remember any of their faces or names. Gabby barely remembered what she had said, as every bit of her energy had been focused on ignoring the duke. *Avoiding* the duke. After their charged dance, Gabby had needed some distance from him. The morning following the party, she had inadvertently collided with him in the hall outside of her bedroom at Casa Inglesa. She'd almost melted when he'd gripped her upper arms to steady her, his azul eyes intent upon hers. Whitfield murmured some sort of apology, but Gabby had been unable to attend to his words because all she could think about was the heat radiating from his palms and streaking through her limbs. With a rushed apology of her own, Gabby had slipped from his grasp and sought out her sister. Fortuitously, Isabel had just received a note from their mother, inviting them to join her for lunch, and Gabby had immediately agreed. During their visit, María Elena had invited her to spend the week with her and her father, and again, Gabby had accepted. While being in such proximity to her father was not ideal, Gabby also did not trust herself around the duke. He was due to return to London soon. Surely, she could find a way to steer clear of him until then . . . especially when the thought of his hands on her skin made heat coil low in that sensitive spot between her thighs.

Yanking the drapes closed, Gabby stalked to her chamber door and flipped the lock. Setting her cup of chocolate aside, she climbed back under the sheets. Staring at the ceiling for a moment and listening for any sounds in the hall beyond, Gabby eventually closed her eyes. Whitfield was imprinted on the back of her eyelids. That taunting smirk curled his lips before they shaped the word *hungry* . . . just as they had during their dance. Gabby shivered at the memory.

Dragging her night rail up her legs and over her hips, she slipped one hand into her drawers, sighing as her fingertips stroked where she was wet and aching. Biting her lip, Gabby allowed the memories of his voice, his scent, his touch to turn her boneless.

Sometime later, Gabby joined her mother in the sunroom for a late breakfast. The room was her favorite space in the house, for while it was tastefully decorated in that regal manner her father insisted upon, it was also comfortable. Her mother had ensured there were pillows of varying textures on every armchair and settee, and soft blankets encouraged visitors to relax. But what really drew Gabby to the space was that two sides of the room were encased in glass. Glass on such a grand scale was a lavish choice and spoke of her parents' wealth, but it also brought the outdoors in. While curled up on the settee, Gabby could admire the craggy slopes of Cerro Grande and the surrounding mountainside. It was a different landscape than what she had grown up with in Mexico City, and certainly what she had come to know in London. But the sight brought her peace.

A bit of peace she should have known she'd need to survive staying under her father's roof.

"You've had a lazy morning, mi hijita," her mother said, glancing away from the newspaper she was reading to greet her with a smile.

After serving herself a plate of fruit with a concha, Gabby seated herself on the armchair next to her mother.

"I sleep well knowing you're near."

María Elena chuckled softly before bussing her cheek. "Mi amor, I've missed you."

"Y yo te." Gabby watched her mother while she popped an orange segment into her mouth. "Have you adjusted to life in San Luis Potosí?"

Her mother released a long breath, and she turned to consider the sweeping vista outside the windows. "We haven't been here long, but it feels more like home than any place we've stayed."

Gabby nodded. After she and her sisters had been sent to London, her parents had traveled all over the central and northern part of Mexico seeking safety. Wherever Presidente Juárez took refuge, so did they. It had been an anxious time for the sisters, for reliable reports of the conflict were sparse, and there was no convenient way to communicate with their parents. Tío Arturo had an extensive network of contacts within Mexico, however, and news filtered through them in irregular waves. Thus, Gabby and her sisters spent many sleepless nights worrying over not just Elías and María Elena, but the president and the state of their beloved Mexico. Gabby could only imagine how stressful it had been for her parents to experience that tumultuous period.

"I'm glad the city has been welcoming to you. From what I

understand, the French attempted to use it as an outpost to solidify their hold in the north."

María Elena turned to quirk a brow. "How did you know that?"

"I have done my best to keep abreast of the Liberal forces' efforts, despite the patchy news coverage." Gabby toyed with an orange rind. "Ana, Isa, and I would read aloud the letters Tío Arturo received from his contacts."

Her mother's forehead crinkled. "Arturo would share his correspondence with you?"

"Of course." Gabby snorted. "He knew we were desperate for any news from home. Not once did he withhold information from us, even when he knew it would frighten us."

It was a jab at her parents' lack of transparency, and they both knew it. Neither her mother nor her father had ever been forthcoming with information surrounding the war, even when there was a chance their daughters would be in danger. Instead, Gabby and her sisters were expected to follow their edicts without question . . . which had become impossible for her.

"It's been so long since I've seen Arturo." Her mother's expression was wistful. "He was always so protective. He didn't want me to marry your father, you know."

As if an invisible hook had tugged on her spine, Gabby sat up straighter. "I did not know that."

Leaning back in her chair, María Elena slid her gaze to the closed door before she said, "Arturo believed your father was only interested in marrying me because of my dowry and familial connections, and he wanted me to have a love match."

Gabby tried to keep the scowl off her face, but it was so very hard. "Mother, but that *is* why Father married you. You must know he doesn't love anyone but himself."

She wasn't sure of the response she expected to receive, but her mother's exhausted sigh was not it.

"You know that, don't you?" Gabby set her plate aside and leaned toward her mother, her hands curled like talons around the armrest. "Surely you understand that his love has only ever been conditional."

"Of course I know," María Elena snapped. Primly folding her hands in her lap, she speared Gabby with a look. "Despite what you may think of me, I'm not a fool."

"I've never thought you were a fool." Gabby's chair squeaked as she pushed it back, and she stalked to the other side of the room. Anger fired in her veins. "But why do you allow him to make you out to be one?"

María Elena gaped at her. "Because I love him, querida."

Her anger fled her in a whoosh, and Gabby sank onto the settee. The words were not a surprise. But to hear her mother confirm her feelings, and in such a dejected way, was crushing.

"I was not ignorant of your father's motivations when I entered this marriage"—María Elena's voice broke—"but he was who I wanted."

Her mother had settled . . . and had convinced herself to be content with scraps ever since.

Tearing her gaze away, Gabby stared at the landscape. Was that her future, too? Hadn't she fled London because a titled man had tried to trap her into a loveless marriage? He'd only valued her because of her family fortune, and not for any of the things that made her Gabriela Luna. Had any man ever inquired about her interests? In the things she was passionate about? Had any man ever bothered to look beyond the sarcasm she used as a shield?

If all you see is her beauty, you're missing the fire, the depths that make her incomparable.

Biting her lip, Gabby buried her face in her hands.

"When do you plan to bring the rest of your luggage from your sister's house?"

Peering at her mother through her fingers, Gabby frowned. "What do you mean?"

María Elena cocked her head. "I just assumed that since you've been here for a fortnight, you should return home officially."

The icy fingers of dread circled around her neck. "Home? Do you mean Mexico? Or . . . *here*?" Gabby twirled her finger, indicating the room around them.

"Here." Her mother frowned. "Surely you'll be living with your father and me."

Gabby was shaking her head before her mother finished speaking. "I wasn't sure what I was going to do, but Isabel and Sirius said I could stay with them indefinitely."

María Elena shook her head in confusion. "Your father expects you to live with us going forward. I understand you may want to stay with Isabel, but she's married and deserves her privacy."

Gabby knew she couldn't truly live with Isabel and Sirius long term, but she also wasn't prepared to return to her parents' home. Not now . . . and maybe not ever.

"I know I cannot stay with Isabel forever, but I've missed her and am not ready to say goodbye," Gabby tossed out blithely, even while her fingers twisted in her skirts.

Her mother sighed, but something about her mien gave Gabby pause. "Is there something you're not telling me?"

One of María Elena's dark brows rose. "Why do you ask?"

Answering her question with a question did nothing to douse the suspicion firing in Gabby's gut. "Has Father said something?"

Immediately, her mother dropped her gaze. "He's made a comment or two regarding you."

Coming to her feet, Gabby crossed to crouch before her mother, grasping her hand. "What did he say?"

María Elena's hazel eyes darted between Gabby's. "He mentioned that several gentlemen have asked after you. Apparently you made an impression with your red gown."

Gabby pressed her lips together as her mind raced. Did that mean—

"He's invited Señor Espinoza to join us for dinner tonight. He's been overseeing the delivery of correspondence between here and Mexico City." Her mother patted the back of her hand. "He's a nice young man. Even a little handsome."

With an exhale, Gabby collapsed back onto the floor, her skirts billowing around her. "So he's already trying to find me a husband. Does he truly not think I can find one on my own?"

"He doesn't think you want to, Gabriela." María Elena tossed her hands into the air. "You return to Mexico without telling us because an Englishman asked you to marry him—"

"Carlisle tried to compromise me!" Gabby exclaimed.

Her mother exhaled a long breath. "I know, and I'm sorry that happened. But perhaps it would have been better had you accepted him."

Gabby's head jerked back as if she'd been slapped. "Better? You believe I should have accepted the marriage proposal of a man capable of such horrid behavior? Who does not love and respect me?"

"Mi hija," María Elena sighed, rubbing her temple, "you've had four years to marry for love. Your sisters have. Why not you?"

Recoiling, Gabby stared at her mother with wide eyes. *Why hadn't she married?* As if her mother agreed that all Gabby was good for was a marriage bargain. Possibly even a broodmare.

Her breathing grew uneven. "Why even ask about my plans when you and Father have already decided for me?"

María Elena tapped her fingertips against her lips as she considered her. When she eventually spoke, her tone was one of sadness. "Gabriela, you had your chance. But now that you're home, your father expects you to do your duty. And your duty is to the Luna familia."

Gabby pressed her tongue to the roof of her mouth, hoping it kept her from crying.

Her mother continued. "Your sisters married British men. Well connected, influential they may be, but British nevertheless. Your father believes that with your light skin and light eyes, you could attract a Spanish husband who could bolster the family's legacy and help lead Mexico into an era of reconstruction and reform."

"He wants me to marry a peninsular," Gabby whispered.

"Surely you're not surprised by that." María Elena waved a dismissive hand. "You look like a Spaniard, more so than your sisters. It has been your father's hope for the majority of your life. I believe he was relieved when you returned home without a husband."

Her legs were wobbly as she returned to her seat. Although she longed to pull her knees into her chest and curl into a ball, Gabby sat straight backed on the chair. "I understand."

María Elena's expression brightened. "I'm delighted to hear it, querida. Your father will be pleased."

As Gabby listened tight-lipped to her mother as she chattered away about Señor Espinoza and the other young men—and *not*-so-young men—who were eager to align themselves with Elías Luna and his family, she grew more and more nauseated. Gabby should have known this would happen. She had been arrogant to believe she could return to Mexico a different

Gabriela Luna than the girl who had fled it. Stupidly, she'd thought she could show her father that she'd changed and grown more mature, but he would always view her as the same silly girl he deigned to pay attention to only when it suited him.

She was the fool.

But no longer. Gabby had been wrong to return, but that did not mean she was helpless. Isabel and Sirius would help her. And didn't Whitfield say he would always be available to assist her? Swallowing, Gabby knotted her hands together in her lap and prayed her countenance gave away nothing of her impatience to her mother. She had a note to send to her sister, and Gabby was desperate to see to the task before her new-found resolve was tested.

Throughout dinner that night, Gabby did her best to play the role of a dutiful daughter. She dressed in her navy brocade silk gown with the black lace underlay, and wore the simple sapphire and silver drop earrings Ana María and Gideon had given her for her last birthday. The maid had styled her hair in a simple updo, and Gabby had even applied a touch of color to her lips. Her mother had gasped when she walked into the sitting room, her face alight with admiration as she pressed a kiss to both of Gabby's cheeks. And while her father had not said a word, Elías had nodded his head after taking in her appearance.

Señor Espinoza proved to be a friendly enough gentleman, if a little pompous. The son of a wealthy banker from Barcelona, he'd only emigrated to Mexico after the War of Reform had ended, but he'd quickly risen through the Liberal ranks. Gabby could understand why her parents wanted a match between her and the young peninsular, for Espinoza practically fawned over her father. Oh, he'd paid compliments to her beauty and engaged her in conversation—just enough to not tax Gabby's already frayed nerves—but then Espinoza had spent the majority of his time trading tales and discussing strategy with her father. She tried multiple times to add to the conversation, not accustomed to being so completely overlooked during a dinner party, but her father would simply cut her a glance and then ignore her.

It infuriated her, but Gabby did her best to hide it. She replayed happy moments she'd spent with her sisters in London, and imagined what her friends with the women's group were doing to shape a franchise bill. Gabby even allowed herself to reflect upon the voyage to Mexico, when Whitfield had encouraged her to speak about politics and share her opinions about the occupation. Or when he teased her while they played hopscotch with the children. Or when he'd danced el jarabe tapatío with her, his breath caressing her lips whenever the steps brought them close together. She even allowed herself to imagine what his lips would have felt like against her own. What they would have tasted like—

"Gabriela," her mother hissed in her ear. "What are you doing?"

Starting, Gabby darted her gaze about and realized her father and Señor Espinoza were already making their way from the dining room to enjoy drinks and cigars on the patio. She hadn't even noticed when they'd risen from the table.

Placing her napkin aside, Gabby thanked the servant who pulled out her chair and turned to her mother. "I apologize. I was woolgathering."

María Elena sighed. "You've been doing so well, mi amor. Don't make a mistake now."

Anger surged up her throat, and with as much grace as she

could muster, Gabby asked, "What sort of mistake do you believe I will make?"

"Ay, Gabby," her mother grumbled, "must I list the multitude of ways you've acted out over the years?"

Holding her mother's gaze, Gabby moved a step closer to her. "Did you ever wonder why I acted out so much as a child?"

"Because you wanted things to be your way. If you desired something and it was not given to you, you became upset." María Elena ran her knuckles over Gabby's cheek. "You've always wanted more. You were never satisfied."

It was a soul-crushing realization to learn one's own mother didn't truly know her. And Gabby rather doubted her mother cared to know her. Not the real Gabby, at least. It assured Gabby that her decision to send a note to Isabel earlier in the evening had been prudent. Ignoring the cold, empty certainty that took root in her chest, Gabby shook her head.

"It's not that I always wanted more. It's that I wanted *enough*." Gabby stared at the doorway her father had walked through, a bitter resignation settling over her. "I was starved for attention, yes, but more so I was starved for love. You gave me what you could, but you alone couldn't give me what I *needed*."

With her shoulders sinking, Gabby walked to the doorway but paused, glancing back at her mother. "I'm done grasping for crumbs."

Not giving her mother a chance to respond, Gabby slipped away. She knew María Elena would not follow her as they still had a guest, so she quickly gathered the small number of her dresses, gowns, and undergarments she'd brought with her and packed them in her trunk. Racing around the room, she snatched up her books, jewelry, hats, and hairpins, shoving them into a satchel. Taking one last glance around the space, Gabby released a long breath. She had been comfortable here, but this was not home. Her mother was not her home anymore, and at some point in the future, Gabby would allow herself to mourn the loss of their relationship. For now, though, she needed to leave.

Throwing her satchel over her shoulder, she hoisted her trunk through the doorway as best she could. Thankfully a servants' entrance led to the narrow alley that ran behind the villa, and Gabby did not have to drag her trunk for long before she spied the sleek black carriage waiting for her. Without a word, the carriage door flung open and Sirius ran down the alley toward her.

"Let's hurry. I'd rather not have a confrontation with your father," he murmured, taking the satchel from her shoulder.

The driver grabbed her trunk and stored it while Gabby climbed into the cab. She gasped when she spotted Isabel waiting for her in the dim interior.

"Oh Isa," she exclaimed, launching herself into her sister's arms.

"Ay querida," Isabel crooned, stroking the hair back from Gabby's brow. "I was hoping your note had just been a precaution, but of course we came. I'm sorry that things have gone this way."

The carriage lurched forward, and Gabby glanced out the window over her sister's shoulder. Her parents' brightly lit villa moved farther from view as they rumbled over the gravel street, and she bit her lip to keep the tears at bay. Gabby felt like a failure.

"Your parents are obviously going to know you've left to stay with us, and I assume they'll give you a few days to *calm* yourself." Sirius emphasized the word with a roll of his eyes.

"But if your father is intent on securing a Spanish husband for you, he will only be patient for so long."

Gabby nodded. She had two or three days, at most, before she'd be summoned to another dinner or event where she would be paraded about like an empty-headed doll. Her stomach dropped at the thought.

"So we have a few days to make our plans." Isabel paused and then slowly pulled back from Gabby. Her sister's dark eyes snared hers. "What do you want to do? If you want to stay in Mexico, say the word, and Sirius and I will search for a place you can go. Maybe with your friend Señorita Moreno?"

"Maybe," Gabby murmured dejectedly. Lucia had mentioned in her last letter that she'd fallen into a comfortable routine with her abuela, and Gabby didn't want to disturb her friend's peace.

"Of course you can return to England. Ana and Gideon would be happy to have you as well, you know."

"The thought of seeing baby Estella again does make me happy." And perhaps any gossip that arose after the Wright ball had been put to rest, and Gabby could make a quiet return. An idea occurred to Gabby, and she swung her head to look at Sirius. "When does the duke depart?"

Her brother-in-law jerked his chin back. "Sebastian travels to Altamira the day after tomorrow."

Gabby nibbled her lip. That gave her a day to convince the duke to allow her to accompany him. Would he say yes? Faith, she hoped so.

"Querida," Isabel uttered the word like a sigh, "you can't travel with the duke unaccompanied. You need a chaperone."

"First, I don't know that Whitfield will even consent to me traveling with him," Gabby said, ignoring Sirius's soft snort. "And second, I would need to purchase a ticket, if there are any still available."

"I'll have my secretary inquire about tickets." Sirius held up a hand when Isabel made to speak. "I will ask him to do so anonymously."

Isabel nodded, and turned back to Gabby. "So we have a day to find you a chaperone."

"If Whitfield agrees, that is," Gabby said, unease twitching along her limbs.

"He'll agree," Sirius said definitively.

"This is Whitfield we're talking about." Gabby arched a brow. "The Whitfield who's delighted in antagonizing me since we met."

The corner of Sirius's mouth tipped up. "I'm well aware. I've heard many complaints about the youngest Miss Luna."

Isabel chuckled, and even Gabby felt a smidge of amusement.

"But I know my friend, and he'll say yes." Sirius crossed his ankles and propped his elbow on the narrow window ledge. "I have no doubt in my mind."

Gabby glanced at her sister, who smiled at her reassuringly. If Sirius and Isabel believed the duke would come to her aid, then she would cling to their confidence. Because she had very few options at this point but to rely upon the Duke of Whitfield.

15

The house was silent when Sebastian stepped from his room the next morning. In the weeks that he'd stayed with the Dawsons, the house had always been full of laughter and carefree chatter. Which made sense, really; Sirius and Isabel were happy, so their home was happy.

It had been disconcerting at first, as Sebastian was used to silence. Aside from the servants, he'd long been the sole occupant at Whitfield Manor, at least after his mother's death. James and David's arrival had revived the old manor house, but the boys occupied the nursery on the top floor, so Sebastian rarely heard them. He'd only adjusted to the lively atmosphere at Casa Inglesa once Gabriela had departed to stay with her parents. Before that, Sebastian had been on edge, constantly aware of her presence. Her laughter. Her cutting witticisms.

It had been a lonely two weeks with her gone.

Brodie exited the chamber door a moment after him, the Scotsman pulling up short when he spotted Sebastian standing in the dark hall.

"Is something the matter, Yer Grace?" he asked.

Sebastian's brows knit together. "It's abnormally quiet, don't you think?"

"Hmm," Brodie murmured, his weathered face scrunched in thought. "Perhaps it's because Miss Luna returned last night. I reckon the servants are being quiet to allow her to sleep."

Ignoring how his pulse jumped into a sprint, Sebastian aimed for curious when he said, "I wonder why she returned. And at night."

The Scotsman shrugged. "I don't rightly know. What I do know is that I spied her crying with Mrs. Dawson in the sitting room. If you ask me, it's a crime against nature for a woman that pretty to cry."

Sebastian didn't dare voice his agreement. Instead, he set off, calling out over his shoulder, "I better search out Dawson and inquire if I can be of assistance."

Finding Sirius was not hard, for he sat with Isabel on the patio, a pot of champurrado and an arrangement of panes dulces between them on the table. When Sebastian's shoes clicked on the Saltillo tile, they both glanced up, and he knew immediately that something was wrong. Sirius's hair was mussed, as if he had been dragging his hand through it, and Isabel's eyes were red.

Never one to prevaricate, Sebastian asked, "Has something happened?"

Sirius rubbed his temple and then gestured to the chair next to him. "Have a seat."

Soon Sebastian had a steaming cup of coffee and a bigote on a plate before him. He toyed with the pastry, although he'd lost his appetite. "I understand Miss Luna returned last night."

"She did." Isabel slowly stirred her chocolate with a spoon, but made no move to actually drink it. "We had thought she would stay with our parents for the rest of the week, if not longer, so her return is a surprise . . . and yet not."

Sebastian inclined his head but held his silence.

Isabel stared at her champurrado for a few seconds longer before she sighed, her shoulders sinking in defeat. "I do not know how much longer my sister will be here."

Sebastian frowned. "Here at your home?"

"Here in Mexico."

Whipping his gaze to Sirius, Sebastian raised his brows questioningly.

For his part, Sirius stared at his wife for a long moment, before he turned to Sebastian. "Mr. Luna is determined to find a husband for Gabby."

It felt as if he had been kicked in the stomach, and it took Sebastian several seconds to regain his breath. "I suppose that's what you meant by not being surprised."

"Indeed." Isabel's chuckle was devoid of amusement. "My sister knew that if she returned home, our father would eventually want to see her wed. He may have largely ignored her for the majority of her childhood, but my father is keenly aware that Gabby's beauty is an asset to be exploited."

Sadly, Sebastian could understand that. The Mexican society he'd spent weeks socializing with was acutely aware of one another's antecedents. Whoever could claim close ties to Spain was held in high esteem. Gabriela Luna was not only the daughter of an important Juárez government official, she was the granddaughter of a powerful Spanish family, with the light skin and light eyes to complement that association. Sebastian had seen the way gazes followed Gabriela at social events, as if assessing her worth. The sight had set his teeth on edge . . . but now it made him want to put his fist through something.

Sebastian did his best to suppress his mounting anger, mindful there was more to the story than what Isabel and Sirius had yet told him. Taking a sip of coffee, he allowed the hot liquid to ground him.

"It happened much sooner than Gabby or you expected, though." Sirius glanced at his wife, who nodded. "It caught Gabby off guard as she had yet to decide her plans going forward."

And Sebastian had never asked her plans. As a young unmarried lady, he assumed Gabriela would return to her parents' home and resume her life here much as she had in London. Sebastian should have known better. *There are those in Mexico who will delight in stripping her confidence away.* Fox had warned him . . . he just hadn't expected the perpetrators to be Gabriela's own family.

Clearing his throat, Sebastian chose his words carefully. "I can imagine Miss Luna is feeling frustrated to be in this position considering the reasons she returned to Mexico in the first place."

"Indeed, I am."

Glancing over his shoulder, his gaze collided with Gabriela's as she stepped onto the patio. While he rose to his feet, Sebastian noted her pallid complexion but also the hint of fire in her eyes. Fire was good, and its presence encouraged him.

After she exchanged morning greetings with her sister and Sirius, Gabriela slid onto the seat next to him, where she brought her freshly served cup of champurrado to her lips. Sebastian tried not to stare at her, but after not seeing her for almost a fortnight, his gaze was greedy to take her in. Aside from her pale, brittle appearance, Gabriela seemed well.

"How did you sleep, querida?" Isabel asked, reaching out to pat her sister on the back of her hand.

Gabriela shrugged. "Fitfully."

"I'd imagine so," Sirius added. "Your sister and I are happy you've returned, though."

Isabel nodded readily, and Gabriela flashed them a small smile. When she slid her gaze to him for a passing second, he held his breath, hopeful she would address him in some way. Instead, she returned her attention to her sister, and Sebastian listened while they chatted about the weather and their plans for the day.

Once again, Gabriela avoided meeting his gaze, and Sebastian tried not to take offense. If their dance the night of the Ortiz dinner had rattled her even a fraction of the amount it had rattled him, he could understand her discomfort. Pair that discomfort with the stress of her current situation, and Sebastian knew she was out of sorts.

And strangely enough, Sebastian wanted nothing more than to pull Gabriela into his arms and hold her tight. Remind her that she was driven and smart and worthy of love and respect, two things Elías Luna seemed intent on withholding. Sebastian watched her covertly as she fiddled with her napkin, her anxiety bleeding into the innocuous movements of her hands. Was her behavior apparent to the others at the table? He had no doubt Isabel noticed, for she knew her sister better than anyone. But how Sebastian should note such a detail about Gabriela, he did not know.

Or rather he did, but refused to consider the deeper implications. Implications he had told himself over and over he did not have the time or interest in unraveling . . . even while his heart urged him to consider the knot that was Gabriela Luna.

His bloody heart was an idiot.

"Your Grace?"

Sebastian blinked back to the moment and found Gabriela

considering him with a pucker between her brows. Lud, had he been staring at her this entire time?

"I beg your pardon, Miss Luna." He coughed into his fist.

Sirius snorted, but Sebastian ignored him.

Gabriela nodded and dropped her head. Sebastian waited, trying hard not to stare again but unable to look away from her downturned face.

"Your Grace," she repeated, her voice softer than he'd ever heard it. "I was wondering if you would be willing to accompany me for a turn about the garden?"

Oh. Surprise tangled his tongue, and Sebastian pressed his lips together as the warring emotions of confusion and pleasure clashed in his chest. Had she ever asked for a private moment of his time? Of course not, for she'd made it clear he had destroyed any goodwill between them on the night they met.

But she wanted to speak with him now, and he would not tell her no.

Sebastian's gaze moved to the small garden that sat beyond the tiled patio. It was not a large space, but they would be afforded a degree of privacy, even with Sirius and Isabel looking on.

"Of course," he finally responded, rising to his feet and tossing his napkin on the table. Pushing his spectacles up his nose, Sebastian followed her silently along the gravel path that meandered through the agaves and shrubs.

When they reached the end of the walking path at the adobe wall that surrounded the house, Gabriela paused, her back to him and her gaze straight ahead. Sebastian held his silence, mindful not to rush her. The Gabriela Luna he knew would not take kindly to being pressured into sharing anything she was not ready to. Instead, Sebastian paced to a nearby tree and leaned back against its supportive trunk.

"I'm sure you were hoping you would not have to see me before you returned to London," she murmured, still not looking at him.

"Why would you believe that?"

She glanced at him over her shoulder. "Come now, Whitfield, I thought we had become friendly. And friends don't tell lies to each other."

"It seems to me that friends wouldn't accuse the other of lying, either," he shot back, raising his brows.

Gabriela rolled her eyes, but finally pivoted to face him. She crossed her arms over her chest. "Obviously Isabel and Sirius told you why I returned."

Sebastian nodded. "I'm sorry you find yourself in such a predicament, and placed there by the two people you should expect to make you safe."

Her throat bobbed on a swallow. "Yes, well, I'm not exactly surprised. My father has only ever acted in his own self-interest. I just expected more from my mother. I had hoped she would be an ally, but . . ."

But she wasn't. María Elena Luna had proven herself to be her husband's ally first and foremost, and from Gabriela's expression, it had been a bitter revelation.

"You are not without allies, though." Sebastian pushed off from the tree and took a step toward her. "Despite the aspersions you cast on my honesty, I was not lying when I told you I would be willing to assist you should you ever need my help."

Her hazel eyes snared his, a trace of vulnerability in her gaze. After their years of antagonism, Sebastian was not surprised to see it. He guessed she felt she may be taking a risk asking for help, and Sebastian had no way to truly express his sincerity except to show her.

"I'd like to return to England."

The words were ragged and soft, but Sebastian heard them just the same. An odd sort of sadness filled his chest.

"But I thought you wanted to return to Mexico." His forehead crinkled. "You've always made it clear that your time in London had an expiration."

Her chest rapidly rose and fell, and Gabriela's gaze darted about the small garden. "I envisioned my reception very differently. I may have come back too soon."

Sebastian didn't know what to say. He'd seen firsthand the cheap and snide manner in which Elías Luna treated his youngest daughter, and how his cutting remarks had chipped away at Gabriela's confidence. Gone was the poised young woman who had bewitched the ton, and in her place was often a colorless impostor. He was angry for her, so Sebastian could only imagine how frustrated and helpless she felt.

"I depart for Altamira tomorrow. Will you be ready to depart?" he asked. "Or is that too soon?"

"No. I'll be ready," she said firmly.

"Very well." Sebastian pulled his timepiece from his pocket to note the hour. "I believe Brodie has already packed the majority of my belongings, so I will ask him to depart for Altamira ahead of us and purchase a ticket and lodgings for you."

She closed her eyes, her shoulders dropping. "Thank you. I can't tell you—"

"And you don't have to," Sebastian interjected. "I know that the only reason you would subject yourself to my company is because the alternative is much worse."

Her lips quirked. "I don't know how much worse, but definitely a bit."

Sebastian chuckled, pleased to see some color returning to Gabriela's face. He pivoted to return to his coffee, but paused. "You're allowed to change your mind. About returning to

England or staying here in Mexico, or any of the other everyday choices that affect your life. You're in a privileged position to make your own decisions, and you must protect that autonomy from those who would manipulate you for their own gain."

She glanced up at him, her throat bobbing. Finally, Gabriela nodded again.

With that, Sebastian strolled away, determined to find Brodie and see him off to Altamira. It was a long trek, but Sebastian didn't trust anyone else to see to the task. He didn't want word to reach the Lunas that Gabriela was preparing to depart, for Sebastian knew Mr. Luna would not allow her to leave so easily. It was clear that he had decided to use her hand as a bargaining chip among his potential allies, and with Maximilian and the imperialists in danger of losing their hold on the country, many men were intent to align themselves with Juárez and his supporters.

"Did she ask you?" Sirius asked as Sebastian walked by the table where his friend still sat with his wife.

He nodded but did not pause. "I'm making travel arrangements now. Will you help me secure a chaperone?"

Sirius nodded. "Of course."

Just before he disappeared into the house, a voice called out to him. "Thank you, Your Grace."

Sebastian turned to find Isabel Dawson walking toward him, her hands clasped at her chest.

"I know I don't have to tell you that Gabby is very special to me. She's long been a fearless defender of mine, and now I don't know how to defend her in turn."

"Sometimes it's the ones we love who hurt us the most," he said quietly.

Isabel's eyes turned glassy. "Sadly, I think this experience has shown her that perhaps Mexico is not her home after all. I appreciate your willingness to help her, especially considering your contentious history with one another."

Not wanting to think of the rancor that had always percolated between them, Sebastian simply nodded. "Whatever our history, I am a gentleman and will be at Miss Luna's service."

A small, knowing smile curved Isabel's lips. "I'll help Gabby prepare for tomorrow."

With that, she turned back to the table and her waiting husband, and Sebastian was left to determine a way forward when everything had abruptly been thrown upside down.

"Juana said you told her you could pack your gowns on your own. Are you sure you don't want help?"

Gabby glanced up from her trunk to find Isabel standing in the threshold of her room, her mouth a slash of displeasure. Without waiting for a response, her sister wandered to the bed, where Gabby had laid out the various gowns she had brought with her from London.

"You looked stunning in this," her sister said, her fingers tracing the embroidery on her red silk Worth gown. "Is it any wonder why half the men in San Luis Potosí have petitioned Father for your hand?"

"All of this mess because of one red dress," Gabby snorted.

"If it wasn't the red one, it would have been the blue one, or the primrose, or the mauve." Isabel cocked her head as she studied her. "You're charming, clever, and thoughtful . . . but I'm sorry that the only trait Father seems to value is your beauty."

Gabby tucked her chin into her chest, a long sigh slipping from her lips. "I truly believed I would be able to show him that I had more to offer than just my face. Like you and Ana have."

"You do have more to offer, querida. So much more." The rustling of skirts told Gabby her sister had moved closer. "But maybe this wasn't the time to show it. Maybe it wasn't the place."

Jerking her head up, Gabby frowned. "Do you really think so?"

Her sister raised a shoulder. "I don't know. But it seems to me that it's hard to be someone new when a mold has already been fashioned for you. There was no mold for you in London."

Isabel was right. While Tío Arturo and Lady Yardley had been their caretakers, Gabby and her sisters had largely been left to their own devices. That freedom had allowed her to explore ideas and concepts she found interesting, and interact with people from different circumstances than the narrow, sheltered life she had lived in Mexico City. Despite the rainy, dreary weather, Gabby had bloomed in her new independence, and was more confident in who she was and who she wanted to be.

Clearing her throat, she flashed Isabel a smile. "You sound very wise, hermana."

Isabel chuckled. "So the duke has agreed to escort you to London."

She nodded, her throat suddenly dry. Whitfield had agreed without hesitation, and she was thankful. "He has"—she licked her lips—"been surprisingly agreeable on this trip."

"High praise, indeed." Isabel pulled the red Worth gown over her lap, her fingers once again tracing over the embroidery. "Sirius mentioned that despite Whitfield's reputation as a haughty rake, he's also genuinely well liked among the ton."

"Because he's a duke, no doubt," Gabby said, wrinkling her nose.

"That probably plays a part." Isabel toyed with the lace overlay on the gown. "But Whitfield has always struck me as a protector. For all that he can be intimidating, he's come to the aid of more than one wallflower or widow whose dance card had been woefully empty. Me included."

Gabby could not argue with her sister's observation. Whitfield was an intimidating figure, even if she herself had never been intimidated by him. But as Isabel mentioned, Gabby had noticed that the duke danced with a handful of wallflowers at every ball, but she assumed he did so because they were heiresses whose fortunes he could benefit from. But perhaps that had been unfair of her . . .

"Sirius suspects that Whitfield's close relationship with his late mother sparked his inclination to protect women in need," Isabel added.

Her interest snared, Gabby turned to face her sister. "I don't understand."

Once again, Isabel shrugged. "Sirius said that until Whitfield arrived at Eton, he had never left the family estate in Gloucestershire. The late duke abandoned him and his mother there, with only the servants for company. Sirius called old Whitfield cruel and neglectful."

"Oh," Gabby murmured dumbly, remembering past remarks the duke had made about his father. Apparently she was not the only one who had been shaped by a formidable parent.

"So that's why I'm not surprised the duke has come to your aid." Her sister's smile was gentle. "Perhaps you've acquired your own defender, querida."

Gabby scoffed, the sound more harsh than she'd intended. But better for Isabel to think her skeptical than for her sister to realize Gabby's heart kicked into a sprint at the thought Whitfield might actually possess gracious regards for her. "The duke has been kind to me, but remember this is still Whitfield we're talking about. He's still haughty and self-serving."

"Mayhap." Isabel waved a hand. "But he didn't have to help secure you a ticket to London, and he certainly didn't have to defend you at the Ortiz party."

"You heard about that?" Gabby gasped.

Isabel rolled her eyes. "Of course I did. I hear all the gossip working for Señora Maza de Juárez. Many were impressed that he praised you so highly."

His words had been a tonic . . . even while their dance afterward had sent her scurrying from his presence like a frightened hare.

Yet Gabby would concede nothing. "He's a duke. One kind word from him is shared in a tizzy."

"You're probably right about that." Isabel stared at her for a moment, and Gabby tried to pretend the intensity of her sister's gaze didn't perturb her. "Why didn't you tell me what happened that night? Why did I have to find out through gossip?"

Gabby picked at a thread on her waistband, weighing various excuses in her mind. This was not the discussion she wanted to have with Isabel. But . . . another part of her wanted to share the heartbreak their father's callous words caused. How holding her head high while her chin trembled with unshed tears had taken every ounce of strength Gabby possessed. How Whitfield's cutting response had quickly ended the conversation. How she was thankful to him for his sentiments, but also angry at how easily he was able to shame her father when not once had Elías Luna ever felt shame for how he treated her.

She met Isabel's stare, glimpsing the well of love her sister always saved just for her. "Have you ever had your emotions pulled in various directions until you have no notion of how you feel about anything?"

"Oh yes. It's rather"—Isabel's gaze grew unfocused, as if she was remembering something in the past—"alarming."

"*Alarming* is an excellent word for it."

Isabel moved from the bed to sit on the floor next to Gabby, their skirts billowing up around them. "Would you like to tell me how the events of that night made you feel? When you depart on the morrow, I won't be available to lend you my sisterly ear."

"I wish I didn't have to leave tomorrow," Gabby whispered, reaching out to grasp her sister's hand.

"You don't have to leave tomorrow," Isabel said, stroking her thumb over Gabby's knuckles. "But if you don't, you may not become the Gabby Luna you were meant to be."

Tears abruptly clogged Gabby's throat, and it took her several seconds to swallow them. "I would so like to meet that Gabby."

"Igualmente." Isabel raised Gabby's hand to her cheek and held it there. "Now talk to me, hermanita, for soon I will be homesick for your voice."

Ignoring the watery quality to her laugh, Gabby rested her head on Isabel's shoulder. Thankful she could steal this time with her older sister, Gabby recounted what occurred at the Ortiz dinner party and how it made her feel. And, with a gulp for bravery, she divulged all the contradictory emotions the duke provoked within *her*.

16

Later that evening, long after Sebastian had seen Brodie off on his expedited trip to Altamira, he sat ensconced with Sirius in his study. They discussed the progress of the mine at length before the conversation turned to his own impending departure.

"It's been almost eight weeks but feels as if you just arrived, and now you're already returning to London." Sirius took a sip of whisky and peered at Sebastian over his glass. "I'm glad you came."

Swallowing a healthy mouthful of whisky, he swiped the back of his hand over his mouth and said, "It's done me good to see you happy here. Considering the condition you were in when you departed London, I've wondered if you made the right choice."

Sirius snorted, although his gaze was a hundred miles away. "I was not in a good place when Isabel returned to Mexico, and I didn't think I would see her again. But I have loyal friends who thankfully knocked some sense into me."

"Someone needed to," Sebastian grumbled.

Sirius had been in a terrible state after Isabel had left London, and Sebastian had been concerned he would fall back into the depressive hole he'd lived in when he returned from the Crimean War a decade prior. Thankfully Fox had helped Sebastian convince Sirius that if he wanted to make a life with Isabel, he could do so in Mexico.

And what a life his friend had created. Sebastian took a moment to let his gaze drift about Sirius's comfortable office, with its shelves filled with books of every size and language, to the window where the scenic and quaint town of San Luis Potosí existed. Sirius appeared more lighthearted, more unfettered, more content living under the Mexican sun with his bride than he had ever been in London.

Sebastian was happy for him even if, once again, a longing throbbed against his ribs.

Rather than rub at the ache, he was reminded that much awaited him in England. Now that Sebastian had toured the mine operations himself, his confidence in the venture had grown, and he finally allowed his thoughts to consider how he could use his returns to benefit the dukedom. The manor was in dire need of renovations, and he planned to schedule them as soon as he set foot on British soil. Sebastian was determined for it to be the comfortable, happy, and loving home that James and David had been denied thus far in their lives.

His chest swelled with resolve. After being indolent for so long, Sebastian welcomed the responsibilities he'd been given, and would see to them to the best of his ability . . . even if a certain Mexican siren would now be underfoot to distract him.

"So will you and Gabby successfully arrive in London without one of you trying to murder the other?" Sirius asked abruptly.

Blinking at the change of topic, Sebastian frowned. "I think

Miss Luna and I have come to share a cordial regard. Surely you've noticed the difference."

Sirius smirked. "Oh, I've noticed."

His words felt like a trap, and Sebastian had no desire to fall prey to his friend's innuendos.

"I am sure Miss Luna will daydream daily about pushing me head over feet into the Atlantic, but she is too well bred to actually attempt such a ruthless act." Sebastian pointed a finger at Sirius. "Duke-icide is frowned upon, no matter how deserving the duke in question may be."

"Duke-icide?" Sirius groaned. "Why am I not surprised you would coin such a term?"

"Because you know that I am clever and quick-witted." Sebastian sighed. "Yet easily preyed upon by those who would wish me harm."

Sirius barked a laugh. "If you don't stop talking about yourself in such flowery terms, I may be charged with duke-icide myself."

"It would be a memorable way to end this trip."

"I'm glad you came, Sebastian." Sirius raised his glass in a toast. "And I am in your debt for how you've helped Gabby."

Sebastian tugged on his cravat, which suddenly felt tight. "You owe me nothing. And neither does Miss Luna. I'm in a position to help her, so I will."

And he would, even if she did try to push him overboard.

Saying goodbye to Isabel, *again*, was just as gut-wrenching as it had been the first time.

Gabby sat tucked in the corner of the carriage Whitfield had rented for the trip to Altamira, her eyes glued on the passing landscape. They had departed from San Luis Potosí an hour earlier, and her emotions were still a raging storm. The idea she would once again be separated from her older sister left her heartbroken, but knowing she had fled from her mother without so much as a goodbye devastated her, and it was all Gabby could do to keep from weeping.

Yet the knowledge that the duke sat across the cab from her, a week-old newspaper from Mexico City spread open in his lap, forced Gabby to swallow her tears. No doubt Whitfield already considered her melodramatic, and she certainly didn't need to reinforce his opinion by releasing the sobs that burned the back of her throat and singed her eyes.

"How long will we travel today, Your Grace?" Señora Lopez asked from next to her. The older woman worked for Isabel and Sirius as a maid, and had agreed to accompany Gabby to Altamira as a chaperone. Word had arrived the week prior that the older woman's newest granddaughter had arrived, and as Señora Lopez longed to meet the new baby, she was only too happy to make the long trip to the coast.

Who would be Gabby's companion on the voyage back to England had yet to be decided.

"Only five or so hours, depending on the horses," Whitfield replied, glancing at the older woman over his paper. He didn't smile, but his expression was genial.

Gabby wanted to ask him about their lodgings for the night, but couldn't bring herself to shape the words for she was certain she would cry if she tried to speak.

"My man, Brodie, left before us, and will be securing rooms for us to stay in along the way." The duke glanced at her. "Many of the inns and hostels will be ones we stayed in on our way to San Luis Potosí."

Swallowing, Gabby nodded. Whitfield's thoughtfulness no

longer surprised her, and when she was fully in control of her emotions again, she would thank him.

The carriage bumped and dipped along the road, and Gabby was eventually lulled into a fitful sleep. Her dreams were haunted by visions of her father, his stinging criticism ringing in her ears. She kept reliving the night of the Ortiz party, forced to hear her father's cruel words over and over. No matter what she tried to say in reply, every defense she mounted, was trapped behind her stuttering tongue. Worse still, Whitfield was not there to defend her when she could not. Instead, her father had gripped her upper arm and jerked her toward the nameless, faceless man he demanded she marry, and Gabby cried out in panic.

"Miss Luna. Miss Luna."

Struggling, Gabby shook her head back and forth.

"Gabriela, you're dreaming."

Gabby's eyes flew wide, and she gasped as she blinked against the light. She gave a start when she noticed Whitfield kneeling before her, his hand on her arm.

"I'm sorry to scare you," he murmured, his hand tightening for a moment. "We've stopped to switch teams, and I thought you might welcome the chance to stretch your legs."

"Oh," she responded, the edges of her vision still clouded by dreams. Turning, she found the space on the squab next to her empty.

"Señora Lopez has already disembarked," he said, as if reading her mind. "She said this inn makes delicious pozole, and wanted to eat before we departed again."

Gabby licked her lips but said nothing.

Whitfield's eyebrows stitched together. "Were you hungry? I noticed you didn't eat breakfast this morning."

She hadn't. Gabby possessed no appetite, certain whatever she tried to eat would taste like wood chips.

Mindful the duke was waiting for her response, she cleared her throat, noting that it was raw from her unshed tears. "No, gracias. But I think a walk will do me some good."

Whitfield climbed from the conveyance and extended his hand to help her down. Gabby exhaled a long breath and reached for it. When both of her feet were planted on the ground, however, Whitfield did not release her. She glanced up at him and raised her brows.

"The driver informed me of an arroyo that runs adjacent to the horse yard here." The duke's voice carried his signature bored tone, but his pale blue eyes traveled over her face with a familiarity that hinted he understood how tenuously she was holding herself together. "I thought it might be an idyllic place for a quiet, private walk."

"That," she said on an exhale, "sounds lovely."

Whitfield nodded but didn't release her . . . nor did Gabby pull her hand from his. Standing this close to him, with his woodsy scent seeping into her lungs, she felt her turbulent emotions ease. Just a smidge, of course. But try as she might, it was impossible for her to deny that the duke was being sincere. The Gabby of old would have assumed he was mocking her, but over the past eight weeks she'd learned, quite against her will, that the Duke of Whitfield was truly a thoughtful man.

It was hard to remember Whitfield was a scoundrel when he gazed at her as if his next breath depended upon whatever words her lips formed.

"Your Grace?" a voice said behind her.

Gabby sucked in a gasp as she stumbled back a step. Whitfield steadied her and then promptly released her hand. They both turned to see the driver standing several feet away, his hat in his hands.

"There are several teams available. Would you like to select which one you'd prefer?"

"I'd be happy to review the selections, but I trust your judgment." Pivoting back to her, the duke dipped his head. "If you'll excuse me."

She stared after him, her stomach flipping when she noted how he flexed his hand, as if her touch were imprinted on his palm.

Whirling about, Gabby smoothed wrinkles out of her skirts before she adjusted the fit of her hat. It had become askew while she slept, and Whitfield was probably staring at her so intently because she looked like an idiot. Setting off in the direction he'd indicated, Gabby tried and failed to convince herself of that notion.

The terrain had become more verdant the closer they moved to the coast, and the arroyo was lined with anacua and texana trees, their boughs providing relief from the afternoon heat. Gabby noted that the tavern's proprietors had placed benches along the arroyo for guests and travelers to enjoy, and if she hadn't been sitting for so long in the carriage, she would have happily found a spot under one of the shade trees. Instead, she paced along the arroyo bank, her thoughts once again drifting to what she had left behind in San Luis Potosí.

Gabby knew now that she had returned too soon. She may have matured in the years she was away, but with no outstanding accomplishments to her name, her father would always view her as a daughter to marry off for his own gain. Isabel returned to Mexico after quite literally saving Presidente Juárez's life and with a position working with the First Lady awaiting her. Her sister possessed power that Gabby lacked, and she should have known better than to assume her reception would be anything like Isabel's.

She'd been so eager to leave London. Excited to be present for the fall of the empire and Presidente Juárez's triumphant return to Mexico City. So desperate to flee the impending scandal of Lord Carlisle's actions. Word had already begun to spread that something untoward had occurred between them, and Gabby had no doubt about whose version of events the ton would choose to believe, for it was her word versus an earl's. Ana María's letters had assured her that the gossip had ceased, but Gabby was still nervous it would rekindle upon her return. But what choice did she have? Whether in Mexico or in London, it seemed Gabby had no safe place to land.

Slipping under the flowering boughs of an anacua tree, Gabby pressed her back to its rough bark and covered her face with her hands. With only the calls of doves and the chittering of squirrels as they rustled through the foliage to serve as witnesses, Gabby let down her emotional guards and finally shed a few tears.

17

Sebastian experienced one of the most uncomfortable moments of his life when Gabriela Luna returned to their hired carriage with her eyes red-rimmed and swollen from weeping. He hadn't known whether he should comfort her, ignore her, or sweep her into his arms and implore her not to cry. It was very disconcerting, and Sebastian despised being disconcerted.

They traveled in relative silence for the rest of the day, with Señora Lopez making occasional observations about the terrain or commenting on the history of the small towns they rumbled through. Gabriela remained withdrawn, her gaze empty as she stared out the carriage window. Sebastian found himself brainstorming questions he could ask her or things he could say to elicit a response from her, but in the end, he held his tongue. She was grieving the loss of the future she had envisioned for herself here in Mexico, and thrown by the abrupt departure from her sister. She couldn't be pleased to have to share a cramped compartment with *him* when her world was crashing down about her ears.

So Sebastian did his best to give her privacy, or as much as he could in their circumstances. He opted to ride next to the carriage some days, welcoming the breeze and admiring the changing flora as they moved farther east, and smiling as he imagined how David would be whooping and hollering as he explored the countryside. In the evenings when they arrived at the inns Brodie had reserved for them on his way to Altamira, Sebastian escorted the women to their rooms, but did not join them for meals. It was an act of self-preservation. He had no notion of whether Gabriela's opinion of him had changed over the weeks they'd been forced together, and for reasons Sebastian was still wrestling with, he was too anxious to find out. Therefore, instead of offering to be a sympathetic ear to share her heartache, Sebastian kept his distance.

But Sebastian learned that distance would be impossible to come by when they finally arrived in Altamira several days later.

Brodie met them at the docks after they delivered Señora Lopez to her daughter's house, clutching his hat, his mien pale. Sebastian was instantly alert. Ushering Brodie several feet away, Sebastian listened as his valet spoke, watching as a ship porter unloaded the trunks.

"What do you mean there are no cabins available?" Sebastian bit out when Brodie was done.

The Scotsman shrugged. "Exactly that, Yer Grace. I was able to secure a boarding ticket for Miss Luna, but there were no available first-class cabins for her, let alone her and a companion. I haven't bothered to inquire after one because where would the poor lass sleep?"

"What of second-class cabins?" Sebastian ripped his hat from his head and dragged his hand through his hair. "She can have my first-class cabin and I'll stay in second class."

"None there, either, Yer Grace." Brodie scratched behind his ear. "Apparently the ship is full with passengers wanting to return to Europe now that the collapse of the French empire seems nigh."

Bloody hell. "And you made sure to throw my title around? What good is it to be a duke if you can't make impossible things possible?"

"Of course. I know how to leverage yer lofty title to get my job done." The Scotsman threw up a hand. "But there's nothing available, Yer Grace."

"Fuck," he bit out. Sliding his gaze to where Gabriela waited silently by the carriage, he clicked his tongue on his teeth. "What the hell are we supposed to do now?"

"It seems to me, Yer Grace," Brodie began, in that singsongy tone that immediately put Sebastian on guard, "that Miss Luna will have to share your cabin with you."

Sebastian slowly looked down at him. "Now is not the time to jest."

Brodie's face darkened. "I'm not jesting, Yer Grace. There are truly no cabins available. Now if you would like me to offer Miss Luna to share my cabin, I will certainly do so. Sadly, I'm sleeping on a bunk and the other bed is occupied, but I'm certain we can figure out some sort of arrangement. Miss Luna is a delightful young woman, after all, and the other gentleman will no doubt be pleased to wake up to her pretty face."

"You'll do no such thing." Just the thought of Gabriela sharing such an intimate space with other men, even out of necessity, made anger flare in his chest. It was a preposterous suggestion, and Brodie knew it.

"Well, then, what do you plan to do, sir? I suppose we can try to dredge up an empty bunk or cot in steerage."

Curling his lip, Sebastian ignored how the Scotsman crossed his arms over his chest and stared at him with arched brows, instead locking his gaze on Gabriela. What was there to do?

He supposed he could offer a sum to another first-class passenger in exchange for their cabin, but Sebastian doubted anyone would accept.

So that left Brodie's idea. An idea that made Sebastian just a bit breathless.

Without saying a word to the valet, Sebastian spun on his heel and prowled toward Gabriela.

She watched him as he approached, her brow slowly lifting with every step he took.

"Did something happen?" Her gaze moved over his face. "You don't appear particularly pleased."

Sebastian tapped his cane on the wooden planks beneath their feet. "There's a problem. With our lodgings on the ship."

She tilted her head to the side, waiting for him to continue.

"Brodie was able to book you passage, but there are no first-class cabins available." Sebastian cleared his throat. "Nor second-class cabins."

The color in her cheeks fled, and her mouth opened and closed several times before her teeth snapped together.

Pausing to gather his thoughts, Sebastian glanced about them. A steady stream of passengers made their way up the wide gangplank, some dressed in expensively cut clothes and servants ladened with boxes trailing behind them. Others possessed only a simple coarse knapsack slung over their shoulder, hope in their gazes. Dozens of carts, wagons, and carriages were lined three deep along the docks, the calls and cries of drivers, passengers, and sailors melding into a roaring clamor. Still, Sebastian heard Gabriela when she spoke.

"Do you know when the next ship will be departing?"

Swinging his gaze back to her, Sebastian's chest squeezed to see the forlorn expression on her face.

"Miss Luna, I'm not going to leave you here by yourself," he said softly.

Her eyes darted to his and away again to scan the bustling crowds. "Do—do you think there's availability in steerage?"

Sebastian shook his head. "Brodie suspects that every cabin and room is booked."

"Oh," she murmured, her throat bobbing before she dropped her gaze to the ground.

Licking his lips, he moved a step toward her. "I have an option for you to consider, and I completely understand if you reject it outright."

Gabriela jerked her head up. "What is it?"

Widening his stance, Sebastian stomped his cane for a moment and then blurted out, "You can stay in my rooms."

Her response was not what he expected. Sebastian was certain Gabby would issue an immediate refusal. A *sharp* refusal. He would not have been surprised if she accompanied her denial with a slap to his face. But Gabriela did neither of those things. Instead, her mouth dropped open and she took a minuscule step closer to him.

"You would let me stay in your cabin?"

Christ, after he spent over a week avoiding her company, the idea that Gabriela Luna would be quite literally sleeping in the same room with him made desire flash like lightning in his blood.

Which would absolutely not do. She needed his help, not for him to be battling his attraction to her. Especially when she had made it clear, over and over, that she despised him.

Sucking in a breath around his teeth, Sebastian nodded. "There is a large sitting room off the bedroom chamber, and I can sleep on the settee there."

"Or I can. Surely a man of your"—Gabriela paused, her gaze traveling down his frame—"stature would find it quite uncomfortable. Especially for a ten-day voyage."

It would be hell, but he was too much of a gentleman to argue otherwise. "I'll be fine."

Her teeth sank into her bottom lip. "You would really allow me to share your cabin?"

Sebastian smirked. "It's certainly not my first choice. Heaven knows you'll probably be plotting my demise by the time we reach London."

"Oh, it wouldn't take me nearly that long," Gabriela shot back, her lips tipping up ever so slightly.

"There's that fire," he murmured, brushing a curl off her cheek with the back of his hand. Sebastian didn't even realize he'd done it until she inhaled sharply.

But she didn't pull away. Instead, Gabriela leaned ever so slightly into his touch, and Sebastian was certain he could drown in the greenness of her hazel eyes.

"Shall I have the porters bring all the trunks on board, Yer Grace?"

Sebastian clenched his jaw for a moment, willing away his annoyance with his valet. "Yes, Brodie. Please ensure all the trunks are delivered to my cabin," he said.

The Scotsman looked between him and Gabriela for a moment and then nodded. "Very good, Yer Grace. If I can be of any service, Miss Luna, please let me know."

Gabriela inclined her head. "I am in your debt."

"Nonsense, miss." Brodie tugged on the brim of his hat before his mouth split into a toothy grin. "If anyone owes me, it's His Grace."

"As if you aren't rewarded handsomely for your services,"

Sebastian growled, moving away from Gabby and her alluring violet and amber scent. "And you *can* be of service to me."

"What else do you need me to do, Yer Grace?" the Scotsman asked, the smallest hint of teasing in his voice.

But Sebastian didn't have time for teasing, not when their moves over the next ten days could see them safely to London or bring scandal down upon their heads.

Dropping his voice, he gestured to the ship behind them with his head. "Miss Luna needs to be escorted to the cabin without being seen."

Brodie's expression immediately turned serious. "Of course. I can take her through the servant passages."

"Excellent." Sebastian allowed himself a free moment to consider Gabriela. "Do you have a dark cloak or pelisse?"

Her brow furrowed for a second before understanding lit her face. "I do. In my carpetbag in the carriage."

"Make sure to put it on. We want you to blend in as much as possible, and even your travel ensemble speaks of quality."

She pivoted back to the hired carriage.

To Brodie, Sebastian asked, "Is there anyone on the passenger list I should be concerned about?"

The Scotsman shook his head. "I reviewed it, and didn't see any familiar names." He rubbed the side of his nose. "Not that I know every toff in London, of course."

"Of course," Sebastian murmured, watching Gabriela as she flung her dark brown cloak over her shoulders and brought the hood up to cover her head. "It's imperative that we do what we can to protect Miss Luna's identity. Her reputation could depend upon it."

"And what about your reputation?"

Sebastian flicked his fingers. "A man of my stature will

recover from any social impropriety. Surely you've heard tales of my father."

Brodie went still. "Here and there, Yer Grace. But I never presumed they were true."

"Presume away." Sebastian snorted. "He was guilty of every wicked, vile deed people have ever whispered about. And yet he was still welcomed into every drawing room in the United Kingdom. A disgrace—"

"Will this do?"

His gaze swung to Gabriela, who stood just behind him. Her gaze sparkled from within the depths of the hood.

Coughing into his fist, Sebastian nodded. "Brodie will escort you to my cabin. Please stay there until I arrive. It's imperative you keep a low profile."

"I understand." She blew out a breath. "Thank you for your help, Mr. Brodie."

The Scotsman's expression softened. "It's an honor to assist you, miss."

Sebastian rolled his eyes, yet was also thankful for his valet because he knew Gabby was in safe hands. He stared after them as they disappeared into the crowd, the lump in his throat no longer threatening to choke him.

Squaring his shoulders, Sebastian grasped his cane and meandered up the gangplank. He stopped to exchange pleasantries with other passengers on the deck and in the first-class lounge, taking the opportunity to sniff out who was also traveling to London, and who might prove dangerous.

Yet Brodie's estimations proved accurate, because Sebastian did not recognize anyone. Most of the passengers had connections to the imperial government and were eager to return to Europe. Sebastian sought out an introduction to Captain

Brown, a crisply polite gentleman whom he instantly liked. Yes, Sebastian thought, he and Gabriela may just make it back to London without being discovered.

The sun was a deep ocher descending into a pool of midnight blue when he finally spied Gabriela on the deck at the back of the ship. She was staring at the ship's rippling wake in the dark water. He came to a stop beside her, his hand wrapping around the rail right next to hers. Long strands of her mahogany hair had been pulled from her coiffure by the sea breeze, and danced about her face. Her gaze remained locked on the distant horizon where Mexico lay.

"I know I was supposed to stay in the cabin, but I needed some fresh air." Her voice was almost a whisper, but he heard her just the same. "I figured since most passengers would be at dinner, I might go unnoticed."

"Are you hungry?" Sebastian could have kicked himself for not considering how famished she may be. It had been two hours since the ship left port in Altamira. "I apologize for not thinking of it."

Gabriela held up a hand. "I'm fine, Your Grace. Brodie brought me a tray. There's one in the cabin for you, as well."

God bless his valet. He dropped his head to his chest.

"How are you feeling?" she asked, glancing up at him. When Sebastian frowned, Gabriela continued, "Are you feeling seasick again?"

Oh. Sebastian's face grew hot. "I'm slightly nauseated, but it's manageable. I followed Señora Lopez's suggestion to sip on hot water with a generous amount of lemon juice, and it has helped. She would be pleased."

"She'd be *delighted* to know a duke listened to her," Gabriela said, her lips twitching over a smile.

They stood quietly watching the waves for several moments, and the tension Sebastian had not realized he held began to ease from his limbs.

"I didn't expect to be standing on a ship deck with *you*, saying goodbye to Mexico. Again."

Sebastian propped his hip against the rail. "*I* didn't think we'd ever be able to have a cordial conversation."

Her gaze darted to his. "And I didn't think I would ever be able to look upon you without disdain, but I was mistaken."

A fiery warmth sizzled through him . . . but was quickly extinguished when Gabriela's face crumpled and she choked on a sob.

"I was mistaken about so many things," she cried brokenly, covering her face with her hands.

Unsure of what to do but knowing he needed to touch her, Sebastian wrapped his arm about her shoulders, sighing in relief when Gabriela turned to cry into the folds of his coat.

Impotent anger and heartache clawed at her chest and throat, and after containing them for the better part of a week, Gabby was desperate, so very desperate, to set them free. That Whitfield was the one to hold her while she did it should have struck her as ironic, but instead all she felt was gratitude. Over and over he had taken care of her, his solicitousness never cloying or overbearing. The duke had been a calm, if occasionally wry, presence over the last two months, and his strong arm around her now, holding her close, made her feel safe and comforted.

When her sobs had turned to hiccups, Gabby pulled back to wipe at her cheeks. "I actually thought I could be a new Gabriela here. A confident, intelligent, savvy woman my father would finally see. He'd finally feel compelled to listen to my ideas, understand how they've been shaped by the things I experienced in London . . ."

The fight fled her on one long exhale. All it had taken was one disdainful look from Elías Luna, one arch of his brow, one sneer of his lips, for Gabby to feel as if she'd been left in a large ballroom alone with all the candles extinguished. If that weren't devastating enough, Whitfield bore witness to her father's indifference. The duke was a spectator to her great shame, and while she felt she knew Whitfield better now and didn't think he would make snide comments at her expense, she would not blame him if he did. Gabby had not been nearly as kind to him as he had been to her.

It was another source of shame.

"Do you believe you're only deserving of your father's approval if you do something grand or noteworthy?" he asked, tucking a wayward lock of hair behind her ear. The simple gesture chipped away at the armor she had wrapped around her heart.

Abruptly, Gabby remembered he'd asked a question. That sardonic lilt that accented the majority of Whitfield's words was absent, and Gabby risked a glance up at his face. He was staring down at her, his spectacles slightly askew because of the crinkle in his nose.

Gabby pondered her response. "Look how he treats Isa. He used to ignore her, wanted to send her to a convent, but my clever sister had grander plans for herself. She saved the Juárez cabinet from capture, and now works for the rightful First Lady." Gabby looked down at her feet, toeing her boot into a groove in the wood decking. "She's married to Sirius, who is obviously besotted with her . . . as he should be, of course. And don't even get me started on Ana María."

The duke rubbed a circle into her back. Dios mío, he was

marvelous at this. "Your sisters are lovely, accomplished women who have found happiness doing something they're passionate about, with someone they love by their side." He paused, and when he continued, Whitfield's voice was softer. "Do you feel that if you don't have what they have—success, recognition, *love*—that you're a failure?"

Yes. Her mind screamed the answer, but Gabby kept her mouth closed. It seemed like a horrible thing to admit. Her sisters were not just deserving of admiration and praise because they had accomplished great things for Mexico, but because Ana and Isabel were exceptional women. Gabby, in comparison, had only ever deserved empty compliments to match the empty head so many people believed she possessed.

She couldn't stop the helplessness, the despair that wrapped its insidious hands around her throat and squeezed it tight.

"Aren't I?" She bit her lip to keep it from trembling and weighed what she wanted to reveal to Whitfield. Seeing as how she was already wrapped up in his arms, the linen of his waistcoat under her cheek, and his woodsy scent filling her nose, Gabby wagered she was in for a penny. "A young woman of my position is expected to marry. Is expected to have children and care for her home. And here I am, with neither a husband nor children. Two times in as many months, I have fled a *continent* to escape being forced into marriage to a man I did not love."

Gabby buried her face in Whitfield's chest and whispered, "I wanted to be more than a pretty face. I wanted to matter because of the thoughts in my head and not my surname and the connections I offer. I want to be more than the children I could give my husband. Yet how can I be more if I don't belong *anywhere*? Not here in Mexico, and not in England. I just . . ."

And she was weeping again. Her cries were not as noisy this time, but her shoulders still shook and Whitfield's coat grew damp with her tears. Frustration and despair coalesced into a ball of anger in her throat.

That was until a gentle hand curled around her chin and tilted her face up. Sniffling, Gabby took a shuddering breath and met the duke's gaze.

"Please don't cry, Ella darling." His thumb brushed a tear from the crest of her cheek. "I would rather you insult me all day than to see you shed another tear."

"What did you call me?" she asked on a ragged breath.

The duke's cheeks turned scarlet, but he didn't drop her gaze. "It just came to me. I apologize for saying it aloud."

A very different kind of emotion weaved its way around her chest and hugged it tight. The Duke of Whitfield had given her a nickname? A lovely name no one had ever called her before. A name born not of teasing or even contempt . . . but perhaps of the very same emotion that made it difficult for her to draw breath.

Exhaling shakily, Gabby summoned her bravery and slid her fingers over the ones that still cupped her chin. "It seems appropriate that you would coin your own name for me."

The corner of his mouth tipped up. "My hubris knows no bounds."

Gabby shuddered a breath. "And I've always done my best to rein in your pride, so I would've expected a humbling nickname in turn."

His fingers slid down her back to cup her waist, and she felt the scorching heat of his touch through her various layers of clothes. "Not once have I ever wanted to humble you. I've relished your cutting wit. Your piques of temper. The lightning that flashes in your mercurial eyes when you fix them upon me."

Her skin tingled, from the crown of her head to the tips of her toes, and Gabby clutched his hand within her own.

"I've watched you contort yourself into shapes, cram yourself into molds that could never possibly contain everything that you are. All for the approval of a man who has no interest in understanding you. Could never possibly comprehend your brilliance." Whitfield's blue gaze was anything but icy as he stared down at her. "And it's been maddening to observe, because you should never have to dampen the fire that blazes so brightly inside you. Those who claim to love you should want you to glow."

"They should, shouldn't they?" she sniffled, smiling weakly when he laughed.

"Absolutely," the duke said, his fingers flexing around her waist. "Despite your inclination to distrust me, rest assured I'm not wrong."

Gazing up at him, Gabby marveled that she was in *this* moment with a man she had once despised. Whom she thought despised her in return. But she'd been wrong; what else had she been wrong about?

Her gaze dropped to his mouth, and suddenly Gabby wanted to put all of her previous notions to the test.

Straightening her spine, she held his stare. "I would very much like it if you kissed me."

Gabby gleaned an immense amount of satisfaction from the way Whitfield whipped his head back.

"Christ," he growled, hitching her higher against his chest, "I've been desperate to taste you for too damn long."

And without a second thought, without a moment for Gabby to draw in breath, the duke's lips came down upon hers.

It was not Gabby's first kiss. She'd flirted and teased any

number of young men, and granted a kiss a time or two. They'd been rather messy, awkward affairs, but she'd liked them well enough.

That was before she kissed the Duke of Whitfield. Or rather, that was before the Duke of Whitfield showed her how divinely toe-curling a kiss could be.

He wasn't rough or impatient. He didn't paw at her. In fact, he was almost gentlemanly . . . if one overlooked how closely he held her. As if Whitfield was afraid someone would steal her away. As if she would allow such a thing. As if she wanted to be anywhere else, with anyone else, but *him*. Certainly not with his lips moving over hers, his tongue teasing along the seam of her mouth until she opened to him and he dipped inside for a taste. Without even knowing what she was about, Gabby dragged her hands over his shoulders and sifted her fingers through his hair, absurdly pleased she was not wearing gloves so she could enjoy the silky texture.

The Duke of Whitfield knew how to kiss . . . but more importantly, he knew how to kiss *her*.

Eventually Whitfield broke away, but not before bussing a kiss to her cheek and temple.

"Dinner will end soon, and I don't want us to be caught."

Right. Of course. Gabby stepped back, brushing loose curls from her cheeks with trembling hands.

"Shall we retire to the cabin?"

Whitfield uttered the words casually, but Gabby saw only caution in his gaze. She suspected he was concerned he had overstepped, but truly, there were only so many places she could go on the ship.

With that in mind, Gabby reached to grasp his hand. "That would be the prudent thing to do."

The duke chuckled, pausing to smooth his thumb over her smile. "Thank you for trusting me with . . . this," he ended, gesturing to the air around them.

"Thank you for giving me reasons to trust you," she replied, relieved to know it was true.

18

He'd kissed Gabriela Luna, and he could not wait to do so again.

Kiss her and so much more.

No, Sebastian growled to himself as he splashed his face with water and stared at his reflection in the bathing room mirror. Gabriela trusted him; not just to deliver her safely to London, but with her fragility and her fears. She certainly trusted him not to molest her.

Sebastian glanced down at the bulge in his trousers. The one he had been sporting since Gabriela had eagerly returned his kisses on the deck. He needed to get himself under control. Sebastian Brooks, the eleventh Duke of Whitfield, would be damned if he ever gave Gabriela a reason to look upon him with disappointment again.

Gripping the sides of the basin, Sebastian willed his cock to relax. It had been entirely too long since he'd been with a woman, and Sebastian had always had a healthy sexual appetite. Yet the stresses of finding James and David, as well as the construction process of the Camino Rojo mine and what its success meant for the dukedom's coffers, had curbed his inclinations. He'd fielded plenty of come-hither stares and overt flirtations while in Mexico, but Sebastian had not been tempted. After tasting her lips and holding her in his arms, Sebastian knew it was because no other woman captivated him quite like Gabriela did.

Once he was certain she had fallen asleep, he would take himself in hand and relieve the pressure that had damn near unmanned him when she'd asked for his kiss.

Just thinking about how enthusiastically she'd responded to him made Sebastian hard again. He bit back a snarl.

Sighing, he turned to consider the nightshirt Brodie had laid out for him. Sebastian never slept in a nightshirt, for he hated how the material tangled about his legs, instead preferring to sleep in his underpants and nothing else. But the nightshirt was Brodie's warning against impropriety, and Sebastian heeded it.

After slipping into the underclothes and a banyan, he knocked on the door leading into the bedchamber.

A faint "Come in" drifted through the wood.

Inhaling, Sebastian pushed the door open and stepped into the room.

Gabriela sat in the center of the bed, her lustrous locks loose about her shoulders. In a modest night rail and robe, she looked girlish . . . and so beautiful Sebastian's chest hurt.

They stared at each other for several heartbeats, and Sebastian suspected she was trying to think of what to say. He certainly was. So much about their relationship was new, and he wanted to proceed with care. Gabriela deserved all the care and gentleness he was capable of.

"Are you sure this sleeping arrangement works for you?" she asked into the silence, biting her lip.

Sebastian was nodding before she had finished speaking. "Of course. Brodie prepared a sleeping cot for me on the sofa."

He was not looking forward to ten nights spent on the velvet sofa, but seeing Gabriela comfortable would relax his mind even if it did little to relax his muscles.

She drew her knees into her chest and wrapped her arms about them. From his vantage point, Sebastian could see her toes peeking out from the linen of her nightdress. It was adorable.

Shit, he was in a bad way.

Yanking on his banyan sash, Sebastian cleared his throat. "Well, good night, then. I hope you sleep well."

"Que duermas bien," Gabriela murmured, her cheeks pink.

Sebastian studied her a moment longer, simply taking in her demure state. She appeared innocent in a way he'd never seen her. The Gabriela Luna he'd always known had been fearsome, cutting presumptuous men and haughty women down with a few words. But the last few weeks had shown Sebastian that her poised veneer hid a depth of vulnerabilities. The need to protect her, not just from those who would exploit her and her good name for their benefit, but also from himself, grew every day Sebastian was with her. And now she would sleep just feet from him.

"Dulces sueños," he finally said, before he slipped out of the room.

The sofa was just as uncomfortable as Sebastian imagined. It took him several minutes to organize his long limbs on the narrow piece of furniture in a manner that didn't send him sprawling onto the parquet floor, and then additional time to relax enough to sleep. But Sebastian's sleep was fitful, filled with nonsensical scenes from both Mexico and London, a meld of faces and a mess of dialogue he could not decipher. At one point, Sebastian was at Whitfield Manor, lined up on the old limestone steps, fidgeting in his best knickerbockers and collarless jacket as he waited for his father to make his bi-annual appearance. When the old duke had stepped from his carriage, Sebastian had turned to run away but slipped and tumbled down the stairs. The wind had been knocked from his lungs, and he'd stared up at the cloudless sky . . . until his father's glowering face eclipsed the sun.

Suddenly, Sebastian could see nothing at all, although a throbbing pain radiated from his elbow.

"Dios mío, Your Grace, are you all right?"

Sebastian blinked his eyes open and winced when he inadvertently put pressure on his elbow. Was he on the floor? A dim beam of light cut across his face, and he turned to it, spying a blurry Gabriela as she hurried to him from the other room.

"Let me help you," she cried, dropping to her knees beside him. Grasping his arm, she urged him to sit up.

"How bloody embarrassing," he groaned, perching on the edge of the sofa. Sebastian slowly extended his other arm, gritting his teeth when his elbow pinged with a dull bite of pain. "I haven't fallen out of bed since I was a child."

"Is it really fair to call this a bed?" Gabriela arched a brow, first at the sofa and then at him. "I'm surprised you were able to fit on it at all."

"It was a close thing"—he shrugged—"but not impossible."

Her answering snort made him chuckle.

Rising to her feet, Gabriela jerked her chin to the bedchamber behind her. "Well, come along."

His forehead crinkled. "Come where?"

"To bed, tonto," she said, splaying her arm.

"But"—Sebastian slowly shook his head—"I can't share the bed with you."

"Why not? The bed is large enough for both of us, and this thing"—she scowled at the sofa—"is barely large enough for one of your legs."

Turning to the offending piece of furniture, Sebastian realized she was right. How he managed to contort himself to fit on it in the first place was beyond him. Still, how could he possibly sleep in the same bed with her without . . .

"Ella, this isn't a good idea," he eventually managed, refusing to meet her eyes.

"Maybe not," she whispered. Her throat worked on a swallow. "But it's the only option I'm comfortable with."

Sebastian dared to glance at her, finding her staring back at him resolutely. He wasn't sure if Gabriela was agreeing to simply share a bed with him or perhaps—no, he wouldn't even think it. They would sleep in the same bed out of necessity and nothing more.

It was a declaration he repeated in his head as he watched Gabriela climb under the sheets, and he followed suit. They already smelled of her, and he fought the urge to bury his face in the pillow. When she flashed him a smile over her shoulder and then turned to douse the bedside lamp, Sebastian reminded himself of the declaration once more. And as the mattress shaped to the lines of his body and his eyelids grew heavy, Sebastian willed himself to keep his distance from her, even in his dreams.

Her eyes ripped open, and Gabby blinked for a moment, trying to orient herself. Faint rays of sunlight streamed through the cracks in the drapes, and the distant cawing of seabirds and the dip and roll of the ship reminded Gabby of where she was. On board the ship heading to London. With Whitfield.

Thinking of the duke sparked a new realization; her cheek was not resting on the pillow, but rather on his broad chest, in the spot directly over his heart.

Gabby was afraid to move. Nervous to inhale. Unwilling to do anything to draw attention to herself, especially when the steady cadence of Whitfield's breaths told her he was still asleep. A small part of Gabby was also loath to disrupt the snug position she'd inadvertently found herself in. She and the duke lay facing each other, the long lines of their bodies touching, Gabby's head tucked under his chin, and their feet tangled together. Her arm was thrown over his hip, the other fisted in the front of his nightshirt, and she bit back a gasp when she realized the backs of her knuckles sifted through the soft hairs on his chest. His *bare* chest. He felt firm and strong everywhere she touched, and ay Dios, he smelled divine. Gabby permitted herself a moment to inhale deeply of his now familiar scent, her eyes closing as it filled her lungs.

"Should I compliment Brodie on the new soap he acquired for me?"

Heaving a breath, Gabby would have jerked from Whitfield's embrace if he had allowed her. But his arms kept her close, and she hid her face against his neck.

"It's quite . . . pleasant," she finally mumbled, pleased her voice contained none of the anxieties pulsing through her.

"Pleasant? Surely it's better than pleasant. It's Mexican soap, after all."

Gabby rapped her fist against his chest before she could think better of it. "If I had known it was Mexican soap, I would have been more effusive with my praise."

"You know I covet your praise," he teased.

"Until recently, I had no notion you did." Gabby angled back to see his face. "You've never acted as if you desired it."

Whitfield slowly raised a brow. "Come now, Ella dear, surely you know that a man of my prodigious ego is always hungry for a beautiful woman's praise."

Her cheeks heated, and Gabby prayed the duke could not tell. That telltale sign alone would make him insufferable. "I'm sure you've never wanted for praise."

The duke dragged the hand wrapped around her back to her chin, and he smoothed his thumb along her jawbone. "And yet I wanted *your* good opinion, Ella."

This was the Duke of Whitfield at his most powerful. Not when he lounged in his club, a glass of whisky dangling from his long fingers, surrounded by sycophants, or when he commanded the attention of a ballroom simply by stepping into it. Rather it was when he focused his blue eyes on you, murmured a dry quip, and smirked while he watched you melt. Even now, molten heat coalesced low in her core.

But Gabby had always prided herself on not being swayed by pretty words from a pretty face, and she was not about to fall prey now.

Meeting his gaze, she tsked. "Whitfield, why do you deserve my praise?"

"It's Sebastian," he said, his voice gravelly and clipped, "and it seems I should remind you of what I'm capable of."

And after searching her eyes for a heartbeat, he lowered his head and kissed her.

Gabby shivered as white-hot sparks of desire licked up her spine. "Sebastian," she sighed.

Faith, but his name tasted delicious on her tongue. Gabby twined an arm around his back and sank her nails into his skin.

He smiled against her lips. "Christ, darling, that is the best compliment I've ever received. Shall I give you more reasons to sigh my name?"

Sucking his bottom lip into her mouth, Gabby nibbled on it. "I'm willing to see if the whispers I've heard are true."

Whitfield—Sebastian—shifted, until he loomed over her, his pelvis nestled in the valley between her legs. Her nightdress had hitched about her thighs, and suddenly Sebastian's warm palm slid under the hem, his thumb smoothing across her skin and leaving tingles in its wake. Gabby had never been in such an intimate position before but she wasn't afraid. Wasn't apprehensive. This was the duke, after all. The man who had verbally tangled and tussled with her for the better part of four years, who'd seen her at her worst, at her most vulnerable, and had held her in his arms while she fell apart. Staring into his glacial eyes now, Gabby finally understood that Sebastian was the only man she'd ever truly been herself with because he made her safe to do so.

In this moment, though, with her life in turmoil and her future uncertain, Gabby craved an escape. She longed to put her worries aside and simply be. Simply *feel*.

He must have read something in her gaze, some sort of decision she'd unconsciously made, because Sebastian dropped his head to her chest, his breath coming in pants. The gesture made her heart lodge in her throat.

"Ella love, I didn't invite you to share this cabin with me because I expected anything"—his shoulders rose and fell on another great exhale—"*physical* to occur between us. I understand you're in a precarious position, and I'm not trying to take advantage of it."

"Perhaps I'm trying to take advantage of you."

Sebastian pulled his head up, a sardonic tilt to his mouth. "You are ruthless, darling."

Gabby laughed, but the sound tapered off when she spied his expression. Her arms tightened around him. "I know this situation is not a result of your machinations. You certainly weren't encouraging my father to auction my hand off to the highest bidder."

Dragging his knuckles along her cheek, Sebastian whispered, "I'm sorry you were made to feel that your worth was based not on who you are but on what others could gain from you."

"A woman's worth is always weighed by what she can give . . ."

The words were shaded with a bitterness she couldn't—*wouldn't*—hide.

Sebastian pressed his lips to her jaw, and surprised a laugh out of her when he nipped at it. "Darling, surely you know the thing I value most about you is your sharp tongue."

She grinned. "Is that so?"

He nodded solemnly, but his blue eyes burned. "Shall we try putting it to a different kind of use?"

A powerful wave of heat surged through her, and Gabby pulled him down until they shared the same breath. "Will you show me?"

"God, yes," Sebastian groaned, crashing his mouth down on hers.

Gabby couldn't fathom how Sebastian could be so gentle while he trembled with desire. Even as his tongue leisurely explored the recesses of her mouth, his hands content to coast along the contours of her face, his shoulders shook with barely restrained fire. Gabby was certain she would vibrate out of her skin if she didn't feel more friction in that molten hot place between her legs that only her fingers had ever touched.

Unwilling to submit to Sebastian's torturous pace any longer, and with a primal instinct urging her to move, Gabby tilted her hips up and ground against his thigh. A whimper slipped from her mouth when she could get no purchase.

Sebastian froze above her, his pupils blown wide. He stared at her for a heartbeat before he rasped a "Goddamn it" and reached up to tug his nightshirt from his shoulders.

Any rational thought still pinging about in Gabby's mind vaporized like mist when her eyes landed on Sebastian's naked torso. In the wisps of light peeking through the drapes, he appeared otherworldly. Like a dark lord intent on absconding with her to the underworld. His skin was pale and smooth like marble, with a scattering of moles and dark hair. But when Gabby dared to reach out and touch him, he was warm and very much alive. Her hungry gaze followed the trek her fingers took mapping the muscles of his chest, down the bands of his abdomen to the trail of black hair that disappeared into his sleep trousers. When her questing hands made to follow it, Sebastian captured her wrist.

"Darling, if you do that, this will be over before we've begun." He kissed her knuckles. "Now do I have leave to see you, explore you, just as you did me?"

"But I wasn't done," she complained, scowling. Her objections died, however, when she met his deep arctic gaze.

Holding her stare, as if searching for any sign of fear, Sebastian reached for the hem of her nightdress and dragged it up and over her head. The cool air of the room swept over her skin, but when Sebastian finally lowered his eyes to her body, fire burned through Gabby's limbs at the look of awe that bloomed across his face.

"Exquisite," he breathed, shaking his head. "But of course you are. It's *you*."

Flooded with that unknown emotion, Gabby surged up to snag his lips with her own.

In that moment, with her bare breasts pressed to his torso, every one of her senses was aflame. The soft hairs on his chest abraded her tender flesh. The luscious flavor of his lips danced along her tongue. His excited breaths teased her ears. Gabby held him tighter, desperate to crawl into his skin.

When Sebastian released her lips, she blinked her eyes open in confusion.

"Ella love," he murmured, his hair mussed and his cheeks flushed, "let me look at you."

Willing herself to relax, Gabby lay back on the mattress. A pair of drawers were the only item of clothing she wore. Knitting her fingers in the sheets, Gabby allowed Sebastian to look his fill.

And look he did. His smoldering perusal went from the tips of her toes to the crown of her head. However, it wasn't until his fingertips trailed a meandering path across her skin that Gabby began to squirm. His touch, the fervent light in his eyes, sent liquid heat coursing through her veins, coalescing once again in the juncture between her thighs. Gabby thought she might scream from the heavenly torture of it.

Sebastian seemed oblivious to her discomfort, for his focus had become her breasts. Skating his fingers up her rib cage, he gathered one in each hand, his thumbs raking over the sensitive tips.

"If you only knew the amount of times I imagined these beauties. The moments I'd glimpse you across a ballroom, your smiles for everyone but me, some fashionable confection hugging every one of your curves in the most sinful manner."

His brow arched as he met her eyes. "And I'd think of you when I stroked my cock at night."

Gabby didn't have time to do more than gasp because Sebastian leaned forward and closed his lips around one puckered nipple.

Blistering bolts of pleasure radiated through her limbs, and Gabby cried out as she arched her back into the sensation.

"But the reality of you is so much more than I could've ever dreamed up in my simple mind." Sebastian blew a warm breath across her wet, throbbing flesh. "*You're* a dream," he purred, dipping his head to lick a stripe across her other nipple.

Thrashing about in the sheets, Gabby alternated between clenching her eyes closed as she struggled to maintain her composure or watching Sebastian suck, nibble, and tug at her flesh, inching her ever closer to losing control. Gabby had no notion she was undulating her hips in response to his ministrations until he lifted his head and chuckled.

"My darling girl, am I not giving you what you need?" Sebastian danced his sinful fingers down her stomach to the secret place that had been begging for his attention.

The first caress of his fingers through her folds left her moaning and canting her pelvis to chase his touch.

"Christ, Ella, you're so wet," he crooned, tugging her drawers down and off her legs. Tossing them over his shoulder, Sebastian grasped her thighs and spread them wide, his gaze hooded as he stared down at her. "Grab the headboard, love. I want a taste."

Coherent thoughts evaporated into the ether when Sebastian settled between her legs and swiped his tongue through her folds.

"Ay Dios," she cried out, her hands scrambling to anchor

herself as he licked and sucked at her flesh. Gabby thought she should be scandalized; perhaps embarrassed. Yet it was so very hard to be those things when Sebastian and his wicked, wicked tongue made her feel so good. And making her feel good appeared to be his priority, because he watched her, gauging her reactions and focusing on those actions that she enjoyed. But it was his words, broken and voracious, that threatened to drive her out of her mind.

"I knew it. I knew you would taste divine." Sebastian flicked his tongue against the sensitive spot at the crown of her sex. "Does that feel good, Ella?"

Whimpering, Gabby choked out a "Sí" as she scoured his scalp with her fingernails and directed his tongue to that spot that made her see stars.

"My greedy girl," the duke growled, then sucked her flesh between his lips and sent Gabby's body into the heavens. Her legs quaked and her back arched, and her scream was only contained because she clamped down on her tongue until she tasted iron.

"So beautiful, darling. You are so beautiful in everything you do." Sebastian kissed the insides of her thighs, before he smoothed his palms up her sides to cup her breasts, his lips snaring hers in a scorching kiss. Gabby tasted herself on his tongue, and the intimacy of the gesture, the earthiness of the taste, fanned the embers of her desire.

"Sebastian," she sighed against his lips, clutching him closer. Without thought, she wrapped her legs around his waist, the seam on his trousers teasing the tingling flesh between her thighs.

He tore away from her lips, his chest heaving and his eyes wild. "Ella love, I'm barely hanging on. If you do that again, I'm going to spill myself all over your pretty breasts."

Although she delighted in torturing him, that wasn't what Gabby wanted. "I want to *feel* you," she whined, undulating her hips again.

Sebastian groaned, tucking his face in the valley between her neck and shoulder. "Do you know what you're asking for?"

She nodded. Gabby had overheard enough talk from the widows and matrons to understand what physical congress entailed. Inconveniently, she recalled more than one woman praising Sebastian's skills as a lover. Ruthlessly pushing those memories away, Gabby forced herself to focus on him. On his kindness. His clever tongue. His overwhelming beauty. The way Sebastian made her feel as if every word out of her mouth was interesting and noteworthy.

It did not take much to set her blood boiling again.

Turning her head, Gabby kissed him, teasing her tongue along the seam of his mouth, just as he'd taught her.

"I want you"—she panted against his lips—"to be my first."

Jerking back to meet her gaze, a devilish grin lit his face with an unholy light. "Gabriela Luna, I will never survive you."

In one fluid motion, the duke rose and prowled to his dressing room. Within the span of a heartbeat, he returned, a satin satchel in his hand. Standing at the end of the bed, Sebastian's heated gaze wandered over her body as he opened the satchel and extracted a sheath. Without ceremony, he shoved his trousers down his hips, and Gabby bit back a gasp at the sight before her. His manhood—his cock—was thick and ruddy, standing tall and proud against his abdomen. Gabby refused to look away . . . especially when Sebastian gripped it in his palm and stroked it, that damn smirk on his teasing lips. Expertly, he slipped the sheath over his length and tied it.

"Do you know what this is?" he asked, his voice iron and silk.

Gabby nodded. Isabel had told her about condoms when she'd asked why her sister and Sirius had not yet had children. Sebastian's thoughtfulness sent a warm rush of gratitude coiling about her.

Crawling onto the bed, he grasped one of her ankles and propped it on his shoulder, while his other hand smoothed down her thigh and pressed it wide. She was stretched open, and anticipation and fear lanced through her blood in equal measure. Fisting her hands in the pillow above her head, Gabby clenched her eyes closed.

"Look at me, Ella," Sebastian commanded.

Her lashes fluttered, and Gabby met his gaze.

"There will be no grinning and bearing it with me, darling," he whispered, dragging his cock through her folds. The muscle twitching in his jaw was the only indication he was affected by the sensation. "I only want to bring you pleasure, and I intend to. So stay with me."

Stubbornly holding his gaze, Gabby felt the blunt head notch at her opening and push in. When she would have tensed, Sebastian laved his thumb with his tongue, and pressed it to the hood of her sex, gently circling it until sparks flickered in the corners of her eyes and her legs lost their starch.

The stretch was uncomfortable but not unbearable, especially with Sebastian softly murmuring, "That's it, love. Let me in. Look how beautifully you're taking me."

Gabby enjoyed being contradictory . . . but not when being obedient felt so damn good.

After what felt like a lifetime, Sebastian's hips were finally flush with her own, and Gabby felt full. Gloriously full, with only a slight sting to indicate how her body had stretched to accommodate his girth. Biting the inside of her cheek, Gabby gave her hips an experimental roll.

"Good God," Sebastian hissed, his head falling forward.

Pleased with his response, Gabby clutched his rear and did it again. Pleasure streaked up her spine, and she groaned at the decadent slide.

Rising on his forearms, Sebastian narrowed his eyes. "You're not playing fair, love."

Undulating her body again, Gabby grinned when he moaned. "I'm not trying to, Your Grace. I'm trying to feel good."

Sebastian twined his fingers in her hair and pulled her head back to growl, "Darling, I'm going to make you feel so much more than good."

And he thrust forward, surprising a gasp from her lips. Sebastian didn't slow his pace, rolling and grinding his hips in a seductive dance that hit a spot within her that Gabby didn't even know existed but had quickly become the concentrated focus of her being. She dug her heels into his lower back, her hands scrambling to grip his shoulders as she canted her pelvis to allow him to hit that spot again and again. Euphoria danced like streaks of azul light in her gaze, and her mouth hung open as she tried to catch her breath. Tried to moor herself in the storm Sebastian unleashed on her.

His lips latched on to a spot near her collarbone, and Sebastian sucked on it before soothing the sting with his tongue, all while his hips snapped between her legs. The influx of sensations made Gabby's eyes roll to the back of her head. She keened, her back bowing when his next thrust caused his pubic bone to grind against the nub at the top of her sex.

"Fuck, darling," Sebastian snarled, punctuating his excitement with a firm thrust.

Completion hovered just beyond her reach, and she grit her teeth in frustration. "I'm so close."

"I can tell," he murmured, smoothing a hand down her

cheek and neck to her breast, where he ran his thumb over a hardened tip. "Let me help you."

Grasping her knee with one hand, he angled it wider while he massaged her sex in time with his next thrust.

Gabby's shriek echoed through the room as her climax barreled through her. Her limbs shook and her nails sank into his shoulders as wave after wave of bliss whited out everything but him. Everything but his triumphant expression . . . which quickly slackened as his thrusts lost their rhythm and he shuddered his release.

She clung to him for several minutes, drawing comfort from his warm, clammy skin and the drumming of his heart. When Sebastian did eventually rise, he discarded the sheath and then brought her a glass of water, encouraging her to finish it before using the washroom. When she was done, Sebastian welcomed her back to the bed and quickly enfolded her in his arms. With his face tucked into the crook of her neck, and feeling safe and satiated in his arms, Gabby fell into a deep slumber unlike anything she'd experienced . . . possibly ever.

19

The next several days passed in a blur. Sebastian did his best to take at least one meal in the first-class dining room, mindful he needed to keep up appearances. While he was the only British lord on the ship, he'd learned there were several well-connected executives and men of business among the passengers. He accepted invitations to dine with them, play a game of billiards or a few hands of cards—all at Gabriela's urging, because if he had a choice, Sebastian would have been content to lock himself away in their cabin and stay tangled up in the sheets with her.

As it was, Sebastian spent the majority of his days with Gabriela. They dined together, read side by side, and discussed all manner of topics. She told him of her childhood in Mexico City, and he spoke of his mother and the happy home she made for him, in spite of his father, at Whitfield Manor. She teased him and Sebastian teased her in turn, their verbal bantering often an aphrodisiac, for inevitably they found themselves in bed afterward, their bodies continuing the bewitching dance they had been lured into. Gabriela was passionate and uninhibited, and Sebastian was pulled more and more into her thrall with every laugh they shared or kiss they exchanged.

He had no notion of how he was expected to let her go after they arrived in London.

Sebastian found himself considering this inevitable reality as they lounged in the sitting room, the double doors propped open to welcome in the salty sea breeze and warm Gulf of Mexico sun. He was supposed to be reading the newspaper Brodie had managed to secure in Altamira before they departed. It was more than a week old, but Sebastian had been interested to learn if Maximilian had surrendered, as well as the nature of affairs in the United States. Yet instead of reading the paper spread open in his lap, he kept sneaking surreptitious glances at Gabriela. She was curled on the sofa, her eyes glued to the last quarter investors' report from the Camino Rojo mine in her hands.

"Did you have any questions?" he finally asked, setting the newspaper aside.

Gabriela glanced at him over the report. "I do. If you don't mind?"

"Not at all." And he didn't. Gabriela was inquisitive and driven to learn new things. Attributes he admired.

"It appears there is a detailed multiyear plan for extracting the silver deposit the mine sits upon, but what about the copper? And the zinc ore?" Gabby dropped her eyes to the report for a moment, and then met his gaze again. "Surely there are plans for them?

"There are, in fact," Sebastian said, smiling. "The hope is to reuse the existing infrastructure to mine them."

Gabby quirked her head. "What sort of schedule are they working with?"

They discussed the schedule, and Sebastian explained how exactly the silver would be extracted from the earth, and the ways in which the process compared to mining copper and zinc ore. From there, he told her of how he had come to invest in the mine and what it had meant to the future of the dukedom. Sebastian didn't disclose his father's misdeeds and how his anger had almost bankrupted the dukedom's reserves. Nor did he tell her of James and David, because the boys and their place in his life still felt like something to protect.

Eventually, Brodie arrived with a lunch spread and refreshments. Out of an abundance of caution, the Scotsman had seen to caring for Sebastian and Gabby on his own; a strenuous task, Sebastian knew. But they had been concerned about the servants spreading gossip that a woman was staying in the Duke of Whitfield's cabin, and his valet had been adamant that no one would speak ill of Gabriela. Once again, Sebastian was thankful for Brodie and the attention he brought to all aspects of his job.

Over a lunch of egg salad and a cold vegetable salad, Sebastian told her of what he had read in the paper regarding the French, and Maximilian's refusal to leave Querétaro. Gabby seemed unsurprised by this, lifting a shoulder as she speared a potato on her plate.

"From what I've heard, Maximilian is genuinely interested in the welfare of Mexico." Her nose crinkled. "Perhaps Presidente Juárez and the archduke would have been allies in another world."

"Hmm," was all Sebastian could think to say in response. Although he had spent almost two months in Mexico, and much longer preparing for his visit, he would not pretend to understand the complex political dynamics at play. After a moment, he added, "I wonder if your father would agree with that assessment."

He regretted his words as soon as they left his lips. The blood leached from Gabriela's face, and her shoulders sank. *Damn it.*

"I imagine he would . . . but he'd never admit to it," she murmured, offering him a pathetic excuse for a smile.

Stifling a sigh, Sebastian tossed his napkin down and strolled around the table to grab Gabby's hand and haul her from her seat.

"Darling, you're being silly," he said as he arranged her in his lap on the sofa. "Haven't we discussed how shortsighted your father is?"

Gabby glanced at him over her shoulder. "No. We haven't."

Sebastian frowned. "Then I must have thought all those damning things in my own mind. An honest mistake."

The corners of her lips turned up. "You're silly."

"When it comes to you"—Sebastian nuzzled his nose against her neck—"perhaps I am."

She twisted about in his arms to face him, her gaze soft. "Thank you."

"For what?" he asked.

Gabriela bussed his cheek. "For never belittling me. For making me feel as if I have a thought in my head worth sharing."

"I wish I was privy to all your thoughts"—Sebastian buried his face in her sweet-smelling hair—"but then I'd have my feelings hurt."

Leaning into his embrace, Gabriela tucked her head under his chin. "Not as often as you'd think."

Lud, but his throat felt tight. Pushing it aside, Sebastian

said, "I'm sorry that you've been taught such behavior is a nicety, instead of something you're due simply by being you."

She sighed. "I'm not just referring to your willingness to listen to my thoughts."

He arched a brow. "What are you referring to, then?"

Gabriela raised a shoulder. "You think of everything. Ever since we left Isa and Sirius's, you have seen to *all* the details of the trip. You arranged for my ticket, and when all the cabins were taken, you offered me a place in yours."

"Yes, well"—Sebastian brushed a loose curl from her brow—"I was not about to leave you behind."

"It's not just that, though. You've also been generous"—her throat bobbed on a swallow—"in bed. With my pleasure. I've heard the rumors, you know. But I was sure they were exaggerations."

"Exaggerations?" Sebastian pushed until she angled back to meet his gaze. "Did you doubt I would bring you pleasure?"

"There's no reason to be upset," she murmured, smoothing her palm over his cheek. "I was simply unsure if women were being complimentary because you were a thoughtful lover or because you were a duke."

"Aah." Considering the previous nature of their association, Sebastian could understand her thought process . . . even if he didn't like it.

"And I've also appreciated how protective you've been," she continued, her eyes darting between his.

Sebastian scoffed. "The least I can do is protect a woman in my care."

"And I appreciate that your protection extends to pregnancy, as well."

Growing still, Sebastian blinked down at her.

Gabriela nibbled her lip. "We didn't discuss it. And frankly,

I was so caught up in"—her cheeks turned crimson—"I didn't even consider it. I'm thankful you did."

"Yes, well," he said, twirling his finger in the satin sash around her waist, trying to ignore the heat that rushed up his neck to crowd his face, "I've never left a woman with a child of mine, and I don't intend to now."

Gabriela smirked. "And I have absolutely no interest in falling pregnant—"

"But if you did, there would be no reason for worry, because I would marry you and make you my duchess." The words were clear. Firm. Sebastian was almost proud. "You would be well cared for."

Much to his chagrin, she snorted. "Sebastian, you should know me well enough by now to know I have no interest in your title."

"Of course I know that." He glared at her. "But you could have feigned interest in it. Or in my declaration. Quite rude of you, really."

Her hazel eyes turned gentle, and Gabriela moved to straddle his lap. Sebastian planted his hands on her waist. "Have I offended your pride?"

"More times than I can count." Unable to have her this close and not taste her, he nibbled along her jaw to whisper in her ear, "And yet I keep coming back for more."

Gabriela dropped her head to the side, presenting the fragrant skin of her neck to him. "I never would have thought you a masochist."

"Only for you, darling." Sebastian sucked at the delicate spot behind her ear, heat rushing to his groin when she shuddered.

He would marry her. But only if she fell pregnant.

Gabby didn't know how to feel about that declaration. She

was elated by Sebastian's words, stated so staunchly, his blue eyes flashing with resoluteness—but would he even entertain marriage if pregnancy weren't a consideration? Did it matter when the idea of marrying *anyone* unnerved her? Hadn't she fled England, and then Mexico, to avoid being forced into marriage? Gabby couldn't bring herself to be hurt by the contradiction, and he didn't give her time to consider her warring emotions, for Sebastian moved to set her on the sofa and then dropped to his knees on the floor before her.

"Open your legs, Ella," he ordered, ripping his spectacles from his face and tossing them on the armchair.

With impatient hands, he unhooked her skirts and shoved them down her legs. As she rarely left the cabin, Gabby had shunned her corset and caged crinoline in favor of a simple petticoat under her day dress. Such attire had also made dressing and undressing easier, a fact she celebrated as Sebastian shoved her thighs apart and wedged his shoulders between them.

He glanced up the line of her body to meet her gaze, his eyes blue fire. "I no longer taste you on my tongue."

Gabby speared her fingers through his soft black hair, anticipation making her breath short. "Was this morning not enough?"

Sebastian leaned forward to softly blow across her already wet slit. His lips twisted when she sighed. "I fear I may never have enough."

Before Gabby could respond, Sebastian leaned forward and caressed her sensitive bud with his tongue, and any coherent thoughts were wiped from her mind. Every one of her senses focused on him. On the feel of the broad strokes his tongue made through her folds; the hungry sounds that slipped from his lips as he devoured her; the sight of this powerful man kneeling before her, intent on bringing her pleasure; the tinge of blood in her mouth from clamping down on her lip to keep from crying out; his woodsy cologne on her skin, infusing her lungs, her *soul*, with him. And when he thrust his fingers inside of her, Gabby cried out his name.

"That's it, darling," he crooned, his fingers working her harder and faster than they ever had before. "You may think me a cad, but you'll never again hear the name Sebastian without growing wet."

"You talk too much," she managed.

Sebastian chuckled, placing a kiss to the inside of her thigh. "You're right. My mouth could be doing more pleasurable things." And he ducked his head to put it to work.

Soon Gabby lay quaking before him, her legs limp. A flush encased the entirety of her body, and she flung her arm over her eyes as she tried to catch her breath. But Sebastian had other ideas, for he suddenly grasped her knees and pressed them into her chest.

"We're not done."

She blinked her eyes open and found him stroking his cock as he stared down at her. He had already donned a condom, and while he held her gaze, Sebastian ran his member down her tingling flesh. Gabby whimpered.

Sebastian was silent as he slid inside her, but she hissed as her body worked to fit him. Her reaction was swallowed by his lips when they snared hers. His hands cradled her cheeks so gently, even as his hips snapped between hers at a frantic pace. His eyes—the pupils dilated—focused on her as he ushered her to the peak once again and watched in satisfaction as she keened her pleasure. When she finally exploded around him in a burst of lights and moans, he whispered how perfect she

was as he continued to stroke within her, prolonging her release. Before he followed her, Sebastian gathered her close
against his chest, his mouth nestled near her ear. She heard the
words he whispered, words Gabby was sure he hadn't meant
for her to hear.

"Never enough."

20

He wasn't ready for the trip to be over.

Sebastian emitted a quiet sigh as he stood on the first-class deck, his gaze fixed on the London harbor as it slowly came into view. Once the ship docked, the idyllic accord he'd enjoyed with Gabriela would be over. Yes, he was eager to be reunited with his brothers and share tales of his adventures in Mexico with them, but the thought of no longer seeing Gabriela, of awakening next to her, was a cloud on the horizon Sebastian could not outrun. For while they had never outright discussed the terms of their affair, there seemed to be an unspoken agreement that it would end when they reached London.

And the city was now within sight.

Tapping his cane on the deck, Sebastian wondered how he would say goodbye to her. Should he make it casual? Offer to stop by during visiting hours at Yardley House and take her for a drive through Hyde Park? Host a homecoming ball at Whitfield Place simply so he could invite her to attend? Mayhap she'd wear that heart-stopping red gown again . . .

He pounded his fist against his forehead. There was no way Sebastian could let Gabriela step off the ship and act as if the last two months had not happened. As if holding her in his arms, losing himself in the warm, wet embrace of her body had not completely knocked him off his axis. Sebastian could not possibly be satisfied with fleeting glimpses of her across ballrooms or salons. He needed more . . . and he could *be* more for her.

"I thought you'd be relieved to finally be home."

Sebastian swung about to meet Brodie's questioning gaze. He shrugged. "I look forward to returning to the manor and seeing the boys. It feels as if I've been away for a lifetime."

"Young James and David will be happy to see you," Brodie said, stepping forward to wrap his hands around the deck rail.

"And I them," Sebastian murmured.

"But I'm sure you'll be sad for other goodbyes."

Sebastian didn't dare meet his valet's gaze. "Goodbyes are never easy."

"Especially when it's the end of something unexpected." The Scotsman paused. "It's been good to see you happy, Yer Grace."

"It's not a foreign emotion to me." Sebastian made a rough noise in the back of his throat.

"Perhaps not," Brodie allowed. "Or perhaps you've confused happiness with contentment. For I've seen you smile and laugh more in the last few weeks than I ever have before."

"Yes, well"—Sebastian coughed into his fist—"whatever the case may be, I should check on Miss Luna and ensure she's packed."

"She is," Brodie stated. "I stopped by the room to ask if she required any assistance before I found you here."

"Ah," Sebastian said dumbly, unsure of what to say. Eventually, he said, "You're certain Fox or Señor Valdés will be waiting to collect her when we arrive?"

The Scotsman slowly nodded his head. "As I've said, I sent

a telegram to Mr. Fox from Altamira alerting him of the change in plans."

"Very good." Nothing about how Sebastian felt was good. In fact, he would very much like to kick something. "I appreciate your forethought."

Brodie dipped his head in acknowledgment.

"If you'll excuse me." Without waiting for a reply, Sebastian hastened away.

He didn't knock when he reached his cabin, instead unlocking the door and slipping inside without preamble. Sebastian's heart pounded as he wandered about the rooms until he saw her standing on the veranda from the corner of his eye.

"I was wondering if I would see you before we disembarked," Gabriela said as he joined her at the rail. Her gaze was fixed on the London skyline emerging from the thick fog that shrouded it.

"As if I would be so rude as to let you depart without saying goodbye." Sebastian's throat worked on a swallow. "Or did you prefer for last night to be our goodbye?"

The night prior, they had made love several times, each time more frantic, more desperate than the last. And when they had finally collapsed, exhausted and sweaty, Gabriela had wrapped her arms around his waist, buried her face in his chest, and fallen into a deep sleep. Sleep had eluded Sebastian, however, and he'd held her close, curling the satin strands of her hair around his fingers, and silently hoping the lurching rhythm of his heart was a suitable lullaby.

To his embarrassed relief, Gabriela reached out to grab his hand, knitting their fingers together. "Last night may have been enough of a goodbye for some, but not for me."

The urge to ask her what she meant sat on the tip of Sebastian's tongue, but he couldn't bring himself to voice the question. In his thirty-two years of life, he'd never been so tempted to make himself a fool.

They stood side by side for a spell, watching as the docks, and the dilapidated and dingy buildings that lined them, slowly came into view. Already the stench wafting across the water masked her violet and amber scent, and Sebastian gripped his cane to resist the urge to draw her to his chest and bury his face in her neck. The Duke of Whitfield had already allowed himself to be brought low, and his pride—his very survival—demanded he not drag himself any lower.

"I'll miss you," she murmured. Her voice was soft but strong. How Sebastian wished he could be brave like her.

Instead, Sebastian pressed his lips together until he was certain none of his lovesick emotions snuck into his tone. "It's a good thing we will still see each other on occasion."

"Perhaps. But I'm sure you'll welcome a reprieve from me."

"I'll have a reprieve from London completely, because I plan to retire to Whitfield Manor for the summer."

Gabriela turned to him then, her hazel eyes wide. "You do?"

He nodded. "There are several renovations planned that I'd like to oversee. Plus, winter crops will be planted soon, and then we'll harvest mature crops afterward." Sebastian looked down at his hands, the urge to tell her about James and David was overwhelming, but what point was there in revealing the boys' identities if Gabriela would never have cause to meet them? "Already the Camino Rojo mine has allowed me to care for the old manor in ways I've long wished to, and I want to be there to see it all happen."

"I think that's wonderful, Sebastian." A smile slipped across her lips. "You are the steward of a great legacy, and of course you should do all you can to ensure its future is bright."

Great, hardly. But he was trying to do his part to erase the sins of the past.

"And what of your future?" Sebastian hadn't meant to ask the question, but it now hung in the air between them.

Gabriela gazed ahead, her throat bobbing on a swallow. "I'm not sure. Now that the plans I had for myself have come to naught, I'm a ship without moor. Perhaps I will ask Gideon to help me plan out my financial future as a spinster. I have no intention of being a burden to him or Ana."

Sebastian snorted. "You will not be a spinster."

"There's nothing wrong with being a spinster. I daresay that marriage proves to be nothing but heartache for many women." She huffed a breath. "Indeed I'd rather remain unmarried than find myself shackled to a man who's more concerned about my dowry and connections than any of the thoughts in my head."

"As you should." Sebastian nodded. "Especially as the thoughts in your head are quite intelligent and interesting."

Gabriela froze, her eyes unblinking on his. He merely stared back at her, his heart threatening to tremble from his chest. What was it about this firebrand that loosened his tongue and made him weak in the knees?

"You're only saying that because—"

Her sentence was cut off by the sound of footsteps behind them. Sebastian watched as Brodie came to a stop before them.

"They're preparing to lower the gangplanks."

In unison, Sebastian and Gabriela swung their heads about to see that the docks were now so close they could see sailors bustling about, preparing for their arrival. Sebastian reluctantly turned to her.

"May I escort you to the gangway?"

She nodded mutely. They walked to the stairway in silence. Soon they were joined by other passengers, many of whom greeted him politely while casting furtive glances at her. None of the guests spoke to them, and Sebastian was thankful for it. As it was, he was fighting the desire to tuck Gabriela against his side or clasp her hand. He knew their parting was quickly approaching and he was desperate to delay it for just a few moments longer.

The bright rays of sunlight assaulted his eyes the moment he stepped onto the gangplank, and Sebastian pulled on the brim of his hat to block out the glare. Of course London would choose this day to be sunny and merry when his mood was anything but.

Sebastian glanced ahead toward the street to see it lined with carriages and hackneys. He immediately spied his carriage and then several spots up the road Fox's nondescript black conveyance. It would only be a matter of moments before he and Gabriela were spotted, and Sebastian had yet to tell her goodbye.

Gripping her hand, Sebastian pulled her from the stream of disembarking passengers off to the side, herding her behind a stack of trunks and crates that would be unloaded from the ship. Gabriela glanced back at the crowd and then looked up at him, her hazel eyes luminous. Christ, what could he say? What words could possibly express how much he had relished his time with her? How she'd gone from being an infuriating shrew to the most enchanting woman he'd ever known.

So instead of words, Sebastian tossed his cane aside and stepped forward to drag his palms along her jaw to tangle his fingers in the silky strands of her hair. Staring deep into her wide eyes, noting with satisfaction how her pulse fluttered at the base of her throat, Sebastian slowly pressed his lips to hers.

Would he ever tire of this simple pleasure? Of the chaste yet erotic slide of her lips against his own? Perhaps Gabriela shared his whimsical thoughts, because to his delight and infinite sadness, she twined her arms around his neck and rose up on her toes to deepen the kiss. A small moan escaped her, and Sebastian dared to hold her a little tighter. Their affair had come to a close, but Sebastian's desire for her would be unending.

Sebastian slid his hand down her back to hitch her closer, unable to get enough of her.

A sharp gasp somehow broke through the roaring in Sebastian's ears—or perhaps it was Gabriela stiffening in his arms—but he jerked his head up. Over her shoulder, his gaze landed upon two older, well-dressed women staring at him with mouths agape, uncaring for the crowd of passengers stumbling to a halt behind them. The older of the two women looked familiar, and Sebastian frowned as his memory searched for a name.

"It's Lady Ambrose," Gabriela hissed, breaking from his embrace and darting around the stack of crates to hide. "Did you know she was a passenger?"

"Of course not," he bit out. He was infuriated with his own lack of circumspection. How had he not known they were passengers on the ship? How had Brodie missed them?

"They must have boarded in Nassau," she murmured.

"Maybe," he allowed. Sebastian pushed those thoughts from his mind when he saw Gabriela covering her face with her hands. His heart instantly moved from his chest to his throat.

"Ella, don't worry—"

"I am going to worry," she snapped. Dropping her arms, Gabby stared at him. "Do you honestly think Lady Ambrose is going to hold her silence? All of London will know by the end of the day."

Sebastian opened his mouth to argue, but instead shut it with a snap. She was right. The older woman, and whoever her friend was, would spread word of their kiss far and wide. It would be a scandal of dreadful proportions.

"I'm sorry, darling," he murmured, reaching to grab her hands, but she jerked back from him.

"I know," she sighed, her brownish-green eyes roving his face before she clenched them closed. "But let's not make things worse for ourselves."

"Right. Of course." Sebastian flexed his hands, and then turned to peer around the crates. "Your sister and Fox are waiting not far away. I'll escort you to them."

Her eyes flew open. "You can't escort me! We can't be seen together."

Sebastian snorted. "We've already been seen together, so we may as well raise our chins and disembark as if we're not embarrassed. I'm certainly not."

"You're not?" she whispered, her brows stitched together.

He shook his head. "I wish we weren't spotted, and scandal is no doubt brewing, but I'm not *embarrassed*. And I refuse to skulk off this ship as if I'm not a goddamn bloody duke." Sebastian arched a brow. "And I was under the impression *you* were Gabriela Luna, who's never been intimidated by the ton."

"You're right," Gabriela murmured, glancing toward the docks. "This wasn't the homecoming I was hoping for, but I refuse to return to British shores and slink about as if I'm a pariah. If they want me to wear a scarlet letter, they're going to have to pin it on my sleeve themselves."

"I do enjoy a good literary reference," he quipped. Sebastian cupped her cheek. "Now lift that chin and walk down that gangplank like you're a duchess."

Because you will be soon enough . . .

To his relief, Gabriela exhaled deeply and then squared her shoulders. Looping her arm around his, she flashed him a jaunty look. "Let's go put on a show."

Her fierceness of spirit would be needed in the days to come, and Sebastian patted her hand. Whatever happened, they would brave it together.

"Well, hermanita," Ana María said, "your return to London was done in the most dramatic way possible."

"Are you surprised, though?" Gideon huffed a laugh. "Between her and Whitfield, how would it not be dramatic?"

Gabby glared at her brother-in-law before she pointedly turned back to baby Estella. She cuddled with her niece on a velvet love seat in the private drawing room in Ana and Gideon's home, trying to grasp some quiet time after her *dramatic* arrival in London that morning.

"Querida," Ana María began, pausing until Gabby reluctantly met her eyes. "You know there will be a scandal."

Her sister hadn't phrased it as a question, so an answer didn't seem warranted. Instead, Gabby blew a raspberry on her niece's cheek, laughing when Estella shrieked in delight.

"Perhaps Lady Ambrose will hold her silence—" Gideon began.

"Impossible," Gabby and Ana said in unison, exchanging an amused look.

"I didn't want to say anything, because I selfishly wanted to enjoy your company," Ana said, her dark eyes large as she stared at Gabby holding her daughter, "but Lady Yardley has sent around a note. Apparently, word of your kiss with the duke has already begun to spread."

Somehow Gabby managed not to cringe. What a fine pickle she and Sebastian had found themselves in. They had been so

careful the entire voyage to keep their affair a secret . . . until
the very end. When her own grief over saying goodbye had
caused her to act recklessly and disembark with Sebastian instead of doing so discreetly. Gabby knew she was risking not just
her good name, but her independence, if they were discovered.
And he knew how important it was for her to maintain her autonomy, so she'd assumed Sebastian and his title could protect
them from any scandal. But now scandal had come to call . . .

Acid touched the back of her tongue, and she pressed her
cheek to Estella's chubby one and inhaled deeply of her sweet
baby scent. It calmed her, but only just so.

Gabby could imagine the gossip. The acrimony that had existed between her and Sebastian was well known throughout
the ton, and she should have anticipated how the news that
they'd been seen engaged in a passionate kiss would spread
like an inferno. But after they had left the ship, acting to all
the world as if nothing were amiss, Gabby had almost believed
they could out muster their critics. Sebastian had promptly escorted her to Ana María and Gideon's carriage, and before
he'd departed, he'd squeezed her hand and kissed it, whispering that he would visit the following day. And then they were
rumbling down the streets toward Mayfair, Ana María holding her close and peppering her with questions.

She'd still not given her sister any answers.

Bless Ana María, for she had not pushed. Instead, when
they arrived at her home, her sister had promptly ordered a
coffee tray, invited Gabby to sit on her cozy love seat, and delivered Estella into her arms. Ana María seemed to understand
that Gabby needed comfort, and she was only too eager to
soak up her sister's gentle caretaking. Her eldest sister was so
very good to her, and Gabby had missed her terribly.

Gideon cleared his throat as he set his newspaper aside. "I

think, darling, that we should give your sister today to rest from her long journey, and tomorrow we can ponder this unfolding situation. I'm sure between the three of us, we can strategize an effective way to manage it."

Ana María nodded in agreement, but Gabby said, "Sebastian—" She paused to lick her lips. "*Whitfield* said he would visit tomorrow."

"Bien," her sister murmured, but Gideon just nodded curtly. Gabby wondered at that, but didn't have a chance to ask, for Estella's lips began to quiver as she glanced around the room for her mother.

"Estoy aquí, mi corazón," Ana María crooned, rising to her feet and reaching for the baby. Plopping Estella onto her hip, Ana María smiled down at Gabby. "I'll return after I feed her and put her down to nap."

Gabby watched them leave, marveling at how her sister was a natural at motherhood. She had no doubt that one day if Estella needed her mother's support, Ana María would give it unreservedly—

"Gabby, I have something to ask you, and I hope you will be truthful with me."

Blinking, Gabby swung her gaze to Gideon, who had moved to the edge of his seat and was considering her with a deep pucker between his brows.

"Is something wrong?" she asked, concern raising the hair on her arms.

"I hope not." Wringing his hands together, Gideon stared at the floor, his jaw working. "Did Whitfield take advantage of you?"

"Uhh." Gabby pulled her chin back. "Of course not."

Her brother by marriage visibly deflated, color rushing into his cheeks.

Gabby leaned forward. "Why would you think the duke took advantage of me?"

"Truly, I didn't want to think he did, but I had to ask." Gideon scrubbed a hand down his face. "The two of you have always been at odds, and now you've returned unexpectedly and were seen in an intimate embrace . . . and I just had to be certain he didn't prey on your vulnerability."

"He didn't," she said quietly but firmly.

"I'm glad, because I asked Whitfield to care for you and ensure your safety."

Her forehead crinkled. "You did?"

A frown darkened his expression. "Of course. I was concerned for you and wanted to assure your sister, as well as myself, that you were safe and secure."

Overcome by his thoughtfulness, Gabby dropped her gaze. She'd never had an older brother to look after her, and she suddenly realized that she now had two in Gideon and Sirius. The thought wedged a knot tight in her throat.

Gideon rubbed the back of his neck. "I'm relieved my faith in him was warranted."

"Your faith in him was more than warranted, because he did care for me. He did see to my safety." A fond smile curved her lips. "The duke showed me, many times over, that I had misjudged him."

"Not completely." Gideon chuckled when Gabby narrowed her eyes. "We humans are not black-and-white, but I agree there is more to Whitfield than the jaded, droll facade he projects to the world."

As she had come to understand. "That's why you're friends with him, isn't it?"

Gideon nodded. "Please know that I care deeply about your

well-being, and despite what happens in the days to come, your sister and I will abide by whatever choices you make."

She knotted her hands in her lap and looked away. Gabby knew she had difficult decisions to make, but her feelings were too raw, her frustration and anger too potent, to allow her mind to continue to linger on the changes that were soon to be thrust upon her because of her own lack of circumspection.

Yet knowing Ana María and Gideon would support her, no matter what, was a comfort.

"Thank you," she murmured simply.

Her brother-in-law inclined his head and then picked up his cup of coffee. Gideon had said his piece, and his words had brought her a sense of relief and more than a little dose of confidence.

21

Sebastian had still not come.

It was the thought racing through Gabby's mind as she sat in her sister's drawing room, attempting to drum up a smile at the scores of visitors who had come to welcome her back to London. Visitors only too happy to ask after the duke and the rumors they'd heard regarding her relationship with him. It took every bit of self-control Gabby possessed to respond politely.

"I was under the impression you had intended to stay in Mexico indefinitely, Miss Luna," Lady Natalie Kingsley said, her blue eyes wide. "What made you change your mind?"

"No doubt a certain duke . . ." Miss Walters murmured quietly at her side, pressing her lips together to contain a giggle when Lady Natalie flashed her a censorious look.

Gabby breathed deeply through her nose. "It seems you were mistaken, Lady Natalie. I had only planned to visit my sister Isabel, who I'm sure you know married Captain Dawson. He's enamored of her, and it was wonderful to see how happy they are."

If her voice was a bit syrupy, Gabby did not care. Many people in the room had been unkind to Isabel, and she wanted them all to know not only that her older sister had secured the hand of one of London's most eligible bachelors, but that Sirius loved her. She noted with relish when several women shifted about on their seats at her words.

"You were able to visit with your parents as well?" Mrs. Anderson, a friend of Lady Yardley's, leaned forward in her seat. "After so many years away, I'm sure you were very happy to see them."

"I was." Tension swelled painfully in Gabby's chest. Just thinking of her parents, of her hasty departure from San Luis Potosí without so much as a goodbye, made her want to escape to her bedchamber and bury her head under her pillows. "It did me good to see them healthy and well. The war has been a frightening experience, but there is hope that an end is in sight."

"I'm happy to hear it, dear," Mrs. Anderson said, and Gabby believed her. The older woman was genuinely kind, and Gabby had heaved a relieved sigh when she'd seen her within the crowd of visitors. There were very few in attendance she was happy to see.

"While I'm certain your trip was pleasant, I think most of us here are curious about your association with the duke," the Countess of Tolleston said into a lull in the chatter. She raised her brows as she glanced about the room, as if ensuring she held the crowd's attention. "Lady Ambrose said she saw the two of you in each other's company. Is that right?"

And there it was. The guests crammed into Ana María and Gideon's drawing room were staring at her with bated breath. This was why they were here.

But Sebastian was not. Dios mío, where was he?

Still, she remembered his words. Lifting her chin, Gabby met the countess's gaze directly. "The duke was kind enough to escort me back to London. He is close friends with both of my brothers-in-law, after all."

A murmur ran through the assembled visitors, who no doubt recognized their connection. Yet Gabby noted the frowns and snide glances. She steeled her spine, for Gabby knew the inquest had just begun.

"I understand he's friends with Mr. Fox and Captain Dawson, but from what Lady Ambrose said, the duke was not acting very brotherly toward you." There was a predatory glint in Lady Tolleston's eyes.

Gabby smirked. "Forgive me, your ladyship, for saying it, but do you think it wise to craft a narrative around the supposed account of a person known to have difficulties with her eyesight?"

The countess stiffened. "I don't understand what you mean."

"What I mean," Gabby said, drawing out the word as her gaze scanned the room, "was that Lady Ambrose was not wearing her spectacles when I saw her on the docks yesterday, and it is common knowledge she requires them to see past her hand. So I'd argue that we can't be entirely sure of what she saw."

Gabby lifted her teacup to her lips, doing her best to project an air of indifference when really her heart thudded so painfully she was surprised the whole room could not hear it.

The Countess of Tolleston tittered, reaching for her own cup of tea. "Well, if Lady Ambrose was mistaken, you would think Whitfield would want to rectify the misunderstanding. And yet he's not here. He's left you all alone to satisfy everyone's curiosity. I wonder why that is?"

The ladies who flanked her tutted their agreement, and the other visitors shifted in their seats at Lady Tolleston's unspoken assertion. An assertion that had Gabby clenching her teeth so hard her jaw ached. She shouldn't be surprised the countess had designated herself Gabby's inquisitor. Lady Tolleston had once been the catty Lady Emily Hargrove, and Gabby had verbally sparred with the woman numerous times, sometimes in defense of her sisters, but oftentimes because Gabby simply did not like her.

But now there was blood in the water, and the sharks were circling.

Lady Tolleston winged up a brow. "Or perhaps the duke heard the rumors about you and Lord Carlisle—"

Before Gabby could be outraged by the countess's innuendo, the drawing room door swung open. Gabby could hear excited whispers in the hall from other visitors waiting to pay their respects.

The butler stepped into the room and glanced at Ana María first before sliding his gaze to Gabby. "The Duke of Whitfield."

The guests collectively gasped as Sebastian filled the doorway, but a quiet sigh fled Gabby's lungs. Dressed in a midnight-blue morning coat with a matching waistcoat that set off the glacial blue of his eyes, and his dark chocolate hair styled just so, Sebastian appeared every bit an imposing duke. His gaze lazily moved about the congested room before landing on her. He looked sinfully handsome, and Gabby's breath stuttered as he focused his attention on her. If she had managed to convince the crowd that they were merely friends, the intensity of Sebastian's stare completely eradicated that notion.

"Miss Luna, if I had known you would have a swarm of visitors, I would have come sooner." There was a hint of a smile on his lips, but Gabby noted his eyes had turned hard. "Have you all come to welcome Miss Luna back to London?"

Sebastian knew the ton only too well.

Gabby suppressed a smile when he fixed a steely gaze over

his spectacles on Mr. Norris, who was seated on the love seat next to her. The man flinched, but without a word, he rose to his feet and moved away. Sebastian settled into the vacated spot, sending a whiff of his woodsy scent to her nose. She clenched her hands tightly in her skirts when he stretched an arm across the back of the love seat behind her, at ease before their audience in ways she could only aspire to. How Gabby longed to lean into his side and bury her face in his neck, where she knew he smelled divine. How she wished he would wrap his arms about her and shield her from the curt innuendos she had only just begun to endure.

When had Sebastian turned into a source of comfort for her?

"I'm sorry I didn't arrive sooner," he said quietly, in Spanish. His blue gaze roved over her face. "Has it been ghastly?"

She choked on a laugh, so thankful for this intimate moment with him. Gabby was acutely aware that every set of eyes in the room were fixed on them, yet Sebastian ignored them, conversing in her native language as if it were natural to do so. Gratitude surged through her, and had there not been spectators, Gabby would have kissed him.

"It's been awful," she murmured, "but now you're here to endure it with me."

"Indeed." Sebastian smoothed a hand down his thigh. "You won't have to face them alone again."

Before Gabby could wonder at his declaration, Lady Yardley cleared her throat. "I had no notion you spoke Spanish, Your Grace."

Sebastian dipped his head. "I'm flattered you noticed, your ladyship. I've been taking lessons over the last year. Spending time in Mexico helped to strengthen my skills."

"I'm sure dear Gabby appreciates your fluency." Lady Yardley smiled affectionately at her. "She's mentioned that she misses speaking Spanish, and unfortunately I do not possess your talent for acquiring languages."

"You've done very well learning it, my lady," Gabby argued. Regardless of the ways in which they vexed each other, Lady Yardley had always been good to her, and Gabby appreciated that the older woman was there to be an ally.

Before the viscountess could respond, Lady Tolleston cleared her throat. Loudly.

"Your Grace, we were just talking about you," the countess said, her smile encompassing Sebastian and Sebastian alone. "It's so good that you've returned from your trip to Mexico, and with a bit of a tan, I see. It would seem as if you enjoyed your visit."

"Indeed, I did." Sebastian nodded. "It was productive professionally, and I was gratified to spend time with my old friend, Captain Dawson, and his wife, the former Miss Luna."

Sebastian shared observations about his time in Mexico, and answered questions about the mine and the town they stayed in, but Gabby sensed most visitors were just biding their time. Waiting until they could turn the conversation toward what they were truly ravenous to know.

Unsurprisingly, Lady Tolleston was the one to redirect the discussion.

"So, Your Grace," she began, leaning forward in a manner that showcased her décolletage. "Rumors have been circulating about you. And Miss Luna." The last was added almost begrudgingly.

"I'm sure they have," Sebastian drawled. He said nothing more, merely cocking his head.

Never one to pass up a chance to be dramatic, Gabby raised her brows.

The countess swallowed and glanced about. Tilting her

chin, she finally said, "The rumors are that you and Miss Luna were caught in an embrace."

The room was silent except for the steady tick of the clock on Ana María's escritoire. Unable to help herself, Gabby narrowed her eyes at the countess, who stared back at her almost gleefully. The anger fled her body, however, when Sebastian's knuckles ran up and down her arm.

Several gazes darted to the movement of his hand, before swinging up to move between her and Sebastian. Gabby did her best to keep her mien impassive, even as she revived under his touch.

Sebastian cleared his throat. "Whether Miss Luna and I were embracing is no one's business, my lady. What an affianced couple does is not for public consumption."

Gabby wasn't sure how she contained her gasp. All she knew was that the roaring in her ears drowned out the exclamations of surprise and the enthusiastic congratulations. It felt to Gabby as if she were separated from the excited activity occurring around her by a veil . . . that is until Sebastian gently set his hand on top of hers. The warmth of his palm jerked her to awareness, and she looked up to meet his earnest gaze.

Thankfully Sebastian answered the flurry of inquiries about their courtship and engagement. Gabby could only sit with a half smile on her face, pretending for all in attendance that she was the glowing future Duchess of Whitfield.

But Gabby wasn't glowing inside. Instead, a muddled mess of anger, impotence, and triumph coalesced like a ball of fire in her chest. Sebastian had announced to all in attendance that they would marry, but he hadn't once asked her if *she* wanted to marry him.

She almost choked on a laugh when Gabby realized no one had bothered to ask whom her chaperone had been for the voyage back to London, and shouldn't that relieve her? Yet she was irked, for apparently it did not matter; marrying a duke erased all her supposed sins.

At that moment, she met Ana María's gaze, worry lines fanning from the corners of her eldest sister's eyes. But ever a proper hostess, Ana María held her silence and turned to accept the congratulations of another well-meaning guest.

"When will the wedding be?" Mrs. Anderson asked, her bright smile encompassing Gabby and Sebastian.

"We have not discussed the details yet, but the banns will be printed soon enough," Sebastian replied, his fingers squeezing Gabby's.

"I'm excited to begin planning," Lady Yardley interjected, clapping her hands together. "It's going to be a beautiful affair, and Gabby will be a beautiful bride."

A startled giggle slipped past her lips. Her, a bride?

Sebastian's grip tightened.

"And not only will you be a bride, you'll be a duchess." Lady Natalie's mouth curved into an approximation of a smile. "Congratulations."

Gabby thought she murmured her thanks, but she couldn't be certain.

The next twenty or so minutes passed in a blur, but somehow her sister and Lady Yardley were successful in ushering their visitors out the door, and Gabby found herself facing the women, who wore matching expressions of worry. Vaguely she realized that Gideon had left his study and now stood just inside the threshold of the drawing room, his arms crossed over his chest and his mouth a slash of displeasure as he faced Sebastian.

"So the ton believes you'll marry." Ana María wrung her hands together. "But what do you want, querida?"

"What does she want? Darling, Gabby doesn't have much of a choice." Lady Yardley scoffed. "She was seen kissing the duke. If she doesn't marry him, she'll be ruined."

"Whitfield, I asked you to keep an eye on Gabby," Gideon proclaimed, his inflection just short of a growl, "not put your hands on her."

Gabby wasn't sure she'd ever seen Gideon so angry, and her affection for her new brother grew. Still, she couldn't allow Sebastian to take the brunt of the blame for their current predicament, when she was just as much at fault. Exhaling a deep breath, Gabby stepped forward.

"I kissed the duke just as much as he kissed me. So please do not—" She paused, turning to meet Sebastian's gaze. "Do not paint him as some sort of villain when I was a willing participant."

Ana María closed her eyes and sighed, while the viscountess signaled a footman for a drink. Sebastian grasped her hand, his thumb sweeping back and forth over her knuckles.

"So what do we do?" Ana María finally asked, looking to Gideon, then Lady Yardley, before landing on Gabby and Sebastian.

"I think," Sebastian spoke into the building silence, "that it would be kind of you all to give Miss Luna and me a moment to speak privately."

"I daresay you've already had plenty of private moments," Gideon grumbled, his eyes narrowed on the duke.

A bark of laughter burst from Gabby's lips, and she crossed to her brother-in-law, wrapping her arms around his waist. After a surprised pause, Gideon returned her embrace.

"I can't express how much I appreciate your defense of me, but I promise I'm fine." Gabby dropped her voice to a whisper. "Le tengo cariño."

The fight fled Gideon in a long exhale, and a small smile lit his face. "Bueno."

Stepping back, Gabby pivoted to her sister and the viscountess. "The duke and I need to speak, and then we can discuss what our next steps should be."

Her sister reluctantly nodded as she looped her arm through Gideon's. "Estella should be up from her nap anyway, so we'll return shortly. Come along, my lady."

Lady Yardley's scowl encompassed Ana María, Gideon, and the duke, but the older woman saved the full weight of it for Gabby. After a moment, she waved a dismissive hand. "Very well. The baby is better company than you lot anyway."

Gabby watched them depart, nibbling on the inside of her cheek. Tensing her shoulders, she slowly swiveled about. Sebastian stood several paces away, his arms linked behind his back, and his brows pulled low over his eyes.

Licking her lips, Gabby weighed what to say. She was angry, but a disconcerting mixture of warm sentiments flooded her blood when she met his gaze.

Anger was familiar, so she clung to it. "You could have asked me to marry you before you announced our engagement to the entire room."

He blinked, but to his credit, Sebastian didn't flinch. "I could have and I'm sorry."

She glanced away.

"Ella." Her nickname was a sentence, and it contained so much emotion. "Surely my proclamation wasn't a surprise. There's only so much we can do to stop the scandal from spreading."

He was right. Of course he was . . . yet Gabby was still primed for an argument. "But maybe we could have thought of something else if you had only been here earlier to discuss it." Gabby threw her arms wide as she glowered at him. "I didn't know how to answer their questions, and I was so worried I'd say something I wasn't supposed to. Terrified they would ask about the nature of our return trip. And you just waltzed in with no such concerns, and declared we were marrying without even speaking to me first."

Helplessness wrapped its venomous tentacles around her, and Gabby held her breath until she was certain sobs wouldn't burst free from behind her teeth. Why was she forever jumping from the flames of one fire to another?

Sebastian's throat worked as he stared down at her, and Gabby took a measure of solace to see him just as discomposed as she was.

"I was meeting with my solicitor."

Gabby whipped her head back. "W-what?"

"I wanted to make sure my finances were in order before I approached Señor Valdés and asked for your hand."

"Your finances?" Gabby frowned. "You're a duke. Surely you're as rich as Croesus."

"The Whitfield dukedom was wealthy at one time, but my disgrace of a father did everything in his power to change that," Sebastian bit out, yanking a hand through his hair. "And I wanted to assure your uncle and Fox that I had the means to care for you as you deserve."

Her curiosity piqued, Gabby moved closer. "What do you mean?"

"What I mean," Sebastian said, billowing a breath, "is that my father left the dukedom in crippling debt, and I only managed to save myself from a transactional marriage of convenience thanks to the Camino Rojo mine."

"Oh," Gabby mumbled, her thoughts churning with the

rumors she'd heard of Sebastian's insolvency. Of his need to marry a rich bride.

Without a word, Sebastian grasped her hand and led her to the love seat. Working in silence, he gently arranged her on his lap. Gabby would have protested his high-handed ways if she weren't so pleased to be held within his arms again.

"I was my parents' only child," he began, the words spoken against her cheek. "My mother almost lost her life birthing me, and was unable to carry another child afterward, despite my father's insistence on a spare." She could feel his lips curl in disgust. "I would rather bathe in the Thames than subject any woman to the disrespect my mother endured in the name of my father's ego. The supposed Whitfield legacy."

The more Sebastian spoke, the more she stiffened. Now that the ugly words had been spoken, Gabby didn't know what to do. Her instincts urged her to comfort him . . . but her mind insisted she know more.

His knuckles brushed a curl from her face. "When my mother couldn't give him the spare he wanted, he left. From my understanding, he lived most of the year in London or on the Continent, carousing with his libertine friends and all but ignoring the dukedom, as well as my mother and me. I saw him twice a year, when he arrived at Whitfield Manor and expected me to come to his study and answer his litany of questions about my lessons. He used to terrify me, and I would weep to my mother for days before he arrived. Once I went off to Eton, I saw him very rarely until I graduated from university."

"What happened then?" she asked, her fingers twining with his.

"I encountered him at a gaming hell. Dawson was with me, and he was with his set, including old Tyrell." Gabby scowled at the mention of the earl who had abducted Ana María several years past. "My father's mouth fell open when he saw me, and he looked me up and down as if surprised I'd become a man without his help. He tried to start a conversation, but I ignored him." Sebastian chuckled, but the sound was harsh. "That *infuriated* him. He grabbed my arm and started to scold me . . . that is until I planted a facer right on his jaw."

Gabby gasped, turning about in his arms. "You didn't!"

"I did." Sebastian's voice lacked inflection. "I would have done it again if he tried to get up. But he didn't, and the sight of him sprawled on the ground looking up at me, in front of all his vile friends, is a memory that has fueled me, even while he did his best to bankrupt the dukedom in retaliation."

She sensed there was more to the story than he was saying, and Gabby frowned. "What do you mean?"

Sebastian's grip tightened. "The papers were filled with inflated, often erroneous, retellings of our confrontation for weeks afterward, and other stories appeared that spoke of my father's foul behavior. He was, understandably, outraged. He couldn't take the Whitfield title from me, but he sure as hell could squander my inheritance and leave me its charred ruins. I've been struggling to repair the dukedom ever since."

"Ay, querido," she murmured, cupping his cheek.

"So that is why the Camino Rojo mine has been so important to me. It promises a better future not just for me, but for the staff at Whitfield Manor, the staff at Whitfield Place." Sebastian kissed the back of her hand. "For the people who depend upon me, who trust me in ways they never dared trust my father."

"I'm sorry." Gabby pushed the hair back from his brow, smiling when he closed his eyes at her touch. "I'm sorry I ever believed you to be a lazy, vapid aristocrat, more concerned with his own consequence than the well-being of those around him."

He snorted. "I didn't give you many reasons to think otherwise."

"But you have now." Leaning forward, Gabby pressed her lips to his. It was a fleeting kiss, but it dissolved some of her anger. "I forgive you for not being here."

"Thank you." Sebastian dropped his head to her shoulder, and she carded her fingers through his soft hair. After several long breaths, he murmured, "I have something to ask you, though."

"You do?" she echoed, her brow furrowed.

Pulling free of her arms, Sebastian set her on the love seat before he dropped to his knees in front of her. Holding her gaze, he pulled a box from his coat pocket and placed it in her hands.

"I made an additional stop before I arrived. At Carrington House, to collect this."

Gabby shook her head. "Carrington House? Do you know the Duke of Carrington?" She'd never met the man or his duchess.

"He's my uncle." Sebastian smiled. "He was my mother's younger brother, and he held this in safekeeping for me."

Gabby opened the box to reveal a delicate gold ring. Flanked on either side by a trio of diamonds, a sapphire the color of the bluest blue sat at the center of the arrangement. It was obviously very old, and in a style from a bygone era. Gabby loved it immediately. With her heart thudding painfully in her chest, she looked at Sebastian.

"It was my mother's. And her mother's before her, and her mother's before that." He licked his lips. "And I'd like for it to be yours."

Her throat bobbed as she held back her tears.

"Will you marry me, Ella? Will you be my duchess? Will you be my wife?" Sebastian's eyes were pools of the palest waters. "Will you let me endeavor each day to prove I can be a man deserving of your hand?"

Despite all her maneuvering to outstep first Lord Carlisle's and then her father's machinations, Gabby was once again faced with a marriage proposal. Time seemed to stand still as she waited for the irritation, the *impatience* she usually felt when entertaining such a question to flood her. Instead, her pulse raced and her mouth went dry. Staring into Sebastian's earnest gaze, Gabby felt breathless as understanding fell upon her: She'd been frightened of marriage because she couldn't imagine a man who would respect her and value her as a person, and not as a commodity to possess. A conquest to be made. But that was before Sebastian. Perhaps she could be happy in marriage as long as it was a marriage to *him*.

A jolt of unease tempered her newly dawned insight, because suddenly she had to know if Sebastian would have asked to marry her if their affair had not been discovered. Gabby wasn't sure why it mattered, but it did.

He must have read the question in her eyes, because Sebastian rose to sit by her side, cupping her cheeks with his hands.

"Scandal or no scandal, I want this. I want *you*." He stroked his thumb over her cheekbone. "I may not have been brave enough to ask before, but I'm trying to be brave now."

Gabby wanted to believe him. Yearned to. But there was a wisp of uncertainty that haunted her. "Is there anything you haven't told me? Something I should know if I'm to be your wife?"

Sebastian's expression remained unchanged, yet there was a flash of . . . something in his eyes that Gabby had no time to grasp. "I believe you know the worst of it," he said with a wry grin.

She considered him a moment longer, her unease abating. "Then I want to be brave, too."

"You're fearsome, darling," Sebastian said earnestly.

"Then let me bravely say yes," she whispered against his lips.

And Gabby let go. Of her defenses. Her fears. Her prejudices against this man who had shown her that he wanted her just as she was. Twining her fingers in his hair, Gabby gave herself over to the inevitable.

They were sitting side by side on the love seat, their hands laced together, when Ana María, Gideon, and Lady Yardley returned to the room fifteen minutes later. Estella was in her father's arms, one chubby fist in her mouth and the other wrapped around her father's once neatly arranged tie. She grinned when she spotted Gabby, but the baby's eyes flew wide when they landed on the duke and she reached out her arms toward him.

"Little Miss Fox, I've missed you," Sebastian said as he scooped Estella from an amused Gideon's arms. He held the baby against his chest in a practiced manner, and Gabby's ribs ached.

"I can't believe she went to you over me," she whined, leaning forward to kiss Estella's cheek. "She's *my* niece, after all."

"Yes well, she'll be my niece, too, soon enough." Sebastian bounced Estella until she giggled, and then smirked down at Gabby. "I can't help it if the prettiest little lady in London desires my company."

Gabby couldn't express—nor did she want to—how the sight of Sebastian cuddling the baby close made her want to cry. One of Estella's dimpled hands knotted in his dark hair while her other palm slapped against his cheek as she gurgled at him. Sebastian tucked his spectacles into his pocket and nodded at her, as if he were listening intently as the baby shared a great secret.

"No, I suppose you can't," she murmured around the lump in her throat.

Sebastian glanced at her and then back at the baby. "Little Miss Fox, I asked the most extraordinary woman to be my duchess today, and she agreed. Do you know what that means?" Estella stared at him with large doe eyes, chewing on her fingers. "It means I'm going to be your uncle. Isn't that grand?"

Biting her cheek, Gabby took a moment to study all the faces in the room. Ana María met her gaze with watery eyes, coming forward to clasp Gabby's hand tightly in her own. Gideon was staring at his daughter and the duke, an exasperated but fond look on his face. The viscountess clutched her dog, Dove, against her chest, no doubt planning Gabby and Sebastian's wedding in her mind.

Finally, she looked up at the duke. The man who would be her husband. Sebastian was watching her closely, as if gauging her response. And for the first time, she well and truly exhaled. Then she smiled. A smile that hurt her cheeks but lightened her heart. "It's wonderful."

22

The Duke and Duchess of Whitfield departed for Gloucestershire in the early afternoon.

Sebastian glanced across the train compartment at Gabriela now, warmth spreading through his limbs. She was his wife. They had exchanged vows within St. George's church before half the ton, all of them desirous to see the youngest Luna sister set aside her animosity for the Duke of Whitfield and marry him.

Despite the crowds that watched them pledge their lives to each other, Sebastian had found it hard to look away from Gabriela. She wore a silk gown of sky blue that sat off her shoulders and flattered the gold tones of her skin. With a simple crown of white roses in her mahogany hair and a bouquet of white roses in her hands, she'd taken his breath away. And she'd yet to give it back . . .

After the wedding breakfast at Yardley House, Gabriela had changed into a stylish traveling ensemble for their trip to Whitfield Manor, and they said their goodbyes to their friends. His wife clung to her sister and plied her niece with a plethora of kisses. Even as he escorted her to the carriage and assured her they would be in Gloucestershire only for the summer, Gabriela sniffled and blinked back tears. He hated seeing her so distraught, and had channeled his anxiety by ensuring she was comfortable during every stage of the trip, from the carriage ride to the train station.

Now they sat ensconced in his private train car, and a heavy silence hung in the air between them. Sebastian knew Gabriela was experiencing a flurry of emotions over the rushed state of their "courtship" and marriage, and he tried to be understanding of that. The cacophony that began after Lady Ambrose had seen them together on the docks exploded after their engagement announcement appeared in the papers, and the attention had been exhausting. The gossip rags were intent on dissecting every aspect of their relationship, from their public squabbles and Gabriela's very obvious loathing of him, to their present "love match." The use of the term had made Sebastian cringe. While he could admit, if only to himself, that every fiber of his being had fallen in love with Gabriela Luna, Sebastian was not ready to confess it. Not when the state of Gabriela's feelings remained so uncertain.

Which was why he still had not broached the subject of his brothers. Sebastian could be vulnerable with his heart . . . but he refused to be vulnerable with theirs.

Still, this didn't stop Sebastian from expressing his emotions in other ways. Like when he'd cornered the Earl of Carlisle at their club one afternoon, and warned the man, through gritted teeth, what would happen to him if he looked in Gabriela's direction again. Thankfully Carlisle was wise enough to heed Sebastian's warning, and the man departed for an extended trip to the Continent soon after. He hoped the earl's absence brought his new wife a sense of peace.

Sebastian studied Gabriela now as she gazed out the window

at the passing countryside. In her hand she clutched a letter from her parents. Sebastian had asked her what it said, imagining the sort of recriminations he knew Señor Luna—*his* now father-in-law—capable of. But Gabriela confessed she hadn't opened it yet, and he wondered at her hesitancy.

Still, even in her melancholy, she was so damn alive, and at that moment, Sebastian wished he could give her a reason to smile.

Unsure of what to say, he crossed one leg over the other and blurted, "That color of blue is stunning on you."

Gabriela glanced down at her traveling ensemble, which matched the dreamy blue color of her wedding dress. Her gloved hand ran along the folds of her skirt. "Thank you. I adore it." She met his stare. "It reminds me of the color of your eyes."

His jaw went slack, and Sebastian paused for several long seconds. "It does?"

She nodded, an amused smirk on her lips. "As soon as I saw it, I knew that I would marry you in this color."

Sebastian's throat grew dry, for he didn't know what to say. Gabriela had been withdrawn in the wake of his proposal, and he had assumed she was feeling overwhelmed. She had gone through so much over the past few months, and to suddenly find herself marrying the man whom she once disliked so forcefully must have left her flummoxed. But as one week melded into the next and their wedding day loomed, Sebastian began to wonder if Gabriela regretted her decision to marry him. Perhaps any kind regard she'd developed for him had been swept away in the rush of public scrutiny and gossip, especially as Gabby had tried so hard to avoid marriage in the first place.

For Sebastian knew there had been some among the ton who

believed she had trapped him. That the lively and tempestuous Mexican heiress had secured the hand of the only eligible duke in the kingdom—a man she had openly detested—was a feat some refused to believe. A misconception they clung to even as Sebastian yoked his life to hers. How could a woman, especially a woman of Gabriela's fierce pride and closely guarded independence, not be regretful that their marriage had been foisted upon her?

Yet staring into her eyes now, Sebastian thought that maybe he'd been incorrect.

Without a word, he rose to his feet and joined her on the curved-arm sofa, pulling her into his arms. Grasping Gabriela's chin, Sebastian tipped it up so he could meet her gaze.

"We'll only be at Whitfield Manor for a couple of months," he whispered. "I want to be in London for the start of Parliament."

"You do?" she said, blinking.

He counted the freckles on her nose. "I've been thinking about what you said that night we dined with the Conners. About how I should use my privilege to do more for others. And, well, I'd like to try."

"Sebastian," Gabriela whispered, threading her fingers through his. "Eso es increíble."

His mouth quirked. "It's going to be awful. You know how I despise talking to people."

"You poor man." Gabriela turned his hand to kiss his palm. "Will you survive it?"

"With Fox's help, perhaps. And then only if you attend all those dry, banal events with me." Sebastian smiled when she chuckled.

"I know of several causes you can champion," she said archly.

Sebastian groaned. "I'm sure you do. But . . ." He paused,

licking his lips. "There's another reason I'm intent on returning to London in the fall."

Gabriela cocked her head.

"Your ladies' club is there." Sebastian lifted a shoulder. "I thought you might want to continue the work you did with them. Or perhaps even do something different."

"Oh, I would." Her mouth gaped. "You would let me continue to work with them?"

His brow dropped low. "If I didn't, would you do so anyway?"

"Por supuesto. The new Duchess of Whitfield is a mexicana, and I fully intend to use my title to do some good." Gabby snorted. "Surely you don't believe I would let you tell me what to do."

"It would be a fruitless, frustrating effort, and we both know I'm much too lazy for all that." Sebastian tapped the tip of her nose. He wouldn't dream of clipping Ella's wings . . . but he hoped to give her plenty of reasons to consider him home. "But I will ask that you have a care with your safety. I would hate for—"

"I will be careful," she whispered. Her eyes abruptly filled with tears. "Thank you, Sebastian."

He kissed away a tear. "I didn't mean to make you cry. I just know it's important for you to find your place, and I want to make that search easier."

"Thank you." Gabriela expelled a shuddering breath. "It's been a trying few weeks, and I've been out of sorts."

"Understandable." Sebastian brushed a loose curl from her cheek. "The gossip was . . . difficult."

"Difficult?" Gabriela chuckled. "I think you're being generous, cariño. It was atrocious. Everyone seemed determined to remind me of our past interactions. I already remember all the reasons why I thought you were a scoundrel, and certainly didn't need anyone to remind me of them."

Sebastian sniffed. "Darling, I thought we agreed that I wasn't a scoundrel so much as unfailingly charming."

"¿Qué?" Gabriela's eyes went wide as she stared up at him, mirth and fire melding in their hazel depths. "Unfailingly charming? Surely you mean unfailingly egotistical?"

Pulling back, Sebastian scowled. "You wound me, Ella. And on the very first day of our marriage."

She snorted. "You'll recover, I'm sure."

Stroking a thumb across her bottom lip, Sebastian pitched his voice low. "And will you help me recover?"

A flush swept up Gabriela's throat, and her tongue peeked out to lick her bottom lip. "I suppose I have to since I'm your wife."

"Damn right you are," he snarled before he crashed his mouth down on hers.

It felt as if stars had been born and died in the time since Sebastian had last tasted Gabriela. Since he'd felt her under his hands. Until that moment, he didn't realize how much he'd missed her. Not just the satisfaction he experienced having her in his arms, but the simple joy of being the sole focus of her attention. The blazing warmth of her smiles. The jolt of lightning that was her laugh.

Biting back a moan, Sebastian looped his arm around her back and hauled her onto his lap, cursing against her lips when her skirts amassed between them.

"Shhh," Gabriela murmured, pressing a quick kiss to his mouth before standing. She fidgeted with her underskirts, eventually stepping free of her crinolette and petticoat. With a saucy grin, Gabriela straddled his lap, and he sucked in a breath to discover the only things separating them were her drawers and his trousers. But Sebastian could swear he felt the heat of her core through the garments.

"It's been torture to have you so close yet be unable to touch you," he rasped. Reaching under her dress, he slipped his fingers through the slit in her drawers and hissed when he found her hot and wet. "Is this for me?"

Gabriela mewled softly. "I've missed your touch, too."

Sebastian clicked his tongue. "We can't have that. You shouldn't want for anything." Holding her gaze, he stroked the crown of her sex before he slipped two fingers inside her and ground the heel of his hand against her pubic bone. A long moan slipped past her lips as she tipped her head back, presenting the column of her throat to him. Accepting the invitation, Sebastian leaned forward and laved her skin.

"Sebastian," Gabriela gasped, her hips undulating to match the rhythm of his fingers, "I was told to be firm with you."

Sebastian's fingers slowed. When Gabriela whimpered, he resumed his ministrations. "I'm not a stubborn stallion, darling. Why would you need to be firm with me?"

His wife leaned forward to rest her forehead on his shoulder, her hips beginning to stutter in their movements. "Lady Vale and Lady Montrose cautioned me that a man of your reputation would grow bored having only one woman in his bed. They said I needed to either accept that you would have mistresses or ensure a mistress was superfluous."

"That you can even use the word *superfluous* while chasing an orgasm is astonishing," Sebastian said around a chuckle.

"Y-you married a clever woman." Gabriela clutched his shoulder as she swiveled her hips, and Sebastian's mouth went dry.

"I did indeed, Ella. And as such, I don't see how I could ever grow bored with you. It's impossible." He punctuated his point by affixing his mouth to her pulse point and sucking.

Warmth gushed around his fingers, and Sebastian groaned.

Gabriela snarled in the back of her throat. "It had better remain impossible."

Oh. Sebastian pulled back, a diverted grin twisting his lips. "Is that right? Will you punish me if I do otherwise?"

"You're being a cad again," she panted, baring her teeth at him.

Slipping his other hand under her skirts, Sebastian slapped her once on the arse. "You mean unfailingly charming, love."

Huffing a breath, Gabriela shifted in his lap, his fingers slipping free of her body. His wife arched a severe brow when she grasped the placard of his trousers, and Sebastian almost swallowed his tongue when she extracted his very hard cock from the tweed.

"Fuck," he rasped, dropping his head to the seat back.

"Sí, esa es la idea."

Sebastian opened his mouth to respond, but Gabriela squeezed him within her tight fist, and words became difficult.

He couldn't see Gabriela's hand pumping him up and down, or when she angled his flesh so she could slide her body down to encase it in her heat. But Sebastian could observe how her mouth went slack when she rubbed the blunt tip up and down her slit. He watched as her teeth clenched as she worked to take him. He grunted when she bottomed out, her body enveloping him so perfectly he almost couldn't breathe.

How could Sebastian ever grow bored with such an intensely passionate woman?

The first twist of Gabriela's hips sent his eyes rolling into the back of his head, and he gripped her tightly as he thrust his pelvis into her movements. Her low hiss sent delight curling about him, so Sebastian did it again, quivering with the sensations bolting through his body. This woman—*his* woman—would absolutely be the death of him, but he would gladly pay his coin to Charon if he could do so with Gabriela wrapped all around him.

A chorus of *mine mine mine* looped through Sebastian's mind as Gabriela pressed her lips against his as she came, her broken gasps and stuttered breaths pushing him toward his own powerful release. In the aftermath, his wife held him close even while she continued to rock in his lap, bussing his cheeks, his temples, and his mouth with soft kisses and panting breaths.

Yes, Sebastian thought, his body sated and his chest absurdly tight. He could think of no better way to go.

Whitfield Manor was not what she had expected.

Not that Gabby had any expectations for Sebastian's ancestral home. She assumed it would be grand and stately, a place where generations of Whitfield dukes had been born and died.

Yet as she gazed out the carriage window as they traversed a gravel drive lined with English oaks, Gabby found it was more modest than grand. More cozy than stately. It was lovely.

The Georgian manor house was constructed from Gault brick, and was three stories tall, with sash windows and a Venetian window centered above a stately fluted portico. Ivy clung to the brick facade, and Gabby imagined a young Sebastian using it to sneak from his bedchamber at night. Her eyes could make out a large garden located off the back partition, as well as a small lake sparkling in the distance. The gravel driveway circled in front of the entrance, and at its center was a tall garden fountain, its swirling design topped with a smiling cherub. Gabby grinned at the sight.

"The manor was not initially built to be the dukedom's primary residence," Sebastian murmured, staring out the window over her shoulder.

He had insisted on sitting next to her in the narrow cab, and had spent the entirety of the ride from the train station reading a book while alternating between drawing patterns on her palm and rubbing her knuckles against his lips. Gabby found the gestures endearing, and she'd leaned into his side and dozed. It had been an exhausting and emotional day, and their lovemaking on the train had used up the last of her energy.

But knowing they were close to Whitfield Manor had piqued her interest.

"How did it become the primary residence?" she asked now.

"Whitfield Estates burned to the ground when the eighth duke dropped a lantern in the library during a drunken stupor." Sebastian chuckled when Gabby gasped. "The Brooks family has produced a long line of degenerates and idiots."

"Three months ago I would have said you were living up to the family name," Gabby said, arching a brow.

Sebastian winged up his own brow. "And three months ago I was. It's a wonder you took pity on me."

"Verdad." Gabby smiled, and then turned to look out the window again. "So Whitfield Estates burned down, and the subsequent dukes took up residence here at the manor?"

"Yes. It had once been the home of the dowager duchesses." Sebastian's expression softened. "It's small by ancestral estate standards, but I was . . . content here."

A sad, wistful note colored his words, and Gabby leaned back until her head was cradled between his neck and shoulder. "And we will be happy here."

Her husband bussed her temple. "I hope we can fill the old

walls with happy memories. And new mortar, because the manor is in desperate need of refurbishment."

Gabby understood the true nature of Sebastian's words when they stepped through the front door. She had just been introduced to Roberts, the butler; and Mrs. Evers, the house-keeper; when she followed Sebastian over the threshold and her gaze swept through the vestibule. Everything her eyes touched upon, from the drapes to the carpet to the paintings on the wall, was just a tad shabby. Faded. Worn. Gabby felt terrible for assigning such adjectives to the place when it was obviously well cared for, but a good dusting and scrubbing could only go so far with old and brittle items.

This would all have to change, and Gabby itched to help Sebastian reclaim the manor house's glory . . . and possibly put her stamp upon the old bricks.

"Mrs. Evers had a light dinner prepared for us. I told her we would eat in my—our—chamber," he said, grabbing her hand and leading her toward the stairs.

"We're going to share a chamber?"

Sebastian stumbled to a halt and looked down at her. "I— I . . ." He shook his head, his ears turning pink. "I thought you might feel more comfortable if I was close by. But forgive me for making that decision without asking you first. I can ask Mrs. Evers to have my mother's set of rooms prepared—"

"Sebastian," Gabby interjected, tightening her grip on his hand, "of course I would like to share a chamber with you. I just hadn't expected you to want to share one with me."

He blinked. "Why not? I want you within an arm's reach at all times."

"Surely not at all times," she said, shaking her head.

His brows drew together. "Well, I suppose not." When she

laughed, he joined her. After a moment, his expression turned serious. "I've just always hoped, although I doubted it would happen, that whenever I brought my duchess to the manor for the first time, she would want to be more than just my duchess. She'd also . . . well, she'd also want to be my wife."

There was a difference, and her lungs constricted as she considered how isolated Sebastian must have been navigating the world wearing a mask of haughty aloofness when he was truly anything but. Without another thought, Gabby reached up to cup Sebastian's cheeks and kissed him. She didn't care who saw; in fact, she hoped the servants witnessed how much their new mistress liked her husband.

Liked? What an insignificant word to describe how her body flushed with emotion whenever Sebastian looked at her. Teased her. Kissed her. Yet *like* was the only word she was willing to use.

Resting back on her feet, Gabby grinned up at Sebastian's flushed face. "Will you escort me to our chamber?"

Sebastian's eyes searched hers, and then, rather shyly, he led her up the stairs.

23

Gabby's transition into her role as the Duchess of Whitfield was easier than she had expected, thanks in no small part to her long-deceased mother-in-law.

If the stories told by the staff were true, the late duchess had been a saint. Despite her husband's neglect, the duchess had made Whitfield Manor a warm, inviting home even as the building itself threatened to fall down around them.

While giving her a tour of the pantry and larder, Mrs. Evers regaled Gabby with tales of Beatrice, the late duchess. How she organized events at the manor and invited not just retainers but residents of the nearby village to attend as well. She visited the homes of sick families, bringing them baskets stuffed with food and possets of herbs designed to help the ailing. The late duchess ensured the local schoolhouse was always well stocked with books and firewood.

"Did the duke play with the village children in the surrounding fields and meadows?" Gabby asked, her mind conjuring an image of a young Sebastian in short trousers laughing and running free.

Mrs. Evers's expression darkened. "No, unfortunately. The

late duke was adamant that Master Sebastian not interact with any of the village children."

"But why?" Gabby was astounded.

The housekeeper sighed. "His Grace believed the village families and their children were not the sort of friends befitting a ducal heir. Master Sebastian had only the duchess and his tutors as companions."

Suddenly realizing she was gaping, Gabby snapped her mouth closed. "How lonesome."

"Indeed. The old duke once arrived at the manor earlier than expected, and found Master Sebastian in his shirtsleeves, playing blindman's bluff with several of the village boys. His anger was a sight to behold." Mrs. Evers swallowed. "I don't know what the duke told those boys' parents, but they never played with Master Sebastian again."

"Oh," she mumbled, too stunned, too heartbroken for Sebastian, to speak.

The older woman's eyes were far away and not on the shelves of linens in front of them. "Her Grace, the staff, and I did our best to give him a happy childhood, but he must have been lonely. How could he not be?"

Gabby bit her lip to keep it from trembling. Sebastian was a popular and respected member of society, and women certainly desired his company. It seemed to her, however, that he called very few people friends. Sirius. Gideon. Brodie, perhaps. Now she could include herself in that group. Her husband was devoted to those friends and helped them in any way he could. Hadn't he shown her he cared for her? Hadn't he made her feel valued and cherished, even in their short time together? Every day she came to realize that the notorious Duke of Whitfield possessed a gracious and tender heart.

And perhaps his childhood had been just as lonely as her own.

This thought ran through Gabby's mind as Mrs. Evers continued her tour, and it helped her to see all the details she had initially overlooked or explained away. Like how clean and welcoming the manor was despite its age and dilapidated appearance. How every staff member she encountered greeted her with a smile, their uniforms pressed and tidy. How Sebastian was referenced in affectionate terms. Whitfield Manor, and the dukedom as a whole, may have slid into disrepair thanks to the spiteful inattentiveness of the late duke, but the duchess, and later Sebastian, had done their best to care for its staff and they were loved in return.

Now that Gabby was here, along with her ample dowry, she was determined to help Sebastian repair what was lost and, maybe, create something new together.

After a tour of the family wing of the manor, Gabby paused by the staircase that led to the attic where she assumed the nursery and schoolrooms were located. Was that laughter she heard? *Children's* laughter?

"Your Grace," Mrs. Evers called, turning to look back at Gabby from the landing half a flight below her. "Is everything all right?"

"Did you hear that?" Gabby cocked her head, straining to listen. "I thought I heard something."

The housekeeper frowned, her gaze darting to the attic stairs.

Taking a step toward the staircase, Gabby murmured, "It sounded like . . . children laughing."

"Your Grace," Mrs. Evers exclaimed, her voice sharp, "I'm sure it's just the wind. Cutting through the drafty attic."

Gabby jerked her chin back at the housekeeper's change in demeanor.

The older woman smoothed her hands over her apron and knotted her hands at her waist. "I apologize, Your Grace. I was simply worried you would climb the stairs and catch a cold."

"Catch a cold? From the wind?" Gabby slid her gaze to a window that overlooked the back garden. The trees, bushes, and grass basked in the sunshine, with no breeze to rustle their leaves. She frowned as she glanced back at the housekeeper.

"Or maybe it was roosting birds," Mrs. Evers stammered, her lips pinched.

"Maybe," Gabby allowed, her eyes traveling up the attic staircase. "Should we go look?"

Mrs. Evers shook her head, rather forcefully. "The rooms are boarded up, so there wouldn't be much to see."

"Oh." Gabby bit back her frustration. Why was the older woman acting so strangely all of a sudden? And why was Mrs. Evers so determined to believe the noises she heard were anything but laughter?

Maybe it was a ghost. Gabby paused as she considered the possibility. Sebastian had said the manor was very old and had seen its fair share of births and deaths within its walls. So was it plausible that spirits still called the manor home? With an uncomfortable swallow, Gabby decided it was.

"Would you like to see the brewing house, Your Grace?" Mrs. Evers asked suddenly, gesturing to a smallish building located off the back garden. "Whitfield Manor has been brewing its own ale for at least two hundred years."

"I would like that very much," Gabby said, turning to follow the woman. And she admonished herself not to look over her shoulder at the attic staircase as she did.

. . .

"Good God, boys, I told you it was important for you to be quiet."

David paused in his reenactment of the squabble he and James had found themselves in with the Johnson boys from the village, his blue eyes owlish. Blue eyes strikingly familiar because Sebastian stared into a pair very much like them whenever he looked into a mirror.

"He's sorry," James rushed to say, glaring at David as he smacked his arm. "We're sorry, Your Grace. Please don't be angry."

Any irritation Sebastian felt fled in a whoosh at the panicked look on James's face. He'd worked to make the boys feel comfortable at Whitfield Manor, and in the ten months they had lived there, Sebastian liked to think he and the staff had done just that. It had taken every one of those months to convince James and David that he wasn't going to pack them up and send them back to the cold and threadbare home he'd found them in.

But then he'd departed for Mexico and returned married to Gabriela Luna, and it seemed their old fears had resurfaced. Christ, he'd really made a mess of the whole situation.

Scrubbing a hand down his face, Sebastian dropped to one knee before both boys, waiting for each pair of eyes to meet his. "Of course I'm not angry. And I realize that it can be hard to be quiet when you're very excited to tell the tale of your epic battle." When David flashed him a toothy smile, Sebastian reached out to muss his hair. "But I don't want to disturb my new duchess as she adjusts to her life here at Whitfield Manor."

The boys nodded solemnly, their blue eyes large.

"When will we get to meet her?" James asked, his expression careful.

"Polly says she's ever so pretty and kind, even if she does have a funny accent," David added, already bouncing on the balls of his feet. "I should like to meet her very much."

Sebastian snorted. "And so you shall, soon enough."

As soon as he told his wife about them. Christ, it was something Sebastian should have done weeks ago. He'd had numerous opportunities to discuss the boys with her on their trip to San Luis Potosí and back, and Sebastian still burned with shame that he hadn't told Gabriela about them when he'd proposed. He knew when she asked if there was anything she needed to know about his past that she'd been referring to his rakish exploits . . . but he'd avoided the truth about James and David as if *they* were a scandalous secret.

Yet so much about his relationship with Gabriela still felt precarious. He knew she cared for him; he sensed it when she smiled at him with a gentleness in her eyes. When she clung to him in her sleep. When she sighed his name as he stroked within her body. But did that mean she cared for him enough to stay? Because if he shared the boys with her and Gabriela eventually left, they would be devastated.

James's sober stare was a silent prick at his conscience.

Eager to change the topic from the secrets he kept from his duchess, Sebastian resumed his seat and gestured to David with a hand. "Now what happened after Jesse Johnson tripped you coming out of the confection shop?"

As he had hoped, David launched into an animated recitation of the altercation, albeit at a much lower tone. Sebastian listened intently to the story, laughing when he was supposed to and congratulating the boys on their prowess, while silently making a mental note to pay a call on Mr. Johnson regarding his sons' bullying.

When he pulled out the gifts he had brought from Mexico

for the boys, he watched with satisfaction as they exclaimed over the trinkets, thanking him profusely with hugs. Sebastian then helped the boys set up lines of tin soldiers across the nursery floor, dubbing one side the valiant Mexican army and the other the invading French troops. James and David listened intently as he described the ongoing conflict, and the brave Mexicans he had met on his trip who were fighting to reclaim their country from imperial rule. They laughed over their play battles, and when David teased James for taking the game too seriously, Sebastian complimented the older boy on his battle strategies.

As a child, this was what Sebastian had always wanted: a family to call his own. And with David and James now residing happily at the manor, Sebastian was fit to bursting.

Yet his happiness was tempered, and it was all his fault. The guilt of withholding the boys from Gabriela, and her from the boys, ate at him, even as he lay in bed at night with her in his arms. Even as he laughed and played with the boys.

James seemed to sense something was amiss, for his blue eyes returned to Sebastian's face time and again, a worried furrow to his brow. Apparently his little brother was much more perceptive than Sebastian had given him credit for.

24

Something was wrong.

Gabby couldn't quite put her finger on it, but something was definitely amiss at Whitfield Manor. It was little things, like how Mrs. Evers or the maids would block her from wandering outside during certain hours of the day with silly excuses about the weather or some other such nonsense. Why she wouldn't be permitted to take a turn about the garden after lunchtime Gabby didn't know, but short of barreling through the housekeeper, who planted herself in the doorway, Gabby acquiesced.

There was also the time she'd found Mrs. Evers and Roberts in the foyer talking in hushed voices, and they had jumped in surprised unison when they spotted her. Stranger still was when she inquired after Sebastian, and they had blurted out different answers, with Roberts claiming he was inspecting the construction on the east wing and Mrs. Evers simultaneously saying he had gone to visit some of the home farms. It had taken every bit of good manners Gabby possessed not to call out their duplicity, and instead she had thanked them through gritted teeth.

The real person Gabby knew she should be angry with was

her husband, but ay Dios, Sebastian made it difficult, for when he was with her, he made her the sole focus of his attention. Yet their time together was limited.

After a shared breakfast, Sebastian departed to tend to any number of tasks around the estate. Some days he helped the masons who labored on the restoration of the east wing, while other times he was found in the nearby village, meeting with fellow landowners regarding improvements to the roads, as well as expanding the local train station. On one particular day, Gabby found him holed up in his study with a team of architects and engineers reviewing blueprints for continued renovations to the manor house. When he'd seen her lingering in the hallway, Sebastian had invited her to join them, where he'd painstakingly reviewed the plans with her and encouraged her to make suggestions. Gabby was touched to have been included . . . and yet she was still unsettled, because there continued to be large pockets of time when her husband was unaccounted for.

Every night, though, when Sebastian met her in the dining room for dinner, he had eyes only for her. He asked about her day, her opinions of the people she met, and the work she did. Sebastian encouraged her to speak in Spanish, and Gabby relished the intimacy of their conversations. When their meal was over, he escorted her to the drawing room, where Sebastian sat by her side on the worn damask sofa and listened to her read. Sometimes she shared news from the paper, news he'd no doubt already read himself, or nuggets of information regarding Maximilian's impending execution she'd received in letters from her sisters. He'd laughed when she'd told him that Lucia had written, her letter expressing well-wishes for their marriage and claiming she knew all along there was something special between Sebastian and her.

Ever an instigator, he also picked arguments with her over the most ridiculous things, a fact that initially annoyed her . . . until she realized how much fun it was to bicker good-naturedly with him. Her fondness for it was further solidified when Sebastian revealed he did it specifically because he liked it when she put him in his place.

So, too, did Gabby quickly learn that if Sebastian had a place for her, it was in his bed. Every night and often in the early mornings, her husband made love to her. Passionately. Creatively. Desperately. Sebastian had a talent for making her giggle with laughter one moment and then cry out his name the next. Gabby relished his touch, desired his good opinion, and coveted his attention . . . which was why she was so aware of how distracted he was at times. And it wasn't just concerns for the dukedom that were his focus, for already the profits Sebastian had made from the Camino Rojo mine, as well as the added cushion of her dowry, were evident in the projects being undertaken around the estate and beyond. Yet still, there was an inattentive edge to Gabby's new husband she couldn't decipher.

So when she spied Brodie stepping into a side passage as she was departing Sebastian's empty study, Gabby thought that perhaps he could help her, for surely the valet would know what the duke was about.

"Brodie," she called, smothering a laugh when the Scotsman's shoulders visibly stiffened.

"Yer Grace," he murmured as he slowly pivoted to face her. "How may I assist you?"

"You may assist me by telling me where my husband is."

The Scotsman grinned. "Yer husband, aye?"

Mortified, Gabby could feel her face grow warm. "It still feels odd to say."

"I reckon you'll get used to it if you do it more. Take His Grace, for example. He has no problem talking about his wife this and his duchess that." Brodie rolled his eyes. "You would think yer name is *his wife*."

Gabby rocked back on her heels as she was encased in a warm glow. The fact that Sebastian, the former rake of all rakes, would be so proud to proclaim her his wife delighted her.

So why, then, did it feel as if some part of him held her at a distance?

Clearing her throat, Gabby raised her brows at the Scotsman. "Where is he?"

"I don't rightly know," Brodie said, his voice all calm assurance. Gabby would have believed him if she didn't spy how the tips of his ears turned pink.

Frustration clenched her teeth tight, and Gabby spun on her heel without another word.

"Yer Grace," Brodie called, "I'm sure he's tending to work around here somewhere."

Gabby waved her arm in acknowledgment, but did not stop.

Once she reached her chamber, she flipped the tumbler and prowled to the window. Aside from the gardener working on trimming the hedgerows, and a scattering of laborers hauling lumber from a wagon to the construction on the east wing, Gabby spied no one else. Where had Sebastian gone, and why did everyone else seem to know what he was up to but her?

Releasing an agitated sigh, she sank onto the chair in front of her vanity and stared at her reflection in the mirror. Her familiar hazel eyes stared back at her, hard and unflinching. Gabby was reminded of her mother. Of how she used to crave María Elena's embrace . . . and now she couldn't bring herself to open the letter she'd received from her on the eve of her wedding. Gabby refused to let whatever disappointments and scolds her mother had penned disrupt the happy accord she had found with Sebastian.

But happiness was not what she felt in that moment, and Gabby fought the urge to curl up on the bed and weep out her confusion.

Instead, she pulled out the last letter to arrive from Isabel. It was filled with all the giddy encouragement Gabby had needed when the gossip before her wedding had become almost unbearable. Isabel's elegant script had written of her and Sirius's enthusiasm for her union with Sebastian, and her sister's firm belief that the duke would be a good husband. It had been a stance supported by Sirius, who had written his own short note to reiterate that Sebastian was the most honorable, steadfast friend he'd ever had, and he would treat Gabby with all the respect and regard she deserved.

And hadn't Sebastian done just that? Despite the gnawing sense he was keeping secrets from her, Gabby had no real proof her husband was doing any such thing. In truth, Sebastian showed her day after day how happy he was to call her his wife.

So shouldn't that be enough?

An hour later, Gabby rose from a fitful nap and padded downstairs, clutching the note that had been left on her side table. It was from Sebastian, inviting her to tour the progress of the east wing renovations with him. Reading her husband's neat penmanship had been a balm, and she approached his study door with a smile on her face. That was until male voices met her ears. One was Sebastian, but she didn't recognize the second. Unsure if she should knock, she glanced inside the room to find her husband in conversation with a younger man with deep red hair.

"David has trouble attending. He's distracted by—"

"I hope not by James," Sebastian interjected, pushing his spectacles up his nose.

The red-haired man shook his head. "No. James follows rules to a fault—"

"Ella," Sebastian called, his gaze colliding with hers before it darted to the man across the desk from him. "Let us continue this discussion another time."

"Of course, Your Grace," the man said, jumping to his feet. His dark eyes met Gabby's for only a passing moment. "Excuse me, Your Grace."

Gabby watched him leave, her curiosity sparking. "Who was that?"

"That's Simon," Sebastian said succinctly. He stood and slipped his hands into his pockets. "Did you get my note?"

She blinked at the change of subject, but she held up the slip of paper. "I did. I'd be happy to accompany you. And . . ." She paused, glancing down at the floor. "Thank you for inviting me."

The room was silent for a tense moment, but when Gabby looked up, Sebastian was staring at her with a soft look in his blue eyes. "I'm sorry I haven't been able to invite you to more things."

"So am I," she murmured, turning toward the door. "Shall I meet you in the foyer in thirty minutes?"

He nodded. "I look forward to it, Ella."

Gabby chewed on her cheek as she considered what to say. The urge to ask him directly if he was keeping something from her sat on the tip of her tongue, but she swallowed it. Hadn't Sebastian just greeted her warmly, as if he was happy to see her? Perhaps she was imagining slights where none existed. Ay, marriage had addled her brain, and she chuckled as she made to leave.

"What's so funny?" Sebastian called, pulling her up short.

She looked over her shoulder and reached for an answer. "It's just that as much as I love that name, it also makes me laugh because Ella makes me think of *ella*, and *ella* in Spanish is *she*."

His mouth twisted into a smirk, even as he reached for his pen. "It's apropos, then, seeing as how you're the only *she* who's ever been important to me."

Like a spark against dry kindling, heat roared through Gabby's blood, and before she knew what she was about, she flipped the lock on the door and prowled toward the desk. Sebastian looked up as she approached, his brow furrowed. Holding his gaze, she shoved his chairback, ignoring the surprised noise he made. Without a word, she dropped to her knees and reached for the placard of his trousers.

"D-darling," Sebastian stammered, his hands curling around the armrests. His chest labored with his excited breaths. "What are you doing?"

"¡Cállate!" she ordered, humming in the back of her throat when she pulled his quickly hardening cock free. Gabby had never considered that this part of a man could be beautiful, but it felt beautiful in her hands. It made her feel beautiful and seeing the look of awe dawn across her husband's expression, Gabby felt powerful. And she very much wanted to remind Sebastian of that power.

Staring into his eyes, she leaned forward and circled the rim of his blunt head with her tongue.

A long, low hiss slipped from Sebastian's lips, and he clenched his eyes closed.

"Mírame," Gabby demanded, pausing her ministrations until he met her gaze again. Once his blue eyes were locked with hers, she slowly covered the tip with her lips and sucked, squeezing his flesh with her opposite hand.

If moans and curses were currency, Gabby would be richer than Montezuma, for soon her husband was thrusting into the steady movements of her hand, his cock nudging the back of her throat as saliva dripped down her chin and over her fingers. Reaching for his hand, Gabby placed it on the back of her head, smiling around his length when he cursed loudly and held her a second longer as his cock thrust into her mouth.

"I remember seeing you outside the door *that* night," Sebastian purred, stroking her jaw. "We'd only just met, and yet it was you I imagined taking me in your mouth."

Gabby would have gasped if she were able to. So Sebastian had known she'd seen his scandalous assignation the night they met, and thus why she had come to dislike him. Well, she certainly didn't dislike him now, and seeing her handsome, arrogant duke so undone was a powerful aphrodisiac. Gabby frantically pulled up her skirts so she could slip her fingers in her drawers and caress where she was wet and wanting. Her eyes rolled into the back of her head at the heady combination of sensations.

Her muffled moan must have snared Sebastian's attention, because he focused on where her hand disappeared beneath her skirts, and his expression darkened. Weaving his fingers through her hair, Sebastian gently pulled until his cock slipped from her lips, and he wiped the wetness from her chin with his thumb.

"Stand up and turn around," he bit out, pointing to the desk.

Panting, Gabby obeyed, ignoring how her legs trembled. Placing her palms on the desktop, she peered back at him. Sebastian had dropped his trousers, and he stood behind her with his ruddy flesh in hand, his gaze a stormy sea. Without a word, he grabbed the bulk of her skirts and hefted them to her waist, before he grasped one of her knees and perched it on the desktop. Although her skirts hindered her view, Gabby imagined how she must appear spread before him.

Before she could ask him to touch her, Sebastian dragged a knuckle through her cleft, and Gabby dropped her head forward as she mewled.

"My God, Ella," he growled, swiping his finger across her flesh once again. Sebastian chuckled when she arched her back, greedy for more. "Are you hungry for me, darling?"

Unable to speak, Gabby nodded.

Running his hand along the inside of her thigh, he dragged it around to squeeze her arse. "Did sucking my cock make your pretty little cunny jealous?"

A fresh rush of arousal dripped from her core. "Sebastian, por favor."

"Christ," he whispered, running the head of his flesh through her slick folds, "I can't believe you're mine."

Gabby didn't have a chance to respond before Sebastian thrust inside her, and she shrieked, scrambling her hands against the desktop as her body worked to adjust to him. He curled around her, his arms crisscrossing around her chest, his hand cupping her chin while one of his long fingers slipped between her lips. With a groan, Gabby sucked it into her mouth.

"Ella," was the only word he said, over and over, against her cheek and temple, as he held her to his chest, his hips surging as he worked his length inside her. Gabby anchored herself to the desk, certain it was the only way she'd be able to withstand the pleasure. It was beautiful and wild, and she clamped her eyes closed, allowing the warring sensations to crash over her.

Within minutes—or perhaps it was hours—her legs began

to quake, and Gabby dropped her head and sobbed as her orgasm loomed. Sebastian didn't slow his pace, but quickly maneuvered a hand into her bodice, where he clutched her breast.

"Ella, now. Come for me now."

His imperious tone pushed her over the edge, and Gabby wailed his name as she was swept under. Moments later, Sebastian thrust into her one last time, gripping her hips with bruising strength as he spent deep inside her. With an exhausted sigh, he gathered her in his arms and collapsed onto the chair.

Neither of them spoke, for they had already expressed everything with their bodies. Instead, Gabby rested her head on Sebastian's chest and closed her eyes, desperate to hold on to this satisfaction for as long as it would last.

25

Sebastian's to-do list for the day was extensive, yet when Simon, the boys' tutor, sent a note that James and David wanted to show him the progress they had made learning their multiplication tables, he could hardly refuse.

Which was how Sebastian found himself in the nursery, his two excited brothers rapidly reciting times tables simultaneously. It was a noisy affair, and Sebastian was not sure he properly heard one boy over the other, but he smiled and nodded just the same.

After their showcase, a maid delivered a lunch tray, and Sebastian and the boys enjoyed a meal of cold roasted chicken, cheeses, tart apricots, and thick slices of bread. He felt more relaxed, more carefree visiting James and David than he had in a long while, and only because Gabriela was visiting the rectory in the village to take lunch with the vicar and his wife. When he learned the couple was interested in organizing a health clinic for their parishioners and the residents of the village, he'd thought Gabriela might be interested in the endeavor. Sebastian knew she had been corresponding with her sisters about arranging such a clinic in London similar to the one she'd visited in San Luis Potosí, and he'd been right, for Gabriela had responded eagerly to the suggestion.

So for once, Sebastian didn't have to worry about the boys being too loud and calling attention to themselves. Mrs. Evers had told him that Gabriela had overheard the boys laughing in the attic and had wanted to investigate. Knowing how close they had been to being discovered made his stomach drop.

Which in turn made guilt flame hot in his throat. He loved his wife and wanted her to know the boys; he'd come to believe Gabriela would adore James and David and would not hold their parentage against them. But the omission had grown in proportion, with every person at Whitfield Manor helping him to keep the secret, and Sebastian was at a loss for how to rectify it. Because despite his best efforts, his regret was beginning to sour his relationship with his bride. Sebastian could sense it in the guarded nature of Gabriela's gaze. In the brittleness of her smile. In the way her lips pinched when he kissed her goodbye at the breakfast table. So Sebastian clung to her, showering her with attention whenever the day's events brought them back together. If he were at leave, he would spend every day with Gabriela in bed, chasing one orgasm after another. Sebastian longed to learn every thought in her head, and tease smiles onto her lips until she rolled her eyes in exasperation. *Adoration* seemed such an inadequate word to describe the fiery rush of emotions Sebastian felt whenever she stepped into the room.

Yet his responsibilities to the estate *and* his brothers were never-ending, and try as he might, Sebastian was pulled in multiple directions at once. The crux, though, was that he knew Gabriela was not upset about his dedication to the manor or the people who worked there. She was pulling away because she knew he was keeping something from her.

That something—or rather *those someones* were currently making animal noises as they finished their lunch. Sebastian watched them, his throat tight. Finding the boys had filled him with a sense of purpose, a need to breathe life back into Whitfield Manor again. Yet it wasn't until Gabriela had arrived as the new Duchess of Whitfield, with her generous heart, nononsense demeanor, and tart tongue, that the old manor house had begun to feel like home again. Sebastian hadn't realized how little he laughed or smiled until Gabriela gave him a reason to do so. And he'd taken the sparkle from her eyes . . .

"We saw the duchess yesterday," David said suddenly, around a mouthful of apricot.

He went still, watching as James scowled, reaching out to smack his brother's arm. "Lud, Davey, we agreed not to say anything."

The younger boy ducked his head. "I forgot," he mumbled.

Turning to James, Sebastian frowned. "Why wouldn't you tell me you saw Gabriela?"

"Because she was crying," David interjected.

Ignoring how his stomach sank, Sebastian returned to James. His brother cringed. "It's true. We were coming back from fishing at the lake when we saw her in the garden. On that bench under the wisteria arbor. You know the one."

Sebastian nodded.

James dropped his gaze to the tabletop. "We hid as soon as we saw her, but not before we saw her wiping her cheeks."

"And her eyes were all red," David added, most unhelpfully. "Did you do something to make her cry?"

Stealing a moment to pluck his spectacles from his face and massage the bridge of his nose, Sebastian willed the fire scouring inside his ribs to subside. "There are some . . . things I haven't told her yet."

"Why not?" James asked, his gaze darting over Sebastian's face.

"Because I'm scared." When the boys gasped, he nodded. "It's true. I've kept certain things from the duchess because I'm afraid she'll—" Sebastian rubbed his brow. "And now I don't know how to tell her."

James frowned. "So you don't trust her?"

His brother knew how to get to the heart of the matter. "I don't trust that Her Grace will forgive me. She didn't have a high opinion of me before, and has only just started to think well of me—"

"And you're scared she will think ill of you again," James finished, his blue eyes so much wiser than his ten years.

Swallowing convulsively, Sebastian nodded.

"But you're swell, Bastian." David pushed his chair out with a squeak, and came around the table to stand in front of Sebastian. He placed one small hand on his shoulder. "We all make mistakes, and I'm sure if you tell the duchess you're sorry, she'll forgive you. Polly said she's very nice."

Sebastian glanced to James, who nodded in agreement.

"And no matter what, you'll always have us," David declared, accentuating his words by squeezing his shoulder.

Swamped with love and a touch of exasperation for the precocious boy, Sebastian pulled David into a hug.

Distracted as he was, he didn't see the figure lingering in the hallway silently dash away.

How Gabby made it back to her chamber without weeping, she didn't know.

Sebastian was a father, and from the brief glimpse she had of him with his two sons, he was a loving and doting one. Which did not surprise her, because Sebastian was loving and doting.

He was also a liar.

Sinking onto their bed, where her husband had spent countless hours coaxing pleasure from her body and making her feel cherished, Gabby pressed her fist to her mouth to keep from crying. So this was his secret. The mystery the entire household had worked to keep from her. Two small boys, surely no older than ten, who looked at their father with stars in their eyes.

Boys she would have loved if she'd only been given a chance to.

She felt like such a fool. Of course Sebastian had children. Gabby had known from the moment she met him that he was a rake, and in all the years they'd been acquainted, he'd continued to pursue his amorous and sexual exploits. So it seemed natural that a man of his prowess, with his elevated status and power, would have children. That's not why her heart threatened to wrench itself from her chest.

Rather it was that he hadn't told her. Had lied to her when she'd asked if there was anything she needed to know about his past. Not that it would have mattered, because Gabby would have had to marry him anyway . . .

But worse still, the entire staff at Whitfield Manor had conspired with him to keep the boys' existence a secret. They must have thought her so stupid. A silly Mexican girl who couldn't see past her own nose.

She's hardly bright enough to hold the attention of the duke . . .

Gabby bit back a sob as she remembered her father's words. Her heartache threatened to choke her . . . until it was burned away in the torrid blaze that was her anger.

Jumping to her feet, Gabby dashed away her tears and rang the service bell with more force than was warranted. Not waiting for her summons to be answered, she stalked into the dressing room in search of a trunk. As she tossed day gowns, shawls, and undergarments into the case, the chamber door opened.

"Your Grace?" Lupe, her maid, called.

Poking her head out of the room, Gabby flashed a tight smile. "Please ask Roberts to have a carriage or curricle, even a wagon, brought around."

The young woman rocked back on her heels. "O-of course, Your Grace. Should I tell him where we're going?"

"The train station," she said succinctly, turning back to her packing.

Thankfully, Lupe did not ask additional questions and departed immediately to deliver her request.

Gabby was just fixing the clasp on her trunk when the chamber door opened again.

"Lupe, will you please grab that cream and pomade I brought from San Luis Potosí? The ones that smells like vanilla and violets," she called.

"Yes, Your Grace."

The voice was not Lupe's. Gabby took a moment to fortify her defenses, imagining her spine was fused with steel, before she stepped from the dressing room. Mrs. Evers was just leaving the bathing chamber, the cream and pomade she requested in hand. The older woman did not say anything as she handed them to Gabby.

Staring down at the jars, Gabby debated what to say. Remembering how the housekeeper had kept her from investigating the sounds she heard in the attic just three weeks prior, Gabby decided the older woman deserved no explanation.

That did not keep Mrs. Evers from lingering near the door, observing Gabby as she grabbed books that had been gifts from Isabel. When she snatched up her shawl, the house-keeper finally cleared her throat.

"I understand your intention is to travel to the train station." Gabby glanced at the woman, finding her worrying her hands. "Would you like me to instruct a footman to purchase a ticket for you and Lupe?"

"I can purchase our tickets," Gabby said, and nothing more.

Mrs. Evers swallowed. "Is there anything I can do to assist you?"

Gabby slowly arched a brow. "I believe you've done enough, Mrs. Evers."

She tried to keep the bitterness from her tone, but she knew she failed when the housekeeper flinched.

Still, the woman was not easily cowed, because Mrs. Evers took a step toward Gabby, her complexion pale.

"Shall I have the duke's trunks packed, as well? Will he be meeting you at a later date?"

Her courage faltered at the mention of Sebastian. "I-I'm unaware of the duke's plans. But His Grace appeared to have his hands full when I saw him in the nursery earlier today."

She gleaned a small sliver of satisfaction from the way Mrs. Evers further blanched. Yet Gabby was suddenly exhausted. So very weary of fighting to be seen. To be respected. To matter enough . . . for the truth.

Surveying the room one last time, doing her best to block out all the happy memories she'd made within the surrounding walls, Gabby spied the letter from her parents peeking out from the book on her side table. She grabbed it and slipped it into her pocket before she quit the room. Without a word to Mrs. Evers, Gabby walked down the stairs, confident the housekeeper would instruct a footman to bring her trunk to the conveyance.

Roberts met her in the foyer, his face pale as his gaze bounced between her and the yard beyond. "Your Grace, I'm sure the duke will want to see you off before you depart. Perhaps it would be best to wait for him."

Gabby shook her head as she donned her gloves. "No. Waiting is unnecessary."

The butler and Mrs. Evers exchanged glances but said nothing more. Gabby was grateful because her mask of polite yet firm disinterest was beginning to slip.

The ride to the train station was done in silence, and Gabby was thankful to discover that Mrs. Evers had disregarded her objection and had a footman secure a private car for her. With her arms wrapped around her waist, Gabby watched as the train pulled out from the station, leaving the quaint little village she had come to love behind.

Now alone, she pulled the letter from her pocket and stared at her mother's sloping penmanship. Gabby was already depressed and dejected, so it seemed an appropriate time as any to read her parents' words. Unfolding the parchment, she locked her jaw and read:

Querida hija, felicidades por tu matrimonio con el duque. Nosotros estamos orgullosos de ti . . .

The letter crumpled in her palm, and Gabby pressed it to her chest, finally allowing herself the luxury of tears.

26

Sebastian knew something was wrong as soon as he saw Mrs. Evers waiting near the garden gate.

"Boys, wash your hands and see if Cook has a snack to share. She usually bakes shortbread on Thursdays," he added with a whisper.

"Yay," James and David cheered, sprinting toward the back door without another word.

He watched them scamper away, although his attention had already turned to the housekeeper. "Has something happened?"

"The duchess left."

Sebastian kicked up gravel as he spun to face her. "What? Ella's left?"

"She has, Your Grace. More than an hour ago," Mrs. Evers said, her expression grave.

Panic tore through his body, robbing it of air. Gabriela had left? Why?

Regaining his voice, Sebastian demanded, "Why didn't anyone tell me? I should have been told the moment she asked for the carriage."

"We couldn't find you, Your Grace." The housekeeper swept

an arm in the direction of the lake. "Thomas searched all along the beach for you, and even up to the quarry."

He ripped his hat from his head and shoved his trembling hand through his hair. "We were in the southwest fields with the new lambs."

Mrs. Evers pressed her lips together. Eventually she glanced back at the manor. "She saw you in the nursery."

Only his good manners and the deep respect he had for Mrs. Evers kept him from cursing aloud. As it was, Sebastian clenched his eyes closed as he imagined what Gabriela thought when she'd seen him with James and David.

The gravel crunched under the older woman's feet as she approached. "Since you left for Eton, I've done my best not to interfere with your life. I've never wanted to overstep boundaries." Sebastian glanced up to meet Mrs. Evers's gaze, unsurprised to find her staring sternly at him. It was a look he found just as intimidating now as he had as a boy. "But you were foolish not to tell the duchess the truth."

"I know," he sighed, dropping his chin to his chest.

"And you made us all complicit in your lie." The housekeeper huffed an angry breath. "I had to see the hurt and disappointment in that girl's eyes, and know I helped put it there."

A scorching shame encased him from his head to his feet.

"The duchess has been nothing but warm and genial since she arrived, and has had a smile for everyone. She would have loved our boys, if you had just let her." Mrs. Evers was silent for a moment, and Sebastian simply stood there, disgrace rooting him to the ground. "Now what are you going to do to make this better?"

What could he do? Hadn't Sebastian just confirmed all of Gabriela's worst beliefs about him? That he was a rakish liar with little morals?

At that moment, Sebastian wanted nothing more than to get lost in the bottom of a brandy bottle. He could think of no better way to erase the image his mind conjured of Gabriela heartbroken and betrayed. Fuck, he really was a cad.

"Master Sebastian, listen to me," his housekeeper began, planting her feet before him. "Did the duchess make you happy?"

He nodded, miserable.

Mrs. Evers clicked her tongue. "Of course she did. I've never seen you smile and laugh as much as you have since you married her . . . even when your dear mother was alive."

He turned his head away so she wouldn't see how his throat worked.

"You deserve to be happy, Your Grace. We all want you to be happy."

Happiness now seemed like an impossibility with Gabriela gone.

Plucking his spectacles from his nose, Sebastian covered his face with his hand. "I don't deserve her."

Mrs. Evers was silent until he dragged his gaze to hers. "I wouldn't dare say whether you deserve her or not, but what I do know is that girl loves you."

"Do you think so?" Sebastian asked, ignoring the longing in his voice.

The older woman's expression softened. "How could she not love you? You're your mother's son."

Pivoting on his heel, he blindly wandered several steps away. Sebastian stared at the distant lake, sparkling like a sapphire in the countryside. "I haven't felt much like her son lately."

"Perhaps not . . . but there's always time to do better."

The gentle hum of the breeze and the chatter of birds flitting to and fro in the garden serenaded them as Sebastian grappled with his wayward emotions. Everything he feared had come to fruition, and he had no one to blame but himself. Sucking a deep breath of sweet air into his lungs, he willed it to ease his guilt-addled mind so that he could find a way forward.

If he wanted to earn Gabriela's forgiveness, he needed to swallow his pride. He'd already made Gabriela swallow so much of her own.

Adjusting his spectacles, Sebastian turned to his housekeeper. "Will you have Polly pack a trunk for the boys? They'll need clothes for a week, at least."

The older woman smiled. "I'll make sure it's done right away. Should I have a telegram sent to Whitfield Place, letting them know of your impending arrival?"

"Yes, please." Without another word, Sebastian turned to prowl up the garden path . . . when he stumbled to a halt. "I'm sorry for asking you to act so outside of your character. I'm ashamed I let this go on for so long."

"Now that the duchess knows, you have to decide how you want to proceed. If you love her, tell her. If you're sorry, apologize."

"You make it sound so easy." When Mrs. Evers laughed, he smiled . . . but he quickly sobered. "She might not even hear my apology."

"She might not," the housekeeper agreed, "but you have to try."

Sebastian repeated those words as he packed the paperwork he might need during his time in London. After speaking with his steward and the foreman overseeing the renovations about the work to be done in his absence, Sebastian made his way to the nursery. The sight of the boys excitedly clutching their knapsacks filled with an assortment of books and toys made his chest a tad lighter.

"Are you ready to visit London?"

James and David nodded, but it was the older boy who said, "We're going to help you win back the duchess."

"She'll have to forgive you when we tell her what a great brother you are," David added, with the effortless bravado of an eight-year-old.

"I don't think I've been a great husband, though." Shifting on his feet, Sebastian sighed. "And I've *not* been a good brother. I should have introduced you to Gabriela as soon as we arrived. I'm sorry, boys. I kept you both a secret as if I were ashamed you're my brothers, when I'm so damn proud."

The boys stared at him, their brows puckered in consternation.

"You're truly not embarrassed?" James asked, his blue gaze serious.

"Not at all." Sebastian crouched down until they were face-to-face. "I'm sorry I ever made you believe I was."

James nodded while David clasped his hand. "Then we'll definitely help you."

Sebastian closed his eyes, allowing himself a moment to soak up his brothers' love and support. Surely this was what it felt like to have a family.

It was a feeling he was determined to share with Gabriela. If he wasn't too late.

Gabby had been at Yardley House for exactly one hour when she was summoned to join the viscountess in her private salon.

Standing outside the room now, Gabby mentally prepared herself for the assault that was Lady Yardley. The train ride to London had been uneventful, which she was thankful for because it allowed her to privately let loose the sobs that tore at her throat and the tears that blistered her eyes. A porter had hailed a hackney for her and Lupe, and she hadn't thought twice to direct the driver to Yardley House. Although she craved Ana María's comforting embrace, Gabby was not ready for her sister's questions. She was certainly not prepared to defend her husband from Gideon's recriminations, especially when she wasn't certain Sebastian deserved her defense.

Just thinking his name flooded her with a confusing deluge of emotions . . . emotions she could not focus on if she was to survive this visit with Lady Yardley.

Inhaling a bracing breath, Gabby sailed into the room and took her customary seat on the settee across from the viscountess's armchair.

The older woman peered at her impassively before she leaned forward to pour Gabby a cup of tea. She accepted it with a quiet "Gracias."

Surprisingly, Lady Yardley didn't immediately launch into an inquiry. Didn't say anything aside from benign observations about the weather. Gabby was instantly suspicious.

A suspicion that was proven right when the drawing room door suddenly opened and Ana María appeared on the threshold. Her gaze immediately snared hers, and Gabby flinched. Her eldest sister took a seat directly next to her, and reached out to grasp her hand.

"Right, now that you've arrived, let's get started," Lady Yardley declared, turning her sharp eyes on Gabby. "Why are you here?"

Gabby jerked her chin back. "Well, it's nice to see you, too."

The viscountess snorted. "Oh, now you're concerned with niceties. After you showed up on my doorstep on a random Thursday with no advance notice. Did you really think I wouldn't have questions?"

"I knew you would," Gabby grumbled, crossing her arms over her chest. "I had just hoped you would give me more time to get comfortable."

"Get comfortable?" Lady Yardley cocked a brow. "Will you be staying long?"

"Your ladyship," Ana María snapped, flashing the older woman a censorious look, "you're not helping."

"And what *would* help, Ana dear?" The viscountess tossed her hands in the air. "Gabriela should be in Gloucestershire with her husband, yet she's here. In my home. I think I deserve to know why."

Gabby rolled her eyes. "I thought you'd be happy for me to visit."

Lady Yardley blinked. "You did? What a darling you are."

"Escúcheme," Gabby began, narrowing her eyes on the older woman—

"Ay, Gabby"—Ana María smacked her leg—"you arrived in London with no warning and without the duke, and we're not supposed to ask any questions? You're not being reasonable, querida."

She wasn't. Gabby knew as much, and yet she'd rather verbally tussle with Lady Yardley all the daytime hours than confess how her husband broke her heart.

But the viscountess and her staff had welcomed her and Lupe back without a word of complaint. The least she could do was be more forthcoming.

Even if the thought of confessing what she'd learned filled her mouth with glass.

Staring at the rug for a long moment, Gabby inhaled around her teeth. "I discovered Sebastian has illegitimate children and they live at Whitfield Manor."

That was not at all how Gabby intended to broach the subject, and based on Lady Yardley's and Ana María's slack jaws, neither had they.

Her sister recovered first. "Are you saying"—Ana María coughed into her fist—"that Whitfield has illegitimate children living at his country estate and he never told you about them?"

"Yes."

The women exchanged a glance. Once again, it was Ana María who ventured a response, although it left much to be desired.

"Well . . . surely he meant to tell you."

This ignited her anger, and Gabby hissed, "But did he? We've been married for almost four weeks, and those boys have been there the whole time. Instead of telling me about them, Sebastian instructed the staff to distract me whenever I got too close or heard something I wasn't supposed to. He actively lied to me when I asked where he'd been or who he'd spent time with. It doesn't seem like he had *any* intention of telling me."

Ana María's gaze turned gentle. "I'm sorry. You don't deserve that sort of disrespect."

Gabby leaned into her sister's side, thankful for her presence.

Lady Yardley had remained largely silent during their exchange, but she finally asked, "What exactly did you see to make you believe His Grace has children?"

"I saw Sebastian in the nursery at Whitfield Manor with two young boys." Gabby stared unseeing out the window. "They had his blue eyes. Those pale blue eyes I've only ever seen on the duke."

Just thinking about the resemblance made bile rise to the back of her throat.

"His father had those same striking eyes." The viscountess shook her head. "He was a *very* handsome man, but all that beauty hid a festering heart. He was a notorious hedonist, even after his marriage to Lady Beatrice Moore." The older woman's gaze was far away. "Lady Bea was a duke's daughter and the diamond of her debut season, but more importantly, she was a lovely person. So witty and lively. But once she married old Whitfield, she all but disappeared from society. The duke was seen cavorting all over London and beyond, but not his wife. It makes me sad to think about what she endured as his duchess."

The back of her eyes burned, but Gabby refused to acknowledge it. Sebastian had already told her about his parents, and while her heart ached for his late mother and the boy he had been, it didn't take away from what he'd done *now*.

"That makes me incredibly sad for His Grace," Ana María said, "but that doesn't excuse what he's done to Gabby."

"Of course not." Lady Yardley's brows dipped low. "Tell me, Gabriela, did you hear him refer to them as his sons? Or the boys call him father?"

"Well, no," Gabby admitted, frowning.

"Then maybe they're cousins. Or even brothers." Lady Yardley glanced at Ana María, her lip curled. "I wouldn't put it past the late duke to have bastards scattered throughout the United Kingdom."

Gabby didn't know what to say to that. Despite Sebastian's revelation about his late father's character, Gabby hadn't really considered him beyond that. Could the boys be his brothers?

"Regardless of whether these children are Whitfield's or not doesn't negate the fact that he failed to tell Gabby about them." Ana María scowled.

"Exactamente," Gabby cried, clapping her hands together. "The boys themselves are not the issue. Rather it's that Sebastian never told me about them. Everyone at the manor knew of them except me. I feel so stupid."

The viscountess smiled, the gesture tinged with melancholy. "You have every right to be upset, my dear. You have always despised being left out."

Gabby huffed. "It's not about that—"

"Actually, I think it is," Ana María interjected, shifting on the settee to meet Gabby's gaze. "By not telling you about the children, Whitfield excluded you. He made you feel as if you were not worthy of knowing his secrets. He made you feel as if you were lacking, when it's obvious you are the best thing to ever happen to him."

"You're just saying that," Gabby managed with her broken voice.

"I'm not, querida." Ana María stroked her thumb over Gabby's knuckles. "I know your childhood was often lonely because you were overlooked by Father for no fault of your own. You shouldn't have to settle for the same behavior from your husband."

Unable to keep from crying any longer, Gabby covered her face with her hands. Tears slipped through her fingers, and her shoulders shook with her suppressed sobs, but her sister's presence by her side was a comfort.

"Gabriela," Lady Yardley eventually said, waiting patiently for Gabby to drop her hands and meet her gaze. "You have to speak with the duke."

She sniffled, wiping tears from her cheeks.

"You have to let him explain. He should apologize, and if he doesn't, you need to demand it. You have to begin as you mean to go on, and that means Whitfield must respect you. You deserve respect, and I don't want you to settle for anything less," the viscountess said, her tone firm.

Gabby nodded.

"And, my dear," Lady Yardley began, raising her brows, "you can't keep running away."

"I d-don't understand," she stammered.

"Don't you?" Lady Yardley sniffed. "First you left for Mexico when that rat Carlisle made trouble, and then you fled back to England when your father did. And at the first hint of trouble with Whitfield, you fled here to London. I think I can speak for Ana when I say that we will always be a safe place for you to turn to should you need us. But sometimes, my darling girl, you have to face your problems head-on."

Hiccuping, Gabby turned to look at Ana María. Her sister brought their clasped hands to her lips and kissed the back of Gabby's hand. "You're fearless for everyone else, querida. Save some of that fire for yourself."

Gabby closed her eyes and soaked in their words. They made it sound so simple to face her problems, when her first instinct was to run far away from the pain. As Lady Yardley said, it's what she did.

But if she cared about Sebastian, and wanted their marriage to be successful, Gabby needed to put her fears of rejection aside. She needed to confront Sebastian directly.

"Have I been a coward?" she asked in a whisper.

"Not at all, hermanita." Ana María squeezed her fingers. "You're just used to being treated cheaply by those who should love you the most, and you wanted to spare yourself that hurt."

Gabby once told Sebastian she would be brave for him, and yet here she was in London, suffering over his perceived slight, instead of standing before him and demanding an explanation. She deserved one, and he deserved an opportunity to give it.

She just hoped she was brave enough to listen to whatever he had to say.

Straightening her spine, Gabby released a long, pent-up breath. "I'll depart for Gloucestershire in the morning."

"Would you like me to go with you?" Ana María asked.

Ay, she loved her sister. "That's very kind of you—"

A knock sounded on the door, and the ladies turned to watch the butler open it. "The Duke of Whitfield is here, your ladyship."

Gabby started, her eyes flying wide. But before she had a moment to prepare herself, Sebastian filled the doorway, his gaze immediately finding hers.

27

"There you are," Sebastian murmured, stepping fully into the room. His arctic eyes roamed over her, relief evident on his face. Seeming to realize she wasn't alone, Sebastian stiffened, before turning to Lady Yardley and Ana María. "Good evening, ladies."

"Your Grace," Lady Yardley drawled, crooking one judgmental eyebrow. "I suppose you'd like to speak with Gabriela."

Sebastian nodded, glancing back at her. "If she's willing to speak with me, that is."

Three pairs of eyes turned to her, and Gabby fought not to squirm. Hadn't she just declared she would depart for Whitfield Manor? Yet now that Sebastian stood before her, his painfully handsome face so dear, his gaze so pleading, Gabby wanted nothing more than to flee to her room. She longed to escape the maelstrom of feelings crashing about in her chest, sentiments that always left her off balance.

Gabby's gaze drifted to Lady Yardley, who was staring back at her expectedly. She could almost hear the older woman say, *Are you going to get on with it?*

Setting her jaw, Gabby slowly rose to her feet and skirted to stand behind a nearby armchair. "Ana? My lady? Would you mind giving the duke and me a moment alone?"

"Por supuesto," Ana murmured, immediately making her way toward the door. "Your ladyship?" she said, glancing back at the viscountess.

"Yes, yes, I'm coming." Lady Yardley glowered as she stood, and pinned Sebastian with a gimlet stare. "You may have more than a moment, but only because I've always believed you were more your mother's son than your father's. *Don't* prove me wrong."

A flush swept over Sebastian's cheeks, and he ducked his head. "I won't, your ladyship."

"Hmph." And with that, the viscountess looped her arm around Ana María's and they quit the room.

The air seemed to grow thick and taut in the women's absence, and Gabby curled her hands around the chairback to keep them from shaking. She also pressed her tongue to the roof of her mouth so she wouldn't nervously blurt out nonsense to fill the awkward silence. Sebastian had followed her to London to speak with her, so she would let him speak.

The duke walked to the unlit fireplace, where he gripped the mantel and stared into the hearth. His shoulders were tense, his jaw like granite. At one time, Gabby would have thought him angry, but she knew him better now. He was uncomfortable. *Good.* She was uncomfortable, too.

After another quiet moment, Sebastian raked his fingers through his hair and pivoted to face her. "The boys are my brothers."

Gabby inhaled sharply. It was just as the viscountess had said. A bright beam of relief pierced through her chest, but she refused to let it warm her.

Sebastian paced back and forth before the fireplace. "I only learned of James and David some eleven or so months ago, and managed to track them down to an orphanage in Dover. Their mother had placed them there after my father died and the checks stopped arriving."

She clamped her eyes closed. Those poor boys. "How long were they there?" Gabby finally asked.

"Several years." Sebastian's throat bobbed. "Long enough for James to become a bit jaded. He's fiercely protective of his younger brother, and it's taken me time to earn his trust. I've been . . . protective of him in turn."

His eyes shined like aquamarines, and Gabby could understand his apprehension. Wouldn't she battle La Lechuza with her bare hands if it meant to harm her sisters?

"I'm sure getting to know each other has been a slow process." Gabby thought of Ana María and Isabel, and how they didn't have a relationship until they were sent to England. Forming their sisterly bonds had created the most fulfilling friendships of her life, but it had not been easy. Gabby couldn't imagine doing it with two small, scared boys.

"It has been," Sebastian agreed, glancing down at his feet. "If I hadn't already had my trip to Mexico planned, I never would have left them."

But he had, and the trip had changed everything about their relationship with each other. Gabby could never be sorry for it, even if her trust had now been broken.

"Were you ever going to tell me?"

She hated how her voice cracked.

"Of course." Sebastian took a step toward her, his hand outstretched. He stumbled to a halt, his expression stricken. His arm fell to his side with a thud. "I had every intention of introducing you to the boys. They've asked frequently to meet you, especially David."

Gabby pressed her lips together to keep from smiling.

"It just never seemed like the right time. I wanted you to have an opportunity to adjust to life at the manor." His shoulders fell on a sigh. "I know you were hesitant to marry me, so I didn't want to give you a reason to leave."

Would the news have changed the way Gabby viewed him? Would it have confirmed the fears she once possessed about Sebastian and his rakish past?

The truth must have shown in her eyes, because Sebastian ran a hand across his forehead. "I had hoped that after we'd been married for a spell, perhaps your feelings for me would soften any ire you felt when you learned the truth."

She froze, static filling her ears. "You thought if I fell in love with you, I wouldn't feel betrayed that you lied to me?"

Sebastian's mouth opened and closed. "I suppose . . . yes."

"Well, you pompous idiot, I fell in love with you a long time ago, and I'm *still* livid you kept the truth from me!"

The room was as quiet and still as a tomb. Gabby couldn't believe she had said such a thing, especially because she didn't realize how much she loved him until the moment the words flew from her mouth.

"Ella," Sebastian whispered. He advanced a step but paused, a bit breathless. "I love you, too."

Tears clouded her vision, her chest so full it ached. Gabby mercilessly blinked them away. "You do?"

"Of course I do. How could I not?" Sebastian wandered closer, his blue, blue eyes glassy. "You're the smartest, kindest, most stunning woman I have ever known. There is a smile on my lips when I awake at the simple promise I'll see you. Hear your laugh. Exchange verbal barbs with you."

Gabby pressed a hand to her mouth to hide how her lips trembled.

"I told myself that just being married to you would be enough. I didn't need you to love me because I had enough love for the both of us." He shrugged. "Because even living in the shadow of your smile would have sustained me."

Sebastian loved her. It seemed so surprising, but hadn't he shown her, in ways big and small, that she was precious to him?

Ignoring the tears that trailed down her cheeks, Gabby threw her arms wide. "Why then did you lie to me? You can't love someone if you don't respect them, and you disrespected me when you withheld the truth. When you made me feel like an outsider in my new home."

"Christ, Ella, I'm sorry." He deflated before her. "My intention was not for you to be excluded. I was just . . . afraid."

Gabby moved around the armchair. "Afraid?"

He nodded. "Yes. That you would realize that life with me, at Whitfield Manor, was not what you wanted. That scandal had forced you to settle. I was afraid you would come to believe I locked you away, just as my mother had been." Sebastian roughly yanked a hand through his hair. "Every morning I've had a knot in my throat wondering if that would be the day you finally left, because I knew you leaving wouldn't just break my heart, it would break James's and David's hearts, as well."

Closing her eyes, Gabby swallowed back a sob. Ay Dios, did he think she was so uncaring? *But you did flee the second you suspected something was amiss.* Despite how Sebastian had proven himself to be kind and gentle, Gabby had left for London without a word to him, confirming his worst fears. Regret twisted and churned in her gut.

"Every person in their young lives has abandoned them, and despite the big, loving heart you have, I was terrified that if I wasn't enough, you would do the same." Sebastian exhaled noisily. "Still, I should have told you about the boys the afternoon I asked you to marry me. You should have been introduced to them the moment we arrived at Whitfield Manor, but the secret was already so big, that I knew you would feel betrayed. I'm sorry. If I could go back and change things, I would. Your regard seemed like such a fragile thing, and I wanted to protect it. In reality, I shattered it into a million pieces."

Gabby believed him. Despite her own fears and the heartache she'd experienced that day, the love that burned and glowed in her chest had not been extinguished.

"Not a million pieces. Just one or two. But together"—she reached for her bravery and went to him, wrapping her arms around his waist—"maybe we can glue it back together."

"Together," Sebastian breathed.

She let loose a sigh when he enfolded her in his embrace . . . but to her great horror, the sigh turned into a sob. A violent sob that tore from her chest and rattled her frame. "I'm sorry I made you think your love"—she hiccuped—"and this life we're building together, wasn't enough. But it will never last if you don't trust me."

Sebastian held her tighter, his cheek pillowed against the crown of her head. In between her shuddering cries, Gabby heard him whisper, "Never again, my love. Never again."

Eventually, her sobs quieted, but Gabby was not ready to leave Sebastian's arms. The day they had spent apart had felt like a lifetime, and Gabby was ready to return to the manor. "I'd like to meet the boys," she murmured softly.

He paused. "You would?"

"Of course I would." Gabby looked up to meet his gaze. "Sebastian, you have brothers. After your solitary childhood, you have a family to fill the manor house with love and laughter. I'm happy for you."

His smile was crooked. "You're the most important part

of my family, Ella. The boys have brought a sense of purpose to my life. But you"—Sebastian's hold on her tightened—"my darling wife, have brought it joy, and a love so bright it blinds me."

That emotion she once refused to name, but now knew was love, threatened to burst free from her chest. Gabby rose up on her toes and kissed her husband, allowing that love to flow into him instead.

"You really want to meet the boys?" Sebastian asked several minutes later.

Gabby panted against his lips. "I would. Very much."

"I'm glad, because they're here."

"They are?" Gabby jumped back, peering around him to look toward the door. "Where? Have they been waiting for us this whole time?"

"Relax, my love. I'm certain your sister and Lady Yardley learned they were in attendance as soon as they left the room, and have been entertaining them." Sebastian grinned down at her. "Shall we go find them?"

"Sí, por favor." Gripping Sebastian's hand, she led him to the door, but halted. Biting her lips, she dared to ask, "Do you think they'll like me?"

Sebastian grabbed her shoulders and turned her to face him. His knuckles caressed along her cheek as he tucked a curl behind her ear. "They're going to love you. Just like I do."

Gabby exhaled, confident he was telling the truth.

It was not hard to find the boys, because Sebastian and Gabby followed the sound of their laughter. Opening the door to the drawing room on the first floor, they discovered James and David standing in the center of the room, their faces animated as they gestured wildly. Lady Yardley and Ana María were seated side by side on the sofa as the boys apparently recounted a harrowing experience with a ram. Gabby glanced up at Sebastian in question.

"I'll tell you later," her husband murmured from the corner of his mouth.

For her part, Ana María played the part of a captivated audience perfectly, her dark eyes appropriately large as she said, "You were both very brave."

"I'm sure if you had heeded the steward's warning and not gone into the sheep pasture, you wouldn't have had to worry about the ram." The viscountess cocked her head. "Right?"

The taller of the boys ducked his chin, but the younger one planted his hand on his hip and replied, "Sure, but what fun is there in that?"

A bark of laughter exploded from Gabby's mouth, and all the heads in the room turned in her direction before she could contain it. Ana María's gaze bounced between her and Sebastian, a pleased smile lighting her face when she saw their hands linked.

"I should have known you'd find such behavior humorous. You probably would have been in that pasture, staring down the ram, with them," Lady Yardley drawled, although there was no ire in her voice. She glanced at Sebastian. "Perhaps you could make proper introductions, Your Grace."

"I would be happy to." Sebastian stepped forward and the boys moved to his side. "Duchess, allow me to introduce James White and David White, my brothers." The elder boy bowed respectfully, while the younger boy, David, grinned impishly. "Boys, this is Gabriela Luna Brooks, the Duchess of Whitfield. You will address her as Your Grace or Her Grace."

"Actually," Gabby said, crouching down so she could meet their eyes, "I'd prefer for you to call me Gabby. We're family, after all."

"I like Gabby much better than Your Grace." David scratched behind his ear. "Although I knew a Grace at the home and she was perfectly swell."

"Davey," James hissed, "stop blabbering."

David scowled. "I'm not blabbering. I'm just talking to the duchess." He turned his blue gaze, so much like Sebastian's, on Gabby. "You're just as pretty as Polly said you were."

"It's true, Your Grace," James said quietly, his cheeks coloring.

Gabby, too, flushed to the roots of her hair. She had never put much stock in remarks on her appearance, but no compliment had touched her quite like the one just uttered by these two young boys.

"She's also a talented hopscotch player," Sebastian said, sliding his arm around Gabby's waist.

"You are?" David exclaimed, looking at her with added interest.

James stepped forward, his handsome little face solemn. "Will you be returning with us to the manor, Your—er, Gabby?"

Filling her lungs with air, Gabby glanced up at Sebastian. Her husband cocked a brow, and the ghost of a smirk tipped up his lips. She grinned.

"The manor is my home. There's nowhere else I'd rather be."

EPILOGUE

June 1872

Dancourt Abbey had changed much in the nine years since Gabby and her sisters had taken refuge there, but had lost none of its charm.

"Sirius has been in discussions with O'Brien and the other men about how best to approach the abbey renovations." Isabel squinted as she glanced across the lawn in the direction of the old abbey ruins. "It's been almost three hundred years since the nunnery closed, and the men want to reuse as much of the original materials as they can."

"Because the old materials contain all the character." Ana María raised a glass of lemonade to her lips and took a leisurely sip. "Can you imagine what those old stones bore witness to?"

"Probably a good number of nuns sneaking in and out of each other's rooms—"

"Gabby!" her sisters cried in shocked unison.

Gabby doubted she'd ever grow tired of scandalizing her sisters. Raising a shoulder, she smiled. "But am I wrong?"

"Ay Dios, I've missed you," Isabel said, reaching out to squeeze Gabby's hand.

"And I you," she replied, lacing their fingers together and holding her older sister tight.

With Mexico settling into an era of reformation after Maximilian and his generals were executed and the French were driven back to Europe, the sisters had found ways to strengthen their bonds across the distance between them. Isabel, Sirius, and their twin boys, Daniel and Gabriel, had arrived from San Luis Potosí a fortnight prior and had invited all the family to join them for an extended visit at their country home, Dancourt Abbey. The family had visited at least once a year since they departed to Mexico, but this was their longest planned visit since the boys had been born. After years of planning, Sirius was finally ready to tackle the renovations to the old abbey ruins where Ana María and Gideon had married years before. Most of the blueprints had been agreed upon, but there were still some decisions to be made, and Isabel and Sirius would remain in England until the first phase of renovation was underway. And now that Señora Maza de Juárez had passed away, Isabel's schedule was not as demanding as it had been.

Gabby and Sebastian had quickly accepted the invitation, ready to quit their busy social and political schedules in London for a spell. The preceding months had been particularly grueling for Gabby as she had helped to launch another medical clinic in Whitechapel, near the parish church where Ana María and Gideon attended. The clinic's focus was to meet the medical needs of women in the area, including pregnant women, new mothers, and their children. Gabby continued to be inspired by her visit to Doctora Jimenez's clinic in San Luis Potosí, and after she'd settled into married life, Gabby had turned her attention to the project, more than willing to use her title as Duchess of Whitfield to accomplish her goal. She had planned the endeavor meticulously, with help and advice from Isabel, Doctora Jimenez, and Ana María. The clinic in Whitechapel was the fourth such clinic she'd helped open over the years of her marriage, a feat that had only been possible with the financial support of a group of wealthy patronesses she'd recruited from among the ton. Gabby had courted them methodically, stealthily, and with a barge full of charm, Sebastian declared. It certainly helped that Gabby's duchess coronet had made her more popular than ever. She fought the urge to roll her eyes when she remembered the fawning articles that had been written after their marriage. Society certainly loved the story of a reformed rake . . . and Gabby loved Sebastian enough not to make a fuss about the narrative.

"I'm so thankful you were able to convince Mother to accompany you, Isa," Ana María murmured, her voice filled with emotion.

Pressing her lips together, Gabby allowed her gaze to rest on her mother, who sat under a willow tree with Lady Yardley, the older women watching the children and men play cricket on the pitch. While neither Gabby nor María Elena had ever discussed the fraught nature of their last conversation before Gabby fled back to England, Gabby sensed her mother was regretful for how the situation unfolded. Her mother had never offered an apology, but neither had Gabby provided an explanation. Rather the women had continued on as if nothing had transpired, an act made infinitely easier by the fact that Gabby had married the duke.

Sliding her eyes from María Elena, Gabby sighed when her gaze touched on Sebastian showing their daughter, Sofia, how to field the mid off position. Sofia was several months shy of her third birthday, but she may as well have been anticipating her thirtieth for all the stubborn, no-nonsense attitude she displayed. Sebastian was amused to no end by her toddler antics, and Sofia exploited her father's soft heart, using it to extend bedtimes and forgive her naughty behavior in equal measure. On more than one occasion, Gabby had vented to Ana María of her daughter's headstrong behavior only for her older sister to remind her that Sofia was much more like her mother than her father, and Gabby had not known whether to be proud or disgruntled. The previous evening, Sofia had stomped her foot and pouted, her blue eyes flashing, after being told it was bedtime, and Gabby had not missed how her older sisters had exchanged diverted glances as they watched her tend to her daughter.

Being a mother had been a challenge, but Gabby was thankful she had a partner in Sebastian. Unlike their own fathers, both of whom deigned to notice their children only when it suited them, Sebastian was doting and gentle. He could be firm with Sofia when necessary, but her duke genuinely enjoyed spending time with their daughter, and Gabby was not surprised. Sebastian had shown her, first with his regard toward their niece, Estella, and then with David and James, that his arrogant manner masked a deep well of love.

Thinking of the wonderful father Sebastian was brought her own father to mind. Elías Luna had not wished to make the long trip to England with his old friend Presidente Juárez in poor health. Gabby knew her father wasn't in the best health himself, as he had curtailed many of his duties after he had suffered a stroke the year prior. Isabel said Elías had softened after his health scare, and spent more time with his grandsons, regaling them with tales of his youth. But more often, their father could be found with Juárez, and Gabby thought it almost poetic that the men, who'd been by each other's side through all manner of trials, would spend their last days together.

"When do the boys return to Eton, Gabby?" Isabel asked.

Gabby swung her gaze to the cricket pitch, where David demonstrated an overhand bowl while James explained the mechanics to Gabriel, Daniel, and Benjamin, Ana María and Gideon's son. "September. Sebastian is thrilled he has so much time to spend with them. They're accompanying us when we travel to San Luis Potosí next month."

"Daniel and Gabe will be elated." A small smile curled Isabel's lips as she watched her sons. "The twins are surrounded by extended family in Mexico, but it's different . . . it's *special* when they get to spend time with their cousins."

Exhaling a shaking breath, Gabby nodded. James and David had been integrated seamlessly into the family, and Gabby struggled to remember what life was like before they had become a part of her happily ever after. Although Sofia kept her busy, Whitfield Manor had been quiet since David left to join James at Eton for the summer term. Sofia had missed them terribly . . . and so had Sebastian.

Ana María released a long breath. "I wish we could travel with you, but we won't be able to leave London until after Gideon's committee meeting. They're so close to pushing through a viable Ballot Act, and Gideon is worried the vote will fall through if he's not there to advocate for it."

"Well, of course he needs to be there," Gabby exclaimed. "If anyone can get the legislation before Parliament, it's Gideon. Sebastian has said numerous times that when Gideon is ready to stand for prime minister, he will be his most vocal supporter."

True to his word, Sebastian had eased into politics, using his influential position to argue for a multitude of reforms. On more than one occasion, Sebastian had lamented the frustrating dance required to advance any meaningful legislation, and he marveled at Gideon's ability to do so, especially considering how he'd earned his political power from pure tenacity.

"Don't worry, Ana, we will be eagerly awaiting your arrival," Isabel said, patting the back of Ana María's hand. "And then we can travel together to Mexico City to visit Father."

The trip would be the first time the sisters had been in Mexico together since they fled following the Second Battle of Puebla. Ana María, Gabby, and their respective families had visited Isabel in San Luis Potosí, but never at the same time. After their father's stroke, the sisters agreed that they would visit Elías for what would probably be the last time, before they introduced their children to the city they spent their childhoods in. It would be a difficult trip to take, but Gabby was thankful her sisters and Sebastian would be there to do it with her.

"Do you ever wonder what your life would be like now if Puebla didn't fall?" Isabel asked suddenly, turning in her chair to face her and Ana María. "Would the person you are in the depths of your heart be who you are today?"

Gabby blinked. She'd been so young when they'd fled Mexico City in the middle of the night. Young, scared, and angry. But in the many years since, Gabby had encountered ideas and met people who challenged her and taught her, and shaped the Gabriela she was now. Her father would never have allowed her such freedom had her life in Mexico continued on uninterrupted.

She looked to the pitch again, where Sebastian helped Sofia hit the cricket ball and then scooped her up and dashed with her to the first wicket while her tíos and cousins scrambled to field the ball. Her husband's and daughter's combined laughter brought a grin to her face, and Gabby sat back, rubbing at her gently swollen belly where the newest member of the family was just beginning to make its presence known.

"I don't want to think about what life would be like, because my life is perfect *now*. I know where I belong, and it's with Sebastian . . . and the two of you."

Her older sisters exchanged watery smiles, and then the three of them clasped hands as they watched their perfect lives play in the grass before them.

AUTHOR'S NOTE

And just like that, the Luna Sisters series has come to an end. *Gabriela and His Grace* was an incredibly difficult book for me to write because I knew it was the end, and the idea of saying goodbye to Gabby, Isabel, and Ana María filled me with sadness . . . and yet I'm immensely proud of these books and the stories they told.

When I initially began brainstorming the series, there were certain things I knew for certain: Gideon Fox would one day stand for prime minister, Isabel Luna's story would end in Mexico, and Gabby Luna would marry the Duke of Whitfield. If you've read *Ana María and The Fox* and *Isabel and The Rogue*, the clues were all there, because I wasn't trying to hide the fact that the fiery youngest sister and the sardonic duke would find happiness together. But the path to their happily ever after was not always clear, and I shed several tears when I finally typed the ending.

On the topic of endings, the end of the Luna Sisters series coincides with the end of the Second Mexican Empire. Gabby and Sebastian's story opens in March 1867, which was a pivotal time in Mexico's fight against the imperial French. More than a year earlier, Napoleon III had ordered the withdrawal of troops from the country, thanks in large part to pressure applied by the United States government. With the Civil War over, the Johnson administration increased the aid they sent to Benito Juárez's forces, pushing the French to request the United States remain neutral in the conflict. But US Secretary of State William H. Seward was not interested in remaining neutral and replied that the French withdrawal from Mexico was unconditional. Thus, the French agreed to reduce their troops in phases and ceased sending reinforcements, and on December 19, 1866, Napoleon announced that all troops would be withdrawn, months ahead of schedule. This move was one of the main reasons Gabby was able to return to Mexico when she did. The end of the Mexican Franco empire was near, and battles and skirmishes broke out across the country as Maximilian's supporters struggled to keep their strongholds. During this time, the port city of Veracruz was inundated with vessels and steamer ships departing for Europe, a phenomenon that Gabby and Sebastian encountered in Altamira as they attempted to return to London.

The Battle of Querétaro was mentioned briefly in *Gabriela and His Grace* but was of great significance. Determined to defend the empire, Maximilian and his imperialist supporters began to gather in the city of Querétaro, located northwest of Mexico City. In May 1867, Republican forces (Juárez supporters) laid siege. After an imperial officer betrayed them to the Republicans, the siege ended on May 14 and Maximilian and two of his generals were captured. The archduke had been encouraged to retreat to Mexico City, but he refused, determined to fight with his forces. Instead, Maximilian was quickly court-martialed and sentenced to death, and despite pleas from European royalty and other illustrious individuals,

Benito Juárez refused to commute his sentence because he intended for Maximilian's execution to be a message that Mexico would not tolerate foreign interference again. Thus, on June 19, 1867, Maximilian, along with generals Miguel Miramón and Tomás Mejía, were executed by firing squad on a hill outside of Querétaro. Mexico City surrendered the following day, and Benito Juárez assumed his position as the democratically elected president of Mexico. Although Gabby and Ana María were not there to witness Presidente Juárez's triumphant return to the capital, I like to think that Isabel described it in poetic detail in her celebratory letter to them.

Because of Gabby's deep love for her homeland, I knew a good portion of the action within *Gabriela and His Grace* would take place in Mexico . . . I just didn't know where. After researching the occupation, and tracking where Juárez and supporters were during specific times throughout those years, I landed upon San Luis Potosí, which was an important city throughout the second French occupation. After the Second Battle of Puebla, Juárez and his supporters (including Elías and María Elena Luna) took refuge in the north of Mexico, and Juárez named San Luis Potosí the capital of the country later in 1863. But Juárez's supporters did not stay in San Luis Potosí for long, and by December of that year, they had fled to the northern state of Coahuila as imperialists took hold of the city. However, with the end of the US Civil War in 1865, more money, arms, and supplies flowed across the southern border to Republicans, and Maximilian began to lose control of many regions in the north. Juárez supporters again took control of San Luis Potosí in December 1866 . . . making it the perfect place for Gabby and Sebastian's relationship to flourish. San Luis Potosí has played a pivotal role in several key events in Mexican history, including the Plan of San Luis Potosí, a political document written by Francisco Madero, which advocated for armed resistance to overthrow dictator Porfirio Díaz, who history buffs know served as a general under Benito Juárez during the French occupation and later became president several years after the older man died in 1872.

One last thing I would like to briefly touch upon is the history of healthcare in 1860s Mexico. Throughout much of Mexican history, care of the sick fell upon religious charities. However, when Benito Juárez came to power, his government confiscated church assets, which included hospitals, clinics, orphanages, and even cemeteries. Healthcare services now fell under Juárez's Ministry of Health, and in 1861, Juárez announced the creation of a National Council of Public Charities, which coordinated the conversion of hospitals and clinics to state-run agencies. However, centralizing healthcare often meant that populations in outlying areas were left without services, a void that clinics such as Doctora Jimenez's tried to fill. Whether there were clinics specifically focused on women's healthcare, I don't know, for my research doesn't indicate. But in our modern climate of dwindling freedoms surrounding reproductive healthcare and women's bodily autonomy, it felt more than appropriate to make Gabby's and Isabel's charitable venture be championing the welfare of women. I can only imagine how excited the sisters would be if they knew that in 2024, Mexico would finally elect its first female president, Claudia Sheinbaum!

This is a quick overview of the events surrounding the story within *Gabriela and His Grace*. It's incredibly hard to condense the events of a multiyear conflict into a few paragraphs, so if you are interested in learning more about the second French occupation of Mexico, I encourage you to research this fascinating time in history. One of my goals in writing the Luna

Sisters series was to share a more diverse historical perspective than many historical romances provide because history is vast and vibrant and varied, and we deserve to read stories that explore and celebrate such diversity. My hope is that the Luna Sisters stories added a bit of rich color to the historical romance canon.

ACKNOWLEDGMENTS

Writing the Luna Sisters books has been the joy of my career. There's a sprinkle of me in each sister, as well as a dose of the strong, amazing Latine women in my life. I'm incredibly thankful to a large number of people for helping me bring Gabby, Isabel, and Ana María to life, a group that includes:

Sarah Blumenstock, my savvy editor, who patiently, and expertly, helped me bring every Luna Sisters story to life. My agent, Rebecca Strauss, who responded enthusiastically to my idea of a series focused on three Mexican heiresses and has cheered for them every step of the way. To my amazing team at Berkley, including Liz Sellers, Yazmine Hassan, Jessica Plummer, Hillary Tacuri, Katie Anderson, and Megha Jain—thank you for your unfailing enthusiasm for my sisters and their stories. I will also be forever grateful to, and a fangirl of, Camila Gray, the artist behind the Luna Sisters covers! Each book cover was a work of art and reflected the sisters to perfection, and I remain in awe of Camila's talent!

Special thanks to Madge Maril, Elizabeth Bright, and Lisa Lin, for their steadfast friendship; I've lost count of the number of times you've bolstered my confidence or helped me brainstorm a new idea, and I'll be forever grateful. Big hugs to Flavia Vasquez, for being the best hype person an author could ask for!

Thank you to the LatinxRom crew and the Berkletes, for your continued encouragement. To the independent bookstores who have showcased the Luna Sisters, specifically the amazing teams at the Novel Neighbor, the Ripped Bodice, the Poisoned Pen, Steamy Lit, East City Bookshop, and Changing Hands; I'm so honored to have worked with you!

Most of all, thank you to my amazing readers, especially my Latine readers. The ones who slid into my DMs to gush about Ana María and Gideon, Isabel and Sirius, or to share their theories about Gabby's book. To those who visited me at book signings and showed off their carefully annotated books, and those who shared that they felt seen in the pages of the Luna Sisters novels. Thank you, thank you, thank you for loving Gabby, Isabel, and Ana María, and making all my author dreams come true!

Last but certainly not least, thank you to my family. To my father, who hard sells my books wherever he goes, even if it's standing in line at Disneyland; my sister and brother-in-law, who help me brainstorm (very inappropriate) book titles; and my young daughter, who fondly talks about the fun we'll have when she's old enough to be my book-signing assistant. But most especially, thank you to Matt. Growing old isn't so bad because I get to do it with you.

GABRIELA
AND
HIS GRACE

A LUNA SISTERS NOVEL

Liana De la Rosa

READERS GUIDE

DISCUSSION QUESTIONS

1. *Gabriela and His Grace* opens with Gabby returning to Mexico to escape her British suitors, even though the Second Franco-Mexican War continues on. Have you ever traveled to a place that was in conflict and your safety wasn't guaranteed?

2. Sebastian's investment in the Camino Rojo mine is a lifeline to the Whitfield dukedom, which is struggling to recover from years of neglect. While Sebastian doesn't have to marry Gabby for financial purposes, her dowry certainly helps his cause. What did you think of this subversion of the heiress-saves-the-penniless-duke trope?

3. Gabby is often viewed as the fiery Luna sister; quick to give her opinion and also quick to defend her sisters from derision. Yet Gabby struggles to defend herself from her father's criticisms, revealing she's much more vulnerable than she appears. Do you know a firebrand like Gabby? Do they hide deep vulnerabilities like she does?

4. Both Gabby and Sebastian have/had overbearing, critical fathers. How did their experiences with such a parent shape who they are as people?

5. Gabby and Sebastian's trip to Mexico is right before the end of the Second Franco-Mexican War, and there is discussion around rebuilding a new Mexico. In fact, new beginnings is a theme throughout the book: Gabby returning to Mexico to restart her life; Sebastian's visit to the Camino Rojo mine to ensure his investment will guarantee the Whitfield dukedom has a second chance; and Gabby and Sebastian's antagonism thawing as they fall in love. Why do you think new beginnings are so important to this pair?

6. The deep bonds of sisterhood between Gabby, Isabel, and Ana María continues in *Gabriela and His Grace*. What was your favorite scene between the sisters, and why?

7. As Gabby struggles to find her place and purpose in her new life, she takes on the role of healthcare patroness. If you were in a similar position, what sort of cause(s) would you champion?

8. The idea of legacy is discussed throughout the book: Elías Luna's belief that Gabby needs to marry a peninsular to uphold the Luna family's position within society, and the various people who remind Sebastian that he is much more like his mother than his father. What do you think the Luna Sisters books' legacy will be?

Photo courtesy of the author

Liana De la Rosa is a *USA Today* bestselling historical romance author who writes diverse characters in the Regency and Victorian periods. Liana has an English degree from the University of Arizona, and in her past life she owned a mystery shopping company and sold pecans for a large farm. When she's not writing, Liana is listening to true crime podcasts while she wrangles her spirited brood of children with her patient husband in Arizona.

VISIT LIANA DE LA ROSA ONLINE

LianaDeLaRosa.com

 LianainBloom

𝕏 LianainBloom

 LianainBloom

Ready to find
your next great read?

Let us help.

Visit prh.com/nextread

Penguin
Random
House